efo

BELLA OF BOW STREET

1941, the Isle of Dogs. Neglected by their drunken mother, young Bella Doyle and her brother Terry are left to roam the streets, fending for themselves and skipping school with ease. When her mother's boyfriend turns violent, Bella finds refuge with Micky Bryant, a local ne'er-do-well. After the war, Bella marries Micky, but with her husband falling into a life of crime, Bella struggles to stay one step ahead of the law, cope with Micky's wayward behaviour and control her growing feelings for his elder brother, Ronnie. It takes a shocking tragedy for Bella to realize that she must shape her own destiny...

BELLA OF BOW STREET

BELLA OF BOW STREET

by

Carol Rivers

Magna Large Print Books
Long Preston, North Yorkshire,
BD23 4ND, England.

British Library Cataloguing in Publication Data.

Rivers, Carol
    Bella of Bow Street.

    A catalogue record of this book is
    available from the British Library

    ISBN   978-0-7505-2882-5

First published in Great Britain in 2007 by Simon & Schuster

Copyright © Carol Rivers, 2007

Cover illustration © Rod Ashford

Published in Large Print 2008 by arrangement with
Simon & Schuster UK Ltd.

Magna Large Print is an imprint of Library Magna Books Ltd.

Printed and bound in Great Britain by
T.J. (International) Ltd., Cornwall, PL28 8RW

For some very special young people
Ella and Jessica
Lucy, Beth, May and Lewis
Bella is for you guys, with love and hugs

Chapter One

The London Blitz
March 1941

'You bugger, don't you hit our Terry again!' Eight-year-old Bella Doyle stared defiantly up at the big man whose fist was clenched in readiness to strike.

Jack Router turned his bloodshot gaze slowly from the small boy huddled in the corner to scrutinize the parcel of rags and lice-infested hair gazing up at him.

'What did you say, girl?'

Bella moved cautiously backwards, out of reach of the man who had just knocked seven bells out of her little brother. Drunk and swaying Jack Router might be, but when the occasion warranted it, she knew he could turn on a sixpence.

'I said leave him alone. You're a bastard bully for clobbering our Terry. And I'm telling me mum when she comes home.'

'Oh you will, will you?'

Instantly regretting her quick tongue, Bella knew there was no escape. Above her, the gaping hole in the ceiling where the rafters of the roof hung down and to her right, the closed door and blacked-out window. Not that she'd try running anyway. Not without Terry.

Jack Router curled a thick, grubby finger in her

direction. 'Come here now, Bella. We should be friends you and me. Give your Uncle Jack a little cuddle. That's all he wants. And you like it, you know you do, girl.'

With her back pressed hard against the wall of the derelict cottage, Bella inched her way towards Terry. The man watched in amusement, his belly quivering above his belt as he enjoyed the child's terror.

'What's it to be then, eh? You or him?' He reached out his hand and Bella froze as a look of satisfaction crept over his face. Tilting his head, he shrugged lightly. 'You know, it was just a tap I give him, that's all. No more than he deserved for spinning your mother a pack of lies.'

'It wasn't our Terry's fault,' Bella protested in a whisper. 'It was Rita Moult from number nine. I heard her meself. She told everyone.'

'Rita?'

'She's all smiles and winks to you,' Bella burst out, 'but behind your back she told our mum that you've had more tarts than eaten hot dinners.'

'You lying little cow! She wouldn't dare, the bitch!'

Bella began to panic. 'I ain't lyin', honest.' She watched furtively as the man thrust hesitant fingers across his sagging jaw, his eyes moving slyly in their sockets. After his midday session at the Rose and Crown, he was breathing fumes. Even from where she was standing, Bella could smell him. Her stomach turned as he belched and rubbed his gut.

'Well now, you've got me all confused,' he grunted as his gaze travelled back to the boy.

'Let's see what your brother has to say for himself, shall we?'

Bella knew it was a trap. In a second or two he would swing round and catch her. But she couldn't let him clobber Terry again. Whatever he did to her, was nothing in comparison to what he'd done to Terry.

But this time he surprised her and with a powerful lunge he aimed his boot into the boy's hip. For all the ale in his belly, he delivered a blow that swept the human bag of bones along the filthy floor like a duster.

Without hesitating Bella threw herself forward and sank her teeth into the outstretched hand. Even as he screamed and pulled her up by her hair, she clamped her teeth tight, hanging on like a terrier. He shook her violently but Bella bit deeper, tasting his salty blood on her tongue. She imagined him dying the worst death possible like burning in one of the bombed buildings or boiling in oil. And the wanting of it was so strong it wasn't until all the air was punched from her stomach that her teeth finally parted.

'Look what you've done to me!' the man yelled in pain. His eyes gleamed as he brought her against him. 'Fight me would you, Bella Doyle? I'll teach you, girl. See this?' He tapped her nose with his knuckles as he held her aloft with one meaty hand. His tongue rolled out to lick the dried beer coating his lips. 'This is for girls like you that need to be taught a lesson.' He pushed hard, sliding his fist over her cheek and finally downwards to her chest.

'Whisper to me, Bella. Say the nice things

Uncle Jack likes to hear and it'll soon be over.'

All the struggle was gone from her now. Her legs and arms were suddenly weak as if she'd run up to the top of a hill and down again. It was a familiar pattern and she recognized it, knowing that no power on earth could save her now. Closing her eyes she tried to pretend she was up in the sky above the planes. Her mind began to draw pictures, taking her aloft on the clouds, flying in the blue ocean over the earth where there was release and freedom.

But just as he brought her against him, his fingers peeling away the layers of her clothing, the door flew open. Mary Doyle's faded green eyes flashed as she took in the scene before her. Fully attired in her working clothes, her chipped red nails dug into the worn black skirt that crinkled tightly over her stomach. Above her belted waist, a thin white blouse trembled on her drooping breasts. Slowly, a patch of angry crimson spread over her throat, creeping up into the lifeless red hair that fell on her neck. 'What in the name of Jesus is going on here?'

Jack Router stared innocently at the woman as he dropped Bella to the floor. 'She's an animal, Mary. She bloody bit me. Look! See them marks? All because I was trying to treat her decent.'

Laying still, Bella knew her luck could go either way now. Their mother was as likely to land him a punch as she was to believe him and blame her children instead.

'She was cheeking me, Mary, love. I swear on me old mother's life. All I did was walk in that door and they gave me a mouthful before I'd

14

even taken me coat off.'

Mary Doyle's gaze narrowed suspiciously. 'If you've lifted one finger against my kids–'

The man laughed suddenly. 'What'll you do? Chuck me out?'

'As sure as hell I would and you know it.'

'Ah, you drunken slut.' He pushed his face into hers. 'Well, you'd do me a favour if you did. If I found meself a pigsty to live in it would be an improvement on this shit hole. I'm sick to death of you and your brats. I must've been mad to take the bastards on.'

'You were willing enough at the time,' she reminded him sourly, returning the crude gesture. 'You had nothing, were nothing! And if it wasn't for me you'd be six feet under and still scratching the coffin lid. You're a curse, you bag of shite.'

Bella held her breath, her wary brown eyes looking out from under the tangled curtain of auburn hair. She was waiting for the inevitable, a continuation of the verbal and physical assault that had begun from the moment Rita, alias Mouth Almighty, had set her poisonous tongue free.

The first blow cracked aloud in the air. Jack Router stumbled, the heel of his boot landing heavily on Bella's leg. With a stifled cry she scrambled aside, dragging Terry with her into the only other habitable room of the dwelling. Here they crouched on a filthy mattress, covering themselves with a threadbare blanket.

Bella buried her head against Terry's. He smelled where he'd peed himself but the room stank like the bog anyway. She prayed the planes would soon fly over and when the siren went,

15

Mary Doyle and her man would be off. They'd be screaming at one another still, but thirst would drive them out in search of liquor.

Terry's snuffling grew louder. His mouth fell open as the blood congealed in his nose.

'Tomorrow we'll tell Micky,' she whispered, as a plan formed in her mind. Micky would know what to do. He always did.

Bella comforted herself with the picture of Micky's gun, not aimed at the wriggling sewer rats but pointed lightly against the brow of the man's head.

Bella rubbed her bruised cheek as she sat up.

A pale morning light seeped under the black-out. She stretched her stiff limbs as Terry stirred beside her, his long brown lashes laying softly on his swollen face. He'd rubbed the scabs from his nose in the night and was snuggled down in his coat. Both children were frozen, the temperature in the room at an all-time low.

'Terry, wake up.'

His almond-shaped eyes flickered. He groaned as he sat up. 'Terry hurts.'

'He gave you a bashing, that's why.' Bella took his hand and pushed the blanket from his tight grasp. 'We're going to run away before they come back.'

His eyes filled with tears. He lay down and pulled the blanket back over him. 'Terry don't want to.'

Bella wondered why God couldn't have left just a few brains in his head. Enough to tell him when he was safe and when he wasn't. Enough to make

16

him understand that the man would kill them both after last night. Why had God forgotten Terry?

She ruffled his thin brown hair. 'You've got to be a good boy, now. And do as Bella tells you.'

In the clothes they had worn day and night for more than a month they stumbled into the street. The cold March wind whipped around them and rain spattered down. Bella gazed up and down the rows of cottages. Only the rats, bugs and fleas that infested them moved in the early light. She looked up at the rotting pile of bricks that comprised number three, at the sunken roof and shattered windows lost in the drifting smoke of last night's raid. She shivered. It was the only home they knew and they were leaving it.

'Terry wants to stay.'

'We've got to find Micky.' She pulled his gas mask tighter across his shoulder. Jack would be home first, looking for trouble, so resisting the tears herself, she urged him forward.

'Is the bombs coming?'

'Tonight they will.'

'Terry don't wanna run away.'

Bella didn't want to either. But if only God had given him half a mind he'd know they didn't have a choice. The man had said one day he would put them in a pot and cook them. And after last night, Bella believed him.

Chapter Two

Ronnie Bryant stood in the big kitchen of the rambling three-storey building and frowned out on the cold March morning. He pushed back his hair and stretched his aching arms. From the kitchen window he could see the piles of junk that filled the yards of Piper Street and spilled around the Anderson like a shark-infested sea. No one would ever guess what was hidden under the floorboards of the air raid shelter. That's good planning, Ronnie my lad, he congratulated himself. The dugout had its uses after all. If the law came sniffing round, they were welcome to sort through all Dad's rubbish piled high on the stones. But it would take a shrewd copper to suspect the neat interior of the Anderson where all the booze and fags him and Micky and Sean had nicked from the docks were stashed safely away.

A gentle dew sparkled on the legs and arms of the ancient furniture and junk going back to the year dot. Their dad's treasure trove, his legacy to his sons as he was always telling them.

Ronnie smiled, the quirk of his full, sensual mouth giving his young face a maturity beyond his sixteen years. His cool grey eyes gleamed sharply beneath the heavy shock of raven black hair, missing nothing.

He glanced across the kitchen to his brother dozing in Dad's old armchair by the range.

18

Micky's curly dark hair flopped over his thin face and his size ten boots were filthy from the mud that had congealed on their soles. The lino in the hall needed cleaning before Mum arrived back from Auntie Gwen's. Another bonus that, Auntie Gwen asking her to stay the night. Luckily it was a good bus ride to Poplar from Cubitt Town. The two widowed sisters liked to chinwag and they wouldn't stir once the fire was made up.

Ronnie sighed heavily as thoughts tumbled in his brain. Him and Micky hadn't had a wink all night and hadn't expected to what with dodging the raids and bringing the haul up from the docks in the old van Dad parked under the railway arches. It was a real rust bucket and on its last legs but it had done the job. What a night it had been! They'd worked like stink digging up the Anderson floor and battening down the boards again. When they sold this lot off he was going to give Mum and Auntie Gwen a good holiday. Send them to the seaside. That's what Dad would have wanted...

Ronnie felt a moment of deep sorrow for the father he'd worshipped and the gap in their lives that had never been filled since his death three years ago. His loss hadn't been easy for Mum or indeed for any of them. But it was Sean, who had only been eleven when Dad went, who had taken it the worst. Odd that, as him and Dad had been opposites. Dad a real man's man, and Sean all curls and a mummy's boy. Still was, in fact. Yet Dad's death had knocked him sideways. Micky on the other hand, had been down the market the very next week, trading junk up the Caledonian or Cox Street. Where there was a gap in the market it was up to a Bryant to fill it, Dad said. Mum didn't know the half of his escapades and never would. And when the Blitz had started last September, well, who wouldn't have made the most of what was on offer? The black market had come into its own and you were an idiot to ignore it.

Ronnie was well aware that 1940 had seen the island at its best and worst. Not a night passing without catastrophe, destruction and death in some poor sod's case. But out of the turmoil came the best living they had ever made. Dad would have been in his element. And whichever way the war went, opportunities like last night were priceless.

There was a loud knock and Ronnie started. Quickly he pulled himself together and went to the front door.

There were two children on the doorstep. The girl, taller than the boy, had hair full of knots and the colour of brass, with eyes as round as pennies. Her coat had more holes in it than his mum's crocheting. The boy's hung down to his ankles. At first he had them down as beggars, but then she asked for Micky by name.

'Who wants to know?'

'Bella Doyle.'

'Well, Bella Doyle, you're out of luck. Micky ain't home. Come back some other time, kid.' He was about to close the door, when she stuck her foot inside.

'I'm not a kid. I'm eight.'

Ronnie was impressed. She had a mouth on her all right. 'Yeah, well, the answer's still the same. Micky's out.'

The girl pointed behind him. 'What's he doing there then, if he ain't home?'

Ronnie swung round to find his brother propped against the wall. Micky Bryant yawned and narrowed his bright blue gaze. 'What's up then, Bells?'

'Got something to tell you.'

'Yeah? Such as?'

Her eyes darted. 'Can't say standing 'ere, can I?'

Ronnie looked hard at his brother. 'Not now, bruv. Get rid of them.' He was about to walk away when Micky grabbed his arm.

'Hang on a bit, Ron. These two turn up a few tasty bits now and then. They're as regular as clockwork on the debris come rain or shine. Don't look a gift horse, as they say.'

Ronnie frowned. 'It's not a good time, Micky. And anyway, Mum'll be back soon.'

'Well, why don't we let 'em stay till she gets back?' His thick, dark eyebrows lifted persuasively. 'She loves kids, probably call them dirty-faced angels, feed 'em up and sort 'em out. Take her mind off what we've been up to whilst she's been away.'

Micky had a point, Ronnie decided as he gave the suggestion due consideration. Anything to divert the numerous questions that would come flying at them the minute she walked in. And, with Sean kipping upstairs like Sleeping Beauty, she wouldn't have time to wonder why he was so dead to the world.

He nodded grudgingly. 'Have it your way, but I don't like it.'

'All right, you two can stay for a bit,' Micky said, grinning. 'But no nicking and no pissing on the floor, pal. Okay?'

'What's up with the boy?' Ronnie frowned as the children stepped in.

Micky shrugged. 'Got bashed in the head once too often I reckon. You gotta wind him up and push him in the right direction to get him going. Their mum's one of them dock dollies that works the Rose. Don't suppose she ever give it a thought as to why he's like he is.'

Ronnie noticed the boy did look a bit vacant under all the dirt. He went down on his haunches. 'Here kid, what's your name?'

'Terry,' his sister said.

'Can't he speak for himself?'

'Depends what you ask him.'

Ronnie smiled. She was a card all right. 'Where'd he get all them bruises?'

'It's the joker they live with,' Micky interrupted. 'A big geezer who kips at their mum's gaff over Bow Street. If he ain't on a bender he's knocking off anything in a skirt that moves. Gives 'em a belting every day if they don't make scarce of themselves.'

'Thought no one was living over them places any more,' Ronnie commented thoughtfully. 'Condemned by the council years ago, weren't they?'

'Yeah, but who takes any notice of a bit of paper slapped on a wall?' Micky yawned once more. 'Funny thing is, Jerry's never landed a bomb on Bow Street. Makes you laugh really, when it'd only take a breath to knock it over.'

Ronnie cursed lightly. This was the last thing he

needed; two kids and a bastard drunk wasn't his problem today. He had enough of his own to be going on with.

But he also knew it was way too late to stop the anger that was already building inside him. If there was one thing he couldn't stand it was a bully. Granted, there were blokes who walloped their women and kids and got away with it. Bullying the weak and infirm was a way of life for some on the island, but not for his own kith and kin. Mum and Dad had brought them up to observe family values. The odd ding-dong now and then was only natural. His folks had gone at it hammer and tongs sometimes like all cockneys did. But only a row to clear the air. When an injustice like this got shoved right in your mug, it was hard to ignore it.

'How did they know where you live?' he enquired suspiciously.

'Must've told them, mustn't I?'

Ronnie studied the girl again. Now that he looked he saw she was blue with bruises. The clothes they wore were no more than rags hanging on bones. His mum would have a fit when she saw them like that.

'You two hungry?' he asked.

The girl's eyes widened. They were troubling eyes, Ronnie noted a little uncomfortably; there was so much hidden in the depths of them.

Micky laughed scathingly. 'Don't mention grub. These two are like bloody gannets. You want to see them demolish the rubbish they find in the bricks. Thick with dust it is and tastes like shit. But it goes down their gobs like dripping.'

23

Ronnie stared incredulously at his brother. That he could talk so lightly of what was in effect starvation. He was seriously worried about Micky's state of mind. Nothing seemed to bother him these days. It was as if all he cared about was number one. Though if he was really honest, that had always been so, even before Dad died.

'Come on then,' Ronnie said over his shoulder as he led the way to the kitchen. 'But then you've got to clear off after, right?' Now he'd taken a closer look at them he knew he couldn't let them stay. His mum wouldn't like those bruises any more than he did, a fact that Micky seemed to have overlooked.

In the kitchen he took the loaf from the larder. Carving off four thick slices, he lay them on the oilcloth. There was butter under the china dish, but it was still rationed and if it was one thing his mum loved it was a good helping of her old cough and splutter. The jam though, not that she knew it, was well and truly off the back of a lorry and more where it had come from any day of the week.

The girl wolfed it down and swiped her mouth with the back of her hand.

'See what I mean?' Micky chuckled. 'They'd eat horse dung if you served it up hot.'

'And so would you,' Ronnie answered him shortly, 'if Mum didn't put food in your belly.'

'That's why I help 'em out,' Micky stated quickly. 'If it wasn't for me they'd be brown bread.'

Ronnie sneered. 'Yeah, I can believe that an' all.'

'I ain't kidding, bruv. Nicking from the debris

is what keeps 'em alive. If it wasn't for me giving them a good whack for what they find, they wouldn't be standing here today. As half dead as they look it's me what keeps them breathing. Their mum don't give a toss what happens to her kids and sure as hell the ugly bastard that belts 'em don't.'

Ronnie knew the only reason Micky had half of London's back street kids working for him was for his own gain. He worked them like stink, returning the poor sods a pittance. Ronnie had turned a blind eye so far but now he was thinking twice. As for the nutter who used two little kids for a punch bag...

'What is this bloke to them?' Ronnie asked heavily. 'He ain't family or nothing?'

Micky laughed as he stuffed his mouth with bread. 'He's Mary Doyle's pimp and that's a fact.'

Ronnie cut another slice and halved it. 'Here, put this away, you two.'

They were at it like vultures when someone knocked on the front door. 'Keep quiet,' Ronnie warned them all. 'Not a whisper.' He went to open it. A warden was standing there, his uniform covered in dust.

'Yeah?' Ronnie asked irritably.

'Is this the home of Winifred Bryant?'

Ronnie nodded. 'She's out.'

'You'd better let me in, son.'

Ronnie put up his hand to stop him from entering. 'Why should I do that?'

He looked into Ronnie's eyes. 'The Luftwaffe hit Poplar bad last night ... and your mum...'

Ronnie stared into the warden's face. He must

25

have got it wrong. Somewhere along the line, there was a mix-up.

'We dug this out, well, what was left of it.' He lifted an identity card and his mum's black purse with a metal clasp. Ronnie saw a stain, a dark red one smeared across the felt. Then he knew she was never coming home again.

Chapter Three

Nine days later

Ronnie pushed his hand under his open shirt collar and squeezed the tense muscles of his neck. Mum would have made him wear a tie, but he hadn't worn one since he was at school and never a suit. Removing his jacket he placed it carefully over the back of his chair as Sean and Micky walked in the room.

Mum would have approved, Ronnie thought as he studied his two brothers, dressed in identical dark suits, they would have been her idea of real class. But now she was gone and her sons being done up like a dog's dinner for the funeral was a sting in the tail if ever there was one. For years she had meticulously ironed their shirts and pressed their trousers, nagging them to smarten themselves up. Now she wasn't here to see the result of her efforts.

'How long is this going to take?' Micky peeled off his jacket. 'I've got things to do.'

'Such as?'

'Dunno, just stuff.'

Ronnie narrowed his eyes, the sense of foreboding that had beset him after Mum's death growing inside him. 'Whatever it is Micky, forget it. There's family business to be taken care of this afternoon. Now shut up and sit down.' Ronnie nodded to the seat on his right. He had swallowed his irritation all week as Micky's attitude had gone from bad to worse. He accepted his brother was grieving but he was well out of order today and Ronnie's patience was growing thin.

Micky dragged out a chair and slumped down on it. Sean was already seated; his elbows resting on the big oval dining table polished each day by their Mum for as long as Ronnie could remember. A pang of sadness went through him as he met Sean's red-rimmed eyes. He had wept openly, unafraid to show his sorrow. Of the three of them, Sean had been their mother's favourite and it wasn't surprising to Ronnie that he'd taken her loss as badly as he had Dad's.

When he'd returned home that day after identifying his mother and aunt in the makeshift mortuary, he'd gazed into his brothers' faces, unable to speak. He had felt as if all the life had drained out of him from that moment. Mum and Auntie Gwen had looked as if they were asleep, their faces unmarked by death.

'You're certain it's them?' the warden had pressed as he'd identified the two corpses lying side by side.

Of course he was certain. The dead women were his family, the only family that he, Micky and Sean had.

'We found her bag straight away,' the man had told him gently. 'I know it's no consolation, but she wouldn't have known a thing.'

No, it's no consolation at all, he had thought bitterly as he stared at the marble white face of his mother that had, twenty-four hours before, been full of life and energy. They loved their father, but all three of them worshipped their mother. Perhaps she had been asleep when it happened? Ronnie hoped to God the warden was right and it had been quick.

He could still hear the rustle of the utility tarpaulins as they were replaced over the two still forms, could still see in his mind's eye the uni-formed man who had taken his arm, intending to lead him away, and he could still feel the frus-tration in his gut as he'd tried to decide whether it was all some sick joke.

All he could think of then was the fact that he wouldn't be looking into Mum's eyes again, their expression alert to whatever catastrophe had befallen her sons in her absence. She wouldn't be conjuring up a fried breakfast. Or chewing them off about the way they refused to get up in the mornings. Life as they had once known it had now come to an end.

Ronnie looked hard at his brothers. 'Sean, I know there's no way we can bring back Mum. But if she was here she would tell us to pull our-selves together and sort ourselves out. So that's what we've got to do, right?'

Sean shrugged helplessly. 'Why did it have to happen to her, Ron? I just don't understand.'

'There's no answer to that question, Seany. I wish I could give you one.'

'She never hurt no one. She'd give the coat off her back to anyone who asked. It was us that's done all the nicking. Why didn't that bomb fall on us?'

'I wish it had,' Ronnie muttered darkly. 'But what's done is done and we're still alive and kicking.'

'But that's just it, Ron, I don't feel right about what we did – you know – just before she went. It's as if it was us who made the bomb fall on her.'

Ronnie jerked his head round. 'That's rubbish, Sean, and you know it. Get it out of your head. We loved her, treasured her. And what we did was all for her, to give her a comfortable life as Dad would have wanted.'

Sean swept the tears from his cheeks with a grubby hand. 'I don't know anything any more, only that Mum turned a blind eye to what we did and we took full advantage. She didn't have a clue as to what was happening half the time. If we'd told her we knocked off a load of stuff and wanted to bury it out the back she would have given us all a slap for even thinking it.'

Ronnie's face tightened. 'Point taken, Sean, but the fact is what the eye don't see, the heart don't grieve over. After Dad died it was too late to change what he'd started and I for one wouldn't have wanted to anyway. The old man didn't spend his life teaching us the tricks of the trade for nothing. We was Robin Hood and his Merry Men. Give anyone a helping hand if they asked and bugger the sheriff. He kept telling us them stories over and over again. They came out of him like verbal diarrhoea and we believed every word. Still do.'

Sean blinked his long lashes. 'I know, Ron. But the country's at war and the punters we deal with are all in this lark for a profit, not to give to the poor and needy.'

Ronnie couldn't argue with that. But his priority was family. If he didn't hold them together now, they'd fall apart. 'Look, if it makes you feel any better, I'll agree that expanding the business into black market after Dad died was my decision, and I take full responsibility. I ain't saying I was right to do so, mind. That is a matter of opinion and you are entitled to yours. But I know in my heart it was the road Dad would have gone down. In my book, there was no doubt whatsoever as to continuing the business.' He paused as for a second he saw his mother gazing back at him in the form of Sean's honest blue gaze. God only knew how the old man had worked the flankers he'd done and kept the old girl in such blissful ignorance. But he had and Ronnie commended him for it. Now it was history repeating itself and with Mum gone, it was Sean who had taken up her mantle. But Sean was the new generation of Bryants, and as such had either to support the business or get out of it completely.

'Seany, let me put you straight on one thing. Mum never died because of what we did. It was nothing to do with us, so get that through your barnet once and for all. She died because a maniac in another country decided to start a war.

And that's a fact you're going to have to accept.'

There was silence in the room. Ronnie glanced at Micky who was sporting a face as long as a fiddle. 'Right, Micky, now it's your turn.' Bracing his shoulders he added firmly, 'I ain't sitting here all day looking at moody gobs, so speak your mind or forever hold your peace.'

Micky kicked the table leg idly. 'Since you're asking, Ron, what I don't fancy is Old Bill sniffing round and I've been shitting bricks lately every time the door goes. Stands to reason they know Mum's gone and she ain't here to tell them to sling their hook. So where does that leave us, I ask? And the answer is we're sitting here like three orphaned ducks.'

'So what is it you're saying?'

'I reckon we get shot of this last little bundle that we stuck in the Anderson. Take a dip on our profits if we have to, but just get clear of it.'

Ronnie nodded slowly. 'Fair point. Any suggestions what we do with it?'

'It's too hot for the markets and it would take too long to flog it round the pubs. What about shoving it Luffman's way? He'll rook us something chronic, but we'll have to swallow on that.'

Ronnie begrudged giving Goldy Luffman the contents of his nose, let alone a generous deal, as he was the meanest sod this side of the river. However, Goldy took anything and everything and asked no questions. 'All right. Suits us this time, but from here on in we'll find somewhere legit to stash our Georgie Woods.' He turned slowly to Sean. 'So, are you up for a clean sweep, Seany?'

'What choice have I got?' Sean replied moodily.

'You've always got a choice in life.' Ronnie stared hard at his kid brother who up until this moment had always been just that, a kid. But with Mum gone he was going to have to step into the real world. 'You don't have to come with us on this one, bruv. Me and Micky will do the business. We'll sort out the Anderson and see Goldy.'

'You *what?*' Micky objected, for the first time sitting up and paying attention.

'I said Seany can sit this one out.'

'But it took all three of us to move it before,' Micky protested. 'A whole lorry load it was, squashed six-foot down under a bloody shelter. We was at it like navvies and only finished just before the All Clear went. We need all the help we can get to move it out.'

'We'll manage.' Ronnie's tone was final. 'Sean's staying put.'

'So what if I decide to sit on me arse all night too?' Micky demanded angrily. 'You gonna shift it all on your tod?'

Ronnie sighed inwardly. There was something in both his brothers' attitudes that was worrying him. Sean was frightened of his own shadow and Micky was in love with himself. They both needed to realize they had to give a lot and take a little between themselves. They were family. And if family couldn't hack it, who could?

Micky continued to stare at him resentfully. There were rings round his blue eyes and a hollow look to his face. With his curly dark hair he was like their dad, a charmer. Sean had the same intense blue gaze but with his light brown hair and soft, smooth features he was their mother all

32

over. Now Ronnie looked at his two brothers and knew they would never be kids again, at liberty to fight amongst themselves and be stopped by a cuff round the ear. Now there could only be one leader. And as the oldest, he was it.

'Right then,' Ronnie said decisively. 'I'll dig out the van and bring it round as soon as the first raid starts. There'll be no lights on anywhere and plenty of noise to distract any nosy parkers. I'll reverse up to the back wall and Sean, you can help us load the stuff but then you'll come back in here and lie low. Me and Micky will drive over to Goldy's and be back before first light.'

'It'll be a bloody miracle if we are,' Micky grunted.

'We did it before. We can do it again.'

'That is if Jerry don't drop one on our heads.'

Ronnie smiled. 'He'll have to catch us first.'

Ronnie was prepared for further protest, but Sean hung his head, trying to disguise his wet cheeks, and Micky was busy still kicking the table leg. He had always had a laugh at anything remotely serious. After Mum, he didn't know how to act.

'And just to refresh our memories,' Ronnie continued, his gaze not leaving his brothers' faces. 'We'll keep this gaff shipshape, then. I don't want to find so much as a fag end under your beds – or anything else come to that. In other words, if the law was to shove its nose inside this house, all they'll find is a layer of dust and even that would be sweet smelling. Are you hearing me, you two?'

'Yeah, yeah.' Micky rolled his eyes.

Sean nodded in silence.

'And no outside jobs,' Ronnie added firmly. 'No creeping, no spotting, no fitting. Not even a touch at the market. No nicking wallets, bags or goods. Nothing goes down unless I say so. The Bryants think, act, even shit as one.'

Micky turned to face him and Ronnie was relieved to see a glimmer of humour return to his brother's eyes.

'What about them kids outside?' Sean asked suddenly. 'They've been kipping right on top of the stock.'

Ronnie had almost forgotten he'd allowed the two urchins to sleep in the shelter. After Mum's death he hadn't had the heart to send them back to Bow Street.

'They'll have to go,' Ronnie nodded.

'Lambs to the slaughter, I reckon,' Micky murmured, a glint in his eye.

'But they're not our problem,' Sean said anxiously. 'Are they?'

Micky shrugged. 'I reckon sending them back to Bow Street is like feeding mice to a cat. I'd like to see how handy the bastard is with someone his own size.'

It wasn't often Micky made sense, Ronnie thought, but this time he was in full agreement. He felt a grudging admiration towards Micky. More than that, he knew his brother was no coward and had taken his punishment on the streets as well as doling it out. There was a vicious streak inside him that manifested itself as pure hate for authority of any kind. Ronnie knew that if this trait could be harnessed for the good of the family, they would have a valuable asset in Micky.

'You want to sort it out?' Ronnie asked.

Micky's dark eyes lit up. 'Now you're talking, bruv.'

But Sean was shaking his head. 'I don't like it. Those kids are bad news.'

Ronnie was under no illusions as far as Sean went. He was never cut out for the physical. Mum had spoiled him on the quiet, though him and Micky had understood why in a funny way. He was the total opposite to Micky who would happily take a swing at a bull with a match up its arse given half the chance.

'We're gonna start as we mean to go on,' Ronnie said without hesitation. 'Ask yourself this question, Seany. What would Dad have done if we had a sister and some lairy sod lifted a hand against her?' His face was set hard, its handsome proportions chiselled out in the broad daylight. 'This is our patch and we need the respect.' He paused, assessing his brothers' reactions. When no argument was forthcoming he continued. 'Now, are we all done?'

Ronnie looked round at them again, then he stood up and felt the smooth material of his trousers fall over his long legs. He liked that feeling. He liked the fact that he now had his brothers' undivided attention and made a vow to keep it that way.

Before leaving the room he picked up the newspaper. The polish of the table sparkled. He thought again about his mum polishing it and the joy she took in doing so; it was a big, solid table, like the family he intended to cultivate. This was the first meeting he had called, but it wouldn't be the last. There would be many more to come.

Now he instructed Sean to change his clothes and put on his working clobber. 'Get those kids out of the shelter and bring them in here,' he added sharply. 'We're all going over to Bow Street.' Ronnie had already convinced himself that the action he was about to take to remedy a bad situation, would achieve a result that his dad, if not his mum, would sanction.

Chapter Four

Jack Router was in dire need of a drink. He was also chastened by the nights he had spent squeezed in those bloody shelters with the stink of every Tom, Dick and Harry up his nose. The confinement had made him appreciate Bow Street even if it was little more than a ruin. At least there was only him and Mary and her two brats. Mind, he'd rather cut his tongue out than admit as much to Mary Doyle. He hoped by now she had learned her lesson. No woman gave him the elbow, especially a brass. And what would the bitch do without his protection, for pity's sake? With her spiteful tongue it was on the cards that she'd fall foul of some bolshie punter refusing to cough up the price of a shag. Jack smiled to himself. She needed muscle at her side and he was her man. If she was still alive and kicking after nine days fending for herself, she would welcome him back on her knees.

Damn the Luftwaffe, though! With landlords buggering off the instant the siren went it was hard to find a good drink these days. Not that he'd even set foot inside a pub today.

Jack marched on, his thirst increasing. He first noticed the woman trailing him as he walked up to West India docks. She was on the game, no doubt. Sizing him up at a distance, he guessed. Calculating his worth and wondering how much he kept in his pocket.

At first he ignored her. With that cow Rita Moult on the lookout, he had to be careful. He wasn't about to push his luck. Not in broad daylight anyway and not on the island. But a mile or two more and they'd be into Poplar.

'Fancy a drink, love?' A waft of cheap perfume washed over him as he turned into Poplar High Street.

'Clear off.' His tone was scathing as he glanced furtively over his shoulder.

'Come on, ducks. You look like you need cheering up.'

'I said clear off.'

She grabbed his arm. 'That's not a nice way to speak to a lady.'

'Show me the lady and I'm the pope.'

She smiled, unoffended. 'You're a laugh a minute, you are, sonny boy.' Her fingers slid over his arms and her touch aroused him. Well, why shouldn't it? He was only human after all. And wasn't a man entitled to look elsewhere if his woman spurned him? He was sick to death of Mary's nagging. He didn't know where her two bastards were and didn't care. Good riddance to bad rubbish if you asked him. If she blamed him for their disappearance, so be it. He'd find another bed easy enough.

'Come on, you could do with a quick one, I'll bet.' She linked her arm through his. 'Where you off to then?'

Good question. Where exactly was he going to drown his sorrows? With Mary working the Rose, he'd lost his watering hole.

'I'm on me way to Limehouse.' He didn't care for the walk, but it was the safest option. No one knew him round there.

Her thin eyebrows raised. 'Despite the fact me feet are killing me, I know a cosy spot up the Commercial Road. Nice friendly landlord an' all.'

'Yeah, I'll bet you do.'

She lowered the neckline of her blouse with dirty fingers. 'What's it worth then, love? A drink or two surely? Come on, let's give ourselves a real laugh, shall we?'

Jack soon forgot about his worries as they walked on. He could feel the angle of her hip touching him as he inhaled her scent. A stink that would normally have him gagging. But now it was a promise, a reminder of the man he was, and the desires he'd had to curb for too long. By seven o'clock they were installed on the back benches of the Fur and Feathers listening to the thud of the bombs in the distance. By eight they'd moved down the road to the George where the publican was game enough to still serve ale and curse the Luftwaffe at the same time. By ten, in the middle of a lull, they were staggering into the dim and musty light of some godforsaken alley, his pockets empty.

Blearily he looked for a spot, somewhere dark and sheltered. Seeing a recess in the wall, where rubbish spread across their path, he told himself he wouldn't get much better.

'Come on, gel, get your drawers down,' he growled as he pushed her against the stone.

'Not here, it's too bloody dangerous.' She knew what was expected of her, but had the gall to push him away. He wasn't going to pay her a farthing, since she had emptied more booze down her gob in the last two hours than he himself had consumed in a week.

He squinted at the mask before him, grotesque in the blackout, with only the moon's light to see her by. The cheap perfume now filled him with disgust. She saw his expression and laughed in his face.

He gripped her jaw hard. 'Spread your legs, woman, or I'll do it for you.'

'Not out here,' she refused stubbornly. 'Them bombers'll be back soon.'

He loosened his buttons. 'Sod the bombers, you cow. Now hold still and damn the bloody raid.' He pulled up her skirt and forced himself between her legs. He entered her roughly and she stilled at once, as he knew she would, eager for him to finish his short, sharp thrusts. He placed his hands on the wet wall and groaned aloud at the disappointment of it all.

'Pay up, you bugger,' she demanded as she rearranged her clothes.

'*Pay* you?' A soft mist curled over the cobbles as

he pushed her away. 'You've drunk me bloody dry, you witch.' He kicked her hard and she fell on the cobbles. She was still cursing as he staggered away. He felt no sympathy for a woman daft enough to work the docks alone. Consoling himself for the unsatisfying encounter, he pulled up the collar of his jacket and strode into the high street.

A long walk back to Bow Street ... but he intended to give Mary Doyle another chance. She'd been a nice little earner and he liked his life of leisure. All he had to do was avoid enlistment and with a little dodging and weaving, that hadn't been too difficult thus far. The drawback was her kids, although the girl was growing up fast. Jack grinned lustily as he turned into Bow Street.

He'd have Mary on her knees and begging him to stay. Nine days away from her nagging had shown he didn't care. The whore would welcome him with open arms.

Mary Doyle sat in front of a cracked mirror dressed in a black silk blouse and tight green skirt. Her hair fell loosely on her white skin and the look in her eye told him she was far from pleased at his arrival. Jack also noted she was not on her knees, at least, not to him.

'What's going on?' he demanded as he slammed the door behind him. He looked suspiciously around expecting to find a punter. So she'd been doing trade behind his back had she, the bitch?

'Would you listen to him?' Her smoke-roughened voice was deriding as she glared at him. 'The galloping great eejit returns!'

He strode towards her and grabbed her arm.

'Where is he? Where's the devil hiding?'

She looked at him and laughed. 'The only devil in this room is right before me eyes.'

'Where's your pay, you lying bitch?'

She shrugged carelessly. 'I wouldn't waste me breath on you, Jack Router. Just look at the state of you.' She shook her arm free, her voice scathing. 'As far as I'm concerned your bitches can have you. Rita warned me you was a conniving, scheming bastard and so by Jesus you are too.'

It was a reflex action: an instinctive blow that lifted her off her feet and across the bed. A blow that would have felled any man and Jack was more than surprised to find her still moving. He hit her again and kept on punching as she covered her face with her arms. When his hand was aching from the effort she gave a shudder and he tore away the blouse. 'Mary Doyle, you think yourself so fine. Well, from now on changes are going to be made.' He felt a swell of desire at the sight of her huge breasts. 'Boot me out, would you? We'll see about that.' He squeezed her neck and her eyes bulged.

'You hear me, Mary, you hear what I'm saying? You'll never toss off a punter again without paying me a cut.'

He was laughing at the thought when suddenly his head jerked back. It was an odd sensation, one he had never experienced before. He seemed to be going backwards and wondered if the drink had finally got to him. But he hadn't had that much. The brass had cleaned him out today and he'd had to curb his thirst. Then he felt an excruciating pain, a grip of iron around his neck.

41

The pain intensified as his arms were pinned to the wall, and he felt a series of blows to his kidneys and a crunch on his face.

A figure was dancing in front of him. Or was it two? He blinked before trying a swipe, but was flung back on the wall again. His legs buckled. The taste of his own blood was in his mouth.

The last thing he remembered was begging them to stop. But he knew as sure as a tart was a tart he was a gonner as the dull drum of planes overhead outweighed his screams.

Bella held Terry against her, listening to the beat of the planes as they drowned the noise inside the cottage. Ronnie had told them to stay outside until the business was finished. The sky was glowing pink over the houses and smoke filled the night air.

Just then Ronnie and Micky came out. The man hung between them, arms outstretched and chin on chest.

'Look after your mum,' Ronnie said, slanting his head to the door.

'What's he done to her?'

'Nothing you ain't seen before, kid.'

'I told you, I ain't a kid.'

'No, you're not any more,' Ronnie agreed, dragging the body into the road.

'Where you taking him?'

'For a walk. A long one,' Micky answered her, wrapping one dangling arm around his neck.

'Is he coming back?'

'Go on in now.'

Bella watched them disappear, listening to the

boots drag over the ground, the same boots that had caved Terry's ribs in. Whatever they'd done to the man, she was glad.

'Terry wants our mum.'

Bella took him indoors, closing the door quickly behind them. Mary Doyle lay on the bed, the blanket wrapped over her legs. 'So you two are back, are you?'

'We stayed at Micky's.'

'Ah, so it was him that was here, was it? Him and that brother of his, Ronnie Bryant?'

Bella nodded.

Mary's swollen eyes blinked. 'Well, I hope they teach that useless git a lesson he'll not forget. Lift a hand to me, would he? Strike a defenceless woman? Good luck to your Micky and Ronnie, girl. Now, stop bloody staring and get me my baccy.'

Bella pulled Terry to the sink. She took the filthy tin from the draining board, brushing away the dust. Mary Doyle rolled her own with shaking hands.

'Light me a match, girl.'

Bella did as she was told. Exhaling slowly, Mary sighed in satisfaction.

When the planes grew loud again Bella led Terry into their room. 'Terry scared,' he sobbed as she made him lay down.

'Say your prayers, then. Jesus will take care of us.' She stroked his head and covered him with the blanket. When he was asleep, she went back to Mary.

'You know, that bastard was going to kill me? See what the fecking sod did? See this? And this?

43

But the Almightly sent help this time. Your Micky and Ronnie done me a good turn, girl.' Her face crumpled as she coughed, falling back on the pillow to stare up at the ceiling. Dust fell like rain as the bombs landed. 'The planes are back. Listen to their racket.'

Bella covered her ears as the ground shook.

'I might as well stay in me bed,' Mary Doyle said as she lay back. 'It's as good a place to die as any.'

Bella took the roll-up from her mother's fingers. She pushed it down in the jar with the others and went back to Terry. The bombs fell loud and heavy and the cottage rattled as she crawled beside him.

In the darkness she said thank you to God for answering her prayers. The man was gone. But then she decided there were no more prayers to be said. It was Micky and Ronnie who had delivered them from evil tonight.

Not God.

Chapter Five

July 1947

Bella tossed back her hair and slid her school tie from her collar. Squeezing it into her satchel, she smiled contentedly. It was the final day of school. She was free at last and more than ready to take on the world. Her full lips turned up in a smile.

'I can only stay till half past six because of Terry,' she said to her friend Dolly Taylor as they walked past the Newcastle Arms.

Spilled ale and musky tobacco wafted out from its doors and windows into the hot day. Bella inhaled the cocktail and felt a thrill. She loved everything about the island, especially in summer when the river was full of movement as the ships passed under the bridges into the heart of the docks. Bets were being laid that it would be the hottest summer in years. Bella couldn't wait to be rid of her damp blouse and purpley blue school blazer. It had been worn many times before she had bought it for next to nothing at the market. Over the years she had altered her uniform so much that it looked a total mess. As soon as she started work she was going to buy herself some pretty frocks and her pleasure grew at the thought of it.

'You're always rushing off,' Dolly pointed out, breaking the magic spell of the wonderful summer's day.

'Terry'll be on his own. He could get up to anything.'

'You know, I can't see your Terry going back to school after you leave,' Dolly remarked as they linked arms and turned the corner.

'He might.' But privately Bella had no doubt at all that Terry's schooldays were well and truly over. At twelve years of age, he still had the mind of a child, despite his tall, thin body. It was always Bella that woke him, dressed him and got him ready for school in time.

'What's he going to do with himself all day?'

45

Dolly pressed. 'He can't stay at home, can he? Not with *him* around.'

Bella had been considering the problem for some time. Not that the cripple could easily get off his backside now. It was Terry she couldn't trust. Last week he had started a fire and Mum had threatened to have him put away in an institution. She threatened often enough, but had never seen it through. This time however, the bedclothes had gone up in smoke and Terry's trousers as well. The match had been a plaything to him. He wanted to smoke the same as everyone else. It must have been some kid at school who gave him the cigarette. Thank God, she had smelt the smoke quick enough to extinguish the smouldering bedclothes. Ten minutes more and the fire would have finished the job the Luftwaffe didn't do.

'The man's no threat now,' Bella shrugged casually. 'All he does is sit in the chair or drag himself down the pub. If it wasn't for the stick he'd never get there at all.' Ever since the night Micky and Ronnie had dispensed rough justice in the middle of a disused anti-aircraft battery at the back of West Ferry Road, their lives had changed. Bella smiled to herself as she thought of the drooling figure with a claw for a hand curled over his stomach, unable to touch her now.

'He still gives me the creeps,' Dolly said.

'Yeah, well, he's no oil painting, that's for sure.'

'And all squashed into such a small house–' Dolly put a hand up to her mouth. 'I mean, it's not that bad, but it's–'

'A dump,' Bella said for her, nodding.

'Has your mum heard from the council?'

'There's a prefab empty down the road and she's put in for it.'

'D'you think she'll get it?'

'You never know.'

Dolly shook her head in wonderment. 'You're the last family in Bow Street now. Even old Mr Billings has gone and Rita Moult too. The council's given her a flat at the top of a big block in Dagenham, would you believe?'

'Yes, I would,' Bella nodded, 'just to shut her up.'

The girls laughed. Bella coiled a copper-coloured lock of hair around her finger. 'Your Ray be home, will he?'

'Yeah. He's just got a new job with the PLA, as a guard on the dock gates. With a uniform and all. And the money's good too. Mum's ever so pleased.'

Bella had no doubt Mrs Taylor was beside herself with joy at her son's new appointment. She was desperate for her children to do well for themselves and enjoyed asking people how much money they earned and what their prospects were. But she was good at heart and had always made Bella welcome, which was a lot more than could be said of others.

'Have you got fixed up yet?' Bella asked, knowing that Dolly hadn't.

'No, but Dad said I should go up to Poplar Town Hall and make enquiries. He said he'd put in a good word for me. The thing is, I want to smarten meself up a bit before I apply. I've got nothing nice to wear. I thought about getting a

47

cherry red suit to match me beret.'

Dolly had light brown hair and plenty of curves. But she was also short and in Bella's opinion the bright-coloured clothes she wore didn't flatter her.

'You're good at typing and shorthand,' Bella said, changing the subject. 'Much better than me.'

Dolly blushed. 'Typing's about the only thing I am good at.'

'That's daft, Dolly. You'll never get anywhere if you think that.'

Bella would rather have gone round Micky's but she had agreed to go to tea with Dolly because it was their last day at school. Next week she was starting work at Dixons of Stepney, the furniture people, and she couldn't wait. Not that she fancied her prospective job much, but it paid good money.

'I wish I was confident like you, Bella. I was shaking like a leaf at that interview and me fingers went in all the wrong places. I couldn't even remember the shorthand properly.'

'What was there to be nervous of?'

'I don't know. But I was.'

'You're as good as the next person, probably a lot better.'

'I never think that,' Dolly said, embarrassed, adding quickly, 'So what does Micky have to say about you working up Stepney?'

'Not told him yet. Anyway, why should he have anything to say on the subject?'

Bella knew exactly what her friend was getting at. Micky had wanted Bella to work for the

48

Bryants 'in the expansion of their business' as he put it, but she had refused. Not because she didn't want to, because she did. She owed the Bryants everything. The way they had looked after her and Terry and even their mother, getting her a job as a barmaid at the Rose and doing up the cottage. But she felt she must show she could do something on her own. Her independence was important to her and Micky might not respect that.

'You know what I mean. Stepney's off the Bryants' patch.' Dolly raised her eyebrows as they turned into Chapel House Street. The Taylors' house was a mid-terrace council house with a shining brass horseshoe fixed to the yellow-painted front door. The windows all had lace curtains and to the left by the path there was a small square of mowed lawn edged with a border of flowers. 'Not that it would stop Micky from having something if he wanted it bad enough,' Dolly giggled as they stood on the front doorstep. 'And we all know what that something is, don't we?'

Bella's cheeks flushed fiercely. 'I'm fifteen, Dolly. Not fifty. And for your information Micky doesn't own me.'

'No, but everyone thinks he does.'

'Well they don't know much then.'

'And you're daft about him.'

'I'm not.'

'You are!' Dolly sighed dramatically. 'Anyway, it won't stop our Ray from giving you the eye, so be prepared. He's gonna be all done up in his Sunday best, just you wait. All I hope is I don't wet

49

me drawers with laughter at the sight of him.'

Bella grabbed her friend's arms. 'Dolly, I'll crown you if you've told Ray I fancy him, because I don't.'

'I've not breathed a word! Anyway, what's wrong with my brother? Some girls would think he's a real catch.'

Bella didn't have time to reply as the door opened. Raymond Taylor stood there and was, as his sister predicted, dressed in a suit, his chin supported by a tie and shirt that looked as though it was choking him. He blushed at the sight of Bella who had often thought that her friend's older brother was good looking in a dull, conventional sort of way. Soft brown hair and eyes just begging to be noticed. But as she walked past him, she knew that Dolly had spoken the truth. Micky Bryant was the only one who could make her heart race like a train with just the briefest flash of his lovely dark eyes.

Bella hated eating tea with the Taylors. She did it as little as possible, and only for Dolly's sake. They sat at measured intervals around the big oval table set with the best china and a cake stand and teapot in matching design. The conversation was always the same. How marvellous Mrs Taylor's cooking was, a result of Mr Taylor's vegetable garden just over the railway line. There were questions slipped in about her mother too and her job as a barmaid at the Rose. So Bella was always on her guard, which made eating the unpalatable food even more tedious.

She took a sandwich from the plate and bit into

it, wincing at the concoction of fatty Spam and sliced vegetable pressed inside the bread. Mrs Taylor, always so proud of the miracles she produced from her ration book, smiled at her husband.

'It's Doctor Carrot again, Neville dear. Fresh from the allotment.'

'Amazing little chap, isn't he? Don't know how we'd have managed without him during the war. I mean, Doctor Carrot even helped us to see in the blackout!'

Bella glanced at Dolly sitting beside her. Both girls smothered their laughter.

Mr Taylor munched noisily as he spoke. Bella had heard it all before, as had every other person sitting in the room. The adventures of Doctor Carrot and Potato Pete, happy foundation of curried carrot, carrot jam and a homemade drink, Carrolade, and Lord Woolton's wartime dish, the all veg and meat free, famously indigestible Woolton pie.

'These are lovely, Mum,' Dolly said, making a sly face at Bella.

'The best,' said Raymond as he patted his stomach, clearly full of the watery custard and anaemic-looking spotted dick he had just consumed.

Bella nibbled and between gulps of air, attempted to keep the food down. The Taylors always ate their sandwiches last, to 'fill an empty gap' as Mrs Taylor put it.

'Well now...' Mrs Taylor began to clear the dishes.

'Where is my newspaper, Mother?' Neville

Taylor rose, brushing the crumbs from his grey suit. As a white-collar worker at Poplar Town Hall, he always wore the same clothes, always a tie and white shirt with detachable collar. A custom, Bella noticed, that Raymond had already followed.

'We'll clear the table, Mum.' Dolly winked at Bella. 'And wash up.'

'That's nice of you, dear.' Dorothy Taylor beamed at her daughter. 'Your father and me will sit down then. Raymond, we'll put the wireless on.'

Raymond jumped to attention. 'I'm going down the Settlement,' he said quickly. 'Be back later, though.'

'Don't stay too late at the club,' Mrs Taylor said reprovingly. 'You've got to be up bright and early for your new job.'

Raymond pecked his mother on the cheek. In the kitchen he whispered to Bella, 'What you doing tomorrow?'

'Breathing, I hope,' Bella replied as she lowered the cups and saucers into the bowl.

Dolly burst into laughter and Raymond blushed. 'You know what I mean, it's Saturday.'

'I know it is. Today's Friday.'

He moved closer, out of Dolly's range. 'Fancy coming up the Troxy?'

'To do what?' Bella asked wide-eyed.

'To see a flick, of course.'

'What's on?'

'Dunno, a double feature p'raps.'

Bella shook her head solemnly. 'You don't even know what's showing, do you?'

'Give us a chance, Bella. Ain't the invitation good enough for you?'

'An invitation to what? A quick grope in the back seats?'

Raymond Taylor's face turned scarlet. 'That's not what I meant!'

'Isn't it?' His guilty expression gave him away and for a moment Bella enjoyed his discomfort.

Dolly was clattering the dishes noisily but turned round at the disturbance. 'What's going on, you two?'

'Nothing,' Bella said, glancing at Raymond. 'Much to your brother's disappointment.'

'Now, now.' Dolly came between them. 'Keep it down or Mum'll be in.' She pushed her brother back. 'And anyway, you daft 'aporth, Bella's spoken for. Ain't you worked that one out for yourself yet?'

It was Bella's turn to look annoyed. Her expression darkened. 'Shut up, Dolly.'

'Well you are, aren't you?'

Before Bella could reply Raymond broke in. His expression was hurt but underneath there was anger. 'Micky Bryant is trouble with a sodding great T, Bella. Him and his family. You'll end up on the wrong side of the law. Why can't you see that?'

Bella glared at him. 'And you are the world's biggest snob for looking down on them. What do you know of the Bryants or what they've done for me? I wouldn't be standing here if it wasn't for them and that's the truth.'

'Have it your way,' he agreed sullenly, 'but don't say I didn't warn you.'

53

Raymond Taylor had hit a nerve but Bella wasn't prepared to show it. 'Listen, Ray, you ain't no different to any other bloke but you won't admit it. Added to which you've got the cheek to stand there and criticize me for the way I live my life when there's one or two whispers I've heard about you and a certain butcher that would give your mother a turn if she heard them. Specially as she can't afford to put proper ham in her sandwiches and has to make do with Spam.'

'You little–' Raymond stepped forward angrily, but Dolly jumped between them. Bella smiled into his face. She had brought him down a peg and she was overjoyed at the result.

Dolly pushed against her brother's chest. 'Come on you two, shake hands and be friends. Please.'

But Bella shook her off. 'No thanks, Dolly. I've had enough for one night.'

She flung the dishcloth down and strode into the hall, snapping her bag from the clothes-stand on her way out.

Bella walked with her head held high, satisfied she had had the last word, although she would have preferred to give Ray Taylor the argument he deserved. How dare he tell her what was good for her and more importantly, what was not? He wasn't averse to flogging an off-cut of beef or pork in his spare time, pocketing the proceeds as fast as he made them. A fact that didn't quite fit in with Mrs Taylor's image of her perfect son and made a mockery of Lord Woolton's pie.

Bella exhaled, the anger inside her slowly cooling. It was a beautiful summer's night. Why spoil it? The street was full of children playing in the derelict houses of the bombed sites. The warm evenings brought them out like ants.

Her thoughts returned stubbornly to what Ray had said. So what if Micky Bryant was a big part of her life! It was jealousy that made people like the Taylors scorn him. And it wasn't for the likes of Ray to pronounce judgement when he was such a hypocrite himself.

'Bella!'

Dolly's call was panic-stricken. Bella turned round slowly, knowing that her friend would try to persuade her back to the house. Dolly was running, her plump form stumbling over the debris that spilled on to the pavement above the leaf-filled plane trees. Her thin hair was losing its clips and her round face was full of remorse. She waved, her cardigan falling open over her full breasts.

'Bella, you didn't say goodbye to Mum and Dad.'

'Tell them I said it, then.'

Dolly was sweating. 'Ray didn't mean what he said. I'm sorry.'

'It's not your fault.'

'He likes you, he really does.' Dolly held her stomach. 'He wouldn't hurt you for the world. And what you said about the butcher...' she looked under her lashes, 'you won't let on to Mum, will you? She'd kill him.'

'You know me better than that.'

'It's just a little sideline he's got.'

'I don't care about that. As long he keeps his opinions to himself.'

'He will, I promise.' Dolly groaned. 'I've got a stitch now.'

Bella giggled. 'You ain't got a needle though.'

Dolly laughed breathlessly. 'Oh, Bella, you're a giggle a minute you are.' Her eyes filled with tears. 'I keep forgetting we won't be going back to school after the holidays. I get a rotten sinking feeling inside when I think of that.'

'I don't.' Bella looked at her friend's crestfallen expression and relented. 'You'll get a job soon and be very happy.'

'Yes, but I'll be all on me own somewhere without you.'

'You'll have to learn to stick up for yourself.'

'You always stuck up for me.'

'I know, but it's the real world now. People will walk over you if you let them.'

Dolly looked sad. 'I wish I was you.'

Bella laughed. 'That's a barmy thing to say.'

'You're strong, Bella. You've always got the answers.'

'Only because I make them up.'

Dolly giggled. 'And you're funny. I never am.'

'Oh Dolly, cheer up. Look on the bright side of life. You can wake up in the morning with a smile or a frown. It's your choice, as easy as that.'

Bella looked at her friend and wondered where they would be in ten years' time. Again she had the picture of Mrs Taylor, the neat and tidy house, kids with shiny clean faces and a parrot of a husband.

'We can still go out together, can't we?'

'Course we can.'

'Shall I call round your house?'

Bella smirked. Dolly never called. No one ever called, except Micky or Ronnie. 'If you dare.'

Dolly went pink. 'He won't answer the door, will he?'

Bella laughed. 'Tell you what, I'll come round to you.'

Dolly looked relieved. 'Will you? Promise?'

Bella nodded. 'We'll go up the market. Cox Street or the Lane.'

Dolly flung herself forward and hugged Bella so tight her bones cracked. 'I'm gonna miss you so much.'

As they parted, Bella smiled to herself. She knew that life had only just begun now they had left school and the thought of freedom excited her. She was going to meet new people and make lots of friends, though she didn't say as much to Dolly who was almost in tears, trying to wipe her wet cheeks surreptitiously as she said goodbye.

Chapter Six

Bella typed the last instruction of the day, one Birds Eye Maple bedroom suite consisting of double wardrobe, one kidney shaped dressing table and matching upholstered stool. One double bed and mattress with accompanying bedside tables and headboard. One chest of five drawers and oblong cream skin rug. Invoice for cash paid in full, eighty-nine pounds, seventeen shillings and sixpence. Remember to date, stamp and post...

She pounded the full stop key on the typewriter with a flourish and sneaked a glance at her watch. Only twenty minutes to go till half past twelve. Then she would cover the machine in front of her and say goodbye to Dixons for the rest of the weekend.

The other three girls were concentrating so hard only their fingers moved in front of them. Back and forth went the rollers on the big, bulky typewriters, the clack of the keys reverberating round the walls. No one seemed eager to leave. Bella couldn't wait. Tonight she was going up West with Micky. He was going to visit a club called the Indigo and she was going with him. She had to look at least eighteen to get in, Micky had warned her. She was going to wear a dress that he'd bought especially for the occasion.

He said he intended to open a club on the island just like the Indigo. He was counting on Ron to help him, but at the moment Ronnie was putting the damper on all his ideas. Since his demob in '45, he had changed, Micky said, scarred by his experiences at war, none of which Ronnie ever talked about. But she had to agree with Micky, Ronnie was a harder man all round.

Bella had butterflies in her stomach just thinking about the Indigo. What would it be like and who would she see? Someone famous perhaps. Micky knew all the actors and actresses that went there; it was a really high-class club.

'Finished already?' Evelyn Donald, the girl working at the next desk, broke into her thoughts.

Bella nodded, aware of the disapproving expression in the other girl's eyes. 'Yes, aren't you?'

'It's not half past twelve yet,' Evelyn Donald said as she tapped her watch. 'There's five minutes to go. I'm beginning this pile of orders so I can get ahead for Monday.'

Bella began to draw the cover over her typewriter. 'I don't need to get ahead, Evelyn. I already am.' She looked straight into Evelyn's narrowed eyes and shrugged casually. 'I don't see the point of making extra work for myself. We're just typing orders and adding up a few figures, that's all, not a life and death situation.'

'But you have to make sure all the figures are correct,' Evelyn emphasized as she glanced at Bella's work. 'Miss Conway is quick to remind us that Dixons' policy is accuracy over speed.'

'Well, it would be, wouldn't it?' Bella returned dismissively. 'They are the bosses and we are their slaves. They are never going to die from overwork, are they? We do as we're told, yes sir, no sir and three bags full sir. Now, if you look at your watch again, it will definitely say half past and that's when we finish on Saturdays.'

Bella managed to prevent herself from laughing at Evelyn's horrified gaze as she continued to pack away. She couldn't imagine what these girls' brains were made of. Probably soup. They were all like sheep, running in one direction, following the leader. Bella had done it herself for the last four months, but she was tired of it. How did these girls tolerate the mind-numbing boredom of their jobs? Margery Cooper had been here for fifteen years and Evelyn Donald for ten. All of the six girls in this office dutifully went over their work at the end of their day as if their lives

59

depended on it. This job would have suited Dolly perfectly, Bella thought wryly as she watched Evelyn return her scrutiny to the book in front of her. Instead Dolly was slogging it out at Burlington Dock Fisheries, her clothes reeking of fish!

Bella stood up as Miss Conway, the supervisor, walked in. She was small and stocky with a man's short, straight haircut. From Bella's first day they had taken an instant dislike to one other.

'Finished already, Miss Doyle?'

'Yes,' Bella nodded, adding dutifully, 'Miss Conway.'

'Well, I am sorry to say I have found a number of faults in the work you left on my desk last night. As you know I dislike crossings out. If a mistake is made I prefer the paperwork to be redone completely. Our customers don't expect to be issued with inferior accounts.'

'But I wouldn't cross out,' Bella protested. 'All my work was correct. I check it thoroughly before I bring it to your office.'

'Well, let me refresh your memory.'

Bella took the papers Miss Conway gave her. Someone had carefully crossed through her figures, making an unsightly repair to the total.

Bella's cheeks flushed as she glanced quickly at Evelyn who was typing away and didn't look up. It was Evelyn who had offered to take her work and leave it on Miss Conway's desk as she went out.

'Is this your work?'

'Yes, but–'

'No buts Miss Doyle. Errors are not company policy and quite unacceptable. You'll make out fresh paperwork, check the figures carefully this time and let me see them before you leave.' She turned and marched off in her thick-heeled brogues leaving Bella to stare at the other girls who, without comment, began to pack away and leave their desks. It took Bella a few minutes to realize what had happened. Someone amongst them had successfully sabotaged her prompt departure.

Bella was standing on tiptoe, gazing in the mirror propped against the wall of the room she still shared with Terry. There was no free space even though she kept the worn floorboards clean and tidy; the old mattress on which they had slept as children was gone and two narrow iron bedsteads with horsehair mattresses now replaced it. The only other item of furniture was a small set of drawers. The chest was covered with a broad chintz runner to disguise the woodworm below. Beside it stood the long mirror, broken at one corner but still in one piece.

Bella was gazing into it, admiring her reflection as she stood in the calf-length black dress that Micky had bought her. He didn't even know her size and yet it fitted to perfection. The dress was made of a soft, clinging fabric that must have cost the earth and the transformation had taken Bella's breath away.

'And where in the name of Jesus did you get that dress, girl?' Mary Doyle's voice was slurred as she leaned against the door.

'Where do you think?' Bella tried to ignore the unbridled aggression in her mother's tone. An

61

unspoken challenge that suggested a need for an all-out shouting match. She had been hoping that her mother would have left for the pub, her shift of duty beginning at six. But instead, Mary Doyle had sunk the last of the gin, a bottle she had found in the man's pocket an hour ago. Bella had watched her search him as he lay snoring in the chair. A satisfied expression had crept over Mary's face as she'd unscrewed the top and poured what was left of it down her throat.

'You've got a vicious tongue on you, girl. Talking to your mother as if she was–'

'*What?*' Bella's own anger was surfacing now. 'Someone who really cared what I look like?'

'I'll tell you what you look like in that, girl, a slut. A cheap little tart.'

'And you should know, Mother, shouldn't you?'

Bella had long ago accepted that Mary Doyle would pull out all the stops to spoil any happiness she found in life. It was in her mother's nature to resent her children's existence outside of the four dingy walls surrounding them. Mary's bitter thoughts showed on her face as she stood in the doorway, examining the picture that Bella presented.

'For all the grand clothes he buys you, it's still a Doyle inside them,' Mary persisted drunkenly. 'You'd think the Bryants were saints themselves for the crumbs they've thrown our way.'

'Crumbs is it?' Bella countered angrily as she took a step towards her mother. 'If it wasn't for them, you and that cripple outside,' she jerked her head fiercely towards the next room, 'would be begging on the streets and me and Terry put away somewhere.'

Mary lifted the glass in her hand and sucked down the alcohol noisily. 'Perhaps it would have been better if you had. A fifteen-year-old girl dressed up like a whore and that man himself is responsible and she still can't see it.'

Bella looked coldly into her mother's eyes. 'Micky ain't responsible for what I am, Mum, and you should know that better than anyone. If I've the makings of a whore inside me, it's you that put it there.'

Mary Doyle stepped forward and landed a blow across her cheek that momentarily stunned her. The stinging sensation spread over her skin and down to her neck but the discomfort was brief as she tossed back her disheveled hair.

'Don't ever do that again, Mum,' she warned, her eyes bright with anger.

'I'll not have you speak to me that way, girl.' There was a note of fear in Mary's voice as she stared into her daughter's burning gaze. 'Sure I'll keep you and your brother on the straight and narrow if it kills me,' she added weakly, falling back against the door.

Bella shook her head in amazement at these words. 'Don't worry, that'll never happen. In fact I'd be willing to lay top odds you'll never die of doing me and Terry a good turn. If you did, it would be the first ever since our births and even then it would turn out to be a mistake.' In silence she lifted her coat from the bed and slipped her bag over her shoulder. Straightening her back she walked past her mother to the front door where

Terry stood waiting. Then she turned slowly back to smile at the overweight, overblown body of Mary Doyle.

'Don't wait up for us,' she said as she grasped Terry's big hand in hers. Allowing her gaze to linger for a last few seconds on the harrowed face, she reminded herself that she needed no words from Mary Doyle to keep her on the straight and narrow. The picture before her was lesson enough.

Bella pulled Terry into the fresh air. The door banged noisily and she breathed in oxygen until her lungs felt as though they would burst. Bow Street air wasn't fresh, it was contaminated by the decay of the abandoned cottages and broken sewers. But any air was fresher than the poison under that roof.

The night was cold and dark as Bella and Terry looked around them at the forgotten street. After the war, the council hadn't bothered to light a road that was dying.

The sound of a car's engine rumbled in the distance. 'Micky!' cried Terry excitedly, like a child. 'Micky's coming.'

Bella's heart began to beat fast as she recognized the sound of Micky's car. For the next few hours she would pretend that she had never heard of Bow Street or the one remaining inhabited cottage. She would step out of this apology for a life and into a better one by far.

'Terry's comin' tonight, Micky.'

'No, Terry, not tonight, chum.' Micky's response was soft but final. 'You're staying with

64

Sean and Ashley. They got a nice game of Snap going just for you.'

'Terry wants to come.'

'*No,* Terry,' Bella repeated gently from the front seat of the big car, Micky's latest toy. 'Me and Micky are going out.'

Bella glanced at Micky as he drove. His face was smiling and happy and she hoped Terry wasn't going to spoil the evening. Micky was always very good with him, but Terry could try the patience of a saint sometimes. And Micky was no saint.

He inhaled the smoke from his cigarette and turned the wheel of the car. Bella thought he looked more handsome than ever in his dark suit with the cuffs of his white shirt showing under his jacket. When he caught her looking at him, he grinned.

'You wore it tonight then, doll?'

'Yeah, Micky. It's a really lovely dress.'

'Right size?'

'I don't know how you guessed.'

'Easy. You've got a good figure. I just described you to the girl. You know, with a bit of make-up you could look just like Lana Turner.'

'Lana Turner?' Bella didn't much like wearing make-up as she had a good complexion and wanted to be acknowledged for her own looks, even though Lana Turner was a big name on the films.

'Yeah ... with a few touches here and there you could be the spit,' Micky continued, oblivious to her thoughts. 'My favourite flick with her in was called *Johnny Eager,* back at the beginning of the war. I took that old slag – 'scuse me language –

65

Sheila Belcher to see it. Course, I didn't see much the first time round...' Micky smiled crookedly at himself in the driving mirror, 'but when I went again with a mate, me eyes were riveted. She ain't called the Sweater Girl for nothing. That flick really blew me socks off.'

Bella was engulfed in a wave of jealousy. She wasn't certain whether it was the mention of Lana Turner or Sheila Belcher that made her feel so bad. Lana Turner was blonde and a sex symbol and it would take a mountain of make-up to create even the slightest resemblance between them. As for Sheila Belcher, she remembered her clearly. She still had the vivid memory of seeing Sheila and Micky together, kissing and cuddling on the couch at Piper Street. Through a kid's eyes Sheila had been as voluptuous as Lana was now, all blonde hair and smouldering looks. At least that was how it seemed then. If Sheila was an old slag, Bella hadn't known it at the time.

'I wouldn't mind seeing *The Postman Always Rings Twice*,' Micky added casually. 'She's a real eyeful in that one.'

Bella had always thought that if she looked like anyone, it was Rita Hayworth with her long, auburn hair and flawless skin. Lana Turner wasn't a favourite of hers and anyway, she had always prided herself on being unique.

'Lana Turner's hair is a different colour to mine,' Bella said as she lifted her hand to touch her own. 'It's much lighter.'

'Yeah, but it's that look in your eyes, you know, when you sort of half close them. A bit of red lipstick and you could be a dead ringer.'

'I never wear red lipstick. It looks common.' Micky hadn't ever said anything personal about her appearance before.

Micky turned the wheel, a smooth whoosh coming from beneath his fingers. 'Forgot to say, Ronnie's coming with us tonight.'

Bella forgot about Lana Turner. 'Why's that?'

'Thought a foursome would be nice. He's bringing a lady friend. You wanna have a chat with her, Bells. There's no flies on our Joyce.'

'Joyce' was news to Bella. 'What does she do?'

'Oh, a bit of this and that.'

'How long have you known her?'

'As I said, she's more Ron's friend than mine. Joyce King.'

In all the time Bella had known Micky she hadn't heard a mention of Joyce. Not that she knew everything there was to know about the Bryants but she had always kept her ears and eyes open, as Micky himself had taught her to do. She'd been calling round to Piper Street to wait for her and Terry's orders, or rather Micky's instructions, for many years. When the air raids had lessened after the Blitz, he found a new niche for them, 'running' for the kennel-boys at the dog tracks. She and Terry had carried small parcels in their pockets and handed them over to the boys outside the grounds. They were told these were dog biscuits intended to help the greyhounds run faster. But when an animal had died after eating one of these so-called biscuits, Micky had moved them back to the doodlebug watch and scouting on the debris. And in all those years, as far as she could recall, Bella had never heard mention of

Joyce in the Bryant household.

'Joyce is a cracker, you'll like her,' Micky assured her now. 'She's a woman of the world, if you get my meaning.'

Bella decided to wait and see what was in store for the evening. Micky disliked being questioned. If ever anyone pressed him about something he didn't want to discuss, he would either walk off or get shirty. She would just have to swallow on the fact they weren't going to the Indigo on their own and that Ronnie and Joyce would accompany them.

Bella glanced over her shoulder at Terry who was sitting on the back seat, his big eyes never leaving her. What would this woman of the world called Joyce think of her and Terry?

She snuggled down in her seat, determined not to let the appearance of an unfamiliar female disturb her. She was with Micky and that was what counted. Her beautiful new black dress looked and felt good. Added to which she was wearing a new bra and new silk camiknickers, all hurriedly purchased from a spiv's suitcase at the market last week.

The Indigo was buzzing. Bella gazed through the dizzying trails of cigarette smoke to the other tables. She was on a high of excitement.

This was a real revue club, with real fan-dancers and silk-stockinged girls that kicked high to the music on a stage flooded with coloured lights. Pretty usherettes sold cigarettes and cigars from stacked trays as they moved flirtatiously amongst the party-goers in their skimpy silk skirts and high-heels. There were bubbles bursting from the champagne glasses, including her own, and there wasn't a woman in the room who didn't look like someone famous. Off the shoulder evening gowns and upswept hair-dos abounded and the men all resembled Clark Gable or Victor Mature.

Bella had never tasted champagne before and it was flowing headily through her bloodstream. Neither did she smoke, but tonight was an exception. Joyce used an elegant tortoiseshell cigarette holder that she held constantly and Bella felt she couldn't refuse a cigarette from the delicately engraved silver box that she flipped open.

The slight anxiety that Bella had felt as Micky had driven them to Piper Street had disappeared the moment she had met Joyce. She was a petite Londoner, nearer to thirty than twenty, with carefully bobbed dark hair and a direct gaze. She dressed immaculately, her choice of clothes subtle. The deep purple dress showed very little cleavage but it moulded her shape and complemented her dark eyes.

'So what do you think of this place?' Joyce's husky enquiry returned Bella to the moment.

'I love it.'

Joyce smiled, her gaze going curiously over Bella as they sat at the table whilst Ronnie and Micky talked with the owners of the Indigo, the Stratton brothers. The band had taken a break and the lighting had softened over the stage area. There was to be more entertainment later and Bella was waiting eagerly.

'You're very young,' Joyce remarked after a while as she inhaled the smoke deep into her lungs. Crossing one slim leg over another, she reclined in the luxurious chair. 'How old are you?'

'Sixteen, nearly.'

'And you've never been to a club like this before?'

'No, only the Dockland Settlement.'

'Is that on the island?'

'Yes, but it's just for kids really. Nothing sophisticated like the Indigo. The Dockland's been going years, like a youth club really.'

Joyce nodded interestedly. 'So what do you think about this latest idea of Micky's?'

Bella smiled, a misty look in her eyes. 'His ideas are always exciting.'

Joyce chuckled softly. 'You're crazy about him, aren't you?'

'I don't know what you mean.'

'It's all right, darling. He won't hear it from me. My lips are sealed.'

Bella looked down and into the safety of her lap. She didn't realize her feelings were so obvious.

'But getting back to what we're here for tonight,' Joyce persevered in a careful voice, 'personally I don't think a club like the Indigo would work on your island.'

Bella's head came up quickly. 'Why's that?'

'For one thing,' continued Joyce as she leaned gracefully forward to tap her cigarette on the triangular-shaped ashtray, 'there's the problem of the bridges, an old problem, but a frustrating one for traffic and any business that should come the club's way.'

Bella hadn't thought about the bridges being a

problem. When the ships passed down the river and through the docks, the island was virtually sealed off. Vehicles and pedestrians had to wait till the business was finished with. Access to the island, which was surrounded on three sides by water, was often a problem and she could see Joyce's point.

'For another,' continued Joyce thoughtfully, 'it really isn't your right sort of clientele.'

Bella frowned as she took this in. She thought she had liked Joyce but now she wasn't so certain. 'You mean islanders aren't good enough for a club like this?'

'Don't take it so personally, sweetheart. It's just business. The docks cater for a wide variety of folk, but will they go out and spend like the Indigo's customers? I mean, these girls and boys are having a really good time, no expense spared.'

Emboldened by the champagne she was drinking, Bella looked indignant. 'Islanders still know how to have a good time when we go out even if we aren't done up to the nines like these women are. I mean, their husbands and boy-friends are probably rich and money doesn't mean anything to them but even in the East End we can let our hair down the same as this lot if it's offered to us.'

For a moment Joyce just stared at her. Then very slowly she began to smile. 'Oh dear, I hadn't realized...'

'What?' Bella questioned abruptly.

'You're young and innocent, Bella, and that's your attraction. But you do have a lot to learn.'

Bella shrugged. 'Maybe I have, but I'm not a

snob. And I don't look down on people I don't know.'

Joyce raised her delicately shaped eyebrows. 'I wasn't looking down on you or anyone. But what you said amused me. You see, Bella dear, these women aren't with their husbands or even boyfriends. They're just working girls.'

Bella frowned. 'What do you mean?'

'I mean,' Joyce inclined her head to one side, 'they're hostesses, escorts. Paid by the club to be with the men for the evening and some for even longer.'

Bella sat in silence as she looked around her. Did Joyce mean they were prostitutes? Bella stared at the elegant, smiling beauties dressed in high fashion. 'What, all of them?' she asked, a little giggly now. 'Even that girl over there?' She went to point at the couple sitting to their right, but Joyce took her hand and patted it gently down on the table. The girl was wearing a gorgeous silver lamé dress and her hair was coiled up into a golden pleat at the back of her head. Her companion was looking into her eyes and pouring champagne into their long, fluted glasses.

Joyce nodded, smiling again. 'And that's not champagne.'

'What is it, then?'

'Probably a mixture of lemonade and wine. But her customer's paid the full price for a very expensive drink.'

Bella peered at her glass. 'Is this champagne?'

'Of course. Sammy Stratton's pride wouldn't let him offer Ronnie anything less.' Joyce slid her cigarette between her lips and sighed. 'The

Strattons are a big name in Soho. They're well known for their expertise in this trade. That's why we're here, to suss out their secrets.' She grinned. 'As if there were any, of course.'

Bella caught the note of irony and took a long sip of the champagne. She was mystified by Joyce who gave her a long, quizzical smile. 'Did Micky tell you that Ronnie isn't over the moon about the idea of a revue club?'

Bella nodded. 'He told me everything.'

'Including your part in his proposed plans?'

Bella was feeling light-headed from the alcohol. 'He told me enough. Anyway, I'd go along with what he wants as he's never let me down yet.'

'Then you must be slow on the uptake, my girl,' Joyce said wearily. 'Either that, or besotted.' She lifted her manicured hand and gestured to the room. 'Look around you, then look at yourself. You are a stunner and have a brain on you. So basically, that is where you come in. You'd be working for Micky just like these girls are working for the Stratton brothers.'

Bella felt a chill wash over her as Joyce leaned forward and took hold of her wrist. In a quiet voice she murmured, 'A word of advice from someone who knows. Believe me, I was as young as you are once and in a similar position. I know what I'm talking about. The Bryants are big on the island and Micky wants a slice of an even bigger pie. There are no flies on Sammy and Tony Stratton and Micky has seen the glint of gold in their eyes. That's fair enough, but their business is based on the women, that's how it works. Now, Micky is trying his damnedest to get Ronnie to

73

agree and, darling, you have to wake up and know what you want, or else be dragged into something you won't be able to get out of. Don't be blinded by Micky's charm. And you know how charming he can be when he tries.'

'Micky wouldn't force me into anything I didn't like,' Bella replied, offended, as she tried to make sense of what Joyce was saying.

'Just as long as you are savvy,' Joyce repeated, reclining in her seat. 'The clubs look glamorous I'll grant you and maybe glamour is what you want. But there's another side to it that is quite the opposite. Tell me to mind my own business if you like. But I will repeat this, I know what I'm talking about. And as a matter of fact, so does Ronnie.'

Bella didn't want to accept what she knew Joyce was trying to say. She had known Micky for years and Joyce a matter of hours. But even the champagne hadn't the power to take the sting out of Joyce's remarks. Bella knew she needed some fresh air. It wasn't only the alcohol that was having such a bad effect on her and suddenly Joyce's voice seemed very far away as the room began to spin in front of her eyes.

Chapter Seven

With his mind turning over the events of last night at the Indigo, Ronnie made the tea just as his mum had taught him as a boy. Boil the water and warm the pot, a full teaspoon of leaves for each person and one for the pot. A touch extravagant perhaps, but that was Mum's way and he never deviated from it. The ritual allowed him to think through his problems and Bella Doyle was certainly a problem. One he was going to have to think about carefully.

Somewhere between the making of a brew and the drinking he hoped the answer would come. At least, that's what his mum said. He wondered sadly if she had ever regretted bringing three sons into the world, a man's world, not really hers. As kids all her homespun wisdom had been water off a duck's back to them. Four strapping men that she'd washed, cleaned, cooked and mended for her whole adult life. Then died at only forty-four, in the time it took to light the gas. Gone. No say in the matter, no struggle for survival; just total blackout. And now he was raking over the memories with a fine-toothed comb, hoping for inspiration that he wished he could hear fall from her own lips.

Ronnie stirred the pot as the hot steam rose into his face. He was nearer to Mum making tea than he was anywhere else. Certainly not at her grave where she lay with Dad and next to Auntie Gwen. It was a desolate place that graveyard, and he felt a twinge of guilt at never going there.

Dragging his thoughts back to Bella, he asked the question once more. What was he going to do about her? Last night she'd passed out and now he felt responsible. The kid was only fifteen after all. He'd carried her upstairs and put her to bed in Mum and Dad's room. When he'd looked down at her and pushed the hair from her eyes, it struck him how young she was. How she'd always been around, her small figure following at Micky's heel. When he'd got demobbed and arrived home, the first thing he'd noticed was Bella Doyle sitting on the wall outside the house.

'It's me,' she'd greeted him, a grin on her dirty face. 'Bella Doyle.' He'd stood trying to get his bearings and forget the killing fields and there was this kid, grinning up at him. He'd nodded and moved past her, eager to see Micky and Sean. But she'd followed him, and the boy too, taller and thinner than before, but still with that vacant gaze. They'd watched Micky and Sean embrace him, tears in their eyes. He wouldn't ever forget that day. He was alive, back in the land of the living. Though God only knew how. And now, she was still here, part of their lives for good or bad after the night when they'd taken Jack Router and made him a cripple.

'Shove a couple more sugars in for me, Ron, will you? I'm trying to get me brain in gear.' This from Micky who stood in the kitchen doorway peering out from sleep-deprived eyes. A blanket was draped around his naked shoulders and he was shivering.

'You mixed your drinks as usual.'

'Yeah, well, it seemed like a good idea at the time.' Micky scratched his bare stomach and coughed chestily. 'When is the club deal going down then, bruv?'

Ronnie handed his brother a cup. 'No time soon as far as we're concerned.'

Micky looked alarmed. 'Why's that, then?'

'Because I agree with Joyce. The punters aren't going to trot all the way down to the island from the West End when they've got what they want on their doorstep.'

Micky walked slowly to the draining board and leaned on it, his face ashen from the previous night's bender. 'I reckon they would if the booze was cheap enough.'

Ronnie turned slowly to face his brother. 'Which is where you come in, of course.'

'I told you, Ron, me and Lenny were on to a big earner with the old tiddly we made. It had a real kick to it. I even tried it meself.'

'The answer's no, Micky.'

'Well, I don't see why you're so against it,' Micky countered irritably. 'Knocking out that stuff is child's play. It was only in the beginning that we made mistakes. Me and Lenny got it down to a fine art in the end. Blimey, look at all those Yanks we serviced in the war. They couldn't get enough of it. And we was only using Dad's lock-up just the same. At four quid a bottle, we could be running a little goldmine.'

Ronnie sat down at the table. 'It was industrial spirit, Micky. No matter what the label is you shove on the bottle, the truth is, it's gut rot. I don't want to be held responsible for innocent punters drinking what is in effect, neat poison.' He turned slowly, his eyes suspicious. 'I take it you got rid of any incriminating evidence? You pulled the plug on the lock-up?'

Micky nodded sullenly. 'Yeah, yeah, the place is as tight as a drum.'

'It had better be.'

'And there was no way them dead GIs was ever traced back to me,' Micky persisted truculently. 'They could've picked up the hooch from anywhere in the city. In fact if they'd stuck to ours, they might be alive to this day.'

But Ronnie was having none of it. 'I'll say this again for your benefit, Micky, 'cos you seem to be having trouble with your hearing lately,' he arched heavy eyebrows, 'your distillery career is well and truly over. It's too dangerous for the poor sods who drink it. And His Majesty's revenue men are rubbing their hands in glee at the thought of nicking people like you and Lenny Rigler.'

Micky slid off the draining board. 'It just ain't fair, that's all, we was on to a good thing.'

'And so was Crippin.'

Micky slouched down in a chair. 'So what time did Joyce go home, then?'

Ronnie began to pour another cup of tea. 'I drove her back to Poplar this morning.'

'Ain't you been to bed or is that a leading question?'

Ronnie frowned darkly at his brother. 'It's none of your bloody business. And while we're on the subject, that kid upstairs is going to have one hell of a lump of lead when she wakes.'

'Yeah,' Micky grinned as he watched Ronnie pour milk into a jug. 'She must've drunk more champagne than she let on. She was talking away one minute and out cold the next.'

'It was a bad idea, taking her. I should never have let you talk me into it.' Ronnie lit himself a cigarette.

'But she's perfect for club work.'

Ronnie's grey eyes flashed. 'I hope you don't mean what I think you mean.'

Micky looked shocked. 'Course I don't. Not *that*. But even you, Ron, must have noticed she has potential. A real punter's darling. She'd be perfect just swanning around the club, entertaining like. She's got the gift of the gab has our Bells. She just needs a bit of coaching. And Joyce would do that, easy as wink.'

Ronnie inhaled sharply and shook his head. 'It's all irrelevant, now, Micky. I've told you the club's off.'

'Aw Ron ... just think about it.'

'I have and it's a non starter.' He wagged a finger in his brother's face. 'And as far as the kid goes, she's already got a job and can make it on her own.'

Micky pulled the blanket around his waist and slurped his tea noisily. 'She'd be better off with us though.'

'Says who?'

'You was all for it last week.'

'I was all for her doing the books. The legit side – the market accounts and the scrap. And maybe a bit of driving.' He rattled his spoon around his

79

cup, then paused, narrowing his eyes thought-fully. 'But what does interest me is the fact that the Indigo had a couple of rooms out the back with tables. And they were taking plenty of cash. Now, a sporting club along those lines...'

'What about girls?'

'What about them?'

'You have to have girls.'

Ronnie began to smile. 'That's all you think about, Micky, ain't it? It's a wonder you ain't had more accidents tripping over your dick.'

They both laughed and Ronnie relaxed. He'd thought he was going to have serious opposition from Micky this morning.

'Right, let's get to work.' Ronnie pulled out a big, dog-eared ledger from the drawer of the table. He placed it before them and opened it carefully, sliding his index finger down the left-hand side of the page. 'We've got Foxy Mason running the stalls up Roman Road, right? And Buster on the Lane. What about Cox Street?'

'All done.' Micky rubbed his palm across his mouth to stifle another yawn. 'Lol Partridge and her old man are on the barrows and we got a couple of suitcases at either end.'

'And the running?'

'Six at least, all good reliable boys.'

Ronnie nodded in satisfaction. 'Now there's two or three lorry loads out the back to get shot of. I want the yard clear before PC Plod makes his social call.'

'How much are we slipping him?' Micky asked curiously.

'Five notes for the time being.'

'Saucy bugger!'

'It's an investment,' Ronnie shrugged. 'He's in too deep to back out now and he knows it. And he just got lumbered with another dustbin lid.'

The brothers were grinning at each other when a noise at the kitchen door made them look round. Terry was standing there, his tall, lanky body clothed in a crumpled suit.

Micky chuckled. 'He didn't even get his kit off last night. Just slept on the landing outside Bells' door, curled up like a bloody dog.'

'Cup of tea, Terry?' Ronnie lifted the pot. He knew that the boy hadn't budged an inch all night.

'Terry give Bella tea.'

'Yeah, I'll pour one and you can take it up.'

'Bella sick, ain't she Ron?'

'No, it was just the booze, chum. Get this down her and she'll be okay.'

Ronnie watched Micky studying Terry and he wasn't sure what he saw in his brother's eyes. Whatever it was, he didn't care for it much and he found he wasn't surprised when Micky stood up and said casually, 'You sit down, Terry old son, and rest your weary feet. I'll do the honours.'

But Terry stood where he was. 'Terry take Bella's tea.'

Ronnie watched with interest as his brother hesitated. Ronnie could almost hear the cogs in his brain working, which of course, Terry couldn't. But it was instinct that had Terry standing his ground.

Micky shrugged. 'Have it your own way, pal. I'm going back for a kip on the settee.'

When he had gone, Ronnie handed Terry the tea. 'Tell her to get dressed and come down for some breakfast,' he said quietly and Terry nodded, balancing the china in the palm of his hand.

Alone once more, Ronnie lifted the pot and replenished his own cup. He was glad to see that Micky didn't always get his own way. And in Bella's case, he hoped it would be a long time before he did.

'What was Joyce going on about last night?' Bella asked in a whisper as Micky drove them home. She was feeling sick and her head was still spinning. How much champagne had she drunk last night? 'She said something about me being dragged into something I can't get out of.'

'Did she now?'

'I can't remember the rest.'

'You do trust me, Bells, don't you?'

'Course I do. Why shouldn't I?'

He reached across and grasped her wrist, squeezing it gently. ''Atta girl. I want you with me when we hit the big time. That was all she meant. She's all right Joyce, but she and Ron ain't chancers whereas I am. Ron and old Joycie are a bit negative, if you know what I mean. Funny thing is, I was doing all right whilst Ron was away fighting. Used me initiative and called a few nice shots. But when he came home from France...' Micky thoughtfully slid the wheel slowly through his fingers, 'well, he was a different man. Takes life too serious now if you ask me. Needs to lighten up a bit. But in all fairness, what can you expect after seeing so much blood and guts spilled right in front of your eyes?'

'That must have been terrible,' Bella agreed softly.

'Yeah, but the war's in the past, ain't it? This is the here and now. I respect them both, of course, but I've got me own style and won't have it cramped,' he ended with a sideways glance at Bella who was trying to think through the waves of nausea that still swam around her stomach. 'Anyway, just as long as I've got you with me – and Terry, of course,' Micky added quickly, aware of Terry's presence in the back of the car. 'You are with me, girl, aren't you?'

'You know I am, Micky.'

'So our business is *our* business, right? We'll keep it under our hats, rather than worry Ron.'

Bella nodded slowly, though she didn't really understand. She knew one thing though. She wasn't ever going to get drunk again.

'What's this Dixons like then?' Micky asked, changing the subject so quickly it took Bella a few moments to catch up.

'All right.'

'You could give it the elbow any time you like you know. Come and work for me. We'd make a good team I reckon.'

Bella felt a warm wave of pleasure break into her gloom at Micky's persuasive words. She really did loathe the thought of Dixons on Monday but she didn't want to be a failure in Micky's eyes. And if she chucked in the job now, it might seem she really couldn't stand on her own two feet.

'Anyway, give it some thought.'

She pointed to the corner. 'You can drop us off

here, Micky.'

'We ain't there yet. And you're still looking a bit Tom and Dick.'

Bella nodded slowly. 'I need some fresh air, Micky.'

'What about coming for a hair of the dog that bit you?' he said enticingly.

'I need more champagne like I need a hole in the head, Micky Bryant.' She managed a smile as she reached for the handle. 'Thanks for the lift.'

'Well, it was worth a try.' Micky grinned and stopped the car. 'You gonna be all right?'

She nodded and her heart gave its usual flutter as his smile broadened. If he only knew how much she wanted to take him up on the offer of a job. But her pride wouldn't let her.

He winked. 'I'll be in touch soon, Bells. Good luck with them snobby types at Dixons.'

She stood with Terry on the pavement and watched the shiny black car move away. When it was gone she frowned at Terry who stood meekly beside her. They'd stayed out all night and were actually rolling home on Sunday morning. She laughed at herself despite the hangover from hell. Her mother probably had a worse one.

'Come on, Terry. Let's walk down to the river and sit on the dock. Pretend we're going on the boats.' It was a game they'd played as kids and Terry grinned.

'Terry jump the barges,' he laughed, his eyes creasing up at the corners. 'Won't fall in.'

'You better not, because I ain't jumping in to save you today.' Bella caught her breath and tried to keep down the breakfast of bread and marg that Ronnie had made her eat. If she fell in the water now she'd sink like a brick.

The alcohol was still in her throat like bile. She'd only just managed to keep the tea down that Terry had brought her. Ronnie had said the first hangover was always the worst. Bella was going to make it her last. You weren't in control when your brain was fuddled. And that was a luxury she could ill afford.

Christmas was four weeks away. Bella was going to spend her hard-earned wages on clothes. But Cox Street was unusually quiet; business was taking second place to the big wedding up West. Princess Elizabeth and Philip Mountbatten were getting married and the event was headlines. The BBC had broadcast that hundreds had slept overnight in the Mall in order to catch a glimpse of the couple riding in the Irish state coach. There had been rumours that the wedding dress, sewn with diamonds and hundreds of pearls, had been delivered secretly to the palace last night by the designer himself, Norman Hartnell.

But it wasn't the wedding that Bella was discussing with Dolly as they walked through the market. It was Bella's trip to the Indigo that had Dolly in a state of suspense. 'Did you see anyone famous there?'

'Not exactly. But they all looked like film stars.' Bella didn't want to spoil the impression she was giving Dolly and left out what Joyce had told her.

'Did Micky ask you for a dance?'

'Yes, we danced all night.'

'Was there singers and a band?'

Bella nodded patiently as they came to the stalls decorated with holly and Christmas paper chains. 'It was just like you see on the films, including the champagne.' She giggled and decided to tell Dolly the truth. 'I drank too much and had to stay at Micky's house.'

Dolly's eyes bulged. 'What, all night?'

'What do you think?'

'I don't know. I mean – where did you sleep?'

'In a bed, of course.' Bella laughed. This was just what Dolly wanted to hear and Bella elaborated. 'A double bed.'

'Bella! You didn't!'

Bella burst out laughing. 'Course not. It was Mr and Mrs Bryant's bed when they were alive.'

'Oh!' Dolly looked vaguely disappointed. 'Wasn't it a bit creepy sleeping in a bed that belongs to dead people?'

Bella shrugged. 'It was big and comfortable and anyway, I wouldn't have known if a ghost tapped me on the shoulder as I was out like a light.'

"What about Terry?'

'He slept on the landing.'

'What did your mum say?'

Bella turned to raise her eyebrows at her friend. 'What can she say? She stands to lose the money I bung her each week and she ain't about to give that perk up, is she?'

Dolly looked uncomfortable. Bella knew that even though they had been friends for years and Dolly more than anyone knew everything about her, her friend found it hard to accept the facts.

'Wake up, Dolly, this is Bella Doyle you're talking to not Lady Muck.'

86

'I know, but…'

'Tell me about Burlingtons,' Bella said quickly as the faint whiff of fish escaped from Dolly's plain brown coat. With her unfashionable pill-box hat and brogue shoes, she looked more like her mother than ever. Dolly's bottom lip quivered. 'There's not much to tell really.'

'Is it interesting?'

Dolly giggled. 'Not really.'

'Why don't you change it if you're bored.'

'I couldn't do that. Me mum would kill me.'

'Batter you to death I suppose.'

Dolly burst into laughter. 'Oh, Bella that's what I miss so much – the fun we used to have. At Burlingtons the women are much older than me. The men too.'

'Isn't there a nice young fishmonger?' Bella couldn't hide the sarcasm in her voice and she was surprised when Dolly blushed. Her round face became even redder as Bella stared at her curiously.

'Well, there is one…'

'Really?' demanded Bella, shocked at this confession.

'He works downstairs in the gutting department.' Dolly began to giggle again. 'It's really horrible work, all these slimy heads and big glassy eyes staring back at you when you walk in.'

Bella pushed her hand through Dolly's elbow and they walked on. 'So what's his name, then?'

Dolly trapped her lip under her small white teeth. 'Percy Shine.'

'What's he look like?'

'Well, not handsome like Micky, but he's got a

87

lovely smile.'

'Has he asked you out?'

Dolly looked shocked. 'No! Of course not. We've hardly talked, but he's winked at me. We only speak when I go in the fish shop to take the orders.'

'You should ask him home to one of your mum's teas,' Bella suggested mischievously, but Dolly was impressed.

'I might, if I can work up the courage.'

Bella felt a sudden deep pang of envy. Dolly hadn't had a boyfriend before, she hadn't even been kissed behind the bike sheds at school, but here she was smitten whilst she, Bella, was longing for Micky to take her out on a real date, hoping he would finally see her for who she was and tell her how beautiful she looked. But all that had happened so far was that she had ended up tipsy and couldn't remember much of what had gone on. Bella sighed and curled the collar of her coat up to her ears. 'Let's have a look at the clothes stall.'

She was going to buy something special for herself, something like the purple dress that Joyce had worn, which had looked very classy. The neckline had been just low enough to attract attention, and the design was simple, complementing Joyce's figure. Bella had decided that simplicity was better than all the frills and fancies that had come into fashion after the utilitarian clothes of the war. Christmas was coming up and she wanted Micky to notice her. Not as Lana Turner, but as herself, Bella Doyle who would be a grown-up sixteen in January.

Dolly bounced excitedly beside her. 'I want to

get a nice outfit for Christmas. I'm fed up with dull colours. Look at me, all in browns and greys.'

'Is this new enthusiasm all for Percy's benefit?'

Dolly nodded, her expression glowing as they approached the clothes stall. It was heaped with every conceivable second-hand garment a person could wear. Bella turned over the dresses and cardigans, but nothing appealed. Every Christmas Eve she and Terry went to the Bryants where Sean cooked a roast, a tradition he had managed to keep all through the war. She and Terry helped Sean in the kitchen, though Terry mostly sat on a chair out of the way, while all Micky's friends would turn up and there'd be singing and a bit of a knees-up after. It was the best night of the year. She always hated it ending. At number three Bow Street Christmas was entirely liquid.

Dolly was waving at her, she held up an orange-coloured blouse with a row of frills around the neck. Bella was going to shake her head in disgust but Dolly was delighted. The decision was made and Bella smiled as Dolly searched her purse for coins.

The picture of her friend dressed in a tangerine delight and sitting next to Percy at Mrs Taylor's tea table made her smile. If Percy could survive that encounter he could survive anything.

Chapter Eight

The office was decorated with a few sprigs of holly pinned above the glass-panelled door. Four small faded decorations that might once have looked seasonal hung in each corner of the room. Several decades after their purchase the red crepe paper was brown at the edges and dust had worn down the edges of the limp bells and sad bows.

Bella gazed around her at the bowed heads of her colleagues and counted the minutes to leaving. Four whole days of undiluted pleasure stretched ahead. It was Christmas Eve and Micky was calling at seven and taking her and Terry to Piper Street. Joyce was going to be there this year, celebrating the start of the holiday. Bella was going to wear the dark green dress she had bought especially for the occasion at Cox Street.

'You'd better make certain the first week of January's paperwork is in order,' Evelyn warned as she leaned across to Bella's desk. 'It's a very busy time for Dixons. Don't forget to change the date on the top of all the invoices, as if we write in the old year incorrectly we have to do the whole thing over again.'

'Don't I know it,' Bella sighed heavily, then nodding to the fat ledger beside her she smiled. 'I've also ticked the respective customers off in the book so there's no mistake.'

'You shouldn't do that till they're posted,' Evelyn complained as she folded a sheet of paper and slid it into the envelope. 'Miss Conway's going through all our work with a magnifying glass since ... well...' Evelyn pulled back her shoulders and sniffed.

Bella ignored the hint at her inefficiency and continued with clearing her desk. She had never been able to prove it was not her work that had been at fault and she had stopped trying to understand why the staff at Dixons were so pathetically childish. It was evident none of them expected someone like her to be capable of using her brain and her fingers at the same time. It was patently obvious the other girls disliked her but Bella wasn't about to let that spoil her day.

Putting away her books, she collected her work and went through to Miss Conway's office. It was empty, though she could see Miss Conway's small, stout figure through the frosted glass of the next office. She left her file in the desk tray.

Bella glanced at the big round clock above the door. Three minutes to six. She returned to her desk and noted the other girls were leaving theirs. She heard their voices as they passed through the outer office and Miss Conway's in reply.

Bella took her coat and bag from the hook and glanced one last time at the room that might as well have had prison bars attached to it. How long would she have to work here before she was accepted? And even if she was, could she stand the monotony of the next few years? As she buttoned up her coat and slid her bag over her shoulder, Miss Conway appeared.

91

'Miss Doyle, before you leave...'

Bella looked expectantly into the hard, humourless face. Perhaps this was a seasonal acknowledgement and she smiled in anticipation.

'You dealt with the Harrington account this week, did you not?'

Bella nodded disappointedly.

'Lord Harrington has decided to change his instructions. Unfortunately I can find no record of the original order.'

'But I put my work on your desk not two minutes ago,' Bella protested, glancing over Miss Conway's shoulder.

'You may well have, but the Harrington file isn't there.'

'But that's impossible...' Bella stepped aside. 'I'll look.'

'I already have, but see for yourself if you must.'

Bella hurried into Miss Conway's office and searched through her work. She double-checked and felt her heart sink. Was it possible that she had mislaid such an important order?

'Well?'

'It's not there,' Bella said helplessly as she drew her hand over the top of her own desk. 'I just don't understand.'

'I'm afraid, neither do I.'

Bella stared around the room as if expecting to suddenly see the missing file appear. There was only one other explanation and it was one she didn't want to acknowledge. The other girls had left before her. It would have been easy to slip a random file into a bag or under a coat without Miss Conway seeing.

'Please take off your coat and come into my office.'

'But it's Christmas Eve–' Bella was cut short.

'Indeed it is. And because of your inefficiency, Miss Doyle, both you and I will be spending the last hours of it rectifying a foolish and unnecessary mistake.' She thrust back her shoulders and turned away, her flat heels squeaking on the polished floor.

Reluctantly Bella removed her coat. The buses would be few and far between this evening and a walk back to the island would take her forever.

Swallowing her disappointment, she followed Miss Conway into the outer office and prayed that Micky would wait for her.

'Terry been waiting.'

Bella walked into the empty cottage. Her mother and Jack were long gone to the Rose, but Terry stood in the dark passage, his smile wide when he saw her.

'Terry been waiting, Terry has.'

He followed her into the room they still shared. A curtain made of heavy chintz defined two sleeping areas. Her bed took up the largest part with a small wooden chest of drawers standing at the foot. On the other side of the drape, a mattress lay on the floor. A faded dark blue candlewick bedspread was tucked over it, with Terry's clothes folded neatly into a pile on a small wooden chair. His jacket was threaded around it, his boots tucked underneath. The broken mirror had been returned to its nail on the wall and Bella's new dress lay over her bed in readiness for tonight.

Now the slim fitting gown with the crepe bodice and elegant panelled skirt seemed to mock her.

Tears of frustration filled her eyes. For an hour and a half she had been trapped with Miss Conway, who had methodically trawled through the Harrington account, drawing up new documents. When Bella had finally been dismissed, the night was cold and unforgiving, a hint of snow in the air. Only the pubs she passed as she walked to the bus stop showed any sign of life. She had hoped to catch a bus all the way home but she'd settled for one that left her at the top of West Ferry Road.

'Did Micky call here?'

Terry nodded, lifting his bony fingers to scratch his head.

'Is he coming back?'

'Yeah, Terry going to Micky's party.'

'What time did he say?'

Terry shrugged.

'Did he say anything else?'

'Terry goin' to a party.'

Bella sighed in exasperation. 'That's not what I asked, Terry, but then I know I'm wasting my breath expecting a sensible answer. Go and sit down somewhere while I change.'

Her brother hung his head and moved behind the curtain. Bella pulled it forward harshly, the rings rattling on the iron rail. What a dump this place was, she thought as she hurriedly took off her coat. Even though Micky had distempered the damp walls and Ronnie had got the council to disinfect the house each year, it was still a pigsty. The population of rats had grown and the bugs were relentless, despite the disinfectant. In fact it seemed as though they thrived on it. The cottage would never be anything but a tip, but at least Micky and Ronnie had made it a tip they could live in. If the long-awaited prefab ever materialized – *if* – Terry would get his own room and she hers. Gilda and Ron Ellis and their two kids, a family that had once lived in Bow Street, had been allocated a prefab a short while ago. The asbestos bungalow had three bedrooms and a kitchen with a separate toilet and washroom outside. Gilda had shown the world and his wife around it for weeks as if it was Buckingham Palace.

Bella stripped off her working clothes and rubbed her sore heels. She had blisters from walking all that way. She was also in need of a wash. But there was no chance of that. The sink would be full of dirty dishes and the drain blocked with dog-ends. She sat on her bed in her bra and knickers and gulped down her frustrated tears. It wasn't fair she had to live like this. No wonder the other girls ignored her. They could smell the filth on her no matter how much she attempted to wash it off. Bow Street was like indelible ink, you couldn't remove the stain. It stuck with you for life, filled every pore. She was not like the other girls at the office, never would be. And they knew it.

Bella lifted her dress from the bed, pressing the cloth against her cheek. Undoing the little buttons at the front she carefully pulled it over her head. With the same care she slid her arms into the long, tailored sleeves. Looking in the mirror, her eyes gazed back unhappily. She smiled, causing an immediate transformation. Her white teeth sparkled and her gaze resumed its intensity. Drawing back her thick auburn locks, she lifted her chin.

Lana Turner ... yes, she could see the resemblance now as she lowered the lids of her eyes, assuming the expression Micky had described. He was returning for her and that was all that mattered. She took her bag and searched inside for a tortoiseshell compact she'd bought from the market, the case similar to Joyce's cigarette holder. Inside the compact was a pond of genuine loose powder. Tonight she would apply the full works.

It was five minutes to midnight.

Bella was sobbing loudly into her pillow. A pillow that smelt of must and damp and now looked filthy. She had cried so hard that the make-up she had carefully applied had washed onto it. She stared at herself in the mirror and laughed. No wonder Evelyn and Margery and the other girls despised her; she was a square peg in a round hole at Dixons no matter how hard she tried to fit. And it was the same with Micky. He didn't really care about her. Or Terry. Over the years they had been useful to him, returning him the best of the stuff they found on the debris. Every penny he'd paid them had been hard-earned and she and Terry could have got more from a totter or the markets. But they had always been loyal to Micky. And now he was enjoying himself on Christmas Eve having forgotten them. Was he relieved not to be burdened by them anymore? After all these years, was today the beginning of a future without him? At this thought she wept all the more, burying her face in the pillow. She had tried her best to be independent, but her plan had backfired. Her real intention had been to make Micky want her all the more. She had clearly failed and was now paying the penalty. Life was unfair. She had tried hard to better herself but she was getting nowhere. She shuddered at the thought of what people knew about her. The girls at work had found out where she lived. She'd never told them, just said she came from the island. Then Evelyn had let it out one day, a look of scorn on her face as if Bow Street was a dirty word. Which, thought Bella as she blew her nose, to them it probably was.

'Bella crying.' Terry touched her arm gently. His gaze was full of sympathy. But he was part of her misery too and she shrank away from him.

'Micky coming. Micky coming for Bella.'

She sat up, her eyes accusing. 'Course he's not coming, you daft 'aporth. He's off somewhere enjoying himself. What does he want with the likes of me, anyway?' She stared into Terry's bewildered face. She knew that unlike Micky, he cared about her. That in this world there was only one person who really loved her. And that was Terry.

'Terry sorry.' He reached out again for her hand. She wanted to hit him, to shake him, to make him feel what she was feeling. But she knew she didn't need to do any of this. He was already hurting, without her having to try. Terry had been hurting all his life inside. He just didn't have the wherewithal to know it.

He hung his head, exposing the fleshy parts of his scalp where his hair had fallen out. There were nits crawling in the fine layers and he reached up to scratch them. His nails were bitten and black and his shoulders sagged under the crumpled jacket. How could she love him so much yet resent him at the same time? As if acting of their own accord, her arms opened.

'Terry sorry,' he mumbled again as he crawled into them.

'It's me who's sorry, Terry.' She rocked him and stroked his hair. 'I took it out on you and you don't even know what it's all about.' She kissed his cheek. 'It doesn't matter about Micky, our Terry. It doesn't matter about anyone. As long as we've got each other we'll be all right.'

'Is the planes coming?'

'No, they ain't been coming for years.'

Bella leaned her head against his and true to the pattern of childhood, they fell asleep.

Ronnie lay in the darkness on the big double bed that had been his parents and listened to the noise downstairs. Micky certainly wasn't missing a trick, in the literal sense of the word. Still, it was his home as much as anyone's and if he wanted to have a bit of fun, then why shouldn't he? Ronnie pulled the smoke from his cigarette deep into his lungs. What would Mum have to say about Micky's so-called friends, he wondered? A wry smile touched his lips. He could hear her now, see the look of horror on her face as she studied the women Micky and Lenny Rigler had picked up at the pub.

'You can give her the elbow immediately,' Mum would have declared if Micky had ever had the gall to confront her with a tart. Which, of course, he wouldn't. No more than Sean would ever reveal to Mum the reason why he always hung about with Ashley Crane. Not that he, Ronnie, was in a position to judge either Micky's women or Sean's choice of his own sex. Here he was in the early hours of Christmas morning hooked up with a lady of dubious background himself. He glanced down at the prone figure beside him and wondered if Joyce was still on the game. She maintained she had retired years ago, leaving 'her girls' to do the business. Which, apparently, was true. The times he called round to Joyce's place, they were all well and truly occupied, with Joyce employing a couple of his heavies to look after her investment. Ronnie blew a funnel of smoke into the air. His lads rarely had any trouble from Old Bill, who were well provided for and gave Joyce's drum a wide berth. It was more the odd punter who got lairy and had to be dealt with. Still, that was what good muscle were there for and Ronnie was happy to do business with Joyce. Though this was the first time in all the years he had known her they had slipped out of their professional roles.

A raucous scream from downstairs followed by loud laughter disturbed the sleeping form beside him. Joyce lifted herself on one elbow, frowning sleepily. 'What was that?'

Ronnie laughed softly. 'A good party by the sound of it.'

Joyce slid up on the pillow and pulled the sheet over her breasts. She pushed back her dark hair and leaned her head against the varnished headboard. 'Your brother certainly knows how to enjoy himself.'

Ronnie reached over to the bedside cabinet and tapped a cigarette from the packet. He lit it with his own and handed it to Joyce. In the darkness, the two ends glowed red.

'This reminds me of the blackout.' Joyce inhaled deeply, her body relaxing. 'Even a lit cigarette in the street was classed as a sin.'

Ronnie nodded, feeling her warmth envelop him. It was the first time they had made love and he hoped it wouldn't be the last. 'A long time ago now.'

Joyce turned to look at him. 'Thank God you went away to war and grew up a bit before we did this.' She drew a finger over his shoulder. 'You never talk about it, do you, the war, I mean?'

'What's there to say?'

Joyce smiled. 'Don't worry. I don't want to talk about it either. Just thought maybe you did.'

Ronnie stubbed out his cigarette. 'I'd rather talk about us.'

She gave a soft chuckle. 'So no regrets about bedding a mature lady?'

Ronnie had no regrets even though it was a calculated risk they'd both taken tonight. He'd felt that if Joyce had been game enough to indulge in a little fun, then so had he. 'Truth is, I've always fancied you, Joyce, but never thought it was a good idea to mix business with pleasure.'

'So what made you change your mind?' she

asked huskily.

'You did.' He took her in his arms.

'I like you Ronnie,' she whispered softly, 'always have. But I've a living to make.'

'Look, Joyce, I've got as much to lose as you when we're talking business. We see eye to eye on our deals, with a nice little earner going between us. I wouldn't want to spoil that either.'

Joyce paused thoughtfully. 'Well, sweetheart, you've always played fair by me, looked after me and the girls and if it wasn't for your lads parked at my door every night, I wouldn't do the good trade I do. Most of the brass houses round here have got ugly reputations with even uglier customers. I've managed to keep my nice clean regulars thanks to you. Even though I pay through the nose for it.'

Ronnie feigned surprise. 'I do the job, Joyce. And keep Old Bill happy. The buggers don't come cheap these days.'

'I know that. You take the squeeze off and I've been up and running since the GIs disappeared, God Bless their randy little arses. It's thanks to you I'm still in business and not scratching for punters in some godforsaken little fleapit. I'm really grateful, Ron.'

Ronnie reached out to lift her chin. 'Is this what this is all about – gratitude?'

'I'll give you three guesses.'

He kissed her gently. 'That's what I like about you, Joyce. You've got a man's outlook on life.'

'And that's supposed to be a compliment?'

'In my book it is.'

She pulled his head down. 'Well, I'll tell you

101

this for nothing. I'd be a fool not to take you up on a little fun. You're in the prime of life and a good-looking bloke and could have any woman you wanted. Granted, you are a moody sod at times...'

Ronnie jerked her hard against him and cupped the full swell of her large breasts in his hands. She was a beautiful woman in his eyes and he wanted her all over again.

She stayed his hands suddenly. 'Ronnie, the moment you want out, you will tell me?'

'We haven't even got started yet.'

'I'm not a working girl if it makes any difference.'

He grinned. 'That's reassuring.'

'I'm serious, Ron. There's been no one for–'

He kissed her, pushing his tongue between her lips to explore her soft, welcoming mouth. She responded as he knew she would and, leaving him breathless, slid down the length of his body.

He was vaguely aware of the noise from the front room, but let it flow over him. He was losing himself and it felt good to forget. Joyce knew what he needed and he hoped he could please her too. There was only a brief regret as he thought of the two kids both he and Micky had abandoned tonight, the first Christmas Eve for years. But things just happened sometimes; all their lives were changing. He hoped the girl would grow out of mooning over Micky and find her own way in this miserable world. The moment of guilt passed quickly as Joyce guided him across her and soon Bella Doyle was far from his mind.

The rain was lashing the pavements and gurgling in the gutters. Bella sheltered under the stone arch of Dixons' entrance, shivering. Her collar was turned up to enclose the headscarf that covered her head and her coat was belted tightly, but her legs and shoes were soaking as the force of the downpour splashed over the stone step on which she stood. It was the end of first week of January and at half past six she had missed her bus. Again.

Streamers of lights reflected across the Commercial Road as vehicles chugged their way noisily through the flood. A city bus passed by, a beacon of light travelling west. A car ploughed through a puddle and she stepped back as the spray covered her coat and spattered her legs. The face in the car gazed back at her briefly, then was gone. Miss Conway drove the Morris and in the passenger seat sat Evelyn, her warm ride home assured.

Bella blinked the rain from her eyes as she stared after the car. Well, what did she expect after all? If she was lying flat in the middle of the road, Miss Conway would probably have driven round her.

The drips were trickling down from her headscarf and into her neck. She knew the longer she stood here, the wetter she would get, she had no umbrella so she would be soaked through by the time she reached home. With head bowed and holding her collar together with frozen hands, she stepped out into the night.

The force of the wind made her stoop forward. In a matter of seconds she was drowned. By the time she reached the bus stop there was water swilling in her shoes. Her headscarf was plastered to her head and her blouse and skirt soaked. As she waited, a car drew up and the door flew open.

'Bella!' Dolly scrambled out, pulling her coat around her and squinting through the rain. 'What are you doing here?'

'I've missed me bus.'

'Get in quick.' Dolly pushed her into the car. 'This is my ... well, it's Percy.'

'Pleased to meet you, I'm sure,' said the driver grinning from ear to ear as Bella fell into the back seat. 'I've heard all about you from Doll,' he said, pulling his cap jauntily over his forehead.

Bella untied her scarf and shook her wet hair free. She shivered in the warmth of the car as Dolly slammed the front door.

'Just look at you, Bella, you're drowned!'

'I'll soon dry off.'

'You need a hot bath.'

Bella laughed. 'I won't get one of those unless I jump in the drink.'

'Course, I forgot, you haven't got a–' Dolly looked embarrassed. 'I mean, you could have a bath at our house if you like.'

'No, I wouldn't put you to the bother.'

'It's no bother. Mum's gonna be so pleased to see you. And Ray too. He was only asking after you the other day. It's a wonder your ears weren't burning.'

Bella wondered exactly what had been said about her in the Taylor household. She couldn't believe it was very pleasant. After all, the last time she'd parted from Dolly, she had been angry with Ray and walked out of the house in a huff.

'So where have you two been tonight?' Bella discreetly changed the subject.

'Up the market for some veg. Percy got a nice piece of cod from work and we thought a bit of cabbage would go with it for dinner.'

'Her Mum is a lovely cook,' Percy remarked, causing Bella's wet eyebrows to jump.

'On Fridays Ray and Percy always nip down to the pub for a pint,' Dolly added shyly. 'Have a quick game of darts together.'

'Yeah, I look forward to me Friday nights,' Percy acknowledged as the car jerked forward and Dolly giggled.

'Tell you what, you can have a nice hot dip whilst I help Mum with the dinner and then you can borrow some of my clothes whilst yours are drying by the fire. Come on, Percy, get a move on or this girl will die of pneumonia.'

Bella didn't have the heart to argue. A bath sounded like heaven but she would have to pay the penalty of meeting the Taylors again. Still, as she gazed at the back of Percy's square, dependable head, she had to admit that the cosy interior of Chapel House Street was a far better prospect to the freezing cottage.

Percy landed his palm on the car horn and shook his fist. 'You blooming great idiot,' he shouted at a man on a bicycle inadvertently being blown in their path. 'You ain't safe to be on that contraption.'

Dolly elbowed him fiercely in the ribs. ''Scuse the language, Bella. Ladies present, Percy Shine.'

'Oops, sorry girls. Forgot me manners I'm ashamed to say.'

Bella smiled at the picture they made together in the front seats. Some things didn't change after all. Dolly was the spit of her mother and it looked like Percy was following in Mr Taylor's footsteps. Dolly's startlingly awful taste in clothes, a bright red beret and a rust-coloured raincoat, resembled a young Mrs T right down to the lace-up boots on her size seven feet.

Yet Bella was envious of her friend. Dolly looked happy, even pretty in a sort of disorganized way and Percy wasn't bad looking either. He did have a nice smile as Dolly had said and it was lovely to be chauffeured.

'This is a nice car, Percy.' Bella leaned forward, her wet clothes making her shiver all the more.

'Yeah,' he nodded proudly, turning to wink at her. 'Second only in looks to the girl sitting next to me.'

Dolly giggled loudly, giving Percy another shunt in the ribs. Bella reclined on the seat trying not to inhale the strong odour of fish. Apart from this small disadvantage, she was impressed with Dolly's catch. His suit, apart from the cap, looked reasonably modern and he had a nice straight back and broad shoulders.

'On Christmas Day Percy took us out to the country,' Dolly elaborated. 'It was really lovely, even though Mum and Dad and Ray was all a bit cramped in the back. We went over Bromley way, the posh part, you know. All them lovely houses and gardens.' Turning to Bella she grabbed the back of the seat. 'I'll bet Micky took you up West again to one of them revue clubs, didn't he?'

Bella was trying to forget the terrible time she had had since Christmas. Micky didn't call round until New Year's Eve. He said him and Ronnie had been busy working all hours known to man. Bella hadn't told him how disappointed she had been on Christmas Eve, how every day had seemed like weeks with no word from him. And how finally she'd been forced to accept the fact that she was a long way down the list of Micky's priorities.

Dolly was staring at her and she smiled brightly. 'I had a wonderful Christmas, very busy though. Sorry I didn't send a card, but time just flew by.'

'Oh.' Dolly nodded wistfully.

'Hold tight, girls, we're nearly there.' Percy tooted the horn with familiar ease as he steered the car into Chapel House Street where all the neat terraced houses were illuminated by the lights of their cosy front rooms. A far cry, Bella thought heavily, to the black coldness of Bow Street. She couldn't wait to see the expression on Mrs Taylor's face.

Chapter Nine

Battered cod had replaced the Spam sandwiches, though the five diners sitting at the table appeared to be savouring every bite. That was how it seemed to Bella, who was trying her best to swallow the fish that had been fried to within an inch of its life. Dorothy Taylor had served up the meal with as much aplomb as she served afternoon tea whilst Neville Taylor dutifully complimented his wife on her culinary triumph. Though on this occasion, Bella noted, the vegetables were not given credit as Mr Taylor's allotment was enjoying a 'fallow' period.

Bella, though grateful for the hurriedly drawn bath and change of clothing from Dolly's eclectic wardrobe – a navy blue wool skirt and sunflower yellow blouse – was now wondering how she could politely refuse Mrs Taylor's margarine-lashed white bread.

'No thank you, Mrs Taylor, I'm full.'

'Are you sure? You don't have much appetite for a growing girl.' Dorothy Taylor pushed the plate under her son's nose. 'Come on, Raymond, eat up, there's a good boy.'

'Smashing dinner, Mum.' Glancing at Bella, Raymond Taylor flexed his muscles. He grabbed two slices, dropping them on his plate and smacking his lips.

Bella experienced a strong sense of déjà vu as

she sat at the Taylor's dining table listening to the conversation; nothing had changed in their happy routine and if either Mr or Mrs Taylor or Raymond had felt upset about Bella's abrupt departure at her last visit, none of them referred to it.

'So how is office life suiting you, my dear?' Mr Taylor enquired as he dabbed his mouth with a napkin.

'Very nicely, Mr Taylor.'

'The staff seem all right, do they?'

Bella nodded as she surreptitiously tried to divide up her crusty fish from the stalks of over-cooked cabbage, hiding as much as she could beneath the mashed potato.

'You'll never go wrong with a good team behind you,' Mr Taylor continued as he gazed up at the ceiling for inspiration. 'I can honestly say if it wasn't for the support of my colleagues I wouldn't be where I am today. A good rapport with your subordinates is worth its weight in gold. Twenty years I've worked hard to establish my position, but it's all been worth it.' His gaze slowly lowered to the food-laden table. 'As the old saying goes, "we live like kings and sup like lords!"'

Every head at the table nodded and Bella took the opportunity to guide the last fragment of lordly fish under the lumpy mash. She was smiling as she thought to herself that if Neville Taylor had sold his soul to Poplar Town Hall for the last twenty years then he was welcome. It had taken her only twenty days if that to recognize the fact she would never fit at Dixons no matter how long she worked there. She was the odd man out and always would be. Lately she had even wondered if she wouldn't be better off bottling onions in the pickle factory and having a laugh with the girls in the canteen, than stuck with the boredom of office life.

'Bella deserves her success, Dad,' Dolly broke in earnestly. 'She was always top in English and arithmetic. Dunno how she added up so quick and always got the right answer. Left us all standing she did.'

'You weren't so bad yourself, Dolly.' Bella placed her knife and fork together, hoping she had disguised the leftovers sufficiently to fool Mrs Taylor. If she offered to clear the plates, she could throw them away in the bin. 'You always got high marks.'

Dolly giggled. 'Yeah, but only 'cos I sat next to you.'

Silence suddenly descended and Mr Taylor's satisfied smile disappeared. 'What do you mean by that, Dolly?'

Dolly went scarlet. 'Well, I mean, I–'

'She means that we always practised our tables together,' Bella provided swiftly, glancing at her friend. 'It was a good way of learning them by testing each other. Isn't that right, Dolly?'

Still blushing, Dolly nodded. 'Oh yes, it is!'

'An exceedingly good idea,' her father nodded, a look of relief on his face. 'And a perfect example of working as a team.'

Bella glanced at Dolly. They smiled conspiratorially and Bella remembered how it really was at school with Dolly being totally ignorant of what she was supposed to learn and Bella being streets ahead, passing notes or writing the

110

answers on her arm or fingers. Even on her dirty knees if the case warranted it. It was a perfect arrangement and the girls milked it for all it was worth. In return, Bella had Dolly's undivided loyalty. And considering the wide berth everyone else gave Bella at school, it was a fair exchange.

'I'll help Dolly clear the table.' Bella stood up.

'You're both such good girls,' Mrs Taylor beamed.

Bella glanced at Dolly as they took the plates to the kitchen.

'We are such *good* girls,' Dolly mimicked and they burst into laughter.

'Right little angels in fact.'

'Dad's still upset about me not getting the council job,' Dolly confided softly as they stood at the sink. 'He thinks Burlingtons is nothing more than a dead end.'

'Well, it is for the fish.'

The two girls shrieked. Dolly's eyes were watering. 'Oh, Bella, you're a real tonic you are.'

Bella nudged her friend's arm. 'Where shall I throw the left-overs?'

'Chuck it in the bin under the sink. Mr Attwell collects it every Saturday for his pigs.' As Bella was scraping the remains from the plate, Dolly said enquiringly, 'It's your birthday soon. I expect you'll be seeing Micky … going out somewhere nice?'

Bella tried not to look into Dolly's searching gaze. The chances of Micky remembering her sixteenth birthday were probably zero. 'Well, I'm not sure exactly, what I'll be doing.'

''Cos if you had some free time, Percy and me

111

was wondering if you'd come out with us. Have tea at Lyons and see a film afterwards.'

'That's nice,' Bella murmured distractedly, still thinking about Micky.

'You sound very enthusiastic.' Dolly scrubbed the plate fiercely. 'We wouldn't want you to put yourself out for us.'

'Don't be daft, Dol. I was just thinking.'

'About what? If money's the problem, stop worrying. The treat is on us. And if your precious Micky wanted to come too–'

'Oh, for goodness' sake!' Bella exclaimed, as Dolly's sarcasm finally got under her skin. 'I keep telling you he's not my Micky. And in fact, I probably won't be seeing him anyway.'

Dolly dropped the plate with a splash. 'Pardon me?'

'Don't make a big thing of it,' Bella shrugged, one half of her wanting to tell Dolly the truth, the other half insistent that she keep up a pretence that everything was just as normal.

'What's going on?' Dolly probed, frowning into Bella's pale face.

'Nothing. Nothing at all. As I said, I've been busy at work and made new friends.'

To her surprise Dolly nodded encouragingly. 'At last the penny's dropped, has it? I wondered when you'd realize that lots of boys would give their right arm to go out with you. But you'd never stand a chance of meeting anyone with *him* around.' As Bella glared at her friend, Dolly's full mouth tightened. 'I'm only saying what's obvious.

'Well, you've said it, but don't forget the fact that the Bryants were the only ones who stepped

112

forward to help me and Terry when we was kids. And the only living souls who set foot inside our four walls and painted them. If it wasn't for them the cottage would have fallen down around our ears long ago.'

Dolly dropped her gaze and resumed the washing of the dishes. The two girls worked in silence, Bella's last remark still crackling in the air. Dolly hated going anywhere near Bow Street, a road condemned in more ways than one.

'But thanks anyway,' said Bella, breaking the uncomfortable silence. 'It was a nice thought.'

'You could bring your Terry too,' Dolly said, suddenly hopeful at Bella's softening tone. 'Percy and me will pay for him. He'd love it, wouldn't he? It'd be a real treat then, something special.'

'I wouldn't expect that.'

'I don't want no more argument, we're going, okay?'

Bella hesitated. 'All right. You're on.'

Dolly threw her wet hands around her shoulders. 'Oh, it's going to be wonderful, just like the old days.'

'Here, what's going on?' Ray strolled into the kitchen, a frown on his face as he heard the last few words.

'Nothing, big ears.' Dolly looked impatient. 'We was just talking about Bella's birthday, that's all.'

'When's the occasion?'

'January 31st,' Bella said with a flourish of the towel.

'You celebrating, then?'

'Why?' Bella furrowed her brow. 'What's it to you?'

'I was only wondering.'

'About what?'

He stepped from one foot to the other. 'I'd have bought you something if I'd known.'

'Well you know now, don't you?' said Dolly. 'And this is a private conversation by the way.'

He turned, his shoulders drooping. 'All right, all right. I can see I'm not wanted round here.'

Dolly glanced at Bella and rolled her eyes.

Bella knew they'd hurt his feelings, but he was such an easy target. 'We are going out, but if you want to come you'll have to ask your sister,' she relented.

His face brightened. 'Can I, Dol?'

Dolly looked shocked but pleased at the same time. 'Actually if Ray was there you wouldn't have to worry about your Terry being the odd man out.'

Bella didn't much fancy the prospect of Raymond tagging along but it was a celebration after all and, she supposed, the more the merrier.

Micky slapped the glue on the label engraved with the name of a leading distillers and pressed it firmly into place on the bottle. Passing it to Lenny he lifted another from the shelf. It was just one of the two dozen that Lenny had earmarked for delivery that afternoon. Chewing the end of his cigarette as the smoke streamed into his eyes, Micky grinned at his friend.

'At two quid a bottle, this scotch is a gift.'

'It should be. I was up half the night, nursing it. One awkward sodding batch this lot was.'

'You'd never know. Looks perfect.'

114

'Which is more than I can say for me sex-life at the moment.'

Micky knew by the tone of Lenny's voice he was in one of his black moods. He'd probably rowed with Gina, and Gina being Gina, Lenny had no doubt lost the argument. Gina ran a café in Limehouse and claimed to be of Spanish extraction despite the name of Smith. She had a paddy to match her big black eyes and fierce cockney tongue. Micky had quite fancied her himself, until the day she opened her mouth a bit too much and he'd witnessed her slating Lenny until his big friend had walked out of the house and slammed the door behind him.

'Who've we got on the van?' Micky enquired solicitously, hoping to change the subject.

'Sean and Ashley,' Lenny barked. 'That is, if those two fairies can leave each other alone long enough to drive the thing.'

'South of the river or up West?' Micky asked, aware Lenny's mood wasn't improving.

'Struth Micky, what am I? A bloody encyclopaedia?'

'I was just asking, that's all.'

Lenny was dressed in shirtsleeves and a dirty apron. He wiped his sticky hands irritably down his backside. 'They're dropping in the City first. St James's Street; Dover Street and Piccadilly, all bottle parties.'

'And none of it can be traced back to us, right?' Micky ventured. 'I mean, we're just delivering orders, yeah?'

'You tell me, you're the gaffer.' Lenny shrugged his massive shoulders. As friends they had run the distillery together since '44, but when he met Gina, Micky had seen a change in Lenny. Namely that he was less inclined to put in the hours and more inclined to spend them in the comfort of Gina's bed. Exercising discipline was something that Micky had trouble with himself, he admitted that, but after all, as Lenny said, Micky was the gaffer and as such had certain perks.

Lenny lifted a chaser glass to the light and examined it closely. The amber nectar inside glittered. He threw it to the back of his throat, causing his eyes to water. 'Not bad. Not bad at all.'

Micky grinned. 'You've got guts of steel, Len.'

'Fancy a slug?'

'No thanks.'

Lenny gave a wounded growl, like a bear, Micky thought, a big brown bear with buckshot in his arse. 'Me tiddly wink not good enough for you now?'

'Course it is,' Micky lied, having sworn himself off the poison since his last little 'taster' which had resulted in him losing his memory for a week.

'Belly ache don't bother me. This is good stuff, this is. You going soft or something?'

Micky smiled broadly and tapped his stomach. 'It's only eleven o'clock in the morning, mate. I've not had me breakfast yet. I'm going down the café in a minute for a fry-up.' Micky dusted invisible dust from the lapels of his close-fitting jacket. He wore a dark suit that enhanced his smouldering looks. He'd read books about the Mafia and seen all the films; he liked to look dangerous as well as handsome, his aim in life to attract female atten-

116

tion wherever and whenever possible.

Lenny shrugged once more then bent to lift the huge glass tank filled with liquid to one side. Carefully he inserted a tube and threaded the end into a large opaque jar. A sound of bubbling and boiling could be heard from the far side of the still. The air was filled with foul smelling fumes and the stone walls began to shine with steam.

'You just make sure Ronnie don't rumble we're still in business,' Lenny warned as he worked amongst the apparatus. 'I'll make you thirty-six bottles of fine scotch malt from nothing more than a bag of prunes and raisins, a dollop of water and a pinch of me own special brew. But the thought of Ronnie turning up here does me head in.'

Micky ascended the stack of crates piled neatly by the door. He sat down on top of one of them, examining the tips of his polished black shoes. 'You leave Ron to me, Lenny old son. He's too busy with his new love interest Joyce and that poxy club they just bought. He's not gonna come down here to Dad's old lock-up now. And anyway, even if he did, what would he find? A filthy old room under the railway arches with nothin' in it. We've moved location, ain't we? We're under the lock-up now, safer than ever. To one and all it's just a bombed-out pit. So stop worrying or you'll get yourself an ulcer.'

'It's the stink that I'm worried about not the ulcer. People are gonna sniff it sooner or later.'

'This place smells sweet as roses.'

'Yeah, they're growing everywhere, just look at 'em.'

Micky jumped off the crates and sauntered over to his friend. 'You worry too mu–' A loud hissing noise made him jump. Lenny strode forward and smashed the palm of his hand on the top of the jar. The liquid inside bubbled as Lenny swore loudly.

'Yeah? And you was saying?' Lenny looked murderously into Micky's anxious face.

'Nothing important.' Micky grinned nervously as he edged his way to the door. 'I can see you're busy, so I'll leave you to it. Get out from under your feet.'

'That's right, do your usual disappearing act,' Lenny shouted after him. 'Why should I expect any different?'

'Oh come on,' Micky half laughed. 'I always do me bit.' He was fed up with holding a candle to the devil lately. Lenny's moods were always on the downward spiral and he was getting sick of it. 'Who got out of bed the wrong side today?' he demanded, sending caution to the wind.

'I'd still be in bed if I had any sense.' Lenny stalked him to the door. 'Gina's giving me grief like there was no tomorrow. I'm never there when she wants me and when I am, I'm too flaming tired to perform.'

Micky clicked his two fingers as if this was a joke. 'That's the penalty you pay for bedding a doll like Gina. Someone wants to tell her how lucky she is – on to a good thing with you, Lenny, old son. She can't have the proverbial cake and eat it, can she?'

At this Lenny's swarthy face turned white. Micky stepped back as the big man tore off his

118

apron and thrust it into Micky's arms. 'So that's what you think is it, you selfish sod? Well, you try running this shit hole single-handed and see how your bits of skirt like it. See if you don't start crawlin' up the walls along with the ruddy bugs. I'm taking a holiday.'

Lenny disappeared along the dark and crumbling passage, his big frame knocking the brick dust to the floor as he went.

At a loss for words, Micky stared after him. Then realizing he was alone he yelled at the top of his voice, 'But I ain't got a clue how it all works!'

Lenny's voice echoed back. 'Then you'd better hurry up and find out, hadn't you? Look in the book and read the instructions same as I had to.'

Micky stood in panic and gazed around him. The place felt as if a bomb was about to go off. The bottles were hissing and groaning and liquid was trickling. Cautiously he moved towards the sticky, bottle-laden table that acted as Lenny's desk. It was smothered in piles of forged labels. A book lay open that contained lines of strange hieroglyphics. He turned the grubby, greasy pages as though they were tainted with poison, which, going on what had happened to the victims who'd fallen foul of some of Lenny's contaminated hooch, it probably was.

The writing became a blur. Micky was seriously worried. His lucrative business was a non-starter if he didn't get Lenny back. There was no one else to cook this lot up. His brother Sean and his fancy man wouldn't have a clue. At a push he supposed he could try nailing the bubbly down himself, but it just wasn't in his nature. Not down here, in this pit, all by himself.

Micky sat down on the broken wooden stool and looked miserably around him at what was virtually a laboratory. An unsafe one at that. Danger bubbled in every corner. He'd seen an exploding tank of meths fire Lenny across twelve feet of ground like a ball from a cannon. But if he wanted the revenue from the bottle parties he'd just have to make it himself. He comforted himself it wouldn't be for long. As soon as Lenny got his oats he'd come crawling back. Gina would want her wedge and there was only one place Lenny could earn it.

Picking up the book again, Micky opened it at the first page. He had to laugh. Written in Lenny's careful handwriting, under the heading, 'Emergency mix only', was a list of weird-sounding ingredients, amongst them methylated spirit.

Bella was flushed with excitement as they climbed into Percy's car parked in a side road off Leicester Square. They were all talking about the film they had just seen called *Brighton Rock*. It was a love story and tragedy combined and Bella had been enthralled by it.

'That Pinkie was horrible,' Dolly was saying to Percy as he started the car's engine and switched on its lights. 'I don't know how Rose, who was after all the heroine, could have been so daft as to fall for him. I'd have seen through him straight away. He was an out and out villain and murderer.'

'Good job I've got a clean slate then,' Percy observed with a chuckle. 'I've been a good boy all me life.'

'Yeah, I'll bet,' Ray shouted sarcastically from the back of the car.

'It's true,' Percy said indignantly. 'I've been saving meself for a good, honest girl, I'll have you know.'

'So where is she, then?'

'Ray Taylor!' Dolly turned round to swipe her brother with a glove. 'You've got the cheek of the devil, you have.'

'Well, I think Rose was naïve not daft,' Bella said quietly as she sat between Terry and Ray. Both men wore suits for the occasion, though Terry's was the same one he always wore and looked as though it had been squashed in a mangle, whilst Ray had put on a light grey suit and polka dot tie. 'Most of all she was in love.'

Ray snaked an arm around the back seat behind her. 'Yeah? So what's that supposed to mean? She had eyes and ears, didn't she? We was the audience and it was plain as a pikestaff he was a bad 'un.'

'Yes, but we saw his bad side and Rose only saw the goodness in him,' Bella answered airily. 'Love is obviously an emotion that you're too immature to know about.'

Ray gave her one of his reproachful stares. 'I might.'

Bella was enjoying having a laugh at Ray's expense. She'd actually forgotten all about Dixons and even Micky hadn't come into her mind for at least three hours. Which was a record for her.

'Rose let him soft soap her,' Ray continued in a whining voice. 'Would you marry me if you

121

thought I'd murdered someone?'

'She wouldn't marry you anyway,' Dolly interrupted before Bella could answer and the two girls began giggling.

'Shut up, Dol!' Ray looked embarrassed. 'I was just supposing, that's all. Murdering someone ain't like on the films, all glamorous and exciting. That's not real life.'

'It's not meant to be, you chump,' Dolly replied haughtily as she pushed the little green hat on her head back an inch.

'Well, I felt sorry for her,' Percy intervened as he frowned ahead. 'The poor kid was besotted. After all she was only a waitress and he was flashing around all his dough. She was young and impressionable so it was natural she fancied him as he was rich in her eyes. Wouldn't any girl be swayed by money?'

'Money wouldn't impress *me*,' Bella replied earnestly. 'No, it was something else about Pinkie. He was a gangster and frightening, yet she really wanted him to turn out all right.'

Ray laughed loudly. 'It did, didn't it? Turn out all right, I mean. He fell off the end of a pier.'

'Terry likes the pier,' Terry said, speaking for the first time since they left the cinema.

'Why's that, Terry mate?' Percy glanced over his shoulder.

'Got lots of lights, pretty things in the water.'

Bella smiled as she thought how Terry always took the best from everything. She studied his blunt profile, his blinking eyes and thin brown hair. Hidden somewhere in his head she was sure he kept the bad memories all parcelled up in a little box. She just hoped he never opened the lid. Even if it meant he stayed as he was for the rest of his life at least he'd be happy.

Suddenly she was aware of Ray's fingers cupping her shoulder tightly. His thigh pressed hard against her leg. He bent close to her and whispered, 'How about it then, Bells, coming out with us again?'

'Who's us?' she demanded, loud enough for everyone to hear.

At the explosion of laughter, Ray flushed. 'You know what I mean,' he hissed, glancing nervously at the back of his sister's head.

'No, I don't.'

'He's still dopey over you, Bella,' Dolly broadcast from the front seat. 'Put a collar and lead on him and take him home with you for goodness' sake!'

'Shut up, Dol!' Ray dropped his hand to loosen his tie. 'This is the last time I'm coming out with you lot again.'

'Really?' Dolly lifted her chin. 'You couldn't wait to get in the car this evening!'

'Well, I'm buying a motor for meself soon, ain't I? You'll be quick enough to cadge a lift then, I'll bet.'

'Oh, stop arguing.' Bella put up her hands. 'You'll have to ask me again, Ray. When everyone's not listening.'

This brought even more laughter from the front seats and Ray's face was a picture of shame.

After a while, Bella gave Ray a nudge in the ribs. He refused to look at her and she repeated the action. She felt sorry for him but he could be

123

such a drip. However, he had paid for their meal at Lyons and the cinema tickets, whilst Percy had bought only the ice creams, keeping his money well inside his breast pocket.

Ray was generous if nothing else. If he bought himself a car she might be interested in going out with him. She hadn't been doing anything interesting lately anyway. Softly she laid her hand on his and squeezed it.

She smiled encouragingly. It wouldn't hurt to keep him sweet, she told herself as Ray suddenly looked as though he'd won the pools.

Chapter Ten

Miss Conway's face was a mask of horror. 'Would you repeat that, please?' The thick pile of papers in her hand suddenly trembled as though they had been struck by a force ten gale.

Bella made herself look into her accusing eyes. 'These errors aren't mine. I don't know who did them but it wasn't me.

'You're blaming someone else?'

'I don't know who, but yes.' Bella had decided to speak up for herself at last. Ray would be waiting outside to collect her as they had plans to go out for the evening and she wanted to leave on time. For once she wasn't prepared to be the scapegoat for some other person's pleasure.

'There is no mistake this time,' Miss Conway decided, holding the file aloft. 'The Harrington account was allotted to your care, Miss Doyle. First you lose it and now we have more crossings out and mistakes. If it wasn't you, then pray tell me who it was?'

'I don't know,' Bella replied. 'But I've been especially careful to check my work since Christmas, specifically the Harrington account. I was wrongly accused before and it looks as though that same person is doing it again.'

Kathleen Conway's mouth became a thin line of fury. 'How dare you speak of your colleagues in such a way. You are accusing one of them of a deliberate act of deception.'

Bella shrugged. 'I'm not prepared to take the blame anymore.'

'Miss Doyle, I advise you to retract your accusations immediately,' Miss Conway said, recovering fractionally from the shock of Bella's mutiny. 'It is up to you to remain here after hours and put right what is wrong. As for your outburst regarding other members of staff, on this occasion I'll overlook it, providing I have your immediate apology.'

Bella shook her head. 'I don't see there's anything to apologize for as it's me that's in the right.'

Miss Conway stared at her without blinking, then after a short pause, she spoke. 'Very well. I've given you a more than fair chance to cooperate but now I'm afraid the situation is out of my hands. Dixon's will not tolerate this kind of behaviour. Not in any shape or form.'

'Does that mean I'm sacked?' Bella asked without hesitation.

'The decision is up to my superiors. I shall give

him all the information I have and–'

'And *then* I'll be sacked, I suppose,' Bella interrupted, her tone sarcastic. 'Well, I'll save you the trouble. If you aren't prepared to listen to my side of the story then I wouldn't want to work in a place that doesn't value the truth. And there is someone here who will be clapping their hands at having got rid of me...' Bella turned slowly to stare at the other girls sitting at their desks, their faces all registering shocked fascination at the conversation going on before them. But it was Evelyn Donald who struggled out of her seat and hurried toward her boss in order to protest her innocence.

Bella put up her hand and smiled. 'Don't waste your breath on denials, Evelyn. You've got what you wanted at long last. The seat next to you will be vacant from here on in.'

Bella kept the smile pasted to her face as she held her head high and walked over to collect her coat from the line of hooks on the far wall. Placing it over her arm and sliding the strap of her bag across her wrist she pulled open the door. Briefly she glanced back at the room in which she had worked for the past year. Each face reminded her of what a mistake it had been to try to better herself here. She had never fitted in from the word go and had hated every moment. Well, it was over now and she was glad.

She closed the door quietly behind her to a resounding silence. With her heart beating crazily inside her chest, she ran down the three flights of stairs exhaling a long sigh. Striding into the warm July evening she felt a wash of warm air roll over her. Even though her legs felt like jelly, she knew she had quit her job with dignity. She hadn't waited to be ousted by the powers that be, but gone on her own terms, and that was what counted. Evelyn Donald was welcome to her triumph. In Bella's book, it was an empty victory – they would die slowly of boredom up there and they were welcome to that.

The traffic was homeward bound from the city. The sky was a perfectly clear and radiant blue. Ray's car was parked on the other side of the road and Bella waved, standing on tiptoe to attract his attention.

He jumped out and after she had crossed the road, she threw herself into his arms. 'Oh Ray, I'm so glad to see you.'

Looking startled he gripped her tightly. 'What's all this about then?'

'I'll tell you later. Just let's go.'

He glanced at the deserted entrance of the building behind her. 'You've left before all the others and it's not half five yet.'

'So what,' she shrugged as she pulled open the car door and jumped in. She glanced back at Dixons as Ray started the car and they moved off. She didn't have any regrets, only a sense of relief that was growing by the minute.

Dixons was a part of her past. She looked at the puzzled driver and smiled. Tonight was going to be a very special night. Only Ray didn't know it yet!

'You did what?' Ray's puppy eyes bulged as his mouth fell open.

'I chucked my job in,' Bella said again, as she self-consciously pulled her blouse together, the same blouse that seconds ago Ray had opened with not so nimble fingers, searching for the naked skin of her breast. Tonight, after the film, when they had parked in the street by Island Gardens, she had allowed him to kiss her passionately and as a result, his hot hand had done what it had never managed to do before. But now he was staring at her as though she had just confessed she was an axe murderer.

'I thought you said that.'

'And I thought you'd be pleased but by the look on your face I'm not so sure you are.'

'I just can't believe it.'

'Why not?' Bella pushed herself up and looped the buttons of her blouse back into place. Ray's amorous dithering had been a clumsy encounter but she had been prepared to suffer his inexperienced pawing tonight as he was always complaining she wouldn't let him touch her. Staring at him resentfully she shrugged. 'You know I wasn't happy there.'

'Yes, but not enough to pack your job in.'

'Shows how much you've listened to what I've told you.' Bella was upset at this unexpected reaction. All evening she had been longing to tell him of the argument and the way she had stood up for herself. Instead she'd had to suffer sitting in the back seat of the Troxy as he'd slid his hand under her skirt trying to find her suspenders.

'I have listened – mostly.'

'Then you'll know I've been the butt of their spiteful jokes,' Bella explained patiently, her irri-

128

tation growing at his sullen expression. 'And today I just couldn't stomach anymore.' She looked at him reproachfully. 'Well, aren't you going to say something?'

'I don't know what to say.'

'Try congratulations or well done.'

'What for? You're out of work now.' He swallowed and she watched his Adam's apple go up and down like a ping-pong ball, a part of his anatomy that she really disliked. 'You haven't got any money.'

'Yes, I have. I collected me wages this morning.'

'I mean what are you going to live on? Jobs aren't that easy to find nowadays. You can't just throw it all up and walk into another one. What about references for instance?'

'What about them? I'll never work in an office again. I'll get something else. In a factory even, but never in an office.'

'But why? It was a good job at Dixons. Not as good as mine at the PLA perhaps, but you got a good whack all the same.'

Bella stared at him and laughed nastily. 'You're only a guard at the docks, Ray. A glorified sentry standing outside a box is what it amounts to.'

'Charming, I must say. I don't hear you complaining when I spend all my hard-earned cash on you.'

'You mean a one and six ticket for a cinema seat?' Bella scoffed. 'I'll have you know it's like sitting next to an octopus trying to grab me knickers all the time.'

He turned away. 'You can be really crude at times.'

129

'Well, it's true. And while I'm speaking me mind, would you care to enlighten me as to why you're being so tight-arsed about me packing in Dixons?'

He pulled a long face. 'You know why.'

'For crying out loud, Ray, I don't.'

'It's just that–' he stopped, his eyes looking guilty.

'Go on, I'm listening.'

'Well, as I said, it was a good job, a very good job.'

'I know, it's engraved in capital letters on me forehead, Ray.'

'And we could've done things ... together like ... for the future.'

Bella frowned at him in the darkness of the car. 'For the future? What do you mean?'

'Bella, you ain't making this easy.' He moved uncomfortably in the driver's seat. 'I'm nineteen this winter and I've been thinking a lot about next year. I've got a steady job and we've been courting–'

'*Courting!*' Bella blinked her eyes in shock.

He nodded silently. 'Yes, more or less–'

'We've only been going out a few months,' she broke in scornfully. 'You're talking like it's been years!'

'We see each other regular every week now,' he argued stubbornly. 'And if once or twice a week isn't courting, then I don't see what is.'

'It's just fun,' Bella shrugged. '*Fun*, Ray, like people are supposed to have when they're young.'

He said in a dry whisper, 'Don't you see any future for us, then?'

'I've never even thought about it.'

'But I have, Bella. I want to settle down. A man's got to make plans – know where he's going. And it'd probably take us a year or two to save up for a place of our own anyway.'

'Please tell me you're joking, Ray.'

He shook his head slowly. 'Why should I joke about something so important as marriage? It's a big responsibility to take on a wife and have kids. I've discussed it with Mum and Dad and they said we could stay with them until we're on our feet. Course we'd have to be sensible about the wedding, not go too barking over it, but I didn't think you were the kind of girl to mind too much about a big do.'

Bella was speechless for the first time that day. What Ray had just said had eclipsed even Miss Conway's little gem.

'I can't believe me ears,' she gasped softly. 'You're saying you've discussed me with your parents – marrying me and us living with them? And even having kids?' She pushed her hands over her face trying not to visualize the idea of producing babies that resembled their father and mother as closely as Ray and Dolly resembled theirs.

'What's the matter, are you feeling all right?' Ray leaned across and tried to take her into his arms.

She pushed him away. 'Don't touch me. You don't know what kind of person I am. You don't know anything about me.'

'I only said–'

'I know what you said.' She opened the car

131

door and jumped out. 'I must've been mad to ever go out with you in the first place. Don't bother about me. I'll find my own way home.'

She slammed the door and began walking away, her steps fast and furious as outrage stuck in her chest. She could just imagine the Taylors, all four of them, sitting at the table after tea and deciding whether or not she was a suitable match for their beloved son. What right had they to discuss her behind her back? What right had Ray to assume that she was the kind of girl to settle for what he had planned for his miserable future?

Suddenly the tears flowed down her cheeks and the night breeze dragged them into her hair. Everything was going wrong. She had lost her stupid job today and had just finished with her even more stupid boyfriend. She would have continued going out with Ray if only he hadn't opened his trap. The truth was Ray was just a stopgap in her life. He was as thick as two planks, a terrifying cross between his mother and his father. In a few years' time he'd be planting cabbages and sprouts and bringing them home for his puppy-eyed children to stuff down their ping-pong throats.

'Bella!' Ray caught up with her. 'Come back to the car and we'll talk.'

'No. I told you, it's over.'

'Not till you tell me why.'

He walked quickly beside her. 'I'm not your type, Ray, and never have been.'

'I think a lot of you, Bella, always have.'

'Look, Ray, you say that but I'm not right for you. Take my word for it.'

'I don't understand,' he complained angrily. 'What have I said? Aren't I good enough for you?' He stopped dead, a look of slow understanding on his face. 'It's that Micky Bryant, ain't it?'

'It's got nothing to do with Micky.'

'Are you seeing him?'

'What if I was? It's none of your business.' She tried to walk on but he pulled her back.

'You are, aren't you?'

'Let go of me, Ray.'

'He's no good, Bella. None of the Bryants are. He's a womanizer and everyone on the island knows it.'

Bella pulled her arm from his grasp. 'You can just shut up about Micky because I'll tell you this for nothing. I don't care if he's got women crawling all over him, he's twice the man you are. And he never once tried it on with me like you did and I'll tell you something else. If he had, I would have let him an' all!'

'You little tramp!'

'Yeah, well what do you expect? This is Mary Doyle's daughter you're talking to.'

Out of the corner of her eye, Bella saw the lights flick on in the houses nearby. Ray grabbed hold of her and they fell struggling into the road. He was shouting at her and she was yelling back when a flash of light illuminated the darkness. There was a screech of brakes followed by the slam of a door and Ray was suddenly dragged from her.

She stumbled backwards as Micky took hold of Ray's shoulder and propelled him against the car. 'Who do you think you're pushing around?' he demanded as Bella stood trembling, trying to regain her breath.

Ray recovered quickly, glaring at Bella. 'I might have known he'd turn up. I was right, wasn't I? Only you couldn't look me in the eye and tell me so.'

'I told you, it's got nothing to do with him,' Bella protested but Micky stretched out his arm, separating them.

'Just a minute, what's he on about, Bells?'

Ray stuck his face up to Micky. 'This is none of your business, pal, why don't you just piss off?'

'A pleasure, my son, as soon as you explain to me why you were pushing around a woman. And you're wrong about it not being my business. Anyone who lifts a hand against her answers to me.'

'Just what I was telling her meself,' Ray growled, jabbing a finger into Micky's shoulder. 'And the day she cuts herself loose from your fucking family will be one to be celebrated.'

'Say that again,' Micky muttered as he slapped away the pointing finger.

'Up yours Bryant. I ain't wasting me breath on shite.'

'In that case, nor will I.' Micky turned as if to walk away but then wheeled round and lifting his fist brought it hard into Ray's face. Bella screamed at the sound of fracturing bone as Ray fell to the ground, holding up his arm to deflect the blows.

Bella ran forward. 'Stop it, Micky, stop!' She hung on to his arm.

'I ain't finished with him yet.' He kept kicking as Ray curled into a ball.

Bella sank down on her knees beside him. She looked up at Micky, her eyes full of anger. 'Look what you've done. You've broken his nose.'

'He'll get over it.' Micky reached down and grabbed her wrist, dragging her to her feet. 'He's got off lightly after what he was doing to you.'

'I can look after meself,' she retorted, pushing him away. 'Who asked you to interfere?'

'What was I supposed to do? Drive on past and ignore you?'

'Why not?' Bella demanded as the tears threatened once more. 'I've been invisible to you for the past six months, what's so different now?'

'There's a reason for that if you'll only listen.'

Bella laughed emptily. 'No, you listen to me Micky Bryant, I don't ever want to see your ugly boat race again. From now on, keep your nose out of my business. This is Bella Doyle you're talking to not one of your bitches on heat.'

Micky stared at her then smiled humourlessly. 'So that's the way it is, is it?' He brushed down the sleeves of his jacket and nodded to Ray who was struggling to his feet. 'In that case, good luck with Prince Charming here. Going on what.I saw just now, you should make a very happy couple.'

Bella watched his tall figure stride across the road and jump in the car. Her heart seemed to split in two as she silently mouthed the words she wanted to call but no sound came out.

What had she done? She had been waiting months to see him. Had dreamed of what she would say if he was standing beside her again and she had the chance to tell him how much she missed him. And now, when she had her oppor-

135

tunity, she was sending him away forever.

The big black car roared off. Her hair blew around her face as a feeling of emptiness filled her. She thought she'd had a bad day until now. Micky had been within arm's reach, had even stopped the car to defend her. If only she had responded with gratitude rather than anger.

'That was the most sensible thing I've heard you say all night,' Ray mumbled as he hauled himself up from the ground and stumbled towards her. 'Though I would never have believed it if I hadn't heard it with me own ears. It was worth getting me face punched in just to hear you tell him to sling his hook.'

Bella turned slowly, a look of contempt in her eyes. 'God help me I'm a fool to have done what I did,' she whispered in a shaky voice, her heart untouched by the sight of his bleeding face. 'All I have left to say to you, Ray Taylor, is that if I never see you again in this life, it will be too soon.'

She turned away and began walking. The sobs came up from her chest, but there were no tears now. She was too unhappy to cry. Soon her steps turned into strides and finally she was running. Running home to Bow Street where she belonged.

August began wet and overcast. Which made staying out all day and keeping dry impossible. But she couldn't stay home, not with the cripple in his chair, watching her. The sight of him brought back too many memories. So she had kept to her habit of leaving home at seven-thirty each morning. No one knew, not even Terry, that she had no job. Ray had a point when he said it wouldn't be easy to get another one. Now that she was walking the streets her money would soon run out.

She applied to the construction company at Chalk Wharf and the timber yard and the mangle works but the answer was always no. She would rather work on the shop floor than in an office and had been willing to take any vacancy. But all the firms wanted to know where she had worked since leaving school. She hadn't realized, when she'd acted so impulsively, that getting future employment was dependent on her track record.

It was Friday and Bella was walking down Manchester Road wondering where to try next. The evidence of war was still clearly visible; houses reduced to debris, others ugly and neglected. People had tried to breathe life into them, but the smoke and the soot covered them like grubby shawls. She had never really noticed them before. Hadn't seen them the way they looked today, cracked and broken. The last time she had walked this way was with Dolly. They had been happy and laughing as they walked past the Newcastle Arms. The sights and smells that had excited her then, now depressed her. As did her reflection in a pane of glass. Her hair was dirty and hung down on her shoulders. Her coat was shabby and shapeless. She moved past quickly.

When she came to Cubitt Town, the prefabs now seemed a long forgotten dream. They were a pretty buttermilk colour with flat roofs and a square of green grass at the front. Bella dug her hands into her pockets. She didn't have the inclination to walk to Cox Street where she intended to

137

buy herself a cup of tea. She couldn't afford it anyway.

The factory workers would be turning out soon, flush with their pay packets. For the girls, Friday night was hair wash night. The men disappeared down the pub. The kids stayed up late in the streets on summer nights, knocking a ball about. Friday night was the best night of the week.

Bella walked quicker, already missing the money that she had begun to take for granted. She had lost a good job because of her pride. Now she was walking the streets, tired, hungry and alone.

She had no idea what to do next.

Bella knew something was wrong when she saw Terry sitting on the pavement. He stood up when he saw her coming, his eyes full of confusion.

'What's up, Terry?' Bella saw the bundle of clothes at his feet. He'd rolled them up and they looked damp with rain.

'Terry ain't allowed in any more,' he said as the door was flung open and Mary Doyle stood there, her arms full of Bella's clothes. She threw them on the pavement beside Terry's. 'Ah, so the prodigal returns, does she? Well, not to this house she doesn't. Thought I was daft enough not to know what was going on behind me back, eh?'

'I don't know what you mean.' Bella began to pick up her belongings.

'Don't lie to me, you brazen cow. Gave up that fine job for an easy life did you? Well you'll not find it so fecking easy when you have to pay all the bills, my girl. Sweet Jesus, did you think you could pull the wool over Mary Doyle's eyes?'

'It ain't a crime to chuck a job in,' Bella retaliated, hiding her humiliation at being discovered.

'A common little tart is what I've bred,' Mary Doyle shouted back. 'And she's had the gall to look down her nose at her mother all these years. And now she's working the street herself like any old tom.'

Bella looked astonished. 'Who told you that?'

'Who hasn't!' her mother screamed at her, stepping forward to push her shoulder. 'The Rose is bursting at the seams with the news of me own girl touting for trade. And you're brazen enough to leave the house and come home with your pockets full of easy money, without your own mother knowing it.'

'They've told you wrong, Mum,' Bella said emptily.

She knew that whatever she said in her defence, Mary Doyle would ignore.

'So they have, have they? Me own friends and neighbours are lying eejits, are they? When they tell me they've seen you every day this week walking the island with your arse for sale? And him – that idiot–' she narrowed her eyes at Terry, 'keeping your filthy secret and tricking his own mother – sure, it's a pair of devils I birthed, not babes.'

Bella almost smiled at the thought of Mary Doyle ever having a neighbour or friend who was not a lying eejit. But she didn't voice her thoughts, nor did she try to stop the tirade as it continued. The daughter who had cost her mother a happy life and crippled a decent man. Who deceived her mother at every turn and denied them all a worthy existence. Mary Doyle stood heaving, her face contorted by anger.

'You'd rather believe them, Mum, than me. Your so called friends and neighbours. All me life I've never been able to make you listen. But I'll tell you this before I go. One day you'll be left without them. One day that decent man of yours inside who beat me and Terry to kingdom come as the fancy took him, will cause you more pain than ever I could if I really did sell me arse on these godforsaken streets. So you're welcome to what you believe and I hope it makes you happy. And one thing more: our Terry never knew I lost me job. He's an innocent, Mum. Which is a miracle, seeing the womb he got dragged out from.'

Bella picked up her clothes from the ground. She nodded to Terry. 'Come on, our Terry.'

'Good riddance to bad rubbish,' Mary Doyle cried as she stepped back in the house and slammed the door behind her.

Bella looked at Terry. Now they really were on their own.

Chapter Eleven

That night they slept at the back of the old Islanders. The pub had taken a direct hit in the Blitz but a shed remained with half of its roof. They curled up inside it, too tired to notice the wet or the rats. The next day they went to Hailing House and drank soup for the destitute served up by voluntary workers. Afterwards, they visited the flourmill. Bella asked for work but the answer was no. She did the same at the ropemakers but the factory was full.

That night they slept on a wreck; a coal barge washed up on the mud. Its skeleton was open to the elements and rotting but a filthy tarpaulin left inside was cover enough. The warm winds that blew off the river brought the smell of the sea into the barge as Bella closed her eyes. But she was too exhausted to care if the tide came in and swallowed them up.

For the next two days they walked the length of the river from Limehouse to Blackwall. Bella asked in the café if they needed help, but the answer was always no.

The Salvation Army provided a meal and at night they returned to the barge. It was a dry, hot morning when they walked to Island Gardens. They sat on a bench and Terry groaned. He'd lost weight and was the colour of pastry. Bella listened to his racking coughs. She had to do something.

'Stay here, I won't be long.'

'Terry sick.'

'I know. I'm going to get Micky.'

He lay down on the bench with his head on the bundle of clothes they'd carried with them. She held his hand and said quietly, 'I won't be long.'

Then she ran all the way to Piper Street. If she had to go on bended knee to Micky she would. If she had to lick his boots, she would. She would do anything Micky asked if only he would help Terry.

Micky's black car was parked in the street. She caught her breath and stood still, staring up at the big house where she was now a stranger. What would she do if he turned her away? Or laughed in her face. But there was no one else she could turn to. No one who cared enough to help Terry.

Slowly she walked up to the big door. Like all the houses in Piper Street, the long windows were shielded by lace curtains and Bella recognized them as the ones that had been there since Mrs Bryant had first hung them years ago. Briefly she recalled the memory of Sean washing them, Sean placing them on the line to dry and being ridiculed by his two brothers for the care he took in preserving them. Micky and Ronnie had always left the household chores to Sean who was a natural at cleaning and cooking. Following in his mum's footsteps, they always said. And though Bella had never known Mrs Bryant, her boys always talked about her whenever they had the chance.

She grasped the brass knocker, bringing it

142

down three times. The door opened and Micky stood there. His face was as handsome as ever; he wore a white shirt and red and blue tie and she could smell the soap that he washed with. Everything about him made her heart race.

'Strike a light,' he murmured. 'Look who it ain't.'

'Can I come in?'

'What do you want?'

'To talk to you.'

'Oh, so now you've got the time of day for me, have you?'

'I lost me job and Mum chucked me out.'

Micky nodded slowly, one eyebrow shooting up. 'So nothing new there, then?'

'We've been sleeping rough, anywhere we can.'

'You don't say.'

'Terry's sick, Micky.' Bella was almost pleading. She didn't know what else to do. 'I left him down Island Gardens on a bench.'

His brow smoothed out as he studied her. 'So what happened to Casanova?'

'If you mean Ray, I don't know. I haven't seen him since–'

'Since you told me to sling me hook,' he interrupted her angrily.

'I didn't mean to. I just lost me temper.'

'Yeah, with me. You should have taken it out on fancy pants.'

'Can I come in? I want to apologize.' For a minute she thought he was going to close the door, then he shrugged.

'I really am sorry, Micky,' she said as they stood in the hall. 'I shouldn't have said what I did.'

'And I'm supposed to forget that you was there on your knees mopping him up like Florence Nightingale?'

'He's just a friend, honest, not even that. He's Dolly Taylor's brother, just someone to go out with once in a while. We went to the cinema a few times, but that was all. I soon got fed up. I was telling him I didn't want anything more to do with him when you came along.' She wrung her dirty fingers anxiously together. 'I was mad at you, that's why I said the things I did. Mad because I ... I hadn't seen you ... and I thought you'd forgotten about me.'

He leaned against wall and stuffed his hands in his pockets. 'So what you're saying is, the purpose of this little visit is to ask for my help, right?'

She nodded. 'Terry's really sick.'

'And I'm supposed to jump to it, am I? Just because you've realized which side your bread is buttered.'

'I thought you didn't want me around anymore.'

'That's your excuse, darlin', but I'm a busy man, Bells. Got a lot on me plate and you above all people should know that. And be fair now, me and Ronnie offered you a job and you turned us down. I mean, what was we supposed to do after that? We got more to think about than putting your life in order, which, you got to admit, we've done since both you and Terry was only just out of nappies. And would have gone on doing if you hadn't got all above yourself.'

Bella felt the tears sting in her eyes. 'The truth is I hated Dixons. I just didn't want you to think

I couldn't make it on me own.'

'Yeah, well, you should've known it was the Bryants who knew what was good for you.'

'I know now, Micky.'

He looked at her for a long while, his dark eyes thoughtful. Then reaching for his jacket on the coat-stand, he slung it over his shoulder. 'You've struck lucky, Bells,' he told her as he took her arm and steered her down the path. 'I'm in a good mood today.'

'Oh, Micky, thanks!'

'You know what, I expected more of you though, throwing the job in my face like you did and swanning off to Dixons.'

She nodded slowly, sad at the thought that she had let herself down in his eyes. She knew that her decision to work at Dixons had rebounded on her in a bad way. It had been a hard lesson to learn and she would never forget it.

'Blimey, Bells, your little bruv ain't in the pink by any means, is he?'

'He's going to be all right, though?'

Micky bent over the prostrate form and shrugged. 'How did he get like this?'

'I think he got a chill from sleeping under this old barge. He's always had a weak chest.'

Terry looked almost unconscious as he lay shivering on the bench. And Micky was tempted to get shot of them both, drop them up the hospital and be done with it. He knew trouble when he saw it, yet he also recognized an opportunity when it arose and it had today in the shape and form of Bella Doyle. He knew if he could turn the situation to his advantage, it would pay dividends in the long run. The kid was on skid row and they both knew it. He hadn't recognized her at first she looked so tatty and the smell of her had knocked him sideways. But as she'd talked, it had all fallen into place. A little plan that would get him into Lenny's good books again.

'Right, pal, let's get you in the car.' Micky took one lanky arm and heaved Terry over his shoulder. He was no weight at all and it was easy to carry him through the gates and into the road.

A few seconds later they were laying him on the back seat, folding up his knees to his chest. He was wet with sweat and making gurgling noises and when Micky closed the door he was in two minds as to whether he was calling a wrong shot. The kid didn't look good. What if he popped his clogs right now? But by the time he climbed in the car and Bella jumped in beside him, Micky gave her a wink. 'He'll be right as rain soon. Reckon it's a touch of flu and he just needs to sweat it out in a proper bed.'

'But Mum won't let us back, not even if I went begging.'

'The old cow ain't an option, Bells. She can kiss your arse goodbye.'

Bella looked shocked. 'So where are we going?'

'To a friend's.' He gave her a sideways glance. Although his arrival at Gina's was a bit impromptu, he'd give her a good wedge for her trouble. He reached across and taking Bella's cold hand, he squeezed it. 'From now on, Bells, you leave it to Micky to sort out.' He paused for good measure. 'You with me on that one, 'cos if

146

you've any doubts say now. But I tell you this, a second chance ain't worth ignoring, gel. It'll never come again from Micky Bryant.'

She nodded fiercely as tears filled her eyes. 'I'll do whatever you want, Micky. And I'll never forget this, I promise you.'

He smiled. He'd make sure she never did either.

Micky parked the car outside the café and smiled as he saw the tall, voluptuous woman clearing the tables inside. There was no sign of Lenny as being Friday, he and Sean and Ashley would be down the lock-up making certain that the orders were ready for Friday night's delivery.

Micky shuddered slightly at the near squeak he'd had with Lenny and their last little upset. Four days of hell spent in the lock-up trying to follow instructions that might as well have been double Dutch was not Micky's idea of a good result. He'd felt like a monk in a brothel and drank himself stupid for thirty-six hours and after a hangover from hell, gone cap in hand to Lenny.

Oddly enough it was Gina who'd persuaded Lenny to return to work and Micky had rejoiced at the fact that Gina was business first and last. From then on they had established an under-standing: whatever Gina wanted she was going to get, basically. If it meant the safekeeping of his little hooch empire, Gina could have what she wanted. But it was cash tinkling in the till that made Gina's blood quicken and Micky had coughed up without protest.

147

Now he raised his hand in salute and Gina nodded to him, her shrewd eyes narrowing under her fringe of black hair. Micky smiled exaggeratedly and hoped that her better nature had climbed out of the right side of the bed today.

'Who's that?' Bella asked and without removing his gaze he replied through smiling lips.

'She's Gina, the friend I was talking about. Nice girl an' all just as long as you know the right foot to tickle. Now, listen to me, Bells. You sit here and look after our friend at the back, right? Don't get out. Just wait here till I come back for you.'

'But Micky–'

'Do as I say, there's a good girl.' His tone was firm as he turned to her, his dark eyes hardening. 'Remember what I said? You gotta leave this to Micky now.' He gave her the proverbial wink and jumped out of the car. Tightening the knot in his tie and brushing his lapels he strutted his way to the café. It was early afternoon and he could smell bacon frying. Gina was going to be a hard nut to crack. But then he'd been lucky before, why not again?

She looked at him, smoothing the bib of the white apron that was drawn tightly across her hips. The café was hot and sticky and thick with smoke. Three of the oilcloth-covered tables were occupied.

Terry gave another wide grin as he swaggered his way to the counter. 'How you doin' then, darlin'?'

Gina frowned suspiciously. 'What do you want, Micky?'

'Just popped in to say hello, that's all.'

'You've said it. Now what?'

'Yeah, right.' He blinked, trying to quell his nervousness.

'Lenny ain't here. You should know that.' Her cockney accent was loud and strong. All heads turned slightly and Micky swallowed hard. He didn't want any information broadcast about the lock-up and expected better of Gina who knew it was a nudge-nudge, wink-wink situation.

'Keep it down, gorgeous,' he said softly, sliding his eyes round their sockets. 'It's not Lenny I want, as a matter of fact...' he lowered his voice again, 'it's his lovely lady.'

'Cut the crap, Micky. As you can see, I'm busy.'

'As it happens I'm here on business.'

Her dark gaze narrowed. 'What sort of business?'

He glanced around at the unshaven jaws working mechanically. 'Not here, out the back.'

She eyed him for what seemed an eternity, then jerking her head to the curtain behind the counter she pulled it to one side. Micky walked through.

In the small kitchen behind the shop he could smell meat and bread and a strong undertone of disinfectant. The private quarters were at the rear, a top floor where Gina and Lenny lived and below a jumble of rooms that acted as lodgings and provided extra income for the café. They were partitioned by a door with a hatch and a long glass cupboard full of provisions, next to which was the cooking range and cupboards. Above these ran a long line of pots and pans.

Gina turned to face him and folded her soft

149

brown arms across her chest. 'You were saying?'

'A proposition, Gina,' he began smoothly. 'A straight deal. I'd like to rent one of your rooms.'

She curled her full lips into a smile. 'Ronnie kicked you out at last, has he?'

Micky looked mildly offended. 'It's for two pals of mine, a couple of kids, actually.'

'I don't rent to children.'

'These are what you might call the more mature variety.'

'How mature?'

'Sixteen at tops.'

'Why should they want a room?'

'Long story, my lovely, but I ain't about to take up your valuable time now.' He took out his wallet and counted three five pound notes, flicking the edges and pressing them into the space between her folded arms and apron. 'One of 'em ain't well, so they might need a bit of your home cooking, right? So this is for starters. Same again in a month if you fancy it. If you don't, they're out of here on the double.'

Slowly Gina plucked out the paper money and scrutinized it as though it might be counterfeit. She examined the texture with two probing fingers then frowned. 'What's the catch?'

'None.' Micky lifted his hands innocently in the air.

'Who are they, Micky?'

'Honest to God they're just kids. Waifs and strays that used to work the debris for me. I'm doing them a good turn. Been kicked out of home by an old brass that lives with a pervert down Bow Street. You should see 'em Gina. They'd break

150

your heart.'

'I doubt it.'

'Come on, Gina, give it a go, eh? What have you got to lose? You've got all them big rooms out the back doing nothing.'

'How long for?'

'As long as you want.'

Gina studied him before finally pushing the folded notes into a pocket below the apron. Micky swallowed as his eyes followed her movements. She was a big girl, no doubt about that. Lucky old Lenny. Micky had always been partial to women with wide hips and a big fife and drum. With her black hair and flashing eyes she was what he called a real stunner, but the moment she opened her mouth, the attraction diminished somewhat. She had a vocabulary that equalled any docker's, which wasn't surprising as her dad was a stoker and her mother had run the Limehouse café for years. When the old girl died, she left the place to Gina who knew the business inside out. When Gina's fancy man did a disappearing act, Lenny had spotted his opportunity. Gina had eaten him alive on their first outing.

'Bring them in the back way. But I tell you, Micky, I'm keeping this for my trouble.' She nudged the hidden fivers with her fist. 'I'll give them a night's kip and if in the morning I'm feeling generous, I'll consider the deal. Understand?'

Micky nodded vigorously. 'You're a doll, Gina.'

'I'm a hard bitch, Micky, and you'd better remember it.'

He could smell her perfume under all those fried breakfasts. Her lips were close and her

151

breasts rose in an unexpected way. She looked him straight in the eye. He was tempted, feeling the attraction go straight to his gut.

She moved forward, smiling. 'I don't know what you're up to, Micky, but don't think you can screw me over. Because if you try – I just say one word to my Lenny. Your Mars and Venus would end up in the mincer.' Still looking at him under her lashes she pulled back the curtain. 'Bring them up the lane to the back of the shop.'

Micky ignored the glances as he walked out. But his heart was still pumping. Out on the pavement he took his handkerchief from the breast pocket of his suit and dabbed his sweating forehead. She was a girl, was Gina!

Ronnie strode through the billiard room and nodded to each player as they bent over the large slate-bottomed tables covered in emerald baize. They played with concentration, chalking the end of their queues and sizing up the opposition. Lamps hung down above the tables spilling pools of light on their surface.

Dressed in a formal dark suit, he savoured the respect the men gave him. He congratulated himself again on the decision to offer only limited membership to his handpicked customers. He intended to keep the riffraff out and the club clean.

Negotiating his way through the onlookers, he made his way to the bar and stood for a moment studying his little empire.

He had been in business for six months now and had secured a legitimate licence. He'd taken a gamble when buying the bomb-damaged working men's club, transforming it into the place it was today. Having cost an arm and a leg to refurbish, the gamble was worth it. As he and Joyce had anticipated, Poplar was a critical location. Positioned just off the high street, they were no time at all from the city. A club for men that was strictly legit and turning a profit.

Ronnie watched his young manager, Dino, who in turn was watching his stewards. They all looked the bees' knees, dressed in black waist-coats and bow ties, their slim figures reflected in the triple mirror behind the bar. The glassware sparkled on the shelves and the ale pumps were all oak handles and chrome bracelets whilst members sat at the bar or in leather club chairs, enjoying the atmosphere.

Ronnie smiled in satisfaction. Life was good. He had a partner he could trust, a lucrative business and reliable staff. And to add icing to the cake, he had received no further opposition from Micky. His little brother was back on track running the markets and suitcases again. All in all, life couldn't be better.

Just then his attention was caught by a move-ment at the top of the blue carpeted stairs. Joyce, wrapped in a fur stole and looking more like royalty than an East End madam, smiled at him. He returned her smile as she turned into the foyer.

Ronnie had always admired her elegance. In some ways she reminded him of his mum in her younger days. He'd seen photos of Mum and Dad, all done up to the nines. But in every other way Joyce was different, a shrewd lady and tough with it. Mum's heart was all marshmallow; Joyce's, reinforced steel. But Ronnie knew he had a good partner in Joyce and he hoped he could keep it that way.

Moving slowly across the floor he followed her, ascending the steps and making his way past the cloakroom. He entered the office and found Joyce waiting for him, idling a finger over the rich, dark wood of the desk.

Ronnie felt a stirring inside him. She was a wonderful woman and he thought the world of her. She reassured him in every sense of the word, a quality he had found in no other woman.

'What took you so long?' she purred as he closed the door and took her in his arms. Her dark eyes were ebony, her skin smelt sweet.

'What took *you* so long, beautiful?' he whispered as he took her in his arms.

'A small problem at the House, that's all.' Her voice was smoky and low as she folded her hands round his neck.

'What sort of problem?' He sensed she was disturbed in some way.

'It was nothing.'

Ronnie kissed her cheek briefly and raised an eyebrow. 'Come on now, spill the beans.'

She smiled then. 'A few clowns cut up rough. Not the usual idiots though, these were more organized, stopped short of a slap as if they had planned it.' She paused, her eyes narrowed. 'They distracted Bernie and Sid just enough to get one upstairs.'

'To your quarters?'

'As good as. Luckily, I caught him on the stairs, looking dead shifty. Said he'd lost his way. But he was clever enough to have got where he was whilst the others entertained your boys.'

Ronnie drew his thumb across her chin. 'Are you all right?'

'Course I am.' She laughed, but Ronnie saw the concern in her eyes. He ran his fingers through her hair and murmured reassuringly, 'Leave it to me, I'll make enquiries.'

'It's probably nothing...'

'Relax, Joyce. I'll put more men round with you, double up on security.' He didn't think it was necessary as he felt she was reading too much into it. But he'd talk to Bernie and Sid and keep her happy. He didn't like to see her upset.

'Oh, leave it a while,' she shrugged dismissively. 'A storm in a teacup, I expect.' She lifted her hands to his face. 'Don't let's talk business, eh?'

He smiled, feeling good as she clung to him. 'To think there was a time when it was only business between us,' he whispered, pressing his lips against her fingers and feeling the passion erupt inside him.

'Yeah, but we changed the rules, didn't we? You're not sorry that we did, are you?'

He tipped her face to the light. 'What a thing to ask!'

'I'm asking it though.'

'Joyce, I want you in my life and not just to make the sums add up right. We're good together, we understand each other and I haven't had a minute's regret since I first kissed you.'

She took his face in her hands. 'I'm a girl again

when you tell me that. You give me all that I've ever wanted, not just the physical but the trust and respect that I've failed to find in another man. No one has ever done that for me before and it's bloody worrying at my age.'

'You'll always be a girl to me, Joyce. My girl.'

'You say the nicest things, you charmer.'

As she pulled him with her towards the next room, Ronnie thought for the second time that evening how life was definitely on the up and up.

Chapter Twelve

Bella was laughing and joking as she served the early morning regulars of Gina's café. Six months ago she had been living on the streets with Terry, at the end of her tether. Now it was the beginning of December and she was a working woman and Terry was earning a few bob too. For someone who couldn't put more than a few words together at one time, never mind enlarge on the thought behind them, this was a miracle. Helping Lenny at the lock-up had changed Terry's life. And becoming a waitress in Gina's café had changed her own. The dark and desolate days of Dixons were well behind her and thank God for that.

'Have a butchers at this, sweetheart.' A big, burly man sitting with his two friends at one of the café tables, waved the newspaper in her face. 'It says here that jam's supposed to be off the rationing list now. Does that mean I get an extra dollop with me breakfast this morning?'

'You'd get an extra dollop anyway,' Bella laughed as she lowered a large china plate overflowing with eggs and bacon in front of him. 'We like to keep all our customers sweet. Now don't touch the plate or it'll fry your fingers.'

'I wish you was my missus,' he grinned, poising his knife and fork before the plate hit the table. 'All I get from her is "Get your great big mits orf you greedy great pig!" Or "Sod off down the pub and buy yourself a pasty". That's why I come here for me nosh. I get treated like a gentleman.'

'Which you ain't,' his friend pointed out, thrusting a rasher of streaky bacon into his mouth as he spoke. 'It's your poor old lady I feel sorry for. Fancy having to live with you for forty odd years. Working with you's bad enough, but waking up in the morning and seeing that great ugly mush of yours beside me I'd have topped meself in by now.'

'Yeah, well, you ain't no Errol Flynn yourself,' the first man replied, zipping open a sausage as soon as Bella let go of the plate. 'Don't listen to him, love. I treat me missus like a queen I do.'

'Yeah, he kisses her arse once a year if he's lucky, and she crowns 'im afterwards!'

The café erupted in laughter and Bella joined in as she stepped lightly round the table, collecting the dirty plates and expertly piling them on her forearm. Under Gina's tuition she had soon learned how to be the perfect waitress and her quick sense of humour had endeared her to all the customers. Bella couldn't wait to turn the notice on the door in the morning to Open. By

157

which time she had prepared the food in the kitchen for breakfasts and buttered four loaves, piling them up in readiness for the orders. Gina had taught her how to cook brown crinkled bacon, crusty fried bread and eggs with a soft yellow eye; food that was unheard of in Bow Street. Gina knew all the customers' individual tastes, right down to the way each one liked the strength of their tea or coffee, served almost immediately they walked in the café door. They were busy men with only half an hour to spare sometimes. The food and drink had to be on the table without fuss or delay. From the very first moment Bella had tied an apron round her waist, she seemed to sense the customers' needs.

'Two fry-ups over here, love, and four more on the way in,' called someone else in the corner. Bella nodded, wrote the order swiftly on the pad attached to a string on her belt and hurried out to the kitchen. Gina was at the cooker, dressed as Bella was, in the regulation white pinafore.

Bella lay the order on the table with the others. 'Two breakfasts now and four to arrive.'

Gina indicated two meals already prepared. 'There you are, love. Regular as clockwork, my Friday boys. We'll have all the blokes in soon from the building site round the corner. I'll double up the bacon as they've got stomachs as big as elephants.'

'Shall I tell them the Christmas dinners are on next week?' Bella asked as she filled up the water heater.

Gina nodded and flipped over the eggs in the frying pan. 'We'll start dishing up from midday.

And don't take any nonsense from them either. If you get any lip then tell me and I'll sort them out.'

Gina had warned her that all the customers were in high spirits at this time of year and she had to be ready for jokes to be played on her. Bella was a little nervous, but she wasn't going to show it. She knew how to work quickly and please everyone. She could add up faster than Gina could and Gina was quick. All the men left the café with smiles on their faces and Gina had told her that in the six months she'd worked there business had improved.

Bella almost danced her way out with the breakfasts, her eyes twinkling as she served the hot meals.

It was the end of the working day and Bella and Gina were relaxing. They sat together at one of the tables at the back of the café, gazing out on the dark night. There was less traffic now and at seven o'clock in the evening, very few pedestrians. The café had been closed for half an hour but the smell of tobacco and cooking was still heavy in the air.

On the table in front of them was a large brown ashtray of the workmanlike variety. Balanced on it was Gina's half-smoked Craven A filter tip. Beside the ashtray stood two mugs of coffee and arranged by these were the accounts for the week. The ledger was open beside them and Bella's careful handwriting filled the pages. With a satisfied smile Gina reached across to a small pile of receipts which she quickly tore in half.

159

'What the taxman doesn't see, he doesn't know I've cooked,' Gina intoned as she inhaled deeply on her cigarette then crushed it out.

Bella was accustomed to this little procedure. She had needed no instruction on how to balance the books; Dixons had taught her all she needed to know about figures.

'You know, Bella, at this rate, one day you'll have a business of your own.'

'I like working here.'

Gina laughed and lifted her long legs, crossing one slim ankle over another as she lowered them to the seat of a chair. 'You're young yet. You won't be here long. You'll get bored. Go off somewhere.'

But Bella shook her head. 'After what you've done for me?'

'What did I do for you?' Gina lifted the palms of her hands. 'Apart from the job – which you can do, may I say, standing on your head.'

'You gave me and Terry lodgings and he was sick at the time. It was only your grub and looking after that got him well. I'll never forget that. Never.'

'I helped you out for a price. Micky bunged me fifteen quid to be exact.'

Bella eyes widened. 'You never said before.'

'Did you think I did it out of the goodness of my heart?' Gina's face softened despite her harsh words. 'Everything has a price tag in this life and you'd do well to remember that. As it turns out you've been a good investment for this café. You can charm the customers round your pretty little finger and you know the figures backwards.' She

160

grinned. 'You remind me of me when I was your age.'

'Were you working here then?'

'I've never worked anywhere else!'

'Did you ever want to leave?'

Gina looked surprised. 'By the time I left school I knew the business backwards. Mum had to scrimp and scrape to get this business going, and I was right alongside her, barely out of nappies when she did it; washing, drying, clearing up, cooking, you name it we did it. Dad was away at sea and no help at all. The most he could boast was a girl in every port.'

'Didn't your mum mind him being away?'

'She was too busy trying to keep us afloat. Mum was terrified of poverty and had good reason to be. She was the ninth child of a family of fourteen, immigrants from Spain, poor devils, who risked life and limb to get here, believing the English streets were paved with gold. After discovering the hard way they weren't, most of them died destitute. But Mum got taken in as a little kid by this old widow who used to run this place as a sweet shop. She helped in the shop and looked after the old girl until she died, then turned it into a café. Dad was a customer and she married him in between one of his trips away, God help her, poor love. They never had any more kids after me, she was terrified she'd end up with fourteen. So in a way I 'spose Dad had every reason to wander.'

'Did she look Spanish, like you?'

'She did once, but she worked so hard she had bags under her eyes the size of Bow bells. I watched all her beauty fade and I promised myself I'd never end up like that.' Gina frowned gravely. 'And if it's one bit of advice I'd give you for free, it would be to take good care of that skin of yours. It's flawless now but it won't last forever.'

Bella nodded quickly. 'I'm going to buy a good cream to rub in.'

'You want olive oil, love. Use it every day. I've got some in the kitchen. Help yourself.'

'Thanks.' Bella smiled hesitantly. 'Despite all you've said about being paid to keep me, I'm still grateful. You've been good to me and Terry. We've two nice rooms and a bit of privacy that we never had before. And Lenny's kept Terry out of trouble down the lock-up and even says he's a good worker. Plus I've got money in me purse and food in my stomach.' She paused, smiling shyly. 'And best of all Micky and me are back on speaking terms, something I thought wasn't going to happen again.'

At this, Gina laughed. 'Oh Bella, you don't know your Micky very well, do you? He doesn't do nothing that doesn't pay him. He is in love with himself and why not? He's a good-looking bugger and knows that what he wants he's bound to get. He could see what an asset you are to him and he wasn't going to let you get away. It's second nature to him, collecting people, having control over them and reaping the rewards from their labours. Which, I assure you, are great.'

'But it was me who had to ask Micky for help,' Bella argued.

Gina frowned, leaning forward. 'Look, Bella,

you know that my Lenny means the world to me, don't you?' Bella nodded, suddenly ill at ease as Gina's black eyes gazed straight at her. 'Well, he's a good man underneath, but he couldn't walk a straight line to save his life. When we first met I tried to persuade him to come half shares into the café with me. But, oh no, he turned his nose up at cooking and waiting tables on other blokes. Micky convinced him they were going to make a fortune on the booze and the result is Lenny winds up doing all the hard slog.' She sighed deeply, scooping the receipts together and tucking them into the pocket of her apron. 'Anyway, I've given up fighting Lenny's battles now. Come to the conclusion I'm better off like me mum, feathering me own nest. Lenny will have to learn his own lessons. Just as you will.'

Bella frowned hesitantly. 'But I thought you liked Micky.'

Gina shrugged. 'He's a fact of life and I accept him.'

'That's a funny thing to say.'

'Bella, I think you think you owe him. But you know, you don't. Your first responsibility is to yourself – number one. Now, here's your money, you've earned it.'

Bella gasped. 'Three pounds?'

'You scratch my back, I'll scratch yours. Do you know we plated over two hundred and forty fry-ups this week? That's not counting rolls and sandwiches. You do the sums. At one and four a breakfast, we hit the jackpot. And considering we're still on rationing, that's not bad. All I can say is long live the black market. Now take it.'

Bella grinned as she accepted the money. 'I know what I'm going to buy.'

'What?'

'A new dress for Christmas.'

'You deserve it. You're a beautiful girl and you should have beautiful dresses to wear.'

'I've still got all the clothes you gave me when I came here. I didn't have nothing, just a bundle of rags. If it wasn't for what you bought up the market for me and Terry–'

'I wouldn't have found myself a nice little waitress, would I?'

Bella knew that behind Gina's hard façade there was really a heart of gold. 'This is the best job I've ever had. And the best place I've ever lived.'

'In that case, you've got my sympathy.' Gina grinned as she rose to her feet. 'Now come on, we've all that washing-up to do before tomorrow. As the door opens they'll be lining up on the pavement for their grub. And they'll need it to soak up the beer they put away on Saturday night.'

Bella felt her pulse race at the thought of tomorrow. Micky was taking her out. He said he'd collect her at six if she could get away. And this time she knew he wasn't going to let her down. Gina had overheard him making the arrangement and warned him he better not be late as she was letting her staff off duty early. As Bella had worked out tonight, Micky relied heavily on Lenny and therefore went out of his way to please Gina.

'Sit tight, Bells, I've got to see a man about a dog.' Micky smoothed back his hair with the palm of his hand and stood up.

'But Micky–'

'Five minutes, that's all darlin'.'

Bella watched him weave his way between the tables acknowledging almost everyone as he went with handshakes and winks. Since the moment they had entered the club, he'd been engrossed in conversation with one person or another. Mixing a little business with pleasure, he'd explained to Bella, who at first hadn't been in the least disappointed, but flattered that he'd brought her to Club Afrika off the Tottenham Court Road. The owner was a man called Ivor who wore a small moustache and tuxedo. Micky talked to him at the bar whilst Bella sat on her own at a table. Unlike the Indigo, Club Afrika lacked entertainment and although Micky had bought drinks in tall glasses, Bella hadn't drunk hers. She'd asked for lemonade instead but it hadn't arrived. Micky seemed to have forgotten all about her.

Looking round the club, which at first glance had seemed mysterious and unusual with its big potted ferns and mosaic archways, Bella saw on closer inspection that it was rather shabby. Most of the tables were occupied by young men wearing jumpers and baggy trousers and the women wore shapeless skirts or dresses. The older variety of customer looked a bit seedy and Bella hoped they weren't going to stay here all evening.

By ten o'clock she was wondering when Micky would come and sit by her. She'd taken a lot of trouble with her appearance and borrowed a deep rose-coloured sheath style dress from Gina as she hadn't managed to get to the market to buy an outfit. It was big on the hips, but with a few tacks, Gina had made alterations. As it was an off the shoulder gown Bella had pinned her thick auburn hair up into a pleat. A lot of olive oil, black mascara and red lipstick had gone in to her make-up and though she disliked it herself, she hoped Micky would notice. Gina had commented that she was definitely a young Rita Hayworth though by the way Micky was carrying on, Bella was beginning to think all her efforts were wasted.

'Sorry about that,' Micky apologized eventually as he strolled up to the table. He lit a cigarette with his lighter and kicked out a chair with the tip of his shoe. 'Look at all this.' He sat down, pulling crumpled pieces of paper from his pocket. With the cigarette dangling from his mouth he sighed. 'Never was any good at paperwork. Look at all this! I need to get meself one of them posh secretaries.'

'What for?'

'Business is booming, ain't it? Need to keep track, start books and all that. We did all right during the war, but I'd never have believed it would be this good afterwards. With all these bottle parties in fashion, I can't see an end to the demand.' He laughed. 'If I could get Lenny to work nights I'd soon be a millionaire.'

'What's a bottle party?' Bella asked, feeling stupid.

'Bottle parties, doll, are the future for Micky Bryant. You can keep your market stalls and suit-

166

cases, your knocked off whistle and toot. Bottle parties are a legit way to render the British public a service and make a fortune into the bargain.'

'So bottle parties are legal, then?'

'Course they are! Would geezers like old Ivor over there stay trading if they wasn't? The onus, you see, is on the punter, Joe Bloggs let's say. He signs an order form for his booze to be brought into the club by an all-night wine merchant, see? That way, it's classed as a private booze-up, nothing to do with the club. At least that's the way it looks on paper, all official like. Me and Lenny supply the booze at special discounted rates and everyone is happy as Larry.'

Bella still didn't really understand Micky's explanation, but she felt it was her intelligence at fault. 'It's just that I don't want Terry to get in any trouble,' she murmured bewilderedly.

'Put your mind at rest then, Bells. No more mucking around under an old lock-up. As of this week we are going into kosher premises. A nice little warehouse at the docks with a sign over the door, proper books to keep and moving in Monday.'

'Oh, Micky, that's wonderful.'

'Yeah, thought you'd see it that way.'

'What does Ronnie–' Bella began but didn't finish as Micky interrupted her impatiently.

'Christ, Bells, this has got nothing to do with Ron. And I don't take kindly to you bringing him up all the time.'

'I don't mean to–'

'Then leave it out, will you?' He glared at her. 'Look, I've brought you out for a good time and

167

all I get is Ronnie this, Ronnie that. He's a busy man, isn't he? Got his club to look after now.'

'Couldn't we have gone there tonight?'

'Strike a light, Bells, ain't you never satisfied?' Micky's face darkened as he pushed himself roughly from the table. 'Look, I've brought you out for a drink, despite me being a very busy man, and still you're nagging.' He stood up and jerked his head to one side. 'Come on, I'm taking you home.'

'But it's only early yet.'

'Well, I ain't suffering any more nag. I come out to enjoy meself not be interrogated by the bloody inquisition.'

'I'm sorry, Micky.' She stretched out for his hand. She had that cold feeling in her stomach and she knew all his danger signs. Somehow she managed to make him angry but she didn't know why. 'I promise I won't say anything more, I'll just sit here and keep quiet.'

'Strikes me, you think more of Ron than of me.'

'I don't Micky. I only care about you. I ... I care a lot.' She blushed as she folded her fingers over his and gave them a gentle squeeze. 'Sit down, please.'

It was a moment before he did as she asked and shaking a fresh cigarette from the pack, he offered her one. She took it, her fingers trembling. 'Micky?'

'What?' He sucked the smoke slowly between his teeth.

'Do you really need help at your new place?'

A smile crept over his lips. 'Yeah, why?'

'I could help you on Sundays.'

He shrugged. 'If you want. But it's a case of zipping this.' He pointed to his mouth.

'I will. I promise.'

'Okay then. I'll take you down the new gaff as soon as it's sorted.'

Bella felt a thrill of excitement. She got bored on Sundays if there were no jobs to do for Gina. She liked Mondays best when the week stretched ahead. She had always hoped Micky would call round one Sunday and take her to Piper Street to see Ron and Sean like the old days. But he hadn't and she'd given up hope of that ever happening.

'But listen,' Micky said in a hard voice that made Bella anxious all over again. 'I'm the boss, you'll be on a good earner if you can do the work, but I want no verbal in the meantime.'

Bella nodded silently.

After a long pause he pulled one of the chairs from another table beside him. 'Come over here.'

She got up slowly and sat on it. He reached up and slid his hand to the back of her head. 'I want my Lana Turner back, the girl with that smouldering look in her eyes. The look that was only for me. Or at least I thought it was till I found you with Casanova.'

'I've told you, Micky, Ray meant nothing to me.'

Bella felt his arm slide around her. His fingers released the grips in her hair and it tumbled down on her shoulders. 'That's my girl, my beautiful Bells. I've watched you grow up and tried to protect you and I may have my faults, but my heart's in the right place. I've got to know where I stand, see? And that whatever I do, you'll be by my side.' His mouth was so close that his breath floated over her face, making her feel as though she wanted this moment to last forever. He was touching her the way she wanted to be touched, holding her as if she was a real woman, the way she wanted to be for him.

He pressed his mouth against her cheek, kissing her skin tenderly. She closed her eyes, expecting him to kiss her but just as his lips found her waiting mouth he whispered, 'Let's get out of here.'

With his arm around her waist he hurried her out of the club. She felt a sense of urgency as he held her hand and walked with her into the dark City night. He had never been like this before. Never said these things before. With the sound of late night traffic in their ears, Bella looked into his eyes.

They were dark and exciting; they promised her so much. In that moment she knew she would do whatever he wanted. Go wherever he took her. He was hers now and she was his.

Chapter Thirteen

It was late on Christmas Eve and Bella had begun serving fry-ups at eight o'clock that morning. At midday there had been a rush for the Christmas menu, roast chicken and Christmas pud. They had sold out by three. But none of the regulars had wanted to leave the carefree atmosphere of the café. They knew they had to return home to face the demands of their wives and family before they could get down to the pub for some serious drinking that evening.

'Let's park ourselves on a comfy chair and have a tipple before we clear up,' Gina suggested as she turned the sign on the door to Closed and walked back to the kitchen. 'Open that cupboard there and you'll find half a bottle of gin. Don't worry, it's kosher, not Lenny's rubbish.'

'The till was going non-stop today.' Bella's cheeks were flushed as she took out the gin and two glasses, following Gina into the café. 'If they'd been available, we could have sold twice as many dinners.'

'To be honest, it caught me on the hop,' Gina admitted as they sat at the back table. 'I've never had a Christmas like it. At least, not since before the war and even in the old days, Mum only opened for a couple of hours on Christmas Eve. You know what? I'm going to spend all morning in bed,' she sighed as she pushed one shoe from her foot and massaged an unsightly corn. 'You and Terry are coming to us tomorrow teatime, right? I've saved some cold ham and we'll use the leftovers in the kitchen for bubble and squeak.'

Bella smiled but secretly she was disappointed. Even though Micky was supposed to be taking her out tonight, there had been no mention of taking her back to Piper Street for Christmas.

'So how are the two love birds?' Gina asked, unable to hide the note of sarcasm in her voice as she poured gin and a splash of lime into their glasses. 'He can't keep his hands off you lately.'

'You know Micky,' Bella said, blushing. When he came in the café now he followed her out to the kitchen and kissed her. She found it embarrassing in front of Gina and always quickly pushed him away.

'Oh, yes, I know Micky.'

Bella had thought that making love with Micky would be the most wonderful thing in the world. From the time he had taken her to the Indigo and she had woken up at Piper Street in the big double bed that belonged to Micky's parents, she had imagined their first romantic night of passion. The dream had been so real that she thought it would come true one day. She wanted to wake up like they did on the films, safe in the arms of her hero. To find herself in a dingy hotel room on the Tottenham Court Road had shattered her dream. There had been nothing romantic about the single electric light bulb hanging by a cord from the ceiling above them or listening to the dripping of water from one of the rusty taps ground into the dirty sink. Micky had taken off his clothes at once and jumped into the rumpled-looking bed. He didn't seem to notice the dowdy setting or Bella's apprehension as she shyly removed Gina's lovely dress, trying to still her trembling fingers. Micky had just laughed and grabbed her, pulling her roughly down beside him. Without pausing for the tender moment that she had expected, his lovemaking had been rough and over quickly.

Lying awake as he slept, she had stared up at the dim light bulb and wondered what she had done.

'What's the matter, ducks?' Gina asked as if she could read her thoughts.

'Nothing. Just a bit tired that's all.'

'In that case, get a drink down you.' She slid the glass closer and reluctantly Bella took a sip.

'So where's Micky taking you this evening?'

'I don't know. He just said he'd call round if he can get away in time.'

'The question is, get away from what?' Gina raised her eyebrows.

'Work, of course.'

'I'm sure.'

Bella didn't like the way Gina kept making hints about Micky. It was the same with Micky who was always sniping at Gina. They had a strange relationship and sometimes Bella felt trapped between the two of them.

'What about Terry?'

'Micky said he could come with us.' He hadn't; it was Bella who had insisted they take Terry along. It was Christmas Eve and she didn't want him to be alone.

'Well, chin-chin,' Gina said, raising her glass. 'Let's drink up and be merry.'

They grinned at each other and just as Gina threw back her head and swallowed her drink there was a knock at the front door.

'Who's that?' she demanded, thrusting down her glass and jumping to her feet. 'Can't they read? We're closed and the sign says so.'

Bella saw two familiar faces pressed up to the glass. 'Oh, it's Dolly Taylor and Percy! Could they come in for a minute?'

Gina peered at them. 'As long as they don't

want feeding, they're welcome.' She went to the door and slid open the bolt. Dolly entered, full of apologies. Percy stood uncertainly, looking very decent, Bella thought, dressed in a smart grey tweed coat and polished brown shoes. His hair had grown to collar length and his smile was wider than ever. 'Season's greetings one and all,' he cried. 'Hope we ain't disturbing you?'

'Not if you're friends of Bella's you're not,' Gina said as she closed the door and held out her hand. 'I'm Gina.'

Dolly shook it. 'I'm so pleased to meet you, Gina.' She gazed at Gina in open admiration.

'Me felicitations,' Percy beamed, pumping Gina's hand.

'Dolly and me was at school together,' Bella explained as Gina led the way back to their table. She felt guilty that she hadn't made any effort to see Dolly since the summer. When they were all seated she looked at her friend and frowned. 'I meant to get in touch, Dolly, but I've been busy. How did you know where to find me?'

'I saw Micky and asked him.'

'When was that?'

'Last weekend when me and Percy went up West to see *The Red Shoes*. Oh, it was lovely, all about a beautiful ballerina and a handsome composer–' Dolly stopped as she saw the look of impatience on Bella's face. 'Anyway, we was in the queue and Micky was walking by. He was with his pals, said he was going up Hammersmith Palais.'

Bella didn't say that Micky hadn't taken her out last Saturday because he said he was too busy working. She didn't want Dolly to know that he'd

174

lied to her.

'Anyway, Bella, I've got some news for you,' Dolly hurried on, eager to expound as she pushed out her hand. 'Look, me and Percy are engaged!'

Bella gazed at the sparkling engagement ring on Dolly's finger. It glittered expensively and made Dolly's plump, square hand look almost attractive. 'Oh, Dolly, congratulations!'

Gina picked up the bottle. 'This calls for another toast.'

'Oh, not for us, Gina, thank you,' Dolly refused politely as Percy looked disappointed. 'I'd be tipsy before I got home.'

'When did you get engaged?' Bella asked.

'At the weekend. When Percy asked me I nearly fainted.'

'Yeah, she nearly did an' all,' Percy nodded. 'Had to give her a dose of her mum's smelling salts. Thought she was a goner.'

'Oh Perce, I wasn't that bad. Not really.'

'Good job I didn't ask you to elope with me.'

'You can never take him seriously, you know.' Dolly fluttered her eyelashes. 'And anyway, we didn't need to elope. Dad gave his permission as soon as Percy asked. Then we went out and bought the ring in Oxford Street. Do you like it?' She splayed her short, stubby fingers on the table. 'It's a real diamond, isn't it, Perce?'

'Course it is,' Percy nodded. 'You can get two and six on it up any pawn shop.'

Dolly's eyes rolled. 'Oh, be quiet you.'

'It's lovely, Dolly, gorgeous.'

'When is the wedding?' Gina enquired.

'Next summer.' Dolly went redder than ever.

175

'Bella, would you be my bridesmaid? I know it's a long way off, but you're always so busy I thought it was best to ask you now. And of course, it would be lovely if Micky could come, and you Gina and–' Suddenly tears filled Dolly's bright eyes and Percy put his arm around her.

'What's up, my treasure?'

'I don't know. I'm just being silly.'

Gina sipped at her replenished drink. 'Tears of joy no doubt.'

'It's all been such a shock,' Dolly gasped. 'I never thought this would ever happen to me, plain old Dolly Taylor.'

'You'll be Mrs Percy Shine,' Percy pointed out as he squeezed her shoulder. 'We'll be two shiners together.'

Dolly and Percy laughed.

'Where are you going to live?' Bella asked.

'We're saving up to rent a place. Somewhere up Poplar we thought. It'll only be a couple of rooms but at least it will be ours.'

'One for me and one for you,' Percy winked.

Dolly began to talk about her wedding and what they had planned already. It was to be held at Christ Church, the reception at Chapel House Street and the honeymoon in Devon.

Bella was envious. Her friend had everything that she had always wanted herself. A romantic fiancé, a real engagement ring and a white wedding with all the trimmings, not forgetting the honeymoon. But most of all, Bella knew that Percy respected Dolly's wishes and would wait until their wedding night to make love to her.

Bella felt sad. There was no way she could see

Micky walking up a church aisle and sliding a gold band on her finger. The last time he had been to church was when his mother died. He had vowed never to go near one again. She didn't even know what his views on marriage were. There was so much she didn't know about him. So much they hadn't talked about or discussed. And yet they had done the most intimate thing that two people could do together. Why hadn't she made him wait? Why had she gone to that dreadful hotel and thrown away her dignity?

The answer was, because she had been desperate to have him, call him her own. And she had been willing to do anything that he wanted. When it should, of course, have been the other way round.

The months leading up to Christmas had been a big success for the Blue Moon. Ronnie was a contented man; 1949 had arrived and business was brisk. He had installed more billiard tables and games of dice and even though February was a known black hole for cash, the tables were busier than ever.

Ronnie surveyed the discreetly lit room and listened to the hum of conversation, the soft laughter and occasional joke. There was no trouble to be found here, no escorts, bottle parties or vice. His members sought the thrill of a challenge and a discreet wager. He provided all this without fuss, eliminating the element of real danger that came from being directly outside of the law. He was gaining a reputation for fairness and respectability and he liked that. Although it wasn't to say that he would turn his nose up at a good deal if it was offered. And he had plenty in mind over the next few years. He was going to buy bomb-damaged properties, do them up as he had done with the club and sit on them, bringing in rents from those who could afford it. He would keep books and see that it was all legit. At least, as legit as it was possible to make it.

He had seen the effects of extortion, the protection rackets and black market when he had returned from service. The rich had got richer and the poor, poorer. And this had depressed him. The Watney Streeters had been top dog in the war, a gang known for their violence and greed in the East End. But even these men were now looking for new pastures as the Hoxton boys and Islington mobs, the Italians and Maltese, even the Jamaicans and Jews were cutting themselves a slice of cake. It was like the Wild West. The gold was there, and in Ronnie's eyes he had discovered it. He was now about to stake his claim officially, so it couldn't be taken away again. Even Micky saw the sense in becoming legit. Dad would even see it, if he was here. And at that thought Ronnie smiled inwardly. The old man had been a canny totter, one of the best. A creeper of the first class, he had indulged in everything a bit iffy unbeknown to Mum, because where there was a profit Dad had his own philosophy. Take from the rich and give to family first and then to the poor and his sons loved him for it. It was a wonder they hadn't all been kitted out in Sherwood Green on the day they were born. But the world was a different place now and the Blue

Moon was proof of it.

Just then Ronnie saw Gino nod in his direction. He walked casually to the bar and smiled at the customers. He sat on a stool, watching Gino expertly pump ale into a pint glass.

When the money was taken and rung into the till, Gino approached him. 'Not to worry you unnecessarily, Mr Bryant.' Barely moving his lips the young man slid his gaze to the right. 'It's them over there. They're the Indigo's boys.'

Slowly Ronnie adjusted his position. He noted two men sitting at a table in the corner. 'You're certain?'

'Positive. The big one is Sammy Stratton's doorman, the other is a runner for Tony. I used to work there, only for a few weeks, but I never forget a face.'

'Any idea why they're here?' Ronnie asked curiously.

'I wouldn't like to guess. But just now I got a touch of the old eyeball.'

Ronnie studied the two men, then nodded. 'Okay, leave it with me.' Turning to make his way up the blue-carpeted stairs to the foyer, he reflected that Sid and Bernie weren't due in for an hour, after their stint at Joyce's. That left him only with Gino and the waiters and his doorman, Henry.

Ronnie approached the well-padded, dark-suited figure and smiled. 'Henry, a word in your ear.'

'Sure, Mr Bryant.'

'How did Tweedledum and Tweedledee over there, get in?' Ronnie glanced over his shoulder.

'They had cards, Mr Bryant. I wouldn't have let them in otherwise.'

'Remember their names?'

'Jones or Smith, I think, something ordinary anyway.'

'Have you seen them before?'

Henry squinted, narrowing his small eyes in his big hairless head. 'Nah. Are they trouble?'

'Probably not, but Gino tells me they're the Indigo's men. Leave the door to me and go round to Piper Street. Fetch Micky and Sean, okay?'

'I'll be back before you know it.'

'Good man.'

Ronnie watched him unlock the door and leave. Casually turning back to study the room he wondered if it was coincidence that had two new faces turning up on Saturday, the busiest night of the week. All the club chairs were taken and tables booked.

Ten minutes later the two men rose and made their way to the bar. The bigger of the two rudely pushed in between the customers, spilling drinks and causing a disturbance. Ronnie felt his stomach contract. An argument broke out and the other man grabbed Gino. Ronnie was down the steps and across the room in an instant. He registered shock on his customers' faces as they quickly scattered. An impromptu visit from the law was a result none of them welcomed.

'You two-faced little runt,' the big man snarled. 'Call this a full measure?' He threw the contents of his glass into Gino's terrified face.

Ronnie clamped a hand on the man's shoulder.

'What's your problem, pal?'

The large, domed head turned slowly. 'Ah, Mr Bryant himself.'

'You know me?'

'Let's say, I'll be getting to know you.' He looked around him, screwing up his eyes in his fleshy, red face. 'And I'll be getting to know your turf even better. Sammy said this club was a joke and he was right. Look at all them ponces, running off like girls.'

'A matter of opinion,' Ronnie replied smoothly. 'Now, my compliments to your boss, but you're taking up valuable time. If you've got something to say, say it. Then you can get the hell out of here.'

The big man smirked. 'Perhaps you ain't noticed but your muscle has just walked out of the door. You're on your own here and my mate is a real nutter.'

A nasty laugh came from behind him. 'Yeah, Mr Stratton said you was a hard nut to crack. Which is why I brought me jemmy along. It's just the job for smashing up a spot of resistance.' With a smile on his face, he demolished the glasses on the bar and taking another swipe he put paid to the row of optics. Ronnie tried to move but a bear-sized paw stopped him. 'You ain't going nowhere, sonny boy. You got a ringside seat for this act.'

Ronnie watched the last of his customers flee, Gino and the waiters among them. Angry with himself for not heeding Joyce's warning, he cursed himself for not having taken her seriously, doubled security. He had ignored good advice to his own cost. Sammy Stratton had tested his strengths and found them to be lacking. The man was evil and this was going to be an all-out howler.

As he listened to the splintering of glass around him, he considered his options. Without a weapon, he was powerless. As much as he valued his property, he valued breathing more. Unless Henry arrived back with the reinforcements, he was going to be totalled. What was troubling him the most was the Strattons' motive. It was hard to believe they had any, except jealousy. They knew he would retaliate. His revenge would be sweeter than anything they could accomplish, he would make sure of that. It would be war and they knew it. But did the Strattons need that kind of aggravation? They were big names, had fearsome reps and were respected. What had he done personally to upset them?

Looking into the ugly face before him, Ronnie said lightly, 'You've made your point, I am listening. Are you going to tell me what Sammy wants and save us all a lot of trouble?'

'You'll find out soon enough,' the man grunted, pushing Ronnie backwards. 'When we've finished with this dump, you're making a little visit, chauffeur driven, to the other side of town, where Mr Stratton's got a few questions for you and that runt of a brother of yours.'

'Micky?' Suddenly Ronnie felt a chill go over him. Whenever Micky's name came up and it had cropped up once or twice lately, there was trouble. But Micky had sworn he was clean. And Ronnie had believed him.

Ronnie landed hard against the wall. He was growing tired of this big ape pushing him around, he wanted to retaliate. But he knew his satisfaction would be short-lived. He would have to wait until reinforcements arrived.

If they arrived … his gut was telling him the fun was likely to be over by the time they got here.

A stool sailed through the air, fragmenting the mirror on the wall. It was worth a small fortune and Ronnie had been glad to pay it. Now he was yearning to rip these two clowns apart.

Two fat fists reached out and grasped his lapels. He could smell his assailant's bad breath. Another stool smashed through the remains of the booze. 'Suddenly run out of conversation, have we? Need a little light entertainment? Well, my boss has got a nice quiet room for you back at the Indigo and a comfy chair. All you have to do is sit in it and me and my friend there will do the entertaining.'

So that was the score, Ronnie thought dismally. No chance of waiting for Micky and Sean. Suddenly he wondered if he would ever see the inside of the Blue Moon again. Whatever Micky had done, he had excelled at it.

'Thanks for the offer,' Ronnie replied with a forced smile. 'Some other time maybe, when the odds are more even?' He thrust his head forward and chinned the man facing him. Blood from his mouth spurted on impact, spraying over them both.

'He nutted me! He's broken me teeth, the bastard!'

Spinning sideways, Ronnie was free. He

183

listened with satisfaction to the shrieks of agony. Then felt a prickle of fear as he saw the glint of a knife. He dodged sideways, but the blade glinted, sharp and close. Ronnie backed slowly up the stairs, but the weapon swept into his jacket. If it had penetrated him, Ronnie told himself he couldn't feel it. He turned and vaulted the cloak-room counter. Melted into the shadows and listened to his own rapid breath, wondering how much time it would take Micky and Sean to find him.

Sean Bryant and his friend Ashley Crane were laughing together in Sean's bedroom. There were two suitcases open on the bed and Sean was sitting by one of them, a frown on his forehead as he held up the jacket of a shiny grey suit. His blue eyes twinkled under his shock of light brown hair that was plastered up and away from his forehead. He liked to dress snappily and his recent investment pleased him. The suitcases were filled with gents' clothing, recently acquired from a West End store. Sean's smooth features and expressive mouth were highlighted by the mid-grey dullness of the cloth but Ashley, dressed in a striped green shirt and dark trousers, shook his head in disgust.

'It's definitely not you, Seany. Grey is so dull, you need a colour to lift your complexion, not swamp it.'

Sean looked disappointed. 'But it's a dead ringer for the type of suit that Cary always wears. Look at the stitching, feel the quality.'

'But Cary Grant is tall – and dark – and tanned.'

'So what are you saying, Ashley?'

Ashley Crane drew his short, expressive fingers over his pale hair, almost always worn as a crew cut. 'You're not a Cary, if anything you're more a Bergman, ducks.'

'Now that's being rude.'

'I'm only teasing. Don't get shirty.'

Sean impatiently thrust the jacket back into the suitcase. He adored him but sometimes Ashley just didn't understand the burning desire to look good. No, not just good, unique. Sean's two passions in life were inherited from his parents. Cooking from Mum, who had taught him everything she knew, and clothes from Dad, whose family were royal weavers, so the story went. Sean smiled at the thought because Dad's tall tales were legion. That being said, he was a real sharp dresser. Sean liked to think if he didn't have the hard-edged masculine lines of his two brothers, he was right up there in the fashion stakes.

'So what's this?' He drew out a white vest and held it under his chin. Without waiting for his friend to reply he laughed derisively. 'This is supposed to be Oxford Street and I wouldn't be seen dead in it, whatever it is.'

Ashley put his hand on his hip and looked thoughtful. 'Well. It has a certain something, if it is a bit common. You know who you remind me of?'

'No, who?'

'What would you say if I said Montgomery Clift?'

Sean's blue eyes widened. 'You serious?'

'Absolutely. White vests are all the rage in America.'

185

A little put out that he hadn't known this information himself, Sean frowned again. 'How do you know?'

'I read all the magazines, don't I?'

'And I suppose you've seen Montgomery Clift wearing one?'

'I got hold of a copy of *Life* last year and he looked gorgeous. I tell you, that boy is going to be big in Hollywood. Honestly the photos would make you drool.'

'You never mentioned him before.'

Ashley smiled flirtatiously. 'No, well we've all got our fantasies.'

Sean dropped the vest back in the suitcase. 'I can't see the attraction myself; he's just a kid. Now if you're talking steamy, Cary is the tops. That kiss on the balcony in *Notorious!* It went on forever. Wasn't that our first film together?'

'No, it wasn't,' Ashley replied, looking hurt. 'Our first film was Bogie and Bacall, remember? *The Big Sleep.* Oh God, it was lovely.' He blushed. 'And we held hands when it was dark.'

'We must have been daft to chance it,' Sean breathed excitedly. 'Anyone could have seen us. One of them usherettes for instance, always shining their torch in your face! I really don't know how we had the nerve.'

'It was lust pure and simple,' Ashley admitted with a grin. 'I nearly died of happiness when you asked me to go to the cinema.'

'Did you really?'

'I never thought we'd last this long.'

'Neither did I.'

Sean gazed at his friend and felt a deep longing

to take him in his arms, making certain he was real and he wasn't dreaming. Instead, he said softly, 'When I was young I felt so confused about being – you know, the way I am. Mum and Dad produced two great strapping blokes like Micky and Ron and there was me, all curls and freckles and terrified that Dad would find out I was a nancy boy.'

'You shouldn't refer to yourself as that.'

'It was what they called me at school,' Sean admitted miserably. 'I didn't even know what it meant. It started after our dad died. I never thought I'd miss the old man so much, especially as he was such a real man and there was me, hanging round me mum all the time and learning how to make apple pies and custard.' He laughed gently. 'But I had a respect for my dad. He was my hero. Then one day he was there, the next minute he wasn't. Everything fell apart in my life. The other kids took liberties at school and it was Ron and Micky in the end that made them stop. I was lucky. They caught Johnny Burrows and Stan Baldrey in the lavs and nearly drowned them down the pans.'

'I wish I had brothers,' Ashley replied enviously. 'Six blooming sisters! Always dolls to play with. No wonder I'm like I am. It's a miracle I don't dress up in frocks.'

Sean giggled. 'We could always try it one night.'

'I might keep you to that.' Ashley opened his arms and a little awkwardly Sean moved into them. They looked into one another's gaze and Ashley stroked Sean's cheek softly. 'I don't care what you wear, Seany. Put on the grey, it don't matter to me. You've got more clothes in those suitcases than a Petticoat Lane spiv.'

Sean grinned. 'I know. They're all knocked off from Cox Street. Some fly boy up there sold me them cheap. I couldn't resist a bargain.'

'Oh, and I suppose you couldn't resist him either!'

Sean looked into Ashley's eyes. 'You're the only one for me and you know it. Oh, Ashley, I wish we could tell everyone the way we feel about each other.'

'We'd land up behind bars if we did. And our lives wouldn't be worth living in clink.'

'One day it won't be like that for people like us.'

'That day's a long way off, in my opinion, but until then, we've got to be–' Suddenly there was a loud banging on the door downstairs.

They leapt apart. 'Gawd almighty,' Sean cursed, putting his hand up to his chest, 'I nearly had a heart attack then.'

'Who is it?' Ashley went stealthily to the window and looked through the lace curtain. 'Looks like Henry, Ronnie's doorman.'

'What's he doing here?'

'Dunno.'

'I thought we wasn't going to be disturbed?' Ashley backed away, fear filling his soft brown eyes.

'I didn't think we would be. Ronnie's at the club and Micky's over at the still.'

'So what shall we do?'

Sean checked the buttons on his shirt and confirming they were in order, walked to the door. 'Answer it, I suppose.'

'Shall I come with you?'

Sean looked back and smiled. 'Any time, big boy.'

The two young men giggled and went downstairs together. As Sean opened the door, Henry was about to knock again and Sean grimaced at the raised fist.

'Give us a chance, Henry,' he said a little coyly as Ashley stood by him. 'Your hand will come through the door any minute if you go on like that.'

'I thought you was out,' Henry said breathlessly as he looked into the hall behind them. 'Where's Micky?'

'Not here, obviously.'

'Oh, Christ,' Henry cursed. 'There's just you two, then?'

'Yeah, and so what?' Sean felt annoyed at the intrusion. It was the weekend after all. Even he had a day off once in while. For the last six months he had been working solid with Ashley, making deliveries to the clubs at night for Micky and the markets for Ronnie in the day. True he just had to collect the takings but it was all leg work. His private time alone with Ashley was rare. He was just about to say so when Henry pushed the door back and stepped in.

'Oy, what's this in aid of?' Sean demanded as Ashley gripped his arm. Sean knew that Ashley was terrified of big men like Henry. Having had no brothers to protect him, he had been bullied to the extreme all his life and it had left its scars.

'There's aggro at the Blue Moon,' Henry explained rapidly, his big ears standing out from his bald head as if he was receiving radio signals. Nervously glancing over his shoulder, he added in a low voice, 'Ronnie wants you and Micky there on the double.'

'What sort of trouble?' Sean began to feel as nervous as Henry looked.

'A couple of geezers from the Indigo turned up. Ronnie thinks they're up for a bundle. He needs reinforcements.'

Sean felt Ashley melt away from him. Ashley's horror of violence was as strong as his need for love. And Sean knew that when push came to shove, the former came first. He was on his own here and yet Micky would kill him if he divulged where he was. He'd been on at Micky forever to bring Ronnie up to date on the still. Cursing Micky for landing him in it with Ron and Ronnie for expecting him to drop everything, excluding his trousers which he could not do now for his own pleasure, Sean reached out reluctantly for his jacket on the hall stand.

'You're not going with him?' Ashley asked incredulously.

'What else can I do?' Sean rounded on him impatiently. Unlike him, Ashley was never called on by his sisters to do anything more than baby-sit one of their kids. Micky and Ronnie only had to crook their fingers in his direction and he was expected to jump to it. 'You could come with me of course!'

'I couldn't fight me own shadow,' Ashley declared, 'and you know it, Seany. Why don't you just go over for Micky and–'

'How can I?' Sean rapidly cut his friend short

and rolled his eyes meaningfully toward Henry. 'We don't know where he is, do we?' Sean didn't want Ashley to say anything that Henry could take back to his older brother because when Ronnie found out about the still, there would be World War Three.

'Look, we're wasting time,' Henry interrupted irritably. 'You'll have to do for now, Sean. Taking your pal here, they'd only die laughing.'

Ashley glared at the big doorman, then snatching his jacket from the coat-stand, he strode out of the front door.

'Thanks very much,' Sean muttered after Ashley had gone. 'You've got a real bedside manner, Henry, that's for sure.'

'Yeah, well, as long as it ain't his bedside, I don't bloody well care. Now hurry up and get in the motor. Or your brother will have our guts for garters when we get back.'

Sean put the thought of garters tied around Ashley's slender legs out of his mind and slouched moodily towards the long, black car in the road. No one understood what it was like to be sensitive. Especially his brothers. Now Ashley was in a strop and it would be days before he calmed down again.

'What are these?' Sean demanded as he went to sit on the front seat.

'Toothpicks, what do you think? Shove 'em in the back.'

Sean struggled to lift the array of heavy iron bars and hammers into the back seat. 'You didn't say it was that kind of trouble.'

'I was a boy scout and be prepared is my

191

motto,' Henry declared as he jumped in beside him.

'I can't see you in a uniform,' Sean murmured, and shuddered at the thought of using the weaponry. He wondered if Henry was exaggerating, but when they arrived at the club and walked in through the door, he knew that he wasn't.

Sid and Bernie were standing with Ronnie. They were holding iron bars and looked as though they'd been pulled through a hedge backward. The two big men dwarfed Henry. They were panting hard, obviously having dealt with the trouble and were about to tie a length of rope around two men who lay on the ground bleeding and groaning. Sean was relieved that Ashley hadn't come with them. He would have fainted at the sight of them.

'What's happened?' Sean gasped as he gazed around the wrecked club. 'Ronnie, are you hurt?' He felt queasy as he saw Ronnie holding his side, his shirt soaked in blood under his jacket.

'Thanks to Bernie and Sid, I'll survive.'

'Shit, Ron. What happened?' he asked again.

'Let me ask you a question. Where's Micky? Or are you going to tell me you don't know?'

Sean was silent, his face grey with shame. He had to tell Ronnie the truth and he wasn't looking forward to it. He began to tremble at the enormity of the disaster that had befallen them. A disaster that clearly involved the two bodies on the floor that were bloodied and bruised. A disaster that in all certainty would now involve him and Micky.

Unable to look his brother in the eye, words

192

failed him. Ronnie wiped the blood from his face with a handkerchief and placed it under his jacket. 'As bad as that, is it Sean?' Sean could hear the pain in Ronnie's rough tone. He dragged his eyes up from the wound in Ronnie's side and finally met his waiting gaze.

Sean nodded. 'You won't like it, Ron.'

'Why am I not surprised?' Ronnie's dark eyes accused him. And Sean's annoyance with Ashley, his feeling of abandonment and the way his day had been spoiled by his family, now paled into insignificance as he began to explain.

Chapter Fourteen

It was Sunday morning and Bella was looking out of the broken window. February felt more like spring. The city was hidden in haze and the tide ran out to sea, a ripple of smooth grey green.

She had been working for Micky since he opened the still in December. It wasn't the palace he had described, but it had become her second home. The first she had ever shared with Micky. Used for storing munitions during the war, the wooden timbers still smelt faintly of explosive. She had bought cushions from the market for the couch and a rug for the floor. There was a cupboard in the eaves and she'd cleaned it, filling it with her clothes. When they were alone, she and Micky made love here. The couch wasn't a bed, but it was heaven compared to the hotel in

Tottenham Court Road. Lenny kept a Primus stove downstairs and sometimes she cooked food on it, pretended she was a real wife to Micky.

'Blimey, Bells, are you a bit mutton or what? I've been yelling meself hoarse down here,' Micky shouted up the stairs.

Bella reluctantly left the window and went down the rickety staircase. Micky was waiting impatiently, his hands thrust deep in his overcoat pockets. 'Just in case you're interested, we're behind schedule and I've got deliveries piling up like farts in a constipated bowel. Sean and Ashley ain't turned up as usual so I'll have to deliver this lot up West myself. There's twelve quart bottles of cherry brandy, fifty assorted spirits and five crates of beers over there. Check them and make sure they've got tops.'

Repeating the numbers in her head, Bella crossed to the table where the crates were piled. There was no paperwork to refer to and no accounts to keep. Micky had decided that all the accounting was safer done in his head. Not that Bella was disappointed. She preferred helping Lenny to refine the alcohol in the big hundred-gallon tank that rumbled like thunder and fermented the contents into a potent wash.

When she had confirmed the bottles were in order, she tied an apron over her coat. It was dirty work as the bottles needed cleaning before they were filled. Bella's fingers often turned blue under the freezing water. She was in the middle of scouring a large green gin bottle when Micky appeared beside her.

'Where's Terry disappeared to?' he asked

194

irritably. 'He's never around when I want him.'

'He's gone for a smoke.'

'One day he's gonna turn into a chimney.'

'He works hard in here, Micky, lugging all them crates.'

'And so he should. Who else would give him a job?'

Bella turned sharply, wiping her cold wet hands on her apron. 'What's the matter with you this morning, Micky?'

'What do you think? I've been out since the crack of dawn looking for that flaming sugar beet. You would have thought it was a life and death situation and yet when I get back here, this place is practically deserted.'

Bella knew that Lenny and Micky were arguing again, which wasn't unusual. It was a way of life for the two men. Usually the quarrel was forgotten by the end of the day, but this disagreement had begun yesterday morning, when Lenny had asked Micky to go out and buy the sugar beet used to aid fermentation. Micky, as usual, had forgotten. The production of crystal clear alcohol depended on this wash. Lenny took pride in the slow and meticulous process necessary to ensure a high quality product. Micky considered it unnecessary. It was a sore point between them and still unresolved.

Micky kicked the pile of boxes at his feet. 'I'm supposed to be boss around here but I don't have a say in anything these days.'

'Leave it out, Micky,' Lenny intervened as he emerged from behind the tank, wiping his sweating forehead with his hand. 'I'm sick to death of

195

hearing you complain.'

At that moment, Terry appeared and shuffled past the tank, giving Micky a wide berth.

'Oh, the wanderer returns!' Micky growled irritably and Bella took hold of her brother's arm, pulling him out of harm's way.

'Leave the kid alone, Micky,' Lenny muttered as he examined the dark brown contents of a large glass container. 'The still ain't gonna fold up just 'cos Terry has a fag.'

Bella watched Micky's face turn red. 'That's rich, that is, seeing as when we was at the lock-up you was always on about me doing a disappearing act.'

Lenny's head jerked up. He drew his muscular forearm across his big nose aggressively. 'Look, those two kids have been more use to me on a Sunday these past months than you are all week. Let's face it, you're a nervous wreck around the still and you're beginning to make me nervous too. So why don't you just push off and deliver them orders.'

Micky looked angry. 'You're talking as if you owned this place,' he accused, taking a step forward and poking a finger in Lenny's shoulder.

Lenny poked a finger back. 'I do, mate. Half of it, anyway.'

'Who says so?' Micky retaliated. 'What collateral have you put up, eh? It's me that pays the rent and just you remember it.'

'Be careful,' Lenny warned angrily. 'You're pushing your luck again.'

'Are you threatening me?' Micky demanded.

'Take it any way you want, you lazy git.'

Micky lunged forward and the two men struggled, falling against the table. All the crates slid noisily to the ground as they wrestled, kicking and shouting at one another, heedless of the spectacle they were making.

Bella grabbed Terry's arm and pulled him under the stairs knowing they would have to wait there until the two men had exhausted themselves.

Sean helped Ronnie out of the car. Together they crossed the wharf frontage. An early morning breeze blew off the river and at the door of the warehouse Ronnie gazed up at the dilapidated shell. Before the Blitz he remembered this place as a timber yard, serviced by the tugs on the river, a hive of industry. A wave of sadness washed over him at the memory. Those days were long gone. When the Bryants were a close family and Dad's word was law. For a moment he was reluctant to go in, but Micky had left him no choice. Like the old building towering above him, their time as a family was running out.

'Ronnie, give Micky another chance,' Sean pleaded, the strain of the night's events evident on his face. 'He should have told you about the still. I don't deny that. But this ain't the time to square it. With Stratton's outfit breathing down our necks, we've got to stick together.'

'Stick together?' Ronnie repeated in surprise. 'Where was Micky last night, when my club was wrecked? Where were you? It's Joyce I have to thank for giving Bernie and Sid an early night. If they hadn't knocked off when they did, you would have found what was left of me floating in

East India docks.'

Sean looked shamefaced. 'I know, Ron. What can I say?'

'Nothing. The damage is done.' Ronnie saw the tears of regret form in his brother's eyes. 'None of this would be happening if you had been straight with me. What possessed you, Sean? If Micky put you under pressure to deliver for him, then you should have come to me. This substance is as reliable as the weather. It knocked out hundreds of Yanks in the war, was more effective than the Luftwaffe's bombs. In fact Hitler should have dropped bottles of it on London to achieve a successful invasion. Now Micky has finally excelled himself and taken out Sammy Stratton's brother.'

'I know all you are saying is true,' Sean nodded. 'But I am scared, Ron. And I don't mind admitting it.'

Ronnie looked into his brother's terrified face. 'And so you should be. If it's an official pardon from Sammy Stratton that you're looking for, you are going to be disappointed. We are all in over our heads now.'

Watching the tears fill his brother's eyes, Ronnie hardened his heart. He loved Sean as he loved Micky, but they had both deceived him and now all three of them were paying for it.

When they entered the warehouse, Micky and Lenny Rigler were staggering to their feet, covered in dust, their boots crunching on broken glass. They looked as though they'd been fighting but he was shocked to see Bella and Terry hiding under the stairs.

'Ronnie!' Micky gasped as he wiped the dirt from his face.

'Don't let me interrupt,' Ronnie growled.

'What are you doing here?'

Glancing round the warehouse, Ronnie said coldly, 'What do you think?'

Micky shrugged, a sudden smile on his face as he stepped over the glass and urged Ronnie forward. 'Matter of fact, I was going to ask you over, give you the guided tour. There's no time like the present, so come on in.'

Ronnie knew Micky of old, understood the workings of his mind and his ability to regain his composure in the blink of an eye.

'Who told you we was operating?' Micky asked casually, glancing accusingly at Sean.

'The Stratton crew. They came to the club today. As you can see, it wasn't a friendly visit.' He opened his jacket to reveal his bloodstained shirt.

'Christ, Ron! What happened?' Micky looked shocked as he stared at the wound. 'They did that to *you*? But why?'

Ronnie let his jacket fall back into place. 'Tony Stratton poured too much of your hooch down his own throat and landed up in hospital. He's in a coma and Sammy now has only one aim in life. To eliminate you or me, but preferably both of us.'

Micky stared in silence at his brother. 'You're kidding.'

'If Sid and Bernie hadn't come back early from Joyce's I wouldn't be standing here now.'

'But I never had no complaints from Sammy

199

before,' Micky protested lamely. 'Me and Lenny make good stuff, we got a good business going!'

'Tell that to the Strattons,' Ronnie muttered, his face tight with anger. 'I warned you often enough. Tried to shut you down but you wouldn't have it, even dragged Sean into delivering for you.' He pointed to Bella and Terry. 'And these two are involved, no doubt?'

'Why not? They're on the payroll fair and square,' Micky stated defiantly. 'I give Terry a good bunce and he's thankful for it. Ask them if you don't believe me.'

But Ronnie was having none of it. 'You have overstepped the mark this time, bringing in kids. But you wouldn't care about that, would you? You would use a cripple chained to a post without a second's thought if it suited your purpose.'

'I swear, on Mum's life, Ron, that my booze ain't iffy.'

'Mum ain't here, thank God,' Ronnie stated flatly. 'She would be sick at heart if she was.'

Ronnie knew time was running out fast. He also knew he was weak from loss of blood. He would be weaker still when Sammy came. A part of him wanted to see Micky take Sammy's punishment and learn from it. But Micky was right. If Mum and Dad were here, they would not tolerate a split in the family. United it stood and united it fell.

As he gazed into his brother's eyes, he knew that Micky's understanding of the world wasn't the same as other people's. But no matter what Micky had done, he was a Bryant. And Sammy Stratton would not be turning up to find him alone.

Ronnie looked hard at his two brothers. 'Go to the car. Henry's hardware's in the boot. Bring it in. Sort it out between yourselves. And have anything else handy that we can use.'

Just then his legs began to fold beneath him. He knew he was about to black out from loss of blood. He shook his head in an effort to rouse himself but even before he hit the ground, he was out cold.

Bella drew the damp cloth over his forehead. Very slowly he opened his eyes. 'It's all right, Ronnie, lay still.'

'What happened?'

'You passed out and Sean and Micky brought you up here. They've gone down to get the things from the car. You're bleeding bad, Ron.' She watched him ease himself up on the couch and press his hand over the blood on his shirt.

'Bella, do yourself a favour, girl, and get out of here,' he told her hoarsely. 'Take Terry with you and get as far away from here as possible.'

She shook her head. 'I ain't going nowhere, Ron. Not without Micky.'

Ronnie's voice was low. 'This doesn't involve you and it promises to be one hell of a night. Sid and Bernie will have dropped Sammy Stratton's two dummies off by now. When they spill the beans to Sammy he's gonna come here and then there will be ructions. I want you to go to Joyce. She'll take care of you both.'

'Don't waste your breath, Ron,' Bella said stubbornly. 'Me and Terry are staying.'

Just then Sean and Micky came up the stairs.

'Are you all right, bruv?'

Ronnie wiped the beads of sweat from his brow. 'Yeah, I'm okay. Have you done what I told you?'

Micky nodded. 'We're ready for them.'

Sean looked worried. 'How do we know if they'll come?'

'They will, take my word for it.'

'It's gonna be a bundle then?' Sean asked, looking pale.

Ronnie nodded as he swung his legs down from the couch. 'Yeah, no doubt about that.'

'You're bleeding bad,' Micky said anxiously. 'Bella, you got anything to put round him?'

She nodded. 'I'll find some cloth. But the wound will need to be cleaned first.'

Micky grinned at her. 'Say no more. A drop of the hard stuff is just what you want.' He went downstairs and returned with a hip flask. 'Here you are, girl, this will do the job.'

'What's in there?' Ronnie demanded, frowning suspiciously. 'Not the rubbish you make, I hope.'

'No, it ain't,' Micky replied sullenly. 'Now go on, Bells, clean him up.'

When they were alone, she opened the soiled jacket and undid the buttons of the shirt. Her stomach lurched at the sight of the knife wound and the blood seeping out of it.

Ronnie caught her wrist and shook it. 'Look at me, Bella. I need you now. Don't faint on me, will you?'

She swallowed. 'I'm all right.'

'Have you ever used a needle and thread?'

'Course I have. Lots of times. But–' She stopped as she realized what he was implying.

202

'Then you can stitch me up,' he continued, his eyes full of pain. 'It's the same principle. Won't be no different to darning a sock.'

'But I've only got ordinary sewing things. Nothing like what they use in a hospital.'

'It'll do the same job, I promise you.' He tilted his head towards Terry. 'Now send the kid downstairs, and give me a swig of that.'

Five minutes later, when she had cleaned Ronnie up and given him the rest of the hip flask to drink, she prepared the needle and thread. It took all her willpower to slide the point into his flesh and when he groaned she paused, trembling at the thought of the pain she was about to inflict.

'Go on, go on,' Ronnie urged through gritted teeth.

Forcing her fingers to move, she brought the two sides of the wound together. Ignoring the blood that still escaped, she sewed carefully, convincing herself with every stitch, that it was Terry's trousers she was mending and not Ronnie's skin.

After it was over, Bella went downstairs. All the men were sitting at the table. Micky lit a cigarette and came over to her. 'How is he?'

'I had to sew up the wound.'

'Christ Almighty! What with?'

'All I had was what I use for mine and Terry's clothes. But the bleeding's stopped at last. I just hope I've done it right.'

'Course you have, Bells.' He tried to kiss her but she turned away.

'What's wrong?'

'Tell me the truth, Micky. Was it the drink that

203

poisoned Tony Stratton?'

'The answer to that is a definite no,' he assured her, his eyes wide and innocent. 'If Tony is in hospital it wasn't me that put him there. Ask yourself this: why should I shoot myself in the foot? Sammy is a good customer.'

'Why won't he listen to reason, then?'

'It's too late now, ain't it? Ronnie has damaged his men, started a war. I'm sorry to say it, Bells, but my brother has cooked the proverbial goose and Sammy has to show balls. His reputation has been damaged and he has to put that right. Given the chance I would have handled it without aggro. Talked to old Sammy, assured him my booze is one hundred per cent kosher and the guilty party is still out there on the loose. And Sammy would have listened, I know it. But no, Ron had to play the big "I am". He wanted to believe it was me because he was envious of what I have created here. That's what it boils down to, I'm afraid. But, Bells, I'm not a man to bear a grudge and I can overlook this.'

Bella listened to what he was telling her. She wanted to believe him and her arms ached to go round him and pull him close. She didn't want to think Ronnie had let him down, but only one of them could be right. 'Will Sammy Stratton really come here?'

'Yeah, Ronnie's right about that. And we're ready for him.' He put his arms around her and hugged her. 'You take Terry and get upstairs with Ron.'

'I'm scared, Micky. But I'm more scared for you.'

'Don't be.' He patted his overcoat pocket. 'I've got me shooter. Remember the rats down at the docks?'

'You're not going to use it, are you?'

'If I have to.'

'Does Ronnie know you've got a gun?'

'No and don't you go telling him. Ronnie don't favour guns, never has. But, Bells, he's not in a position to argue, is he? Look at it this way,' he lifted her chin and looked into her eyes, 'tonight is the beginning of a new era for you and me. Okay, mistakes have been made I grant you. I should have told Ron face to face about the still and I can see his point. But when this is over, the Bryants will be strong in the eyes of the East End.' His eyebrows rose. 'Remember what that bastard Router did to you and Terry? How me and Ronnie took him out? We were on our way up then, lords of our territory. And it's going to be that way again if I have anything to do with it.'

'But Ronnie could have died tonight, Micky.'

'I know and for him being cut I am sorry. But this isn't about Ron, it's about us, you and me. And our future.'

'I want you all in one piece, Micky. I love you.'

He kissed her, pulling her against him and she knew that she loved him more than ever. Ronnie had been as much to blame in all this, she could see that now. Slowly her world slipped back into place as Micky whispered, for the first time, he loved her too.

Ronnie was asleep when the cars pulled up. Their headlights reflected across the timbers and Bella listened to the voices, the sound of car doors banging and heavy boots on the stones. She and Terry waited, the only sound, Ronnie's breathing.

Suddenly there was a crack. Were they the same sounds as when Micky had killed the rats? Would he really use his gun to kill Sammy Stratton? Or would Sammy try to kill Micky first?

Ronnie groaned, shifting on the couch. He sat up, swinging his legs to the ground. Shaking his head, he staggered to the stairs and went down them. A strange smell began to fill the air. Soon smoke swirled all around them, creeping up into the timbers and filling the loft.

'Bella, where are you? I can't see a foot in front of me.'

'Here, Micky.' She reached out for him.

'The still is alight. We've got to get out of here.'

Bella began to cough. The smoke flowed across the floor and into the timbers, thick and powerful; the little nest she had made was burning.

'Follow me.' Micky grasped her hand. She managed to take hold of Terry's hand and they all went down the stairs. The smoke filled her nose and stung her eyes. Sean and Lenny were helping Ronnie past the tank as the wash inside rumbled noisily. Lenny shouted a warning and they ran for their lives, out into the cold night air.

Chapter Fifteen

They followed Lenny down the alley, still coughing from the smoke and covered in ash. The tradesman's entrance, as Gina called it, was locked and Bella heard Lenny curse as he almost fell over the rubbish outside. 'I was out on a bender last night and she ain't going to be best pleased.' He knocked lightly on the door. 'Gina, it's me, open up.' They stood in the darkness, waiting as a light finally came on inside. 'She's gonna kill me,' Lenny muttered. 'Brain me first, then kill me.'

'Who is it?' Gina demanded from the other side of the door.

'It's me, love, and Bella and Terry and–'

'I ain't talking to you, Lenny Rigler. I ain't seen you for two days and now you appear. Look around you at my yard. Stinking it is. Whilst you're doing sweet fanny adams the flies are breeding in my larder as big as rats. And I'm supposed to be running a café!'

'I'll clear up in the morning.'

'Yeah, and I'm a monkey's uncle. It's a wonder you can stand there and not drop from the stink.'

'Gina?' Bella stepped forward. 'It's me.'

'Is he sozzled?'

'No, Lenny's stone cold sober.'

The lock snapped back inside. Gina, wearing a frilly blue dressing gown and no make-up, opened the door slowly. She stared accusingly at Lenny then frowned at the other black faces. 'Blimey, where have you lot been dug up from?' She pointed to Ronnie, who was leaning on Sean. 'Who is he?

'This is Ronnie, Micky's brother,' Bella said.

Gina stared at the bloodstained jacket, then ignoring Lenny, she opened the door a fraction wider. 'You'd better come in, I suppose.' She folded her arms across her chest as she watched them enter, treading over the empty boxes, rotting vegetables and waste that Lenny had omitted to clear. 'So trouble has finally landed at your door, Micky,' she sneered, as they lowered Ronnie onto the nearest seat.

'Don't start, Gina,' Micky warned as he wiped his filthy face in the crook of his arm. 'All we want is a couple of beds for the night.'

'What's wrong with your own?' Gina's tone was scathing. 'No, don't tell me, I already know the answer. As sure as pigs live in shit, it's got something to do with that bloody hooch!'

'Then this next bit of news is going to warm your heart,' Micky replied sourly. 'The piss-shop, as you refer to it, is no more. It went up in smoke tonight, the lot of it.'

Gina looked disbelieving as she stared from one to the other. 'You're having a laugh, aren't you?'

'I wish I was,' Micky growled. 'The tank's gone, the booze, everything. Thanks to some bastard with a chip on his shoulder the size of Big Ben.'

'I apologize for the inconvenience, Gina.' Ronnie spoke for the first time. 'The point is, we need a safe house for the night. I'll spare you the

208

details, but as you can see we need somewhere to clean up, have a bite to eat and get a few hours' rest.' He slumped in the chair. 'I expect nothing for free so look on this as business. Name your price and you'll have it, plus a handshake on top.'

Bella watched Gina's expression change, the lines of anger around her eyes melting away. Her shrewd mind was calculating the odds in her favour and even though she was annoyed with Lenny, had been for some while as he had spent more and more time at the still, Ronnie's words had entranced her.

'If it's business we're talking, then yes, I've got rooms available,' Gina answered with a nod. 'The karzy is out the back, good enough for a quick wash down for you blokes. Lenny will cook you a fry-up after, but I warn you my kitchen is spotless. So make sure you clear up afterwards. As for you, Ronnie, you'd better come with me. Bella, grab one arm, I'll take the other. We'll put him in me mum's room. It's on the ground floor and he won't have stairs to climb. It's not been used since she died but other than a few moths, it's decent.'

Between them they assisted Ronnie along the dark passage. Gina's mother's room was filled with books of all shapes and sizes. A large black mantilla hung down from the wall and an ornate red fan depicting a bullfight was opened above an oval mirror. The window was framed by heavy chintz curtains and under it stood a mahogany sideboard cluttered with personal effects. Beside this was a highly polished wardrobe, the clothes inside it still stinking of mothballs and camphor.

'Well, ducks, me mum never had a fella in her bed before, but I daresay she won't complain from where she is. Bella go and boil me some water, love, and bring the first aid box back with you.'

Gina began to remove his jacket. Bella went to the kitchen, her hands still shaking as she lifted the kettle on the stove.

'You did a good job on those stitches,' Gina told her as they left the room half an hour later. 'Now nature will have to take its course.'

'Should we get a doctor?'

'He says he don't want one.'

'Is that wise?'

'No, but Ronnie's no fool. With what happened hanging over their heads it would be daft to broadcast a wound like that. If he don't get it infected, then I would say he stands a good chance of recovery.'

When they walked in the kitchen the smell of fried eggs and bacon still hung in the air. The others had eaten, leaving the room warm unlike the rest of the house which was sub-zero. Whilst Gina disposed of the soiled dressings, Bella washed her hands and removed her coat. She had worn it all day and the pale wool was filthy, having absorbed all the alcohol fumes and smoke.

'Look at this mess, I told them to clear up,' Gina grumbled as she began to remove the dirty plates, knives and forks from the table, transferring the crocks to the draining board. 'Men believe that women are made by God to wait on them. But tomorrow I'm putting Lenny straight.

He's going to clear this place up and earn a living as long as he remains under this roof. I'm not having a go at you, Bella, but for nearly three months now, you and Lenny have swanned off on Sundays to the still and forgotten that we have a café to run. And despite Micky having lost his little gem, I for one am relieved to hear it.' She took the dirty frying pan from the stove and began to scrub it.

Bella felt guilty. 'I always thought you could manage all right on Sundays.'

'Yeah, well, I wanted you to have a day's rest. I didn't foresee you'd work yourself to the bone for Micky.' She turned and smiled. 'Anyway, now I've got that off me chest, do you want two eggs or one with your fried bread?'

'I ain't hungry, Gina, thanks.' Bella was feeling queasy. Even the smell of food was upsetting her stomach.

'You need to keep your strength up, a growing girl like you.' Gina frowned curiously at her, placing the pan upside down to drain. 'You been off colour lately?'

'No, I'm all right.' Bella sat down at the table.

'You used to eat a good breakfast every day.' When Bella didn't reply she sighed, saying wearily, 'I hope you ain't worrying over Micky because, love, he ain't worth it. He was bound to upset someone; if it wasn't Sammy Stratton, it would have been someone else. I warned Lenny so often I got sick of hearing me own voice.'

'But Micky never intended to harm Tony Stratton,' Bella was quick to defend.

'Bella, ducks, you can't see the wood from the

211

trees where Micky is concerned,' Gina sighed, shaking her head. 'He's an opportunist and lives to make number one happy. God knows what happened today, but that poor sod lying in Mum's room is lucky to be alive. If that knife had gone any deeper it would have come out his other side. The scar he'll bear will be as long as the Commercial Road. And in it all, you know, I can see Micky's hand. Now, I've never met Ronnie before, but what he told me as he laid in that bed, was enough to freeze the blood in me veins. Even he maintains that you and Terry would be better out of it. I'm not saying this to benefit meself, but you kids was doing all right with me. Now you're in the shit right up to your necks and so is my Lenny.'

'I love Micky, Gina. And he loves me.'

'You're sure of that?'

'He doesn't show it, but I know he does.'

Gina pulled her frilly blue nightgown over her full breasts. 'You are only just turned seventeen, girl. I worry over you, can't help it. Now, don't look so sad, love, the world ain't come to an end. I might be an old sceptic, but who knows? Look on it another way, a miracle might happen and Micky'll turn into a straight geezer. If he does, I'll be the first one to admit me mistake. At least the Almighty, in all his wisdom, burnt down that still tonight. Though I suppose we have this Sammy whatshisname to thank for that.'

Bella shook her head slowly. 'It wasn't Sammy Stratton who started the fire, Gina. It was Lenny.'

'What!'

'He made what he called bottle bombs from the

neat wash in the tank. Sammy's men had guns and started shooting and so Lenny and Micky threw the bottles out the window. One of them landed on a car and it burst into flames. The fire spread to the other car beside it and then the warehouse caught light.'

'My Lenny making bombs?' Gina gasped. 'Where did he learn how to do that?'

'From your mum's books, he told us. These Molotov Cocktails were used in the Spanish Civil War against the Russian tanks. Only then they had petrol in them not Lenny's formula.'

The two women looked at one another as Gina's jaw dropped. 'Him and his formulas!'

'None of us realized it was so inflammable. When the wash inside the tank got really warm it exploded and nearly knocked us off our feet. Luckily Sean's car was parked across the wharf or it might have gone up like the others.'

'Was Sammy and his men inside those cars?'

'There was too much smoke to see. It was everywhere, big black clouds of it blowing over the wharf.'

'So that's why Ronnie wants to lie low, in case Sammy is alive and kicking?'

Bella nodded silently.

'A blaze like that won't go unreported,' Gina said eventually. 'The papers are going to love it.'

Bella shuddered. 'They might be reporting us dead if it wasn't for Lenny.'

Gina's dark eyes widened. 'Doesn't bear thinking about, does it?'

Bella had no answer to that. She was still unable to believe it had all happened. Had

213

Sammy Stratton escaped or had he perished in those terrible flames?

Bella was feeling sick again. She had not seen her periods since making love with Micky and the dread that had been growing inside her was now a real fear. Visiting the doctor had been way down on her list of priorities, but she knew now that a visit had to be made. She hadn't let herself think about the baby. Didn't want to believe it could be true. And yet, when she did, a tenderness filled her. If it was a mother's instinct, then it was powerful, lighting up the world before reality set in. What would Micky say if she told him?

Up at the crack of dawn, she washed and dressed in an old blue working skirt and brown jumper. She had taken her good clothes to the still, all part of her private dream to be Micky's wife. Now all her treasured possessions had gone up in smoke.

Ronnie was awake when she went in. As she pulled back the curtains he screwed up his eyes against the pale morning sun. He was sitting up, his broad shoulders bare against the white pillows. The strips of old sheeting that Gina had wound round him were unsoiled and Bella nodded to them. 'You're still in one piece, then?'

'Thanks to you and Gina.' Ronnie smiled, the stubble on his jaw thick and dark.

'I'll cook you some breakfast and bring it in.'

'I ain't an invalid, girl. And if I don't get my arse into action today I'll be laying down permanently, six feet under.'

'You should rest. Let the wound heal.'

'Listen, sit down, I want to talk to you.'

She sat on the chair beside the bed. If this was going to be a lecture about Micky, she didn't want to hear it. But Ronnie's voice was soft when he spoke.

'I've been thinking all night and devised a plan,' he told her quietly. 'Whether or not Sammy Stratton is alive, I will still need to recruit muscle, because I am not getting caught with my trousers down again. I'm going back to the club bright and early, make the place tight as a drum. Sid and Bernie are there and I'll brief them on what to say if Old Bill sniffs round. The story is, the club was closed yesterday because of a ruptured water pipe. A minor flood with witnesses and a wet carpet to prove it.'

'What about Micky?'

'He has been running the club with me and Joyce for the past three months and let anyone try to disprove it. As for you and Terry, I want you both to stay here. Plaster a smile on your face and act as though you ain't set a foot outside this place all weekend. It's business as usual and no one will know any different if you don't tell them.'

But Bella was alarmed. 'It's not me I'm worried about. It's Micky.'

Ronnie looked at her and smiled. 'I don't know what today will bring, but one thing I will say to you, Micky is a lucky bloke. He doesn't deserve you or what you did for him yesterday.'

'It wasn't just for him,' Bella said, unable to stop herself.

'What do you mean?'

Bella looked down. 'I'm expecting our baby.'

Ronnie was silent, his grey eyes staring into hers as he searched her face. 'Does Micky know?' he asked at last.

She shook her head, drawing her fingers across her wet cheeks.

'As I said,' he murmured as his black eyebrows knitted together, deepening the grooves between them. 'He is a lucky man, even luckier now that he has his own family to take care of. His blood will go on into a new generation. What man could ask for more?'

She looked up in surprise. 'I hope Micky sees it like that.'

'If you want my advice, wait until this is over,' he replied after a pause. 'Micky is the biggest of kids himself and his little toy has just been taken away. He ain't in the best of moods. But you are going to be part of this family, Bella, and you will need a tough skin. Develop it as quickly as you can.'

Bella heard the kindness in his voice. Where Micky was concerned she was weak and they both knew it. But it was advice from someone who loved him as much as she did and she took comfort from this.

'Now, I will take you up on that breakfast,' he told her, his tone matter-of-fact once more. 'I'll come along to the kitchen as soon as I'm dressed. Then I'll take Micky and Sean to the club.'

'How will we know what happens?' Bella asked anxiously.

'I'll send word. Now, get yourself out of here, girl.'

She left the room and in the kitchen, tied on her apron, as her stomach revolted at the sight of bacon. But at least she had shared her secret with Ronnie and having done it, she felt better now.

After Ronnie, Micky and Sean had left, Gina sent Lenny out for a newspaper.

'Here it is,' Lenny said as he spread the paper out on the kitchen table. 'It ain't much, would you believe? A couple of paragraphs entitled "Warehouse Fire".'

'Read it out,' Gina said as she fried the bacon.

'"A disused–"' Lenny stopped abruptly, gulping his breath. 'Hear that? *Disused,* meaning they don't know we was in it!'

'All right, all right, don't get excited,' Gina warned over her shoulder. 'What else?'

'"A disused warehouse caught fire on the Isle of Dogs and was dealt with by the fire brigade last night,"' Lenny continued. '"The smoke from the blaze was seen as far away as Nelson Dock south of the river."'

'Go on, get to the important bit,' Gina told him impatiently as she broke eggs into the pan. 'Was anyone found? Did anyone see anything?'

Lenny read on, mouthing silently, then nodded. '"The remains of bodies were discovered in the burnt-out shells of two cars nearby."'

'Oh, Christ!' Gina gulped, handing the plates to Bella.

'Do they say who they were?'

Lenny looked up at them woefully. 'No, they were burned beyond recognition.'

Bella's face paled as she imagined the grue-

217

some discovery and Lenny's face showed he was thinking the same.

'I never intended to kill anyone,' he whispered, his eyes full of remorse. 'I didn't think those bottles were that lethal.'

'Look, Lenny,' Gina said firmly as she turned sharply from the stove, 'stop torturing yourself and us. You been doing it all night, even in your sleep you was tossing and turning and yelling out like a stuck pig. There is nothing you can do to change the past. It was self-defence, pure and simple. Now, does the paper say any more?'

He didn't look down, just stared into space.

Gina nodded to Bella. 'Take those breakfasts out whilst they're hot, love, will you? And as Ronnie said, try to act as normal. Someone has to around here.'

Bella looked at Lenny who seemed lost in a trance, then took out the first fry-ups of the day. She knew Gina was attempting to help Lenny by taking a brusque attitude, trying to rally him round and return him to normality. But even Bella could see that was not going to happen overnight. Lenny had taken the news badly, which showed he had a heart. Something that Sammy Stratton did not possess, because if he was still alive and kicking all three of them knew he would exact his own form of punishment without turning a hair.

Bella served the two meals to the men, smiling brightly as Ron had told her and hoping her worries didn't show on her face.

After the last customer had left, Bella washed

down the tables and cleaned the floor, taking the pig bin into the yard where Gina was watching Lenny at work. She stood in her coat, chain smoking, frowning at his every move. Bella knew that Gina hadn't let him off the hook for his crimes. Which were, in her book, deserting the café for Micky's still. It wasn't dead bodies that Gina was concerned with, unlike Lenny who was suffering under the weight of guilt.

'Shut the shop?' Gina asked sharply as Bella appeared, her face screwing up unflatteringly.

'Yes, and the kitchen's clean. Is there anything else you want me to do?'

Gina's scowl softened. 'No thanks, love. Me and Lenny will be finished here soon. It took us all day to shift the rats. If I had sixpence for every one we found I'd be a rich woman. They ate their way through all me stock in the shed and even through bricks and mortar. That's what taking your finger off the pulse does,' she added, frowning again at Lenny.

As they stood in awkward silence, Lenny pushed the broom in weary resignation, circles of sweat ingrained on his vest. Just as Bella was about to go in, the back gate opened. They all gasped softly as Sean appeared dressed in a long coat.

'What's happened?' they all asked at once.

Sean glanced over his shoulder as though someone was following him. Then jerking his thumb toward the house, he urged them to follow him inside. Sean searched the kitchen and café with worried eyes. 'Are we alone?'

'Course we are,' Gina replied, her patience

growing thin.

'It was Sammy all right.'

'Oh, Gawd,' Lenny gasped. 'How do you know?'

'We don't, not for sure. But there ain't a living soul at the Indigo and no one on the street has seen Sammy.'

'What about the police?' Gina asked.

'A copper called at the club this morning but he is a friendly, on wages from Ronnie. The Old Bill, he said, are doing the rounds, asking questions because Sammy and Tony are into vice in a big way. He controls half of the girls in Soho and is taking a big wedge, causing unrest with the other ponces.'

'And the law don't know where he is?' Lenny asked furtively.

'No, it's quieter than a nun's knickers on the streets.'

'What if someone saw me and Micky at the still?' Lenny said in a whisper. 'What if the police turn up a grass for instance?'

'They'd have to prove it. And anyway, we was only in operation three months and we didn't see a soul, did we?'

'That didn't mean someone didn't see us,' Lenny repeated, his face haggard now.

'What do you want me to do about it?' Sean frowned irritably. 'You was the one who made the stuff.'

'You can stop right there, love,' Gina interrupted, her black eyes flashing as she wagged a long finger in Sean's face. 'Passing the buck won't help. Lenny might have made it, but it would never have been shipped to the streets if it wasn't for you and Micky. As far as I'm concerned, you are all dopes, the lot of you. Doing what you did was the height of stupidity. And if you get away with it, you should go down on bended knee to your maker for the reprieve. But knowing you all as I do, you'll all be jumping in the shit just as quickly again. Only I hope this time, before you do, you will consult with Ronnie, who has had to clean up your mess before.'

They were all silent, then Sean spoke. 'I've got to go. Ronnie wants me back at the club.'

'What do we do now?' Gina called after him as he walked away. 'Sit twiddling our fingers, I suppose!'

Sean chose to ignore this as he disappeared along the lane.

Lenny sank down on a chair, his face white.

Gina looked sternly at him. 'And you can cheer up, you moody sod. Playing with fire will eventually get you burned. The saying couldn't be more apt in your case, Lenny Rigler.'

He looked a beaten man and Bella felt sorry for him. But Gina was intent on pressing her point and she admired her for her strength of character. Like Micky, Gina needed to be in control. The trouble was, with Gina pulling one way and Micky the other, no one could sit on the fence for long, not even Lenny.

Bella knew the time would come when Gina would apply the same pressure to her. But even though she owed Gina a lot, she owed her baby more.

221

It was the last Friday in March when finally there was news of Sammy. Or at least, news of his body parts. Gina was cooking as usual and Bella was slicing tomatoes, helped and hindered by Terry. All action stopped in the kitchen as Lenny, who had been working out in the yard, entered with Ronnie. Dressed in a dark suit, white shirt and tie, he looked his old self and his expression was relaxed as he smiled at them.

'Blimey! Look who it ain't!' Gina exclaimed and Bella's own heart beat fast as she looked over his shoulder for Micky.

'How are you, love?' Gina asked and Ronnie nodded.

'Thanks to you both, on the mend.'

'Is Micky coming?' Bella couldn't wait to ask.

'No, but listen to me. Sammy Stratton's remains were confirmed by the coroner twenty-four hours ago. A verdict of misadventure was given as there was no evidence to the contrary.'

'How did they know it was him?' Gina walked towards him, her mouth falling open.

'They found his gold teeth. The other bodies remain unidentified, which is not surprising as Sammy was known for hiring and firing on a frequent basis. The warehouse itself wasn't insured and no one is claiming an interest. The police are eager to see an end to the matter because of the Strattons' involvement in vice and the thorn in their side that Sammy was proving to be. All in all, I would say we had the best result possible.'

'I can't believe it,' Gina gasped, 'how gullible can the coppers be?'

'One hundred per cent when they choose,'

Ronnie shrugged. 'My informant tells me they are clapping their hands that Sammy is now out of the frame and Tony a permanent sleeper.'

'What about me?' Lenny asked, his face weighted with strain. 'Did my name come up?'

'Not yours or Micky's, so you can relax.' Ronnie took a package from his overcoat pocket and laid it on the kitchen table. 'But I suggest making yourself invisible for a while.'

Gina stepped quickly forward, the cooking forgotten. She opened the large envelope and smiled. Looking up at Ronnie, she nodded. 'This is handsome, Ronnie. It's been a pleasure doing business with you.'

'Can I see Micky now – today?' Bella felt she couldn't wait a moment more, the month they had been separated felt like a lifetime.

'Jump in the motor and I'll drive you.'

Bella looked anxiously at Gina. 'Is that all right?'

'Don't ask me.' Gina looked disapproving. 'You're a big girl now. And anyway, I'd be wasting me breath, wouldn't I?'

'I can't wait to see Micky.'

'Well, you know I think you're a stupid bitch, but you have my blessing.'

It was the best thing that Gina had ever said to her.

Ronnie was standing with Micky in the backyard of Piper Street and his temper was rising. There was a young girl sitting in the front room whom Micky had used over the years for his own gain and although Micky wouldn't see it like that, it was the truth. His nature was to exploit when it suited him, even his own family, as Ronnie had discovered personally. Micky was a law unto himself but it had taken the recent events to open Ronnie's eyes. Now as he looked at his brother and watched the colour drain from his face, he was determined to see fair play done.

'I don't even know if it's my kid!' Micky raised his hands exasperatedly. 'Just because she says it is, I am supposed to believe her?'

'You know it's yours, Micky,' Ronnie answered shortly. 'She wouldn't look at anyone else. She only has eyes for you, always has.'

'Then what was she doing with that prat Raymond Taylor?'

'Nothing, as I understand it.'

Micky looked insulted. 'What would you do if it was Joyce who was seeing someone else?'

'That is a different situation,' Ronnie replied. 'We are business partners first and foremost. And trust each other.'

'I don't trust any female,' Micky said scathingly. 'They've always got an ulterior motive.'

'And you haven't?' Ronnie demanded, his tone incredulous. 'The girl has no idea you were using her at the still, as you and Lenny used Terry and Sean. Odds on she is ignorant of the fact you have been servicing Ivor's women and God knows how many others.'

Micky's face darkened. 'I dunno what you mean.'

'Your presence at Club Afrika has been well and truly noted as I discovered when I chased up Sammy's whereabouts.'

Ronnie watched his brother in grudging admir-

224

ation as he coolly took a packet of Players from his pocket. Lighting one, he deliberately turned his back and walked casually away. 'There's no law against enjoying yourself, bruv.' He leaned against the yard wall, savouring the tobacco. 'You've got your own way in every other respect. I am minus my business, my future income, you should be happy.'

'The hooch was poison, Micky, and you know it.'

His brother suddenly stepped forward. 'Listen, Ron, it was you who buggered off to France and didn't give a toss about me and Sean. We were left trying to earn a crust whilst flaming Adolph nearly wiped us off the face of the earth. We had to survive in your absence, build up what Dad had left us. And we did it. Sean and me. With no thanks to you.'

'I was called up, Micky. I had no choice.'

'Course you did,' Micky returned, disgust in his voice. 'You could've ducked and dived, found ways to stay at home. But no, as usual, you had to play the conquering hero. Well, me and Sean survived the war, but we did it in our own way and would be continuing to do so if you hadn't stuck your oar in with Sammy.'

'You manufactured a volatile substance, Micky.'

'The Yanks didn't care! Why should you? Anyway, I don't believe my booze done in Tony Stratton. It was Sammy's word against mine and you believed him.'

Ronnie felt his temper snap as he listened to the same old record being played. Micky heaped the blame on anyone else's shoulders and put himself

225

in the clear. But not this time. He exhaled slowly to calm himself, watching his breath curl in the fresh air. He walked over to his brother and looked into his eyes. 'I am not arguing with you, Micky. If you are intent on going your own way, then so be it.'

Micky's eyes glittered. 'You ain't telling me what to do, Ron. No one is.'

'Then we had better call it a day.' Ronnie narrowed his eyes, seeing Micky in a new light. 'Take your clobber and get the hell out of here.'

For a moment Micky stared back at him unable to believe his own ears. Then laughing, he shook his head. 'You can't throw me out.'

'I can and I will if I have to.'

Micky dropped his cigarette, his eyes searching Ronnie's as real fear suddenly spread over his face. Ronnie knew that Micky was considering the possibility that he meant what he was saying and it was not going down well.

'I never said I was against you.' Micky's gaze wavered and Ronnie knew that for the moment, he had won. It was a back-down, but he was not going to let Micky off the hook.

'The East End is not what it was when we were kids, Micky. There are major outsiders threatening to carve chunks out of our turf for themselves and their own. So I want no misunderstandings. You resume your business, go your own way but if you do, it will not be from under this roof.' Ronnie stared long and hard at his brother. He had given him an ultimatum, one that was long overdue. It was the making or the breaking of the Bryants and they both knew it.

Chapter Sixteen

It was a dazzling morning in May and Bella looked radiant. Though she didn't have a long white dress and train to walk up a church aisle in, she was deliriously happy. Her wedding dress, made by a seamstress friend of Joyce's, was calf length, white and buff chiffon, with a Peter Pan collar and three-quarter sleeves. It was gathered at the waist to hide her bump and fell gently around her legs. Joyce had clipped a small veil to her white satin, half-moon hat and arranged her hair around it. She felt like a bride, even though she wasn't dressed like one in the traditional sense. Micky stood beside her as they paused on the steps of the registrar's office, his black suit, crisp white shirt and plain tie, a stark contrast to her pastel colours. All the Bryants were handsome men, but with his blue eyes and dark hair, Bella considered Micky outstanding. Lenny and Terry both wore dark suits and Ronnie was in grey. Sean and Ashley were dressed to the nines in Oxford Street suits and cheeky bow ties.

Bella's heart was bursting with pride. This was her new family. She was Mrs Michael John Bryant and the man on whose arm she leaned was her husband. Her dreams had all come true and she was still pinching herself to believe it.

'Say cheese, you two!' Joyce was standing in front of them holding her Brownie box camera.

Bella thought how stunning she looked in a figure-hugging navy and white suit. Even though it was May, she was wearing a single fox fur looped around her shoulders. She looked the most expensively dressed woman amongst them. Even Gina, with her thick black hair rolled up into a cone-shaped hat of bright orange to match her full skirted tangerine frock, didn't outshine her.

Micky and Bella smiled. Then Bella lifted her bouquet of white carnations and roses. She threw them and heard Dolly scream, but the flowers were caught by Joyce.

'Nah, Ronnie ain't the marrying type,' Micky whispered in her ear. 'You should have bunged them in Gina's direction.'

'I closed my eyes so I didn't cheat,' Bella whispered back as he led her down the steps to the waiting cars. Black and sleek with white ribbons and bows, they made Bella feel like a queen. Friends and family threw confetti as they came down the steps. It was the most wonderful day of her life.

Micky lifted the white veil from her eyes. 'Congratulations, Mrs Bryant.' He kissed her passionately. A cheer went up.

'Oh, Micky, I'm the luckiest girl in the world.'

Micky was grinning as Dolly threw herself forward. 'Oh, Bella, you look gorgeous.' Her eyes went down to her waistline. 'You can't even see a bump.'

'I hope not,' Bella giggled, hugging her friend. 'It took me all evening to let out the sides. I'm getting so fat.'

Bella could hardly believe it was herself talking. She loved being the way she was with the baby growing inside her. Even the sickness had gone now and she was eating for two.

'Do you like this hat, Bella? I bought it especially for today.' Dolly was gazing at her expectantly, her hazel eyes wide under her feathered hat.

'You look stunning, Dolly.'

'Percy said I look like his gran's budgie. And I'm twice your size even though you're expecting!'

Bella gasped. 'I hope I get my figure back after the baby in time for your wedding. You couldn't have your matron of honour still wearing her maternity dress!'

The girls giggled and Micky took hold of Bella's hand. They ran along the pavement as the others chased them, throwing confetti.

Bella glanced at her husband and fell in love with him all over again. The family she belonged to now was united and she was determined to keep them that way. She couldn't imagine life without Micky in it. He was her be all and end all. And she dearly hoped she was his.

And, as Ronnie said, new blood was coming into the world. Their baby would be the first of the new generation and Bella's heart raced at the thought.

The Blue Moon was sparkling; there wasn't a glass in the place that hadn't been washed and dried to perfection, nor a table or chair that hadn't been polished to the highest degree. Bella had helped Joyce set out the buffet early that morning before the ceremony at the registrar's. The club had been thoroughly aired, all its windows and doors thrown open.

Ronnie had refused to consider another venue for the reception and even though Micky had hinted that his brother's intention was simply to publicize the new image of the club, he had nevertheless gone along with Ronnie in every respect.

Bella was standing at the top of the stairs welcoming the guests as they gazed admiringly around them. The new ruby red carpet that had replaced the blue one was causing a stir. As was the magnificent new bar that Gino was once more attending. Reflecting the room behind him were new, full-length mirrors that made the club look twice its normal size. The card tables in the next room had been discreetly covered and a buffet spread over them.

Ronnie had honoured them by holding the celebration here. Even though Bella didn't know some of the guests, she greeted them warmly. Well-dressed men and couples who Ronnie told her were connected to his business. And as Bella shyly examined the unfamiliar faces, they smiled back, taking her hand and congratulating her.

The wedding gifts were all placed on a table for opening after the speeches. Micky was going to make one, and Ronnie. As there was no father of the bride, just witnesses in the form of Gina and Lenny, Ronnie had thought it more appropriate that tributes were kept short and to the point.

And even if Bella had fleetingly entertained the thought of inviting her mother, no one had suggested it. Even Terry never talked about home any more. She knew it was becoming a fantasy for them both, a bad dream that time was slowly dissolving.

Someone pulled her round and embraced her. It was Percy, his eyes full of admiration. 'Blimey, gel, this is swish, ain't it?'

'Glad you like it, Percy. Where's Dolly?'

'In the Ladies, fluttering her feathers.'

Bella giggled. 'Go over and get yourself a drink and there's plenty to eat.'

'I'd have worn me top hat and tails if I'd known,' Percy said as he gazed around him. 'The invite just said refreshments after.'

'Ronnie and Joyce put it on for us as their wedding present,' Bella admitted. 'They've even paid for us to stay overnight in a hotel.'

Dolly rolled her eyes as she appeared, hearing Bella's last words. 'Oh Percy, ain't that romantic?'

'It'll be your turn next,' Bella reminded her. 'I'll be a matron of honour because I'll be an old married lady!'

They all started laughing as Gina and Lenny walked into the club with Terry. He was wearing a smart suit and tie that Ronnie had taken him to a gents' outfitter in Poplar to buy. Bella had parted his hair on one side and applied Bryl-creem to keep it in place, although it was still thin and fell out in lumps. He was smiling, looking at everyone and everything and Bella's heart went out to him. Like Micky, he missed the still and working with Lenny and now they were living at Piper Street, he had nothing to do all day.

Suddenly Bella felt someone beside her. She

231

turned expectantly, hoping to find Micky there. But it was Joyce and Ronnie, Sean and Ashley and some of their friends. Introductions were made and congratulations given. Soon the room was filled to capacity, faces she knew and those she didn't, but to Bella, it didn't matter, these people were her life now. She wanted Micky to be beside her though, and she searched the room for his tall figure. Right up to the moment the registrar had married them, she had been unable to believe that Micky really wanted her. In her heart she felt that married life had been thrust upon him because of the baby. But Ronnie had assured her that his brother was a family man at heart, even though Micky was reluctant to admit it.

At last she saw him, standing at the bar. He was head and shoulders above the group of men and she felt a wave of love and pride. He was so handsome that she couldn't believe he was really her husband now. She was his wife and no one could take that away from her. As Ronnie had put it at the last family meeting, the Bryants were respected in the East End. They had been tested and come through the worst.

'Ronnie has done you proud, girl,' Gina said as she swallowed the last of her gin, smacking her lips together as she returned her empty glass to the table.

Bella smiled at her friend's flushed cheeks, jarring slightly with her tangerine dress. It was a beautiful shade of orange though and suited Gina's Spanish colouring. As they sat together in a cosy corner, watching the guests eat, drink and be merry, Bella felt the baby move inside her. Inadvertently she placed her hand over her bump.

'Kicking a ball around, is he?' Gina asked perceptively.

'Well, at least you know it's a boy.'

Bella smiled. 'I'd like a son for Micky of course. But little girls you can dress up, spoil a bit.'

'Whatever you have is going to be spoilt rotten with a family like the Bryants. Just look at them over there, like the blooming Mafia, ain't they?' She nodded towards the group of men standing at the bar drinking, smoking and talking together. Bella studied her husband and two brothers-in-law and nodded.

'I'm still trying to convince myself I'm married to one of them.'

'Don't try too hard. It will dawn on you soon, I promise.'

'Oh, Gina, I know you don't trust Micky, but things are going to be different from now on.'

'Course they are, love. I'm just an old cynic. You know I miss you, girl. The café's not the same without you.'

'I miss you too.'

'Lenny does his best, but he's ham-fisted and don't look as good as you in an apron. He's not a natural mover, that's for sure, and I'll be drawing me pension before he manages to balance a breakfast on his arm! Still, at least I've got him where I can see him now. And, if I'm honest, if he was to settle down to the business, I might consider making us legal.' She put up her hand as Bella's eyes widened. 'Don't get excited now. It's only an if. Lenny has a streak in him for branching out into the unknown. It's a natural trait of dishonesty that I'm working to eradicate and at the moment, because he was scared after the fire, he's behaving himself. But as you can see...' she sighed as she looked at the all-male contingent surrounding the bar, 'he's thick with your Micky and one plus one in their case makes trouble.'

'Ronnie won't let that happen.' Bella sounded confident as she watched Lenny and Micky and listened to their laughter. She felt that Gina was over critical of Lenny, who was trying to please her and doing his best in the café. He had been happier at the still, but Bella would never point that out to Gina. It was more than her life's worth.

'Ronnie's a good geezer,' Gina nodded. 'So is Joyce. I like her.'

'She's been very good to me. A bit like a mum.'

Gina stared at her thoughtfully. 'You heard from yours at all?'

'No, and I don't expect to. Why should I? She chucked me out and told me she didn't ever want to see me again.'

'But she might feel different now.'

Bella said nothing as she tried to hide the feelings inside her that welled up when she thought of Bow Street. She had been tempted, it was true, to go round there, tell Mary that she was getting married and Ronnie had even asked if she wanted him to accompany her. But she had decided against it, as much for Terry's sake as her own. He was happy now, happier than he had ever been, had been given Ron's old room at Piper Street and liked being in the big old house with a family feel.

'Ronnie is going to open up the basement,' Bella told Gina, changing the subject discreetly. 'Me and Micky are going to move there as soon as Ronnie's had it done up. The airey, as it's known, hasn't been used for years, so it needs a bit of doing up. I think it's still got the duckboards on the floor to keep out the damp so it will need a good lot of heating.' She paused, her eyes softening as she thought of her plans to make the airey a real home, the furnishings she would choose and the room full of toys she would transform into a nursery for the baby. 'At the moment we've got Mr and Mrs Bryant's old room upstairs, but when the baby comes we'll need more space and the airey has a lovely big sitting room, scullery and kitchen and three bedrooms, quite enough space to meet our needs.'

'Will Terry move in with you?'

'I said he could, but he wants to stay in Ron's old room. He likes it there, next to Sean. And when Ashley's over they all have a good laugh.'

'Don't Ronnie sleep in it anymore?'

Bella grinned and said softly, 'Most nights he stays at the club with Joyce. Prefers it to going all the way back to her place.'

'The house of ill repute, you mean?' Gina asked.

'It don't seem like it,' Bella shrugged. 'I've been over there with Joyce and she keeps it really nice. The girls are lovely too and Bernie and Sid keep any trouble out.'

'You sound like a Madam yourself, girl.'

'It's a good business if you run it right, Gina.'

235

'You thinking of starting one yourself?' Gina sounded alarmed and Bella shook her head quickly.

'Course not. I was just saying, it's a way to earn a living same as anything else.'

'You know I can hear your Micky talking there.' She rolled her eyes expressively. 'Well, give me my café any day. I know I spend me life cooking and waiting on tables, but I'm only thankful I've got beer bellies sitting on chairs and I'm not lying under them.'

She laughed, but Bella was quick to enlighten her friend. 'Joyce doesn't work any more, you know. She's retired.'

'Don't Ron ever get upset about what she done?' Gina asked curiously.

Bella shrugged as she sipped from the glass of water in front of her. 'It was all in the past, Gina. They've got a good understanding, being friends for so long.'

'Not like your Micky then?'

'What do you mean?'

'Nothing. Just that he's on a short fuse where you're concerned, ain't he?'

'It was only Raymond Taylor that annoyed him once,' Bella dismissed. 'He trusts me and I trust him.'

'Well, take my tip and knock any jealousy on the head straight away if it appears. If you're not careful the old green eye can get out of hand.'

'Gina, we ain't even been married a day yet!'

'It's never too early to put your foot down. And when the baby comes along, men tend to get shirty about being ignored.'

'Well, I'll have all the time in the world to pamper him,' Bella said with a smile. 'Don't forget, I won't be a working woman, will I?'

Gina looked at her and frowned deeply. 'Is that what you want, Bella, ducks? Waking up to washing, ironing, cleaning and changing nappies all day? Tea on the table as soon as he comes home and the carpet slippers ready?'

Bella straightened her back and nodded. 'Well, I can't see Micky wearing carpet slippers, but yes, that's what I want.' She gave a hesitant smile as she added softly, 'A home, a real home, is what I never had, Gina.'

'I know, love. But you've got brains as well. Because you've come up the hard way you've had to use them an' all. You don't want to let them go to waste. That'd be a sin.'

Bella laughed, sliding her hand through the crook of her friend's arm. 'That's what I love about you, Gina, you've always got your feet on the ground.'

'Too true I have,' Gina agreed, knocking back the dregs in her glass and chuckling. 'You can't trust a man any further than you can throw him. Not any man. And believe me, there are no exceptions to the rule. And speaking of which, your bloke is walking towards us, giving me the evil eye for monopolizing you. So off you go and – what did you say you was going to do – pamper him?'

Bella looked up to see that the group of men at the bar had disbanded. Micky was making his way towards her and she stood up, her heart racing at the sight of him.

Gina was wrong, there was one exception to the rule. One that she had found, anyway. Micky had always been her friend, her only ally in the hardest of times, her protector and her lover. And now he was her husband. She had loved him forever, would continue to love him and knew that he loved her in the same way.

One day she would remind Gina of this conversation in years to come. When she and Micky were an old married couple, were still friends as well as lovers, and had raised a family to prove their love had survived the test of time.

Chapter Seventeen

August 1954

It was Saturday afternoon and Micky knew he should be getting up and out of the bed. He had been in it all morning since leaving home. But Leyla felt good next to him, the reason being she was dreaming sweet dreams. And he had been indulging too. The small black pellet in his cigarette had furnished him with a glorious lethargy, a sensation that was now crying out for more of the same. The heel-balls they had just smoked were of the finest quality, a fact Micky had proven for himself. His Limehouse contact, Weng-Weng, was to thank for this, though where the little chink was buying the opium from, he had no idea. But he intended to find out. He had sampled it for himself and knew that it was kosher.

Leyla stirred beside him, her slender black body and full, young breasts always a turn-on as she moved against him. It was only when she opened her mouth that Micky felt disappointed. She spoke with a whining nasal accent and very fast. Leyla Spinks came from Liverpool, a northern brass and a stunner to look at. She was also his link to the drug scene in the north. All he need do now, was leave with his twenty-five quid. He could ask for six times as much for the heel-balls from the bohemian set who favoured the clubs and bars of Soho. They were loaded and would pay fortunes for any substance they could smoke, swallow or stuff up their refined noses like the Indian hemp he had been buying from the Russian. But he had heard that up north there was a lucrative market for opium and he would offer the goods for a song at first, create a demand and then drive up his price.

The girl turned away from him, snoring slightly, her thick, curly black hair twisting around her face. Micky slid quietly out of bed, put on his trousers and checked the room to see if he had left any incriminating evidence. It was a shabby Aldgate dump, but it did the job. His friend, Norman Waters, had bunged him a key and in return Micky passed him a selection of stock, fast cars and the little black beads that were making such an impact on the London scene.

Taking Leyla's bag, he shook out the contents and found her purse. He opened it and took out an impressive wedge of notes. The bitch was loaded! Tipping twenty pellets from his matchbox into the purse he counted out twenty-five notes and a further ten for his trouble. The sum was over and above their agreement but she had come well prepared. He tucked the money inside his jacket pocket hanging from the chair. Lacing. his shoes and inspecting his image in the dressing table mirror he nodded.

'The day ain't even started yet, Micky, old son,' he congratulated himself. 'And a nice bit of skirt into the bargain.' He knew Leyla wouldn't be best pleased at his price, but he also knew she would be back for more.

Unlike him, she now had a habit. He could stop any time if he so wished. But why should he? Sweet dreams as they were called, were a major perk of the opium. They were what he enjoyed, and most of all they relieved him from the mundane. Which, at the moment, was driving him nuts.

After all, marriage and a family hadn't been his actual choice, had it? In fact, he still didn't know if had sired young Michael. The boy had blue eyes, true, but otherwise, he was Bella's double. It was all kids at home; the neighbours' kids, friends' kids, Uncle Tom Cobley's kids. Bella loved it. Revelled in it. She even smelt of kids. He was surprised they'd not had any more, but he wasn't complaining, even though Bella was worried they weren't going to produce again. She had even been to see the old doc, but all he'd said was to relax and things would sort themselves out in time.

Micky knew he should pay more attention to his wife but to be honest, it was a bit of a chore, no excitement left in the bedroom. Forbidden fruit was his cup of tea. Like Leyla, who wore musky smelling scent splashed over every inch of her smooth ebony skin and would always comply with what he wanted her to do.

Still, he wasn't about to complain. Bella kept him sweet with Ronnie and that was important. After the Stratton fiasco, Micky had learned a big lesson. After Tony had died in hospital, there had been a big shake-up in the East End. Ronnie had been right about that. Some hard men had emerged and Micky knew he couldn't go it alone, at least not yet. And when Ronnie had offered to finance buying a garage at Aldgate and stocking it with top quality cars, he'd jumped at the chance.

Micky laughed out loud at his good fortune. He had convinced Ronnie that he actually enjoyed being legit. But the cars were just toys for him to play with. A front for his other more enjoyable interests, like those he had partaken of this morning.

The smile slowly slipped from his face. He had to be careful as he didn't want Ronnie breathing down his neck again. This arrangement was perfect. Until he was ready to change it, he would keep his family happy.

Whistling softly, he lifted his jacket from the back of the chair, drew it on and went from the room.

He stood outside in the hot August air, breathing in the filthy fumes from the traffic and the hot, over-worked tarmac. It was said that where there was muck there was money and he believed it implicitly. The hemp that he had been flogging

241

to the arty set in Soho was about as mucky as you could get. And its users were no better than the old chinks of Limehouse, now a vanishing breed. This generation with their lefty views just pretended to be poor, they had no conception of real poverty. And this annoyed him the most. He took real pleasure in selling them the dope at astronomical prices. It was their comeuppance.

And now he had Leyla. She was rough and coarse, but a pro. He even had a grudging respect for her. Where she was coming from. And bless her little black heart, he would continue to provide her with the best sweet dreams she had ever dreamed.

Winking at a pretty girl as she walked by, Micky smiled. There was no rush to get back to work. Terry would have washed all the motors and swept the site. At least the kid was good for shining up the stock, keeping it smart. And his new salesman, Milo, would take care of any punters. He was a good sort, was young Milo. Put on the airs and graces a bit, but the chicks loved it. Miles Heath-Gash, double-barrelled moniker and dressed to kill. Yeah, Milo could sell ice to an Eskimo any day of the week.

So, having nothing better to do than enjoy the day, Micky sauntered after the girl. She had a round, neat bottom and long legs and he smiled again as she glanced encouragingly over her shoulder.

Carefully, he smoothed back his thick, dark hair, adjusted his tie and walked after her with a spring in his step.

Although the weather had been gloomy, today the sun was shining and Bella was excited. She and young Michael were on their way to meet Dolly and the twins at Cox Street market. She was going to buy small gifts for Michael's fifth birthday party tomorrow. Dolly's four-year-old twins, Anne and Irene, were all glossy golden ringlets and big smiles. They loved Michael who basked in their attention. Michael had reddish brown hair like Bella, but his big blue eyes were his father's. His expression was serious for a little boy, but when the twins made him laugh, he couldn't stop.

The Shines still lived in the Poplar house they had moved to after their wedding. The girls met weekly at the market; it was a good excuse to gossip whilst they shopped or sat on the bench by the arches as the kids played around the stalls.

Today Dolly was already shopping at the clothes stall and Bella smiled as she approached the colourful trio.

The girls were Dolly's doubles, standing on firm, strong legs, dressed in buttercup yellow frocks and green sandals, whilst Dolly herself was wearing a floral cotton dress and a floppy white hat.

The girls saw Bella first. 'Auntie Bella, Auntie Bella!'

Bella stopped as they ran into her arms. After she'd hugged them both, they were soon kissing Michael with their soft lips and making him laugh. He was normally a quiet child and Bella loved the twins for their ability to bring him out of his shell.

'Oh, Bella, you should see what I've bought.'

Dolly rushed up, breathless as usual. 'Look, two identical skirts. Someone must have had twins as old as mine. They're almost new. A bit on the big side, but nothing I can't alter.'

'Lucky you,' Bella nodded with a smile. 'You found a snip again.'

'Let's look for something for young Michael.'

'I need little surprises to wrap up for the party tomorrow. Games like pass the parcel and hide and seek.'

'How many children are coming?'

'Seven in all. There's our three, the two little girls from next door, Emma and Victoria, and that nice girl Phiona's two children who go to the Docklands.'

'Oh yes, they're from Blackwall, aren't they?'

Bella nodded as, engrossed in conversation, they moved on with the children playing around them as they walked to the bench and sat down.

They loved to talk about their world. Their little universe of children, household projects and the other mothers and their families who met at the monthly club held at the centre. The kids belonged to the Dockland Settlement, playing with the toys donated by well-wishers, learning new games and drawing and painting. Skills that would help them when they attended school, as Michael was going to do in September. Bella always tried to meet Dolly there when time allowed. She was very busy looking after her family and keeping the books for the Blue Moon and Ronnie's new building company.

'Don't go out of sight,' Dolly shouted as the children toddled off to the toys and sweets.

'I'm making the jelly and blancmange tonight.' Bella smoothed down the full skirt of her pale blue cotton dress. Her fingers went up to the tiny buttons of the shirtwaister bodice and she twisted them pensively. 'Gina is coming over in the morning to help me with the food.'

'What time does it start?'

'Two o'clock. You'll all be coming, won't you?'

'Wouldn't miss it for the world. Percy has to work at Burlingtons in the morning and help with the early deliveries of fish, but he'll be home by twelve. Course, he'll stink to high heaven and will need a wash or they'll be thinking all your lovely food has gone off!'

The girls burst into laughter, before Dolly asked curiously, 'Is Micky getting time off from work to be at the party?'

'I hope so. He has a nice young man to help him now. Saturdays and Sundays can be very busy. If Miles is there, then Micky will come home.'

'Miles? That's a posh name.'

'Micky calls him Milo.'

'Have you met him yet?'

'No, I only go to the garage when Micky drives us up to Aldgate in the car. It's too far to walk. But Micky speaks very highly of him. He's good with the customers and sells cars almost as easily as Micky. And our Terry likes him too. He told me that Milo tips him two bob from his own pocket when he's pleased with Terry's work.'

Bella hoped that now Micky had an assistant he would have more free time. Although Terry could be relied on to wash and clean, he was unable to sell, or even talk to the customers. He was still a little boy inside a man's body and she knew now that he would never change. At least he could be relied on to use soap and water, shine up the stock and keep it clean.

Dolly sighed dramatically, bringing Bella back sharply from her worries about Terry. 'Percy's really envious of Micky driving all those fast cars. It must be exciting having a job like that.'

Bella smiled proudly. 'Last week Micky took us round the block in a Jaguar. It was white and had a soft, fold-back hood. We was a bit squashed with the three of us, but it went really fast. All the wind blew in me hair and Michael loved it, waving over the top of the window at everyone.'

'His customers must have a lot of money to spend on cars like that.'

Bella laughed. 'Not always. Some can't really afford a car and spend every penny they've saved. Other men just want to look good and impress their girlfriends. Micky takes them out for a spin and before you know it, they're sold. He's a really good salesman you know.'

'I'm sure he is,' Dolly nodded quickly.

Bella wished she could sit on the seat all day boasting about her husband. She loved him so much and was so proud of him. All that was missing was another addition to the family. A sister or brother for Michael. She'd spoken to Dr Cox about it, but he said she was fit and healthy. He'd asked her if she and Micky had any problems with intimacy, but she had been too embarrassed to say that Micky didn't seem to be interested in love-making. She felt it was her fault somehow and always tried to look nice and please him. But the end result was, when they did make love, she was tense and the enjoyment was replaced by anxiety. Dr Cox had told her that when she stopped wanting a baby so much, one would come along. She hoped he was right...

'Bella, can I ask you something?' Dolly's voice broke into her thoughts. 'I was wondering if young Michael ever asked about his granny.'

Bella was taken aback by this. She never discussed Mary and had no inclination to do so now. 'He doesn't know he's got one, does he?' she replied a little shortly.

'But when he goes to school, the other kids will talk about theirs. What are you going to say to him then?'

Bella shrugged. 'I don't know.'

'Have you thought much about it?'

'Course I have, Dolly. But what's the use? I can't provide a granny for Michael by waving me magic wand. And anyway, he's got plenty of uncles and that's more than enough for now.' Bella looked at her friend. 'Sorry, I didn't mean to snap.'

'It's just that we don't ever talk about your mum. And we're close friends, we talk about everything else.'

Bella knew Dolly was being kind and would be willing to listen to anything that Bella had to confide. But Mary was a sensitive subject and one that Bella didn't even like thinking about herself because it was too painful.

'The truth is, Dolly, I'm content with my life now. I have everything I want. A wonderful husband, a gorgeous little boy and family and friends. Bow Street seems like a bad dream. When I think of what that man did to me and Terry I feel physically sick. After all he put us through, I don't think I can ever forgive him. As for Mum, she kicked us out, didn't she? So what I'm trying to do is forget.'

'I understand,' Dolly nodded at once. 'I'd feel the same if it was me.' She paused, looking at Bella from the corner of her eye. 'So you don't ever think about going round there?'

Bella frowned. 'And have the door slammed in me face again?'

'She might not. Not if young Michael was with you. He's her first grandchild after all.'

'What would I say?'

Dolly shrugged. '"Hello, Mum, this is Michael, your grandson." At least you would have given her a chance.'

'Oh, Dolly, I don't know. I can hear Micky telling me I was asking for trouble.'

'Yeah, I suppose you're right.' Dolly bit her lip, a sure sign that she was reluctant to say what she was about to say. 'But if you change your mind, me and the girls would go with you. Your mum would have to think twice with the lot of us standing on the doorstep.' She laughed nervously as one of the grips fell out of her untidy hair and she pushed it back into place again.

'I don't know, Dolly. Even if she invited us in, *he'd* be there.'

Dolly shuddered. 'Yes, but it's your mum you're going to see, Bella, not him.'

Bella was silent, her thoughts in turmoil. Dolly

was forcing her to consider something she would prefer to ignore. She had buried her fear and loathing of the man and had sealed off her feelings for Mary. But her friend was right. Michael would ask after his granny when he went to school. In fact, she was surprised he hadn't already as all his little friends had grannies.

It was a lovely day, the market in full swing with people strolling lazily through it. The fruit and vegetable stall was under siege by its customers and the jewellery and watches next to it had also drawn a crowd. The smell of over-ripe vegetables and horse dung mixed with a waft of disinfectant from the public lavatories.

'I appreciate you saying you'd come with me, Dol,' Bella said gratefully.

'You'd do the same for me, wouldn't you?'

'Course I would,' Bella agreed. 'But that ain't likely with your mum and dad.'

'They're always asking when you're going to bring Michael round.'

Bella often saw Mr and Mrs Taylor at Dolly's house. They always gave her and Michael a warm welcome and amused the children whilst she and Dolly had a nice quiet chat in the kitchen. She and Dolly still laughed when Mr Taylor told the children about Doctor Carrot and Potato Pete. But Raymond was a sore subject with Micky. Although Ray had lost his job at the PLA and moved to Southend to work on the funfairs, Micky had refused point blank to go to Dolly's wedding. She had been forced to tell a barefaced lie to Dolly, saying Micky was ill and unable to attend.

'I'll think about what you said about Mum, Dol,' Bella nodded but as they went on their way, she knew she didn't want to walk down Bow Street again. Her life seemed so far removed from what it was then. And Michael hadn't asked any questions yet, she told herself quickly. As Micky often remarked, love for today and let tomorrow take care of itself.

It was Sunday and Bella's kitchen was filled with succulent cooking smells. Whilst Gina set out the sausage rolls, lifting them cleanly from the greased cake tins on to the rack, Bella poured out the lemonade.

'I wish my sausage rolls turned out so crispy and brown,' Bella said wistfully. 'Mine aren't a patch on yours.'

'Course they are. You are a good cook now, girl, even though I say it myself. I taught you well.'

'You taught me everything I know.'

'I still miss you at the café,' Gina sighed reflectively. 'Little Tina's a treasure and Lenny pulls his weight, but the two of them put together don't fill your shoes, love.'

Bella knew that Gina meant what she said and she smiled. 'Tina is a sweet girl, Gina. She's a good waitress and likes the customers.'

Now it was Gina's turn to smile. 'Likes them too much, that's the trouble. That little arse has been pinched so many times it must be blue not pink under that tight skirt of hers. I tell her to give them a slap when they do it, but all she does is giggle and encourage them.'

Bella had met Tina when she'd taken Michael

to the café for a plate of chips. She was a lovely cockney girl, never short of a cheeky answer for her customers. She had been working for Gina since she left school three years ago and they got on well. Lenny continued to act as cleaner and general dogsbody, a role that he had become accustomed to. The business was still booming, the labourers who ate there ever increasing as part of the regeneration process of the East End. Gina was always considering the opening of another café, but hadn't done so yet.

Gina took off her apron and hung it on the peg behind the door. She glanced in the kitchen mirror, examining her mascara and her thick black hair pinned up in a pleat behind her head. Bella smiled as she watched her friend take a lipstick from her bag and smooth it carefully over her lips, purse them and blot them with her handkerchief.

Gina caught Bella's eye in the mirror. 'Shall I light the candles on the cake? Or do you want to wait for Micky?'

Bella glanced at her watch. Micky had promised to be home for two but it was now four. The children had played all the games and exhausted themselves and now it was time to eat. She nodded to Gina. 'No, let's go ahead, shall we?'

Bella watched Gina walk to the big white cake standing on the table. She lit each of the five blue candles standing upright in the icing, careful to avoid the message written in big loops. 'Happy Birthday Michael'.

Bella hoped that even at the eleventh hour, Micky would turn up. Ronnie and Joyce, Dolly and Percy, Sean and Ashley and all the mothers

251

of the children invited to the party were waiting expectantly in the sitting room. Lenny and Terry were at present entertaining the group of excited youngsters with magic tricks.

Bella watched each little flame flicker alight. The five blue candles represented the five wonderful years of her marriage to Micky. She had everything she could possibly want, even if Micky wasn't here to enjoy it. Nevertheless he was providing his wife and son with a great deal of happiness. Just look at her gorgeous home, she told herself enthusiastically.

The kitchen and scullery were painted a soft green and all the rooms were very spacious. The sitting room on the lower ground floor was accessed by stairs leading up to the front door. The rooms were filled with furniture that Bella had chosen herself. She had taken pride in making her home look elegant on a shoestring. Most of the heavy chintz drapes were from the market, the dresser, table and chairs from a Poplar furniture makers. The sideboard and glossy cocktail cabinet in maple wood was second-hand, bought from a Stepney warehouse. The thick Indian rugs on the floor covered the old duckboards and the large hearth contained an open fire that was always burning in the winter. It was decorated with Mrs Bryant's brass tongs, coal scuttle, muffin fork and brass fender.

The furnishings were traditional and in keeping with the old house and Bella liked to think Micky's parents would have approved of her choice. The exception to the rule was Michael's bedroom which was very modern. A single bed, a slim wardrobe and chest of drawers were painted white and the shelves that filled the walls were full of Michael's books and toys. The two other bedrooms had double beds and suites of solid oak furniture. She had installed a rocking chair in her and Micky's bedroom where, when Michael was a baby, she'd rocked him to sleep in her arms. The window was below the ground level outside and stairs from the back garden ran down to it. For many years they had been sealed off but when Ronnie had opened up the airey for them, he had removed the barricade and cleaned and painted them. Now that it was such a busy house, they were often used, not least by young Michael himself as he ran up and down them into the garden.

'Ready?' Gina asked, lifting the cake on its big china plate.

Bella nodded. How lucky she was to have family and friends around her and a happy, healthy little boy.

At that moment Michael came bounding towards her in his new white birthday shirt and short blue trousers. Ann and Irene followed him dressed in beautiful pink frilly party dresses and black patent shoes. The other children all followed and there were screams of delight as Gina held the cake aloft.

In the sitting room, she placed it on a small table in the centre of the floor. All the adults clapped and the children jumped up and down excitedly. Bella began to sing 'Happy Birthday' as Michael stepped forward to puff out his cheeks.

Bella hugged him as he took a big breath and

blew. All the candles went out and once more everyone cheered. Ronnie lifted Michael on to his shoulders as Bella began to cut the cake. She glanced up for a moment and looked at her son. Ronnie was like a second father to him. He had always been there; present in his life from the day he was born when Micky was out and Bella had given birth in the big double bed that was once Mr and Mrs Bryant's. It was Ronnie who had first held Michael in his arms as the midwife and doctor took leave and Sean went out to find Micky. It was Ronnie who, a year later, had driven them to the hospital when Michael had developed whooping cough and Micky had been at work, unable to be reached. It was Ronnie who last year had taken them up to the City on Coronation Day to see the golden coach carrying the new queen. And it was always Ronnie and Sean who played football with Michael each Sunday in the yard whilst Micky was hard at work.

And now it was Ronnie who was holding Michael aloft on his fifth birthday, making him laugh aloud as he sat on his shoulders.

Bella sighed softly as she watched their antics. Her world would be complete if only Micky was here too.

Chapter Eighteen

Ronnie was standing at the window, looking down on Piper Street. The plane trees were shedding their September leaves. After last night's rainfall, gutters were blocked and puddles had formed in the road. Lost in thought he stroked the fine dark material of his jacket. His long fingers teased the skin beneath, gently irritating the remains of the scar on his chest. The bump brought back memories, the Strattons, the distillery and the fire. How many times had he consoled himself with the fact they had all survived? Fate had spared them and taken others. For a while they had lived in peace but now there was danger once more.

Stronger, harder men had taken the Strattons' place. Like Billy McNee. Ronnie transferred his hand to the back of his head. Pensively he stroked his thick, dark hair styled short above his collar. His grey eyes, fringed with ebony lashes, looked into the distance.

He had made a big decision, but now he was set on it. He'd listened to some of his customers who made their money in the building sector, buying property, doing it up and letting it out. It was hard work, but paid off, they said, if you stuck at it. And Ronnie felt ready for the change. Whilst he was young enough to put his back into a new career, he would give it all he had. Yes, it was a big step but he was prepared to take it. It was

Micky's reaction to selling the Blue Moon that was worrying him. Even though Micky had no financial interest in the club, he revelled in the prestige that the club's name brought the family. The Blue Moon was respected and a good earner too. But now it was attracting the wrong kind of attention. And Ronnie had decided to cut his losses whilst he could.

He turned from the window to face Sean and Ashley. They sat at the big polished table, dressed in silver grey mohair suits and slim jim ties. Their faces were animated, full of the excitement generated by their new venture, a hairdressing salon. Ronnie had given them a start by buying the run-down property in Greenwich and doing it up. Furnished with the latest in hooded hairdryers, comfortable chairs and private cubicles, the customers had soon been fighting each other for appointments.

'Ronnie, can we get started?' Sean looked into his brother's thoughtful eyes. 'We've got shampoos and sets coming out of our ears today and Micky ain't the best of timekeepers, is he?'

'You've got a point there,' Ronnie agreed as he heard Bella and Joyce's voices. They were climbing the steps from the airey where they had been enjoying a chat and cup of tea whilst young Michael was at school.

Ronnie glanced at his watch. It was a quarter to eleven. He hoped to conclude the outstanding business by midday and once more he glanced out of the window hoping that Micky would appear.

Joyce and Bella entered the room and Ronnie

smiled warmly, indicating their customary seats. Joyce took the chair beside him, Bella the one on the opposite side.

'I'm sorry, Ronnie, he must be busy,' she apologized as she sat down. 'He drove Terry in to the garage this morning and must be delayed.'

Ronnie shrugged, hiding his annoyance. 'We'll get on with business, then, shall we?'

All heads nodded and Ronnie kept the lid on his irritation at Micky. His timekeeping was getting worse. But then, to his relief, there was an engine growl outside.

'He's here!' Bella exclaimed and Ronnie glanced through the lace curtains to see a white car pull into the kerb.

Micky soon appeared, looking to Ronnie as though he had just stepped out of a film. His black hair was windblown around his tanned skin and he was dressed in a fawn summer blazer and navy blue trousers. He kissed the top of his wife's head and pulled out the chair beside her.

'Nice of you to turn up, Micky,' Ronnie said.

'Yeah, well, family comes first, don't it?'

Ronnie's eyebrows rose briefly at this remark. It was a blinder, coming from someone who so neglected his family. A problem he hoped would soon be rectified by the addition of Milo. Ronnie for one would be relieved when Micky took more responsibility for the upbringing of his young son. The boy was one in a million, a lovely kid. Ronnie was amazed at his own depth of feeling for his nephew. He tried to make up for Micky's absence but it was not a situation he was happy with.

Ronnie looked into the expectant faces staring up at him. He was reluctant to break the news but it was the reason he had called the family together. The Blue Moon had been a way of life and everyone in here would miss it. He had made many friends whilst running it, even a few enemies. But as much as he regretted the fact, times had moved on. As a family they must move with them.

'This won't take long,' he said abruptly. 'For the last five years we have protected our property, kept out the big crews. The Bennetts and the Sabinis and even new faces like the Donovans. They all saw us as easy pickings and wanted a bigger piece of the East End pie. But now we have to deal with an outsider. Billy McNee.'

'That mug from Notting Hill?'

'Not so much of a mug, Micky. He's taken over other manors recently. And not looked back.'

Micky shrugged. 'It's just a question of tightening up. We never ran scared of no one, Ron. Bernie and Sid have been with us years and we can take on more muscle if McNee threatens us. No one would dare tread on our toes and if they did they'd be sorry.'

'That ain't the true picture, Micky,' Ronnie answered. 'Last week Joyce had a visit.'

'From him?' Micky looked startled. 'Did you, Joyce?'

She nodded, saying nothing.

'They own half of Soho now,' Ronnie continued. 'And you know their reputation, connections with Old Bill included. They've built on their investment and are respected for their pull.'

Micky moved restlessly and Ronnie sensed this was not going to go down well. Micky resisted change and Ronnie knew in his heart that his brother still believed he had been robbed of the distillery. They never discussed it now. But it was there between them and always would be.

'So what if they pull a few strings? Billy's crew is west of us and of no importance. Joyce's place is not in their manor.'

Micky looked astonished as Joyce answered for Ronnie. 'Billy McNee ignores boundaries. He came to the House with an army in tow. It don't take a genius to see which way the wind is blowing. He's buying up all the cream businesses, of which I am one.'

Micky looked nonplussed. 'But you had Ronnie's men on the doors, didn't you?'

Joyce nodded, her expression weary. 'They were outnumbered ten to one. And when Billy left, he took two of my girls with him.'

'He can't do that!'

'He can and he did.' Joyce shrugged her small shoulders and looked into Micky's shocked gaze. 'I'm selling out, Micky. I'm likely to end up with nothing except a severe case of concussion if I haggle.'

'But we can take him! We can soon shut him up.'

Joyce smiled as she shook her head. 'You don't understand, Micky. They had weapons. McNee is a big operator, bigger than you've ever dreamed of. Isn't he, Ron?'

Micky's head jerked round, shock registering in his eyes. 'They came to the club?'

Ronnie nodded. 'Yeah, no surprises there.'

'What happened?'

'What I have been expecting for quite a while. He made me an offer I couldn't refuse.'

'What are you saying!' Micky shouted. 'The Blue Moon is Bryant turf. You can't ditch it. The club is ours, always has been. This is our manor.'

Ronnie felt the anger that he had been forced to hide suddenly fill him again. He didn't want to lose the club any more than Micky did. And he also knew Micky wouldn't understand. He hadn't seen the full force of McNee's outfit. Joyce was right, they were an army, acquiring every club and brothel across the city that Billy fancied. Ronnie had thought hard about the future as he gazed into McNee's cold, shrewd eyes. The man was wearing rings and a quality suit, but underneath he was a new breed of villain. The quality that put him above the rest was his insatiable greed. He took out anyone in his way. Billy McNee was travelling East. He was advancing and if Ronnie opposed him, without doubt there would be loss of life. In that moment of clarity, Ronnie had agreed. He had done the deal, accepted the offer and called it a day.

'I'm quitting, Micky. Time to move on.'

'You are going to be pushed around by the likes of McNee?'

'I'm accepting his price.'

'I don't believe I'm hearing you,' Micky said. 'We ain't cowards, Ron. We've got to fight.'

'Like we fought at the warehouse?' It was Sean who spoke now, his face tense as he looked at his brother. 'I ain't forgotten what happened that night, Micky, and neither should you. Ronnie nearly died then, or have you blanked out Sammy Stratton?'

'Bugger the Strattons and the McNees,' Micky shouted, his fists slamming down on the table. 'They are filth and should be treated as such.'

'Micky – just think about it for a moment,' Bella broke in, her tone confused. 'Perhaps Ronnie's right–'

'McNee is a brainless git,' Micky continued angrily. 'He's struck lucky, putting the fear of God into people just because they let him. And that is what is happening to us – the Bryants. Ronnie, you can't let this happen, bruv.'

Ronnie stared into his brother's ashen face and wished with all his heart that he had the balls to take Billy McNee and rip him apart. But if he did that, it would be World War Three and he couldn't allow that to happen. 'Billy McNee might be a brainless git, Micky,' Ronnie nodded, 'but he's ousted everyone in his path so far. Fighting ain't an option for us. We are small fry in comparison to the big firms. Listen to me, the mob has changed into something I don't recognize now. What is happening today is out of our league. The specialist crews are moving in and taking over, disregarding manors and turf. They are heavies of the first order and we are not. We have had our day. Now we must put our brains where our muscle has been. And we can do it. All above board and legitimate too. Ten years down the line we will be wealthy, with businesses that are not corrupt.'

But Micky was shaking his head as Ronnie

spoke. 'Ronnie, you are making one big error here. The Bryants are a name and will continue to be so if we stop McNee right now. Once this is done, we step into his shoes and *then* we will be wealthy men!'

Ronnie flexed his tight fingers, again amazed at his brother's refusal to learn from past mistakes. 'You have a short memory, bruv,' he reminded him sharply. 'We paid the price in '49. And I refuse to pay it again.'

Micky sat back, his blue eyes cold. 'You are running scared, Ronnie. And you know what, all those that respect us now will be laughing behind our backs. We'll be standing jokes to the hard men of this city. The Blue Moon is our turf and ours alone. If it sinks, then we sink with it.'

Ronnie looked calmly at his brother. 'I have seen this day coming and prepared for it, Micky. That's why I bought the garage, a legitimate business and you must grow it. There's no end to the potential. You can expand into the suburbs and make a name for yourself there.'

'What if I don't want to?'

'Then you would be throwing away a profitable future.'

'Micky,' Joyce broke in, 'listen to your brother. He's right. The clubs are being carved up, and so will you if you don't get out now.'

Ronnie watched the fury fill Micky's face. He admired his courage, his confidence and the desire to be someone that counted, to be a Name. But he could not see reality. He was wanting something he could not have. Ronnie also knew that Micky would never forgive him for selling out. In Micky's mind the Bryants were losing face and the loss of the Blue Moon and the House were the ultimate insult.

Micky pushed back his chair and stood up. Ronnie watched as Bella rose too, fear filling her face as she tried to reach out for him. But Micky angrily pushed past her. The door slammed shut in the hall and there was silence in the room. An engine roared outside and she hurried to the window.

Ronnie watched her shoulders droop. It was the end of an era and everyone in the room knew it. He just wished that Micky could accept the fact too.

Bella was sitting by the fire and the airey was warm, despite the fire having burnt low. The heavy chintz curtains were drawn back allowing the last rays of the sunshine to creep in the big window. It looked out onto the stairs that led up to the front door of the house. Just over an hour ago she had walked up the same stairs with Joyce, unaware of what lay ahead.

She looked at the big moquette chair opposite where Joyce had sat drinking her cup of tea. Joyce hadn't said a word about McNee or the loss of her House. Instead, she had listened to Bella, who never needed an excuse to talk about Micky. Joyce had just let her talk to her heart's content as usual. Now Micky had stormed off and Bella knew he had taken Ronnie's decision hard.

Bella felt alone and uneasy. Like Micky, she too found it hard to believe that Ronnie had relinquished the Blue Moon without protest. She didn't know who this Billy McNee was and she wished that Joyce had shared her knowledge of the man with her prior to the meeting so she could have been more prepared. But then that wasn't Joyce. She was loyal to Ronnie in every way and chose her moments carefully. Perhaps she too was anxious about her future? After all, what would she do when both the House and the club were sold? Ronnie had his other business interests. But Joyce had been an East End Madam for years, loved her girls and the business itself.

As Bella lifted the tongs and dropped a nugget of coal on the fire, she heard the latch go. Looking round, she hoped to see Micky, but it was Ronnie who stood there.

'Can I come in?'

Bella nodded, replacing the tongs. 'Course you can.'

Ronnie closed the door behind him and took the comfortable chair that Joyce had vacated. The fire started to catch again and he unloosened the button of his suit jacket reclining his long legs in front of the hearth. Bella studied his face, the high, proud cheekbones and generous mouth that were a Bryant trademark. Yet when he looked into her eyes, Ronnie's expression was so different to Micky and Sean's. The light grey of his gaze was always a little unnerving. It was sometimes too intense as if he was reading her thoughts and now, as he stared at her, she looked away.

'Don't worry about Micky,' he told her after a moment. 'He was upset, but he'll get it out of his system. I'm sorry he took it so hard, but I have

264

no option.'

'I don't think Micky saw it like that,' she replied, staring at the tiny red flames licking the coal. 'Who is this Billy McNee?'

'He is a thug, pure and simple, but a thug with half the city in his pocket. Joyce wasn't exaggerating when she called his outfit an army. He hires from abroad and ships them over on the boats. Jamaicans, Chinese, Eastern Europeans. They owe their lives to him and more importantly, their families' lives. I'd never met him. Not until the day he went to the House with his entourage. When he came to the club afterwards, he brought Joyce's two girls with him. They were terrified, hysterical. But after we cut the deal he released them. He didn't need to point out that it wasn't Joyce – this time.'

Bella looked up sharply. 'But that's blackmail, Ronnie.'

'It could have been murder.'

'I've never heard you talk like this before.'

'I've never needed to.' He leaned forward and rested his elbows on his knees. 'Listen, Bella, I would be the first in line to row out Billy McNee if I thought it was worth it. But Billy McNee is the first in a long line of villains who will try to own the East End. Before the war it was different. We were trading on the business Dad had built up; the scrap and junk, doing deals from the yard and any street corner. We owned our turf, kept to the island and respected the territory of others. But during the war the black market replaced our totting. And now, after the battle with foreigners, we've got wars in our backyards. Every Tom, Dick and Harry thinks he's tough enough to demolish his neighbour. We have two choices as I see it. Get us back in the frame as is Micky's inclination. Or bow out gracefully.'

'Micky doesn't know the meaning of that word, Ron. He is a fighter.'

'And I respect him for that. But I won't see thirty again and I want peace. If we resist McNee, the repercussions are endless. Would you want young Michael to grow up with his father and uncles carrying weapons at all times? Would you want to see even less of Micky than you do now, when there is a chance with the garage you can have it all? Live without threat or danger and enjoy one another. If the Bryants opposed the new blood then we would challenge the upstarts who have no conception of talking a deal through. They use force at the drop of a hat. Anyone who stands in their way is eliminated.'

'Even us?'

Ronnie nodded slowly. 'Especially us. Until now McNee has kept to his manor. But the word on the street is he is moving across the city and offering a price to let it be known that he is a fair man. That is, fair in his estimation. Of course, he also offers protection; a monkey each month if you prefer. Now you do the sums, Bella. And tell me if a wedge like that is worth staying in business for.'

Bella's gasp was audible. 'Five hundred pounds? For protection?'

He nodded. 'The milk round. Pay up and you don't have your windows smashed or your staff crippled.'

'Oh, Ronnie, Micky would go crazy if he knew that.'

'Which is why I decided to cut loose, make a clean break.' Suddenly his face darkened. 'But I tell you this, it sticks in my craw that I can't help Joyce. And one day I will see justice done. But at this moment in time Billy McNee has scored.'

She had never heard Ronnie speak with such passion before. She also knew now why he was keeping the whole truth from Micky. And she would have to keep it too.

'Will McNee ever be stopped?'

'Oh yes,' he assured her, a cold smile on his lips. 'There are others on the scene, like the twins from Bethnal Green. Billy Hill and Jack Comer, crews with formidable reps who will graduate into the big time. Odds on it will be a turf war like the East End has never seen.'

Bella felt the weight of his words and knew she had reason to be afraid. Not only for Micky but for young Michael. She didn't want to spend her life wondering if Micky would come home in one piece each day, or whether Michael was safe at school. If Ronnie was to be believed, the sooner they adjusted to a new life the better.

'What will Joyce do?'

He smiled distractedly. 'I'd like to put a ring on her finger but she's refused me.'

'But she caught my bouquet, Ron. You two were meant for each other.'

'That's what I told her.'

'She loves you, I know she does.'

'Not enough to marry me, apparently.'

'She'll change her mind, she's just upset.'

He looked into the fire. 'I don't want to lose her, Bella.'

Suddenly she saw the real Ronnie, the man who always kept his feelings in check, the man she looked on as someone even stronger than her Micky. If Ronnie loved Joyce as much as she loved Micky, he would do anything for her, and at this moment in time, the one thing that meant the world to Joyce was her House. And she was losing it. Ronnie had been unable to help her and it was destroying him.

She knelt down beside him. 'Ronnie, it will all be all right. I know it will.'

He nodded, taking her chin in his fingers. 'The family and Joyce, who I consider as part of this family, is what I am doing this for, Bella. My natural inclination is to take hold of Billy McNee and crush him. But I have better sense than to screw up what I have worked so hard to preserve. I would give my life for you all, for Sean and Micky and you and young Michael. I love you all and want the best for each one of you.'

For a moment they looked into each other's eyes. Bella felt a ripple go through her body as he drew nearer. The fire crackled and his full mouth parted as he bent slowly towards her. Then suddenly he jerked back his head and stood up.

The front door closed quietly behind him. She closed her eyes and sank back on her heels. She didn't want to think about what had almost happened then.

Ashley was humming along to Hank Williams singing 'Your Cheatin' Heart' while he lacquered the curly blonde hair of the young girl sitting in the chair next to Bella. The salon was busy, as it always was on Saturdays. And with Christmas in sight, the December rush was on. The six pink-hooded hair dryers in the next room were humming away, the heads beneath them covered in purple hairnets with pads of cotton wool pressed to each ear. Behind each magazine was a face, oblivious to the soft music that was being played in the main salon.

Ashley winked at Bella as he teased the girl's curls into place and Bella smiled shyly, inhaling as she did so the strong odours around her. On the trolley was a box full of pink, blue and white plastic rollers, all of which had just been removed from her own head. Sean had gone off to find a brush that was suitable for the management of her thick, shoulder-length hair. The ponytail that she always wore was about to be styled into a long, glossy pageboy.

'Now, where shall we comb your parting?' Sean frowned intently as he appeared again, his long, artistic fingers rearranging the loose chestnut locks that fell about her head.

'On the right. It always falls back if I comb it any other way.'

'You should use more lacquer.'

Bella coughed gently as Sean enveloped them in another cloud of spray from the bottle.

'Seany, give the girl a break,' Ashley warned, rolling his eyes. 'She doesn't need to be drowned in it.'

'I know, I know,' Sean answered tartly, raising his voice above the strains of the Chordettes singing 'Mr Sandman'. 'But there's a wind blowing out there and she has to walk all the way back through the foot tunnel.' Sean placed a hand on Bella's shoulder. 'You gonna be in time to collect young Michael?'

Bella nodded, grateful the lacquer had now been returned to Ashley. 'It's the school's Christmas party today, so the bell won't go till a bit later.'

'Just you look after yourself then. It's still blowing a gale out there.'

Bella had brought a headscarf with her, although she was reluctant to use it over her new hairstyle. The winds of the last six weeks had been ferocious. As she had walked through the foot tunnel from Island Gardens to Greenwich she had heard it whistling after her like a steam train.

'What about that tornado last week, then?' Ashley said as he removed the white towel from around his customer's shoulders. 'It ripped the roof off Gunnersbury Station as if it was a piece of cloth. And one of our customers told me she was over Acton visiting her daughter and they saw a car lifted bodily into the air.'

'And those poor souls on the South Goodwin Lightship,' Sean added in a whisper. 'All the crew died except one. He clung to the ship for eight hours before he was rescued.' Quickly resuming his normal voice he added, 'Even our customers were afraid to venture out. Goodness only knows how many appointments we had to cancel.' He smiled brightly into the mirror, cupping his hands on either side of Bella's head. 'How is that for you, darling?'

'I love it, Sean.'

'Micky taking you somewhere nice is he?'

'I wanted to see that new film *The Barefoot Contessa* with Humphrey Bogart and Ava Gardner. But Micky said he has something special in mind. I've bought a new dress especially and Gina and Lenny are baby-sitting.'

'Well, he'll have to chain you to his wrist for the night. Ava in person don't hold a candle to you.'

'I wish that was true, Sean.'

He looked into her suddenly sad gaze and bent close to her ear. 'Now listen you. You are a beautiful girl, in your prime, but lately I haven't seen much of that lovely smile. I don't know what's wrong, but it can't be all that bad, as you have your health and your little boy is a credit to you. Money can't be a problem,' Sean added wisely, 'as your old man is making it hand over fist. So, my recommendation is to go out and let your hair down with your new dress and lovely hairstyle. A bit of fun will cure your blues and that's a promise.'

Bella knew Sean was speaking the truth and she dearly hoped that she could win back her husband's attention in such a way. He hadn't been himself at all lately. She knew Ronnie and Micky had quarrelled over Ronnie's decision to sell the club to Billy McNee. Micky believed the family was looked on as a spent force now and he missed the kudos the Blue Moon had provided. Once he hadn't come home and he'd stayed out all night. She had worried herself sick and not slept. But the next morning he had walked in the door, claiming he'd had to work. They had

271

quarrelled bitterly and the rift between them had become even deeper.

Sean continued to try to cheer Bella up, but she was only half listening. Her thoughts were on her family, mainly Micky and his attitude towards her. He was so distant and never told her she looked like Lana Turner any more. He rarely commented on her appearance or the effort she put into looking nice for him. That was why she was here today in the hopes that a new hairstyle would make him notice her again. She wanted their relationship back the way it was. Micky used to be happy at the still. He had been his real self then, always excited about what he was going to do next. Somewhere along the line, he had changed and now she was wondering if Ronnie was partly to blame for this.

Micky had his faults, but he was not a coward. He was a Bryant and a proud one. And she knew that in his heart he believed his brother had chosen a coward's way out. And he had no respect left for Ronnie because of it.

'You should go out more,' Sean was saying as he met her gaze in the mirror. 'All work and no play, you know how the saying goes. Me and Ashley can get real stroppy with each other if we don't have a bit of fun.' He winked at her, comically tapping the side of his nose as they gazed in the mirror. 'So you just enjoy yourself, give your old man a cuddle in the back seats and take Uncle Sean's advice.'

Bella wanted to. More than anything she wanted their marriage to succeed. In the five years she had been Mrs Bryant, she had never regretted marrying Micky. She had a lovely home and beautiful son and she wasn't short of money. Most women would be satisfied with what she had. Perhaps she was blowing things out of proportion. Micky had promised her a treat tonight, something they hadn't done for ages.

Encouraged by Sean's words, a happy vision began to appear in her mind. She imagined her and Micky dancing romantically to some slow, sweet music, alone in their little world in the middle of a crowded dance floor. His whispered words were telling her she meant the world to him and that he wanted her – no, *needed* her – like he used to when they first got together. Then he would drive them home and after taking her to bed and making passionate love to her, in a few weeks' time she would discover that she was pregnant. She could see Dr Cox's face smiling at her, telling her that he had been right in his advice to relax, to enjoy the pleasures of making love.

The dream grew brighter and more vivid by the moment and suddenly her heart started to beat fast. Her smile in the mirror was radiant as she thought of being close to her husband again and the wonderful prospect of a little brother or sister for Michael.

Chapter Nineteen

Bella felt the wind tug at her scarf as she left the salon. Her new pageboy style was protected, tucked into the collar of her raincoat. Soon she was entering the dimly lit foot tunnel that led under the Thames to the island and was well in time to collect Michael. The Christmas party at school was being extended until a quarter past four.

It was growing dark already, the thundery skies over London making the late afternoon seem even wintrier. As she reached the steps of the exit, the chill wind blew hard and with it came a few spots of rain.

Parents were gathering when she arrived at the gates of St Nicholas's. Everyone was dressed for bad weather and the bright lights of the classrooms twinkled as the children ran into the playground.

Bella waved to Michael. He was walking with a little girl whose shabby coat was a washed-out shade of purple. Her red hair was blowing around her small face and her eyes were as big as saucers.

'How's my big boy?' Bella hugged Michael. His serious little face was transformed by Micky's smile and looking into his blue eyes, she saw her own, but his expression was all his father's.

'Did you have a nice party?'

Michael nodded. His little figure was buttoned

up neatly in his gabardine raincoat. He always dressed himself carefully and laced his shoes, tying a perfect knot. 'This is for you.' He pushed a folded sheet of paper in her hands. 'We made Christmas cards today.'

Bella read the big scrawled words, 'To Mummy and Daddy', that must have taken a great effort for him to write, and inside was a Christmas tree crayoned in green.

'Thank you, darling. I'll stand it on the mantelpiece when we get home.'

Bella smiled at the little girl who was still standing there. 'Hello. Are you in Michael's class?'

'Her name's Teresa,' Michael said. 'And she's new.'

'Teresa's a lovely name.' Bella looked round for the girl's mother. The playground was empty now, the cries of the children fading in the distance.

A few raindrops danced down on Michael's nose and Bella hoped it wasn't going to pour.

'Why isn't your mummy here?' Michael said, echoing Bella's thoughts.

''Cos she's ill, I 'spect.'

'Oh, dear. I'm sorry to hear that. What's wrong with her?'

'Dunno.'

Bella searched the child's uncared-for little face. Her fringe was cut as though she had used scissors on it herself. She had such a sad expression that it went straight to Bella's heart. 'Where do you live?'

'Collier Street.'

'We'll walk with you, if you like?' It was out of their way, but Bella didn't like to leave her on her own.

Teresa nodded happily and Bella watched the children join hands. They ran ahead, laughing and playing in the wind. Ten minutes later they all arrived in Collier Street.

'That's me house.' Teresa pointed to one of the prefabs on the left-hand side of the road.

Bella's heart sank. There was no light coming from behind the drooping curtains and the place looked deserted. She hadn't been this way in years and it brought back memories. Once the asbestos prefabs had been the height of luxury. Now they were in a very poor state, covered in mould with all their iron parts rusting.

Bella sighed reflectively. To think that once, when she had lived at Bow Street, she had envied Gilda Ellis and her family who had been allocated one. Now they were no more than damp old huts.

Teresa pushed the front door hard but it was shut tight. So Bella knocked and they waited. When at last it opened, she smiled apprehensively, ready to introduce herself.

But the words died on her lips as she stared at her mother. Mary Doyle's long red hair had turned grey and she wore an old coat buttoned up to her chin. 'Jaysus,' she exclaimed, as shocked to see Bella as Bella was to see her. 'What are you doing here?'

Bella pulled herself together. 'I walked this little girl home.'

Mary looked angry. 'Have you been in trouble again?'

'No, Mum, I ain't, honest.'

'Teresa is yours?' Bella blurted.

'And why shouldn't she be?' Grabbing the little girl's shoulders roughly, Mary pushed her daughter inside the house.

Bella watched in dismay as Teresa disappeared into the gloomy hall. 'How long have you lived here?' was all she could think of to ask.

'A year and it's a year too long, I can tell you. The council pulled down the old house and dumped us here, worse off than we were before. Not that you would care, would you?'

'That's not true,' Bella said, offended. 'Me and Terry slept rough for a week before we had a roof over our heads. And only then because we asked Micky for help.'

'So it was him you went to was it?' Mary sneered. 'I thought as much. Done well out of my misfortune, ain't you, girl?'

'Me and Micky are married, if that's what you mean.'

'Well, a curse on that lying git, that's all I have to say! Him and his brother, them who took all the strength from me man and left me in the shit.' She drew a long, smoke-filled breath. 'So you, Miss High and Mighty, can clear off and look down your pretty nose at some other poor sod that deserves your pity. I don't want you round here and neither does me child.'

Bella was angry now. As Mary went to shut the door, she put her hand on it. 'I ain't pitying you, far from it. I wouldn't waste me time. But if it wasn't for my Micky preventing *him* from bashing your head in, you wouldn't be here now, even though you won't admit it. He would have

277

killed you, me and Terry too if Micky hadn't stopped him.'

Bella felt Michael's eyes on her. She was ashamed of what she was saying and the heated words of their quarrel. How could she explain all the things that had happened in the past? He was just a little boy and this woman was his grandmother. If Teresa really was Mary's daughter, then her blood was the same as his.

Mary squinted at the little figure standing beside her. 'Your kid?'

Bella nodded. 'This is Michael.'

'Like peas in a pod, ain't they? Teresa and him. Same eyes, same hair.' She laughed coarsely. 'You and me and both with kids. Except you are standing there in all your finery and him beside you looking like a little prince, whilst my poor girl has only rags. And all because of what you took away from my Jack who is now dead and buried.' She screwed up her eyes. 'But a fat lot you care about us and that's the truth!'

'He's *dead?*'

Mary Doyle nodded. 'He was nothing but a cripple anyway. Drank his bleedin' self to death and left me with a fat belly, the result of which I'm forced to go out scrubbing floors, despite me poor health.'

'Mum?' The small voice came from the darkened inside of the house.

'What do you want now, girl?'

Bella watched as Teresa slowly appeared.

'I've wet me knickers.' A pool was forming on the floor at her feet.

A girl with dark hair was singing 'Santa Baby' and trying to sound like Eartha Kitt. Bella was watching her as she drew the attention from the men by twisting her hips in a snake-like dress of silver lamé. Two other girls in fishnet tights and short red skirts were sitting astride a sleigh. The scene was supposed to be set amongst the mountains, but the scenery behind showed green hills and trees dotted with white paint. One of the antlers had fallen off the cardboard reindeer's head.

Bella knew that none of the audience was bothered about detail. The Fortune Club in Soho was a hostess club and the men here had come to enjoy what was on offer, namely the alcohol and women.

Bella felt ridiculously overdressed. She was sitting at the table with Micky, wearing her new dress. It was midnight blue nylon tulle, full skirted, with a velvet bow tied at the back of the strapless bodice. The first cocktail dress she had ever bought. She had gone up West with Dolly to buy it last Saturday whilst Percy had looked after the three children. Now Bella wished she had never gone to the trouble. The club was full of old, sweaty-looking men who were ogling the singer and the two girls. Beside them the hostesses sat drinking champagne. Or what really was, as she knew now, just tonic water and lemonade. She would rather have gone to the cinema to see *The Barefoot Contessa* but she didn't want to refuse Micky when he told her he had a surprise in store.

The girl finished her act and there was a half-hearted applause. Micky's was the loudest as he whistled through his teeth. The girl gazed across and smiled, stepping down from the stage on her high heels and crossing to their table.

'Hello, Micky. Enjoying yourself?'

Micky grinned. 'Bella, this is Suzie.' He nodded to the stage. 'Go on then, give us another song, darlin'.'

Suzie winked and smiled flirtatiously as she left.

Bella's mouth had fallen open. 'What was that all about? Who is she?'

'The entertainment of course.'

'But you know her.'

'Course I do. This is me surprise, Bells, and you should be very proud of your old man. I am now the owner of the Fortune Club. Or at least part owner with old Ivor. Remember him? He used to run Club Afrika. Sold it about a year ago and bought this little gaff. Met him again by pure chance. Came to the garage one day to buy a car.'

'Why should you want to do business with him?'

'Because he's sitting on top of a goldmine. I mean, look around you at the potential. It's a cracker.' Micky's smile faded. 'Well, ain't you gonna congratulate me?'

'What for? I don't like this place, Micky.'

'What do you mean?' he demanded, suddenly sobering up.

'Why buy a club? You could have got another garage.'

'I don't want another garage. I want this.'

Bella looked into his eyes. 'Clubs are risky as Ronnie found out.'

Micky glared at her. 'Before you start on about Ronnie, I've already told him about this.'

'What did he say?'

'What does it matter what he said? Why are you always so bothered about his opinion? I bought into the Fortune with my own cash and Ronnie has no part in it. This ain't nothing like the Blue Moon. It's too small for anyone to want to take over. It will do me just fine, until such time as I want to spread me wings. But one day, I promise you, the Fortune is going to make us very rich.'

'I don't want to be rich if the money is from places like this.'

Suddenly Micky got up. 'You are one stroppy mare, Bells.'

She looked round them, embarrassed at the disturbance they were making. 'I'm your wife and I don't like you shouting at me.'

'You might be my wife,' Micky retaliated, 'but you ain't my minder. Now get your coat, we're leaving.'

Without speaking, Bella rose from her chair and walked sedately out to the cloakroom. But inside she was shaking.

Bella watched Micky drive away. The wheels of the car screeched as he sped off in the darkness, missing Lenny's car by inches. He had driven fast all the way home in an angry silence. She had expected him to come in with her but after she had climbed out he had driven off.

She was worried now. Was he going back to the Fortune Club? Was he going to see Suzie again?

Bella shivered in the cold December night. She

looked up at the big house and regretted Ronnie's decision to move out. He now lived in rooms with Joyce and she knew he was the only one who could influence Micky. What had he said to Micky when he told him about the Fortune? Whatever it was, Micky hadn't changed his mind.

Slowly she descended the steps. Light spilled out from the window and as she opened the door Lenny and Gina looked round. They were sitting in front of the big open fire.

'Where's Micky?' Gina asked.

'He had to go back to the garage.' It was a lie but the only one she could think of.

'At this time of night?'

'He forgot to lock it.'

Lenny got up and came towards her. He looked smart in his dark suit and waistcoat, his black wiry hair glistening with brilliantine. 'Is there anything the matter, love?'

'No, nothing.'

Gina got up and pulled her towards the fire. 'Sit down and tell us all about your night. I'll just get you a nice cuppa.'

'I could do with that. How's Michael?'

'He went to sleep all right, despite Lenny telling him a story about a giant.'

Bella smiled. 'Oh, he would have liked that.'

Lenny urged her to the chair. 'Warm up, love, you look frozen.' He took her coat and hung it up, returning to join her at the fireside.

'Thank you for baby-sitting,' Bella said as Gina returned with a tray of tea. Gina had put on the standard lamp and a cosy glow enveloped them, spilling light over Michael's toys and his books on the table.

'Did you have a good evening?' Lenny asked.

'Not bad. We just went for a drink that's all.'

'But you was all dressed up,' Gina exclaimed. 'A pub ain't very exciting.'

Bella decided not to say anything about the Fortune Club and just sipped her tea as she listened to Lenny telling her about Michael. She knew he loved children and Gina wasn't keen to have any which was one reason why she wouldn't consider marriage, or so she said.

'He's such a bright little spark, knows words in books already, don't he, Gina?'

Gina nodded, widening her black eyes. 'Now who is this Teresa he keeps on about? All evening all we heard was Teresa this and Teresa that.'

'What did he say?'

'That she's his best friend and when you walked her home, Teresa's mummy got cross. And then the poor little kid weed herself. Is that true?'

Bella nodded. 'You'll never guess who Teresa's mother turned out to be.'

'No, but she sounds a mouthy cow.'

'It was Mum.'

'*Your* mum?' Gina almost dropped her cup. 'No, I don't believe it.'

'Nor did I at first. This little girl Teresa is the spitting image of Michael. It didn't register at all as we walked her home. Why should it? It was the last thing I expected. When Mum opened the door I was staggered. She said they got re-housed by the council in this prefab in Collier Street as they've knocked down number three.' She paused. 'And by all accounts, Jack is dead.'

'Dead? Are you sure?'

Bella nodded.

Gina's smile was genuine. 'Well, that's one bit of good news anyway. Has she shacked up with anyone else?'

'I don't think so. She's very bitter though and blames me and Micky for everything.'

'That's ridiculous!' Gina exploded. 'Jack Router was a bastard and she must know it.'

'I don't think she does. She even said it was me who walked out, not the other way round.'

'Well, give me five minutes with her and I'll soon put her right. And I mean that an' all. I don't know the woman, but I do know what she did to her kids. Don't forget, I was the one who picked up the pieces and put them together again.'

'Is Teresa really *his* daughter?' Lenny asked, getting a word in for the first time.

Bella nodded.

'Does young Michael know who she is?'

'He don't really understand. He's only five yet.'

'Course he is, poor little mite.'

'What's this little girl like, then?' Gina asked curiously.

'She looks just like Michael. But she isn't cared for, washed or fed properly.' Bella looked down at her lovely blue cocktail dress that seemed even more inappropriate now than it felt at the club. *All her finery*, Mary had flung at her. The words lay heavy on her conscience.

'Did you give them money?' Gina guessed disapprovingly.

'A bit. She says she has to go out scrubbing floors and by the look of the place she doesn't have much.'

'You know you ain't responsible for yer mum, don't you?' Lenny said kindly.

Bella sipped her tea, knowing that whatever anyone said, she did feel responsible. It was her own blood, her little half-sister and aunt to Michael.

Gina sighed, pushing back the elegant wave of black hair that fell across her face. 'I suppose you know what you're doing.'

Bella looked at them both. 'I wish you had seen the state of that little girl. It was heartrending.'

'She will use that kid to manipulate you,' Gina warned.

'I know. But I'm not a complete fool.'

Lenny smiled gently. 'You're far from that, love. Now, we should let you go to bed and be on our way home. Is it worth us waiting for Micky?'

'No, it's late, you go.' She didn't want to tell them what had happened at the Fortune as Gina would throw a fit. It would be one too many outbursts to take in one day. She needed to be quiet now, kiss her son goodnight and then she would sit down and think. Decide on what to do next.

At school the next day, Bella was dismayed to see Teresa dressed in the same old clothes.

'Are you going to walk home with me?' she asked.

'Can we, Mum?' Michael asked.

Bella nodded and the two children joined

hands as they made their way back to Collier Street.

When the door opened Mary was holding on to the wall. Her face was dirty and her eyes looked as though they had fallen to the back of her head.

'Are you all right?' Bella asked.

'What's it to you if I'm not?'

'I was only asking.'

'I'm frozen and I've got a rotten chest.' She coughed loudly. 'There's no heat in the house and the money you gave me I spent on food. Never a mouthful for meself but gave it all to her. Didn't I, Teresa?'

The little girl looked sadly up at Bella. 'I got bread an' dripping for me supper. It was lovely.'

'Did you buy any clothes?' Bella asked.

'What? How am I supposed to walk all the way up the market after a hard day scrubbing floors?'

'I'll take her then,' Bella offered, 'and save you the trouble.'

'We ain't no charity cases–' Mary began, but Bella put up her hand.

'You know I can help you and I will. But I won't stand here and argue. I've had enough of that. It's either yes or no, your choice.'

Mary's white face reddened as she spluttered, 'You've still got a tongue like a knife.'

'If I have, you know where I got it from.'

'Ah, have it your own way, girl. I don't give a toss what you do.'

'I'll call for her at nine.'

Mary laughed scornfully. 'You'll be lucky. I don't draw breath till noon.'

'Teresa can open the door and let herself out.'

Bella smiled down at the child. 'Would you like to come to the market with Michael and me?'

The little girl looked up at her mother. 'Can I, Mum?'

Mary shrugged and walked back into the house.

'See you in the morning then, Teresa.'

The child nodded and watched them go.

Michael took hold of Bella's hand as they walked back to Piper Street. 'Can we have pie and mash at the market?' he asked.

'Yes, and lemonade too.'

'With Auntie Dolly and Anne and Irene?'

'Yes, of course.'

As they walked home Bella realised she had almost forgotten the quarrel with Micky at the Fortune Club. And the fact that he hadn't come back last night.

Michael and Teresa were playing around the stalls. It was Saturday and already very busy. Bella had arrived at the market before Dolly in order to shop at the clothes stall. She had found a nice assortment for Teresa and the stallholder had let them change by the warmth of an open brazier. The lady helped Bella by holding a sheet around them so they had some privacy.

Bella would have liked to wash Teresa first but she had no way of doing so. It was a cold December day, not wet as it had been all month, but very seasonal and excitement was in the air. Christmas was coming and all the stalls were covered in holly and some in sparkling decorations. When Teresa was dressed, Michael peeped round the sheet.

'Are you finished yet?'

'Don't look yet,' Teresa giggled.

'All you need is a pair of shoes,' Bella remarked as she gathered Teresa's old clothes and placed them in her bag. She would give them a good wash when she got home. There were always dozens of second-hand shoes at the market. Lots of them were deformed where people had corns or bunions. Some didn't have proper soles, just lots of Blakies. But there was an occasional bargain and as Bella looked at Teresa, she was pleased with what she had found. 'You look very pretty in your new coat.'

'I like blue.'

'It will be just right for school in the cold weather.'

'It's the right size. I ain't never had one that fits before. It feels funny.'

Bella knew what she meant. As a child, she had lived in the same old clothes that were never washed or mended. It was only when she started work at Dixons that she had been able to take a pride in her appearance.

'Go with Michael and play, but don't go far. Some new friends will be arriving soon for you to meet.'

'Who are they?' Teresa asked doubtfully.

'Two nice little girls the same age as you.'

The lady put away the sheet and smiled as the two children ran off. 'You can have that little lot for two bob, dear.'

'Thanks. I'll need some more as well. A navy blue gym slip and raincoat in the same size and a change of underwear.'

'Leave it to me, do your shopping and I'll sort them out.'

Bella was crossing to the pie and mash stall when she saw Dolly. The two girls looked immaculately dressed in their identical pink coats. Michael and Teresa came running up. The four children gazed at one another. In a matter of seconds Michael was introducing his new friend to Dolly's girls.

'Well I'm blowed,' Dolly gasped, her hazel eyes wide under her big brown hat with a velvet bow. 'So Teresa is your half-sister?'

Bella had poured out her story as they sat on upturned boxes watching the children play. 'Yes, she is.'

'She has your big brown eyes and same colour hair, just a shade more coppery. And she could be Michael's sister too, except he has blue eyes.'

'Dolly, I felt terrible when she wet her drawers. Mum didn't even notice.'

'Oh, Bella, the poor little soul.'

'I asked the woman on the stall to throw away her underwear. It was filthy.'

'She looks lovely now.'

'I wanted to wash her. I don't suppose she's had one in weeks. That's why the other kids were laughing. I got a knot in my stomach. It brought back everything.'

'What does Micky say about it?'

Bella looked guilty. 'I haven't had time to tell him. Well, that's not exactly the truth. He just hasn't been home to tell.'

'What's he doing then?' Dolly looked anxious.

'He's bought a club.'

'A what?'

'A hostess club in Soho called the Fortune.'

'But what about the garage?'

'Milo is running it with Terry.'

'What does Terry do?'

'He washes and cleans the cars.'

'You're in a difficult position, Bella.'

'I know. Micky and me had an awful row over the club. Since then we haven't really talked. He says he has to work late at the club and what makes it worse–' Tears filled Bella's eyes and she brushed them quickly away. 'There's this woman he introduced me to, a girl called Suzie. She's a singer and very glamorous. I know she's sweet on Micky.'

'How do you know that?' Dolly stopped drinking her tea.

'It was the way she looked at him.'

'You can't know for sure, Bella,' Dolly said gently. 'You might just be jealous.'

Bella nodded fiercely. 'I am. I'm extremely jealous. So jealous I could cheerfully strangle her.'

'Don't say that.'

'Are you ever jealous of Percy?'

'He's never given me reason to be.'

Bella thought how she had once looked down her nose at the Taylor family. They had seemed unexciting and boring. She thought of Ray who had annoyed her when he had tried it on, which was, she now admitted, only natural. He wasn't that bad really but she hadn't been able to see his good points. The fact that he wanted a wife, a home and a family, which, like Dolly, made him a sensible and normal person. And as she knew now from Dolly, Ray idolized his little girl and boy and adored his wife.

Micky was at the other end of the scale. She had always known he hadn't wanted to be tied down. She always feared he had only married her because she had fallen pregnant. Is this what happened in a marriage when one person loved more than the other?

Dolly was staring at her. 'I thought Micky was happy selling cars.'

'So did I.'

'He'll soon lose interest in the club.'

'I hope you're right.'

Dolly squeezed her arm. 'Look on the bright side. You haven't got to worry about money, at least, not like you used to. Michael is a happy little boy and loved by his dad and his uncles. You can spend time with him and not have to go out to work. Micky's only bought a business you don't approve of and that's not the end of the world. Really, there is a lot to be grateful for.'

Bella nodded slowly. 'I am grateful, but I love him and want more of a family life. I knew Micky was stubborn when I married him but in my heart I always thought I could change him.'

'But what would you want to change him for if you loved him?' Dolly asked innocently.

It was a good question and Bella had no ready answer. In fact it was a perfect piece of logic that could only come from someone like Dolly. From a woman who loved her husband unconditionally and was loved back the same way.

Chapter Twenty

'Oh, it was a lovely speech,' Sean said wistfully as he stood at the kitchen sink. He was peeling potatoes, a pinafore tied round his waist. Next to him, Ashley stirred custard in a mixing bowl. It was Christmas Day and they were discussing the Queen's Speech, as they drank frothy ginger beer from pint glasses.

'When she said about the rain and wind beating on the windows and the peacefulness inside our homes, it was as if she was here too,' Bella agreed as she polished the cutlery with a cloth.

'I'm not a lover of the old castor oils,' Ashley commented, transferring the bowl to the table where he poured the custard into glass dishes. 'But I must admit she was quite poetic when she said that bit about the light streaming from a Nazareth cottage. Though I don't suppose she's got a clue what the interior of a cottage looks like. Not living in a palace all her life.'

'Well she can't be that out of touch, can she? She baths in a bath same as us. Cleans her mincers like us.' Sean turned to wipe his wet hands on the towel and grinned. 'Sits on the karzy like us.'

'Probably got a gold-plated seat though,' Ashley added dryly.

Sean hooted. 'What difference would that make? She ain't got a gold bum, has she?'

Bella laughed as she listened, gathering together

the knives, forks and spoons and taking them into the front room. Dinner was being eaten at the big polished table, opened to its fullest extent. As usual, Sean and Ashley had cooked lunch for all the family. For years they had eaten together on Christmas Eve, but since Micky had owned the garage, the meal had been transferred to the twenty-fifth. Micky worked late on Christmas Eve but always took Christmas Day off.

Bella heard the front door open and rushed into the hall.

'Hello, beautiful.' Micky stood there, with young Michael sitting astride his shoulders. They had been getting ready downstairs in the airey and Bella was overjoyed that Micky was taking so much interest in his son. Last night Micky had played Father Christmas and delivered a train set into Michael's room wrapped in a large pillow-case. Then he had drawn her close as they watched their sleeping child, imagining his excitement when he woke.

It had been a wonderful moment. Later, they had made love and this too had been so special. He had held her in his arms and told her he loved her. She hoped their quarrelling was over. And after her talk with Dolly, she had felt more grateful than ever for her life now. Micky lowered young Michael to the ground and he ran into her arms. She hugged him, breathing in his smell, Sunlight and water and some of Micky's shaving soap. He was dressed like his father in a clean white shirt and tie.

'Is dinner ready yet?' Michael asked eagerly.

'Nearly.'

'Where's Uncle Sean?'

'In the kitchen. And Uncle Terry's upstairs. You can go up and tell him dinner's nearly ready if you like.'

Michael ran off eagerly and Micky drew her into his arms. 'You look good enough to eat,' he whispered, bending down and kissing her. She slipped her arms around his neck and his lips softly grazed her cheek. 'You happy, Bells?'

'I'm happy.'

'I'm taking you out tomorrow. You and the nipper. Terry too if you want. We're going for a spin in the country.'

'Are you home, then?'

'It's Christmas. No one works at Christmas.'

'I wouldn't have been surprised if you did.'

'Come on now, girl. Let's bury the hatchet.'

'It's just that we love you, Micky, and want more time with you. Is that so unreasonable?'

He held her away from him. 'I'm going to make a New Year's resolution. To keep that lovely smile on your face. I'll put it in writing if you like. Now, come here and shut up while I kiss you.'

They were still kissing when a key slotted into the lock of the front door just as young Michael ran down the stairs with Terry following.

'Caught in the act,' Micky grinned as Ronnie and Joyce entered the hall, their arms full of presents. Bella thought that if Ronnie had been upset over the Fortune he certainly wasn't showing it. There were kisses and hugs all round as they crowded into the front room.

Young Michael jumped up and down excitedly as he was given permission to open his first present. He took the biggest one from under the Christmas tree and began to untie it.

Sean and Ashley rushed in from the kitchen, their faces red with the brandy they had sampled on the quiet. Bella felt a deep sense of wellbeing as she gazed around her. Everyone she loved was here and waiting for a real family Christmas to begin.

Micky was as good as his word. The next day he took them for a drive away from the City and out towards Osterley Park. Wrapped up in their warm winter coats, they stopped for a picnic and Micky and Michael played football. They all drove home flushed with fresh air from their day out. And before bedtime Micky read a long story from one of Michael's favourite books.

The next morning Mickey didn't go to work again. Nor the next. He made breakfast for everyone and even washed and shaved with his son at his side. Bella didn't ask who was looking after the club. She felt so happy she didn't want to break the spell. Her one concern was for Teresa. Was she being washed, fed and dressed in the clothes they had bought from the market? Did they have enough food? Had Mary bought her daughter a Christmas present with the money Bella had left?

Micky was in such a good mood that she was almost tempted to tell him the story. She even thought that young Michael might mention his new school friend. But their days were so busy that Michael seemed to have forgotten all about Teresa.

On the evening before New Year's Eve, whilst Gina and Lenny looked after Michael, Micky drove them out for the evening. They strolled hand in hand along the Embankment and took in the sights. The bridges rose tall over the river and a bright, illuminated Big Ben shone against the navy blue sky. They ate at a cockle stall, sprinkling on plenty of salt and vinegar. When they drove home, Bella laid her head on Micky's shoulder.

Christmas had been wonderful. The time they had shared together had made her feel Micky really loved them. She was going to make a New Year's resolution too. If she could patiently accept Micky's absences, he might be more inclined to spend more time with them. She knew her criticisms annoyed him and from now on she would try to be a more understanding wife.

Snow fell in January, and when Michael returned to school the children were building snowmen or playing snowballs in the playground.

'Teresa ain't here, Mum,' Michael wailed.

Bella looked too but there was no small figure waiting for them.

'Perhaps she's late because of the snow.' The bell rang and all the children went in. Bella kissed Michael and told him to remember to put his coat on at playtime.

Alone, Bella pushed her gloved hands deep in her pockets. For ten minutes she walked up and down the street. Tiny snowflakes landed in her hair and eyelashes, softly covering the path in front of her. Soon she began to grow cold and reluctantly turned for home.

Where was Teresa? What had happened over the holidays? Perhaps she would be at school tomorrow. If she wasn't, then she would go round to Collier Street and see for herself.

By Friday Teresa was still absent. Michael was unhappy that his friend hadn't turned up to school.

'Let's call round, shall we?' Bella suggested.

'Yes, but I don't like her house.'

'There's no other way to find out.'

Hand in hand Bella and Michael walked to Collier Street. The prefabs looked wet and drab and the blocked drains had formed big puddles of dirty water and ice.

'They're not in,' Michael said disappointedly after Bella had knocked several times.

'Let's go round the back.'

Warily they trod over the fallen fence and piles of rubbish half covered in snow. The prefab was covered in green mould. It climbed up the walls like ivy and there were icicles hanging from the broken gutters.

Bella tried to look through one window but she couldn't see anything but darkness. The other window though, was stuck open.

'Teresa?' She could see a figure lying on the floor. 'Is that you?'

'I got a cough.'

'Where's your mum?'

'She ain't here.' Teresa began to cough.

'Can you let me in?' She watched Teresa stand up very slowly.

'I don't like it here,' Michael said as they made their way round to the front of the prefab.

Bella drew him close as they waited. When the door opened Bella was shocked. Teresa stood shivering in an old, soiled nightdress and she looked very thin. Her hair was tangled, full of knots and fell over her gaunt white face.

There was no light and no warmth as Bella helped her back to the dark room. The mattress she was lying on was full of holes and exposed springs and as Bella pulled up the filthy cover a beetle dropped from it and scuttled into the corner.

Bella was angry as well as shocked. What kind of mother would allow her child to suffer like this? Unfortunately she knew the answer.

'When will Mummy be home?' she asked Teresa gently.

'Dunno.'

Michael began crying and Bella hugged him. What as she going to do? A doctor was needed immediately. But she would have to leave Teresa alone again to find one.

Ronnie was coming out of the house when they arrived, both of them breathless and puffing. Full of tears, Michael ran into his open arms.

'What's up, young Michael?' He hugged him tightly.

'Teresa ain't well.'

'Who is Teresa?'

'Me best friend at school.'

'What's wrong with her?' Ronnie's voice was soothing.

'It's a long story, but she's ill and all on her own.

I don't know where her mum is but she sounds bad to me,' Bella told him.

'I'll drive you round to the doctor's,' Ronnie said at once. 'But it will be better if Michael stays here with Sean.'

Bella took her son in her arms. She knew what he had seen today had upset him just as much as it had upset her. 'We won't be long, I promise.'

'Will the doctor make Teresa better?'

'Yes, I'm sure he will.'

When Sean had taken Michael, they climbed in Ronnie's car. 'You'd better be ready for a shock,' Bella said as they drove away. 'This isn't just any little girl, she is a relative, close family, although Michael is too young to understand that at the moment.'

Ronnie took his eyes briefly from the road. 'A relative?'

'She's my half sister,' Bella said quietly. 'Teresa is Mum's little girl.'

He looked astounded. *'Mary Doyle* is her mother?'

'I know it's hard to believe, but yes. They don't live in Bow Street anymore. A year ago the council moved her to Collier Street. Jack died from the drink and left her expecting Teresa. She's only just sent her to school and she was put into Michael's class. That's how it all happened.'

After a pause Ronnie sighed. 'What has Micky to say about all this?'

'I haven't told him yet.'

Ronnie raised his eyebrows. 'I think you should have.'

'I was worried he'd be upset.'

'Has she shacked up with anyone else?'

'No, but she's as bitter as ever and hasn't got two pennies to rub together.'

'Is she still on the game?' he asked sharply.

'No, I don't think so. She said she's scrubbing floors.'

Ronnie drove in silence and Bella knew he was disturbed. He would never forgive Mary for what she had done and she didn't seem to have changed. Now here was another little waif who was suffering what she and Terry had gone through.

Ronnie had to hammer on the door to make Mary open it. Bella gestured to the tall, brown-haired man standing beside her. 'I've brought a doctor for Teresa and you know Ronnie.'

'What d'you bring them here for?'

'I came round while you were out and saw Teresa through the window. You'd better let us in, Mum, as it don't take a genius to know she's ill.' Bella pushed past her and Ronnie and Dr Cox followed.

'There ain't no money for the meter,' Mary growled after them. 'So don't expect any light.'

Ronnie found the meter and filled it. The prefab walls were so damp they had tidemarks running round them. The smell of must was everywhere.

Dr Cox went into the bedroom and bent down to the little girl lying on the mattress. Gently he folded back the dirty cover.

'How long has she been like this?' he asked Mary sharply.

'Oh, she's always coughing. And what do you

expect living in a place like this?' Mary slumped into an old armchair in the corner.

'This place is filthy,' Bella said. 'Don't you ever clean it?'

'In my condition?' Mary laughed derisively. 'Anyway, what's the point? You can't clean away damp. This is how the other half live whilst you eejits enjoy yourselves in your nice posh houses.'

Bella saw her mother was wearing the same old brown coat that she had worn before Christmas. Her hair hung down in matted tangles from her head and her face was grey and unwashed.

'You ain't changed, Mary Doyle.' Ronnie's voice was filled with disgust. 'Not that I believed you ever would.'

'Judge me, would you, you bugger!' Mary pointed a finger stained with nicotine. 'It was you that interfered in my life and took away the only soul that ever cared about Mary Doyle and her kids. You made him a cripple and I'll never forgive you for that. He was my man and he looked after us until you decided to stick your oar in.'

'This child is very sick.' Dr Cox put away his stethoscope. 'She is suffering from malnutrition and neglect and a very bad chest infection.' He stared at Mary. 'Where is her father?'

Mary was too drunk to reply and Dr Cox looked at Bella.

'He's dead.'

'What about relatives, friends?'

'Just me. Teresa is my half-sister.'

He nodded slowly. 'She can't stay here obviously. Her lungs are congested and she'll need penicillin to clear them. If there's nowhere else for her to recuperate I'll admit her to hospital.'

'I'll take care of her,' Bella said at once. 'Just tell me what to do.'

'My girl ain't going nowhere!' Mary shouted suddenly, trying to sit up and pushing the hair from her eyes. 'She's my kid, not yours.'

'So what is your suggestion?' Dr Cox demanded. 'Are you capable of looking after her? Can you provide good food, warmth and care?'

But Mary waved a filthy hand. 'Ah, be off with you, you quack! Can't you see I'm ill meself.'

'Nothing that sobriety won't cure,' he replied, shutting his case with a snap. 'If you fail to co-operate, I shall call the authorities and inform them of the suffering you have imposed on this child.'

'Threats to her are like water off a duck's back,' Ronnie growled as he slid his hand inside his coat. 'There is only one language that Mary Doyle understands.' Opening his wallet he took out a five pound note and dropped it into her lap. Then he walked over to Teresa and lifted her gently into his arms.

'You think money will buy me? *His* money?' Mary cried as they all went out.

'Are you saying you don't want it, then?'

'Jaysus, girl, you have a hard heart. You'd leave your poor mother to fend for herself, would you? Sure, you won't even know if I die.'

Bella felt sick at heart as she left. In spite of everything Mary was still her mother and the ties of blood were strong.

'Here is a prescription and I'll call to see her tomorrow,' Dr Cox told them as Ronnie lay

Teresa on the back seat of the car.

'Thank you for coming, Doctor Cox.'

'It's unimaginable how some people live,' he muttered before he walked to his own car and sped away.

'I hope you know what you're doing,' Ronnie said as they drove back to Piper Street. 'Your mother will milk this situation for all it's worth.'

Bella glanced round at Teresa, covered in that filthy blanket. She knew Ronnie was right. But what could she do?

That night, Bella had Teresa washed, fed and tucked up in a nice warm bed. She wore Michael's spare set of flannelette pyjamas, which had brought the first smile to her face. When she was comfortable, propped up by pillows, Michael brought in his toys.

'She's too tired to play tonight,' Bella whispered when Teresa fell asleep. 'But you'll have plenty of time tomorrow. Now go and say goodnight to Uncle Ron whilst I turn back your covers.'

Bella went into Michael's room and prepared his bed, resting his teddy on the pillow. When he came in, he put his arms round her neck. 'Uncle Ronnie says he'll take me up the park on Sunday.'

'That's nice. Now climb in.'

'Will Teresa be better tomorrow?' he asked as he snuggled down.

'I hope so.' Bella drew the white sheet over him as his eyes began to close.

'When's Daddy coming home?'

'Soon, I hope.'

He yawned. 'I'm not tired yet.'

Bella smiled as she walked to the door. 'You will be soon.'

Outside in the hall she heard coughing. Quietly she went in to the spare room.

'Is me mum gonna be all right?' Teresa asked sleepily.

'Of course she is. It's you that we've got to get better.'

'I didn't want to go to 'ospital. I'm glad I came here.'

'I am too. Now close your eyes and rest.'

Bella returned to the sitting room where Ronnie was sitting by the fire. She sank down in the chair.

'Is there anything I can do to help?' Ronnie asked.

'No, I think she'll sleep now.'

'The doctor said he'd call tomorrow.'

'Yes, he was very good to leave his patients like that.'

Ronnie frowned in the firelight. 'I've seen some bad sights but Collier Street beats most of them.'

'Mum said it was damp when the council put them there.'

Ronnie nodded. 'Prefabs are notorious for it as they were only meant as stopgaps after the war. But it's filthy too, and you can't blame that on the council.'

'Bow Street wasn't much better.'

'As I said earlier she doesn't change.'

Bella glanced at him. 'I don't like the sound of Teresa's chest, Ron. She's very wheezy. It reminds me of how Terry used to be. And he still goes down badly when he gets a cold.'

'How is he doing at the garage?'

Bella smiled. 'He loves it. I don't see much of him now as he's always there. It's his second home and Milo treats him very well, pays him out of his own pocket too, if he's done a good job.'

'It's Micky's job to do that, isn't it?' Ronnie asked, suddenly looking up.

'Micky's not always around on pay-day, so he settles up with Milo when he sees him.' Bella didn't mention that the Fortune was taking up more and more of Micky's time as she sensed it was a sore subject with Ronnie.

Ronnie gave a soft sigh and shrugged. 'Well, Micky knows what he's doing. And Terry seems happy enough.' He stretched his back and stood up. 'I'm off then. When will Micky be home?'

'Oh, soon, I'm sure,' she nodded.

'Do you want me to stay till he does?'

Bella shook her head quickly. 'No, I've got things to do and the dinner to cook.' She walked with him to the door.

'Try not to worry,' he told her gently. 'And if there is anything you want, just ask.'

'Thanks, Ron.'

Bella listened to the sound of his boots on the steps. What would she have done without his help today?

It was past midnight when Micky arrived home. The airey was still warm and the standard lamp was giving out a soft light. He took off his coat and hung it on the back of a chair, flexing his knuckles and stretching his arms as he did so. He felt as though he had run into a brick wall. Which, in a sense he had. The car had glanced him, sending him crashing into the alley and the dustbins, rolling along the cobbles until he'd ended up by the railings. He was cornered then, boxed in when McNee's two heavies climbed out and strode towards him. They would have knocked six bells out of him if Ivor and his mates hadn't come out of the club.

Micky felt the tiredness sweep over him. His body needed time to recover, not that his injuries had affected him last night. The memory of Suzie's hard, firm breasts pressed against him, her lips and her eagerness to please still lingered. He would have to find another gaff though. Her one room was a dump. If he invested in a flat in Soho, she could visit him there. And now that Norman had sold the Aldgate flat to a tight-fisted bookmaker, he needed somewhere else for Leyla. As soon as he had taken care of McNee he would see to it.

Micky stood, massaging his bruised sides and thinking about Leyla, Suzie and the new smoke that was coming in with the Jamaicans. Powerful stuff, their baccy, as he and Suzie could testify. Trouble was, he had lost twenty-four hours from his life whilst smoking it. Now he had to think of an excuse for Bells.

He was about to find himself a beer when he heard a noise, like someone coughing. He moved into the dark passage, following the sounds. He looked in on young Michael who was fast asleep and opened the door of his and Bella's bedroom. The bed was made up with no one it. Puzzled,

Micky continued to the spare bedroom where the coughing noises seemed to have come from.

Bella appeared, closing the door behind her. 'Micky! I didn't hear you come in.'

'Who's in there?' he demanded suspiciously.

'A very sick little girl,' his wife told him softly.

'What's she doing here?'

Bella crooked her finger and whispered, 'Come and sit by the fire and I'll tell you all about it.'

After Micky had eaten his dinner, Bella told him everything. They were sitting by the fire and Micky was frowning into the flames. 'Why didn't you tell me about Mary?'

'I didn't want to upset you.'

'Is she still on the game?'

'No, she's cleaning floors.'

'Huh!' he muttered. 'Are you sure this kid is hers?'

'You've only got to look at her to see she's a Doyle.'

'It's history repeating itself,' he grumbled. 'After what she did to you and Terry, now she's doing it again. At least *he* got his come-uppance and not before time either.'

Bella hadn't told him how bitter Mary had sounded over Jack's death. She knew it would make him angry.

'Is it catching what the kid's got?' he asked.

'No. She's ill because of the damp and dirt they live in. The water is running down the walls and the smell is awful. She didn't even have a bed. I couldn't leave her there, she's me little sister after all.'

'Did the old witch ask after Terry?'

'No.'

'She don't even know if he's alive or dead! All she cares about is getting down the boozer.'

They sat in silence for a while until Bella sat up slowly and said, 'Micky, I've been worried about you. Where've you been?'

He gave her an innocent look. 'At the club, of course.'

'You've been away two days.'

'Now don't start on me, Bells. I've had enough for one week.'

Alarmed, Bella asked, 'Has there been trouble, then?'

He lowered his empty glass to the floor and sat back. 'Yeah, a bit, just don't say I told you so, all right? A couple of locals gave us aggro and we had to show them the door. I stuck around in case they came back, that's all.'

'Were they Billy McNee's men?'

He rolled his eyes. 'Course not. I told you, he won't bother about us.'

'You never know, Micky.'

He sighed impatiently. Micky's brain worked quickly. He hadn't expected to come home to this strange turn of events. How could he use it to his advantage he wondered?

'Look, Bells, I ain't having a go at you about that kid in there, am I? I can see you was in a spot and did the best you could. You never know what's round the corner, the perfect example being your old girl. If I told you last year that a kid sister would appear on the scene you would have laughed in me face, wouldn't you?'

'Yes, but I didn't have a choice in all this, Micky. You did. You needn't have gone in with Ivor.'

'We've been over this before,' he replied irritably, his face angry again. 'The money I earn provides a good life for us, Bells. It allows you to stay at home and look after Michael and not work your fingers to the bone like some have to do. You don't want for nothing, neither does our son. And whilst that little girl is under our roof, neither will she. In fact, I'm willing to bet your old lady has tapped you up already, ain't she?'

Bella nodded, dropping her gaze.

'It's all right, love, don't worry, I know the position you're in. Your mother is skint and you aren't. But she can sniff the ackers a mile off and it wouldn't surprise me if she had all this planned from the start.'

'She didn't Micky. It was me that called on her.'

'Yeah, but how do you know she didn't spot you and Michael at St Nicholas's? She told you herself that she's been a year in Collier Street. Maybe she's been looking for you ever since he pegged it.'

'I never thought of that.'

'Bit of a coincidence all this, ain't it?'

Bella didn't know what to think. Would Mary really be so conniving?

'Picture this. The old sod kicks the bucket. She's on her uppers and ain't exactly coining it in. What does she do next? Go out and find a job like any normal person? You must be joking! Mary Doyle thinks, I'll find me long lost daughter and sponge off her. That crafty old cow is going to use her noddle, despite it being corroded by a lifetime of booze. She ain't got nothing in this world, only you, and she knows it. You are her light at the end of the tunnel so mark my words, you will be dipping into your pocket from here on in.'

Bella was silent. She couldn't argue with Micky's logic because in her heart she knew every word was true.

Suddenly Micky stood up. He reached out and drew her into his arms. 'Come on now, cheer up, I'm just saying watch yourself.'

'Oh, Micky, I know what she is. But there's Teresa to think of now.'

'Yeah, course there is. She's only a defenceless little kid.' He kissed her, stroking her face softly. 'Now, it's late and we've burnt the candle at both ends. Let's go to bed and sleep on it.'

Bella nodded, resting her head on his shoulder. After all that had happened, most men would have refused to have anything to do with Mary Doyle and her child. But Micky was not like most men. How lucky she was to have him.

Chapter Twenty-One

Bella hurried to open the door. A soft April breeze blew down the airey steps sweeping Dolly with it, followed by Anne and Irene. Bella hugged them all tight as they entered the sitting room.

'Where's Michael and Teresa?' the twins chorused.

'Waiting to see you.' Bella took their coats and hats and hung them on the coatstand.

'Are we having tea here?' Irene wanted to know, her curls bouncing around her face.

'It's rude to ask,' Dolly scolded them.

'Course you are,' Bella smiled. 'Go along to the bedroom. All the toys are in there.'

The two girls, identical in their green woollen dresses knitted by Dolly, skipped down the hall to the bedroom. They had been regular visitors during the months that Teresa had been confined to the house.

'What's the latest report from Doctor Cox?' Dolly asked, hanging up her own coat and following Bella into the kitchen.

'He's inclined to think she'll always have a weak chest,' Bella explained as she filled the kettle. 'But she's much better than she was and, thank God, it looks like she's over the worst.'

'Has her mother visited?'

Bella put the kettle on as Dolly sat down at the table. It was set with custard and jellies, cucumber sandwiches and a big sponge cake. 'Only once and then she nearly collapsed from the walk. Sean had to drive her home.'

Dolly paused thoughtfully. 'Did Micky meet her?'

'No. But he's been very generous and offered to buy some furniture for the prefab.'

'That's good of him.'

Bella nodded. 'Yes, I'm not complaining.'

'Oh, go on, why don't you?' Dolly said with a sad smile. 'I do my fair share, don't I?'

Bella frowned as she looked at her friend. 'You

311

never complain about Percy! Only about the price of food or the rents going up, things like that.' Bella sat down and was about to speak again when she saw Dolly's face.

'Oh, Dol, what's the matter?'

'Nothing.' Dolly brought out her hanky and blew her nose. 'Nothing that won't mend.'

'What do you mean?'

'Percy's lost his job.'

Bella gasped. 'At Burlingtons?'

'Yes, they've gone to the wall.'

'An old firm like that?'

'It's awful, isn't it? But you see, there are bigger and better companies outside of London that are cheaper and deliver nationally.'

'But Burlingtons are solid, like the Bank of England.'

'Yes, but some of the old island firms who wouldn't change their methods are not prepared to keep up with the times.' Dolly's voice wavered. 'Their situation is worse than we thought and Percy doesn't even get severance pay as there's nothing left in the pot.'

Bella felt very sad for her friends. 'Could he get a job at Billingsgate? He'd have to travel up, of course, but you've got the car.'

'Yes, it's worth a try, even though the petrol would be expensive.'

'If it wasn't what he wanted, would he try another trade?'

Dolly nodded. 'Yes, but Percy ain't used to labouring and that's all he'd get on the island. There's jobs going at West India Docks, loading ships. But he would only take an unskilled job if nothing else turned up as it's half his usual pay. You see, we bought our house thinking he was safe at Burlingtons and there would be a chance of promotion.'

'How are you managing?' Bella said quietly.

Dolly went red. 'Me Mum and Dad have loaned us twenty-five pounds.'

'What about food?'

'I've pawned me engagement ring. The one we bought in Oxford Street.' Tears sprang to Dolly's eyes again. 'I didn't want to, but it was the only way.'

'Oh, Dolly, I wish you'd told me. I would have loaned you the money.'

'That's very kind of you, Bella, but we'll manage. As you know I'm very thrifty. I make everything we wear, we grow our own vegetables and I'm very careful with the pennies.'

Bella grasped her friend's hand. 'But Dolly, if you're ever in a tight spot please come to me.'

'I hope it never comes to that.' Dolly changed the subject quickly. 'Look at this lovely spread! And the cake – did you bake it?'

'Teresa and Michael helped.'

'She can get up and do things now?'

'Yes, Doctor Cox said it's good for her to move and shift the congestion, but she does get tired.'

'When will she go home?'

'Not until she's completely better. With TB being rife on the island a few years ago, I won't take any chances. I've written to the council and so has Doctor Cox, saying the prefab needs fumigating and decorating. Until that's done, she's staying here.'

'You'll miss her when she goes.'

'Yes, it's like she's always lived here. But, I told myself from the start not to get attached.' Bella sighed inwardly. She wasn't the only one who would miss Teresa when she returned home. Michael and Teresa had become inseparable, liking the same things, reading the same books and sharing the same sense of humour. They got on so well that it seemed as though they were brother and sister.

'Do they know they're related yet?' Dolly asked.

'I told them that Mary is Michael's granny and Teresa is his aunt, but I didn't go into detail. I thought I'd wait until I was asked to answer any questions.'

'And to think we were discussing what to do as regards telling Michael he had a granny. It was as if someone above was listening and helped sort it all out.'

Bella nodded firmly. 'One day I'll take Michael back and show him Bow Street, where his mother and uncle were born and his granny lived.'

'Dad said he walked round that way last week,' Dolly told her then. 'The ground is as flat as a pancake where your cottage was. There's a sign up saying it's been sold for development. To think that it was once people's homes, where families like yours lived and old Mr Billings and Rita Moult. I expect some awful flats, as small as rabbit hutches will be built there instead.'

Bella didn't know how she felt about that. Bow Street had been her home even if it had been a derelict cottage she'd lived in. But the memories she had of it weren't happy. Even Dolly, her best and oldest friend, didn't really know what it was like to live there. Perhaps if she and Terry had had some memories of a father, or even some information about him, it would have forged some kind of link. But Mary said she didn't know who their father was and, more to the point, didn't care. They had been used to different men appearing on the scene and when Jack Router moved in, he had been the worst of them all. So all in all, she wouldn't be sad to see a change. If a block of flats was built there, they would create new memories for the families that lived in them and hopefully happier ones.

Dolly tapped her on the arm and she jumped. 'Bella, our Ray was asking after you the other day when he came round. He's on a week's holiday and visiting with his family.'

'How are they?'

'Got another one on the way.'

Bella grinned. 'He's a fast worker.'

'He was always keen on you, though.'

Bella giggled. 'It would have been funny being your sister-in-law.'

Dolly's eyes widened. 'I'm glad you ain't. They live all the way out at Ramsgate!'

'I couldn't imagine being anywhere else except here in Piper Street,' Bella confessed. 'I've known this house all me life. Just like you. I've known you from when we started school.'

Dolly's eyes moistened again. 'I hope we don't have to move away.'

Bella's jaw dropped. 'Is that likely?'

'Only if we can't afford the house.'

Bella was trying to absorb what Dolly was

telling her as the children came running in. Dolly and Percy must be in serious trouble for her to say that. Was it a sign of the times that things were getting worse in the country?

Bella watched as Dolly drew Teresa on her lap. What would she do if they had to say goodbye? It was then that Bella realized how much Dolly's friendship meant to her.

'Sean and Ashley want to buy the flat above the shop,' Ronnie said as he and Joyce strolled arm in arm in Island Gardens.

'They've saved up enough?' Joyce asked in surprise as they sat on the bench near the entrance to the foot tunnel. It was a soft May day and Ronnie was eager to gain a whole-hearted yes from Joyce or, if she really wanted to end their affair, a definite no. He would be devastated if it was the latter, but he couldn't go on like this. He wanted kids, he wanted a family. He was thirty-one and he didn't want to be too old to play football with his son. Being with young Michael so frequently had made him think seriously about the future. His property business was expanding, he had saved a fair wedge since selling the Blue Moon. And now that Sean was settled and on his way to his first fortune, Ronnie felt as though he was free. He actually knew what he wanted out of life. He didn't like living in rooms and he didn't like the fact they were living in what Joyce called happy sin. He wanted permanence, security, the old-fashioned values his mum and dad had taught him.

Ronnie nodded. 'I'm signing over the deeds

next week.'

'That quick?'

'Well, you see, I've got an ulterior motive.'

Joyce looked at him and smiled her lovely smile. She was a good-looking woman, everything he could want in a female companion. They knew each other like books, he could trust her one hundred per cent and she him. The physical attraction was there – if not red-hot it was still warm. All that could be added was they made it legal and she could bear him a son, continue his name.

'Come on then, spit it out.' She looked at him with those dark, knowing eyes and he noticed for the first time the little lines that grew around them. Neither of them were getting any younger, he was the first to admit it. But she was still a stunner was his Joyce, the bees' knees. And he wanted to let her know it.

'Joyce,' he said, taking a deep breath, 'this is going to come as a shock to you, but I don't want to buy a gaff in the sticks. What I really want is to move back to Piper Street.'

Joyce looked at him in surprise. Her eyes went over his face, as she unconsciously stroked her black hair, cut to the nape of her neck and lying softly on her cheeks. She was wearing her dark purple suit, her colour, and Ronnie thought once more how good it was to have her beside him. 'But what about all those plans you had? Bromley, you thought, or even across the water, Blackheath perhaps.'

'I know and it's what I thought I wanted at the time.'

317

'And you don't now?'

Ronnie could never quite guess Joyce's reaction, which was one reason why he loved her so much. 'That's about the size of it.' He slid his finger inside his collar and loosened it. 'Poplar ain't me home, Joyce, nor would Bromley or Blackheath be. The only place I'm truly happy is on the island. And when Sean and Ashley move out, the old gaff will be empty except for Micky and Bella downstairs. Seems a waste to ... to, well, not live in it.'

'But ain't that a backward step, Ron? We could live anywhere we want,' Joyce said in a puzzled tone. 'You are a man of means and I've got enough put by to see me through to a ripe old age without working again. Putting our cash together we could afford somewhere a bit stylish.'

Ronnie sighed heavily, stretching his arm along the back of the bench. 'I'm not so sure about all the frills and flounces now. There was a time when living in a posh house and driving a big motor meant a lot, because it would say I was a success. But since I've been doing up places and putting families back in them, it's scratched the itch inside me. Sounds daft I know, but when I look into their faces and they shake my hand, that is what counts. I give them back their roots and I've discovered I want mine back too.'

Joyce smiled easily. 'You're going soft in your old age, Ron.'

'Maybe I am.'

'You've changed, you know. Take the Fortune for instance. I thought you'd blow your top when Micky bought it. Instead you shook his hand and wished him luck.'

'It would only have sounded like sour grapes if I hadn't,' Ronnie replied with a shrug. 'And anyway, I'm not my brother's keeper anymore.'

'You were once.' Joyce touched his hand. 'What's happened to the man who wouldn't let go?'

'Was I that stubborn, Joyce?' Ronnie asked a little shocked.

'A bit,' she told him gently. 'But your grip of iron is what I've admired about you. Your brothers always came first and everything else after.'

'Including you?'

She nodded. 'Yes, especially me.'

'Joyce, you know I love you.'

'And I love you, Ron. But you are telling me something today that I'll have to think about. For the first time in a lot of years, I'm not sure we can compromise.'

Ronnie felt his stomach lurch. He knew he didn't see himself as others saw him. He also knew – belatedly – that he had tried too hard with Micky and Sean. But Sean moving out had suddenly made him realize what a home meant. Perhaps Sean and Micky had to leave him before he could find himself? But to be alone and without Joyce? Now that was a different kettle of fish.

'Would Piper Street be a come-down for you?' he asked sincerely. 'The old gaff ain't up to much I'll admit.'

'I'm not a snob, Ron.'

'But you fancied more?'

'To be honest, I don't know.'

'That's good then. I'm in with a sporting

319

chance.' He took hold of her hand, felt the tiny bones of her fingers inside her soft skin and forced himself to go on. 'I want a family of me own, Joyce. A son would be wonderful, but a daughter just as good, 'specially if she looked like you.'

She gazed into his eyes, her face sad although she was laughing and her head was shaking. 'Ronnie, you're mad. I'm too old for a baby. And even if I did conceive and give birth, I'd have to look after it. Can you honestly see me as a mother?'

Ronnie nodded. 'Yes, I can.'

She frowned. 'And when it got old enough I'd have to tell it what I once did for a living. That its mother was a Madam, a brothel owner, amongst other things.'

'And I'll make sure he's proud of that fact.'

Joyce laughed, her voice shaking as she stammered, 'Ronnie, what's happening to you?'

'I've fallen in love.'

A tear escaped from her eye as she lifted her hands and lay them on his shoulders. 'You are a good man, Ronnie Bryant, the best. But the odds aren't in my favour. I can't see myself as a housewife, a mother and I can't–'

'I can.' Ronnie pulled her close and kissed her, keenly aware of her softness and her warmth and loving her all the more because she was vulnerable. 'Marry me, Joyce. This time I really mean it.'

She was half crying, half laughing when she asked, 'You didn't mean it before then?'

'I would have married you years ago given half

320

the chance. But I'll admit I didn't want it then as much as I do now.'

She took out her hanky and wiped her cheeks. Looking under her wet lashes, she smiled. After what seemed like an eternity she said quietly, 'Oh, Ron, I'm speechless for once.'

Ronnie pulled her against him, his heart pounding like a train. In spite of the glances from the afternoon strollers, he kissed her as though he'd never kissed her before. 'So that's a yes?' he whispered urgently.

Joyce pulled away, staring at him with her dark, serious eyes. 'I must be mad, but...' she nodded, 'it's a yes.'

Ronnie pulled her to her feet. Kissing her passionately, he gave a loud shout of joy. The little kids in the sandpit were giggling and he laughed back at them. He wanted to tell everyone that he was going to marry the most wonderful woman in the world.

Teresa and Michael had gone next door for the morning. Daisy Brown was a piano teacher and had a lovely upright piano. She was teaching all the children their scales.

Bella had asked Terry to go with her to Collier Street.

'Can't,' he kept repeating stubbornly, even though it was his day off from the garage.

'Mum would like to see you.'

'Going to Sean's,' he just said over and over again.

Bella knew he liked to sweep up the hair and do all the odd jobs for Sean. 'You can go to the shop after,' she assured him. 'Be a good boy now and come with me. I'll buy you some nougat on the way.'

In the grocer's, everyone was talking about the election. Sir Anthony Eden, the new Tory Prime Minister, was glibly promising people they would soon be able to buy their own homes. East Enders were wondering when and if that could ever happen. Why was the working class represented by a toff who knew nothing about them? If the Prime Minister lived on the island for a week, it would be a lesson in life. But wealthy people shied away from the poor. It was better to arrive at decisions in the comfort of parliament and the discreet interiors of gentlemen's clubs.

Bella thought about the prefab. Had the council called and done as she had asked in her many letters? The fumigation was essential to Teresa's return, not to mention getting rid of the damp.

As they entered Collier Street, Bella saw a man dressed in overalls. He was working outside her mother's, pouring what looked like milk into a bucket. When he saw Bella and Terry, he stopped work. 'Afternoon,' he nodded, tilting back his cap.

Bella smiled. 'Are you from the council?'

'Indeed I am.'

'Oh, that's good. We've been waiting for you to come.'

'Well, I'm here now, ain't I? Mind yer nice clothes now, 'cos this stuff is diabolical. Can rot your skin if you ain't used to it. I'm giving it a second dousing, just to make sure I've got all the little buggers.'

Mary appeared on the doorstep and folding her arms, frowned at Terry. 'So this is me long lost son, is it?'

Bella pushed Terry forward. 'Say hello, Terry.'

'What's the matter with him?' Mary demanded when Terry refused to speak. 'Ain't he got a voice?'

'He's shy.' Bella didn't want to embarrass Terry. 'Can we come in?'

Mary shrugged and glanced at the man from the council. 'You stopping for tea, Gus?'

'Don't mind if I do.'

They all went inside. Bella was amazed at the transformation. All the doors had been painted a nice cream colour. There was even some new wallpaper on the walls. She was pleased to see that her letters to the council, accompanied by the doctor's entreaty, had resulted in action.

Bella also noted the new furniture had arrived; beds and wardrobes, a couch for the living area and a small square table and four wooden chairs for the kitchen.

Mary led the way to the kitchen. 'Sit down, I'll put the kettle on.'

Brushing down his overalls, Gus took a sheet of newspaper from his pocket and placed it on the chair. 'I'd offer to take off me boots, but more would come out of them than's in the bucket outside.'

Terry sat beside Bella. He was still very quiet and Bella could tell nothing from his expression. It was so warm inside the prefab that her summer frock clung to her. Were the mugs that Mary was lining up on the drainer, clean? Or home to old dregs as they used to be at Bow Street?

'So when will you be finished the fumigation?' Bella asked Gus politely as a mug landed heavily on the table in front of her and the tea splashed over the sides.

'End of this week.' Gus gulped his drink, blinking his small, friendly eyes.

'How's my poor sick girl?' Mary asked.

'Doctor Cox said she can come home soon. But how long will it take for these fumes to wear off?'

'Give it a week,' Gus replied, realizing it was only him that could answer the question. 'Meanwhile keep the windows open, let in the fresh air and you'll never know I've been here.'

'Haven't got much food,' Mary grumbled. 'Ain't been well enough to go out and I've got no money.'

'You know I'll see to all that.' Bella felt embarrassed in front of Gus.

'I'm a vegetable man meself,' he said suddenly. 'Got an allotment, a few flowers and greens. I'll bring some bits with me termorra if you like. In fact, if you want, I'll plant a few spuds out the back. Nice to just go out and pick 'em for yourself and the kid.'

Mary was smiling again and quickly Bella finished her tea. She felt they were in the way here. 'We'd better be going.'

Terry stood up quickly, Bella knew he was anxious to leave. It was as if Mary was a complete stranger to him.

'Does that boy ever say anything?' Mary demanded loudly.

'Sometimes. As I said he's just shy.' She smiled at Gus. 'It was nice to meet you.'

He nodded, standing up politely. 'You too, missus.'

On the corner of Collier Street, Bella looked up at her brother. 'Are you all right, Terry?'

'Yer.'

'You didn't say very much.'

'Goin' to Sean's.'

Bella sighed. He had taken to Teresa like a duck to water, as though she had always been part of the family. But this meeting had upset him. However, it was something he would have to get used to and in time she was sure he would. 'Well, you'd better get along then.'

'Frew the tunnel,' he responded like a little child. 'Terry goin' frew the tunnel.'

Bella smiled. It was the most Terry had said all day, but that was Terry. She went on her toes to kiss his cheek. 'Here you are, take the nougat with you.'

Terry's eyes lit up as she pushed the small brown paper bag in his pocket. 'Go straight to Sean's, won't you?' she was careful to remind him.

Terry nodded and she watched him walk away, taking the road to Island Gardens, where he would walk through the foot tunnel over to Greenwich. She waited till he was out of sight. He was twenty years old but he was a kid mentally. At least now he could be trusted to go to places on his own. He no longer dropped cigarettes or started fires. Working at the garage had made him much more responsible. She smiled as she saw

325

him disappear.

It would take time for him to trust Mary again, but it would happen one day. To think that he had been the one who didn't want to leave Bow Street! 'Terry don't want to run away,' he'd said over and over again. Now she was sure he would never want to return there, even if the cottage was still standing.

Bella arrived back at the airey and found Gina there. As she followed Bella inside, Gina looked around. 'Well, I can see he's not here,' she sighed as she collapsed into a chair. 'But then I didn't think he would be.'

'Who's not here?' Bella asked in confusion.

'My Lenny.'

'Why should he be here?'

'It's a long story. Where are the kids?'

'Next door until two o'clock.'

Gina looked very pale. Bella could see it was taking a great effort to speak. 'Lenny's gone. He walked out and took his suitcase with him.'

'Gone where?' Bella gasped.

'We had another row over the café. He's always saying he's fed up with being a skivvy at my beck and call. He said he couldn't stand it any longer.'

'How long has he felt like that?'

Gina lifted her shoulders. 'I don't know.' She looked exhausted as she shook her head. 'Yes, I do. The answer is he's never liked café work. You know that. I suppose I have got a quick tongue and I don't suffer fools gladly. Lenny is no fool but he's a man and men don't think like women. He was happiest making the hooch with your

326

Micky. But after the fire I thought we stood a chance of making the café into a good earner between us. And to his credit these last few years he's cooked and cleaned his arse off. Oh Gawd, Bella, I don't half miss him.'

'Did you say anything to upset him?'

Gina laughed emptily. 'Everything I say upsets him these days. I have to keep me mouth shut or else we're at it like cats and dogs. Can't afford to let the customers see that, or young Tina either.'

'Let me make you a cup of tea and we'll talk about where he could be.' Leaving Gina gazing into the fire, she went into the kitchen and put on the kettle. Where could Lenny have gone?

When the tea was made she took it into the front room and set it on the table. Gina was staring into space, her smart appearance gone and in its place, was an older, lifeless Gina.

'Drink this and tell me all about it.'

Gina looked into her cup. 'You ain't got something stronger have you?'

'I have, but that's the last thing you need now.'

'I need a pick-me-up to help me think straight.'

'You won't be thinking at all if you're tipsy. Now, what was it that started your tiff off?'

Gina lowered her cup and saucer to the floor. 'He ain't been right for some time. Moody and sharp to the customers and going off down the pub every night when we shut shop. Of course I wasn't having that. I mean, if he's going to drink our profits away, then what's the point of all our hard work? The last holiday we had was after the warehouse fire, remember? Well, I suggested we take another one. Margate or Brighton, somewhere by the sea, a nice boarding house. But he wasn't having any of it. He said a week's holiday wasn't going to cure what was wrong with us. I asked him what did he mean and he said he'd had enough. That I didn't make him feel like a man. I couldn't believe me ears. The next morning, Sunday, I woke up to find him standing by our bed, his suitcase packed. I got the fright of my life. There was me without me face on and he's just standing there, looking down at me like flipping Gulliver off on his travels.'

'Did you try to stop him?'

Gina looked away. 'Course I did.'

'And?'

'And – he just walked out.'

'Just like that?'

Gina turned to frown at her. 'Don't you believe me?'

'Yes, but it sounds as if – well, as if he planned it, packing his case like that. I mean did he do it whilst you were asleep or before?'

Gina stared at her for a long time, then suddenly shrugged. 'I don't know. I hadn't given it a thought.'

'Have you asked at the pub?'

'No. I didn't like to. I've got my pride you know and that lot down there would probably laugh in my face.'

'Has he got any special friends he might go to?'

Gina shook her head. 'No. No. Only–'

'Who?'

Gina said uncertainly, 'Well, Micky of course.'

Now it was Bella's turn to look dismayed, but she didn't want Gina to notice so she answered abruptly, 'I'm sure he would have told me if he'd seen him.'

Gina nodded slowly and the two women sat in silence. After a while there were noises above and little footsteps outside. Teresa and Michael came bursting in.

'Auntie Gina,' Michael shouted, throwing his arms around her.

'How's my boy, then?' Gina hugged him, then smiled at Teresa. 'Are you feeling better, love?'

Teresa nodded, grinning.

'Come here then and let me give you a smacker.'

Gina reached out for Teresa's hand and drew her close, planting her full lips on the little girl's cheek.

Bella watched Gina making every attempt to seem her normal self but Bella knew that inside she must be aching.

Chapter Twenty-Two

That night, when Micky came home, Bella explained about Lenny.

'She was always a nag,' he replied abruptly as he ate his dinner. 'And fancy making him work like a woman!'

'That ain't fair, Micky,' Bella said, shocked. 'Lenny didn't have to stay at the café. He could have got a job.'

'I'll tell you why he didn't,' Micky waved his

329

knife at Bella as she sat down at the kitchen table. 'Because he never heard the end of it after the fire. She took away his confidence and tied an apron on him instead. He was putty in her hands and she played on it.'

'How do you know that?'

'He told me.'

'When?'

'Struth, Bells, I can't remember when. Anyway, you know those two, they'll be back to tearing each other to shreds before you can say Jack Robinson. Now, if we could drop the subject, I'm going to have forty winks. I've been on me feet all day and I'm knackered.' He drank the last of his ale and walked out to the front room.

Bella cleared the dishes from the table and put them into the sink. By the time she caught up with him, hoping to discuss the rest of the day's events, he was asleep in the chair. His tie was loose and the buttons of his shirt undone at the neck. His black hair fell over his forehead and his long lashes lay on his cheeks. Bella knew he would be there long after she had gone to bed.

Sighing softly she returned to the kitchen and began to clean the dishes. She thought about Gina and Lenny. Was Micky correct in believing they would be back together again soon? They had been together a long time and even though Lenny might not like working in the café, it had become a thriving business. Could either of them turn their backs on it? The more Bella thought about it the more she became convinced that this was just a quarrel and Lenny would soon put in an appearance.

As for her own evening, it was now past nine o'clock. She and Micky had spent the best part of it discussing problems that weren't their own. She wanted to tell him how good the furniture looked in the prefab. And how Gus had fumigated it successfully and fresh wallpaper was on the walls.

Bella drew a critical eye over her neat and tidy home. She kept it spotless and even though Teresa's presence in the house had kept her busy, she had always maintained a high standard. There would be less to do of course, after the summer holidays. Teresa would be reunited with Mary and Michael back to school. The accounts she still kept for Ronnie had been halved after the sale of the Blue Moon. There were no babies on the way, despite her deep yearning for more children. Michael was growing fast and needed a sister or brother.

Bella switched on the standard lamp in the front room. Micky was snoring loudly. She wanted to discuss her hopes and her fears, her concerns about Terry and Mary, and the dreams she had for the future.

On her way to bed she looked in on the children. Each was fast asleep, the sound of their soft breathing making her feel content and yet disturbed. What would she do if the years passed and no more children arrived? Fear prickled on the back of her neck at the prospect.

What did life have in store for her and Micky? These were the concerns she wanted to share with her husband and attempt to find an answer for.

It was the second week of July when Bella decided to take Teresa home. When she told Ronnie, he offered to drive them as Micky was at work. But when the day came, Bella wondered if Teresa was really well enough? Would Mary look after her properly? But she knew that she couldn't put it off any longer.

On a bright, warm morning Ronnie collected them. 'I don't want to go to school without Teresa,' Michael complained as Ronnie opened the car door, holding out his hand to take him into the playground.

'She'll be starting again in September,' Bella reminded him. 'But today she has to go home.'

'And you'll see her next week,' Ronnie added gently. 'It's the holidays, don't forget.'

Eventually Michael allowed Ronnie to walk him in. Teresa held Bella's hand tightly. She was looking very pale. 'Is me mum going to be in?'

'Yes, of course.' Bella had gone round the previous weekend to confirm the arrangement.

'Will you be all right?' Ronnie asked when they arrived in Collier Street.

She nodded. 'Thanks for the lift.'

He bent down and grinned at Teresa. 'I'm going to miss you, young lady.' He looked at Bella. 'By the way, Joyce and me would like you all to come to dinner the Sunday after next. Sean and Ashley are cooking.'

'At Piper Street?' Bella asked in surprise.

'Yeah, just like the old days.' He grinned, then patted Teresa on the head. 'See you soon, little miss. Be good.'

Teresa giggled as he drove away. 'I like Uncle Ron.'

'He likes you too.'

The door opened and Mary stood there. 'Oh, it's you,' she mumbled and looking down at Teresa, she nodded. 'You're looking better, girl.'

Bella stepped in with the bags and having no further greeting made her way to the bedroom.

'I've got meself a job cleaning the grocer's round the corner,' Mary announced, coming up behind her. 'Don't pay much, but it's better than lavs.'

Bella was surprised to hear this, and to see that Mary hadn't returned to her old coat and slippers but wore a navy blue dress and a pair of decent flat shoes.

'I'm glad to hear it.' Bella continued to make up the bed with the fresh sheets she had brought. 'You'll be able to buy some nice veg as Teresa needs to eat well–'

'She'll eat what I eat,' Mary interrupted sourly. 'I ain't got enough for fancy stuff like you been spoiling her with.'

Bella folded the sheet over the rose-coloured candlewick spread that Teresa had helped her to choose from the market. 'In the summer holidays,' Bella said, as she deposited Teresa's freshly washed clothes in the new wardrobe, 'I'll take Teresa to the park if you like.'

'Please yourself,' Mary muttered. 'And where is me son and heir today?'

'He's at work at the garage.'

'And couldn't find time to visit his mother?'

'It wasn't that. He just has a job to do, that's all.

333

Is there a cup of tea going?'

Mary looked at her then walked away. Bella sat on the bed with Teresa. She was not going to get much co-operation from their mother. But she wasn't going to let it upset her. 'Do you like your new room?' she asked Teresa.

'Yes. I ain't ever had a real bed before.'

'You'll sleep like a top in this one. And all your new clothes are in the wardrobe.' Bella combed back Teresa's hair, taking each silky strand and carefully plaiting them, adding a ribbon as a final touch.

'When are you coming next?'

'On Monday. We'll go to the park as it's the holidays.'

'Did me mum say I could?'

'Yes, she said it's all right.'

'Can I come round your house too?'

Bella nodded. 'You and Michael have birthdays in August. Would you like a party?'

'Oh, yes please! Can Anne and Irene come? And Emma and Victoria?'

Bella laughed softly. 'Yes, everyone.'

Teresa wrapped her thin arms around her and they sat quietly together. Although Teresa was much better, she still had that weak chest that Dr Cox had warned her about even though she had put on weight and her cough was gone.

Micky was talking with Milo and Ivor. They were in the small office attached to the garage. Micky had instructed Terry to stand outside and knock on the door if there were any customers. Through the window he could see Terry standing stiff as a

334

sentry beside a 1950 Austin. The kid wouldn't move from there unless he saw a punter and Micky relaxed. The door was locked, no one would enter.

On the table in front of them was a large map. They were all concentrating on one particular area circled in red, with a large X drawn across it.

'Downey Manor,' Micky said in a low voice as he glanced at Miles. The young salesman had a frown on his handsome face. 'It's a blinder,' continued Micky enthusiastically. 'I can guarantee it. My eyes nearly popped out of my head when I saw the rooms all chock-a-block full of paintings and antiques. I wouldn't be surprised if Lady Muck is worth a fortune.'

'She may well be,' agreed Ivor, also looking doubtful. 'But those kind of goods would not be easy to dispose of.'

'It's not them I'm interested in,' Micky said with a sly smile. 'You see, the old girl took quite a shine to me. Told me all about the family fortune, most of which is stashed away in the banks. But her hubbie was a bit of a gambler, liked his gee-gees. Must've been a winner too as he stuffed the cash where he could put his hands on it. She paid me for the motor with all these rolled up fivers.'

'From under the floorboards no doubt?' said Miles sarcastically.

'No, from a hole in the wall behind one of her Rembrandts.'

'How much?' Ivor asked, stroking his small moustache. The office reeked of his foreign tobacco. Micky had closed the window tight so they couldn't be overheard.

'There was wads of it, so much that she was fighting to push it back in again. The two hundred quid she paid for the Jag didn't even make a dent in it.'

'She showed you?'

'Yeah. Didn't bat an eyelid. She's a bit off her trolley, see? Eccentric. I could have been anyone, couldn't I?'

'You are,' agreed Miles. 'You're planning to steal it.'

'Borrow it, Milo. Swap it for funny money. She won't ever know the difference. I mean, most of it is just gathering dust. I was sitting at this big table that was more like a skating rink and clocking every move she made. There's notes in boxes and bags and rubber bands and she's short-sighted an' all, so she has to shove it up to her nose to see what it is.'

'Weren't there any servants?'

'No, she only has someone come in to cook and clean and a gardener cum driver. She said she don't trust no one.'

'Only you?'

Micky grinned as he lifted his foot to a chair and leaned his arm on his knee. 'Look, I built up the trust see? I was giving her the old flannel; these old biddies love flattery and a bit of attention in a department that has been sadly lacking for years. I took her for a few spins, whizzed her out in the fresh air with her poodle on her lap and the force of gravity taking twenty years off her double chins.'

'You are a smooth bastard,' Miles laughed. 'I

was only thinking last week how that Jag was sticking. Then you call in one day and chat my customer up in a matter of seconds.'

'Yeah, it was love at first sight.' Micky laughed loudly at his joke.

'This doesn't sound healthy to me,' Ivor said suspiciously.

'And those fags don't look it either,' Micky came back with quickly. 'Your insides must be blacker than an incinerator.'

'Can we return to Downey Manor?' Miles intervened, glancing at the map again. 'Let's go over this one more time. What precisely would I be expected to do?'

'Drive,' Micky told him easily as he adjusted his white cuffs under his sports jacket. 'You wait for the boys outside and when they've done the job, chauffeur them home.'

'And I am expected to provide finance for the er – funny money?' Ivor looked down his long nose.

Micky nodded. 'We need a good printer and that costs.'

'You know of one?' Miles asked in his faultless accent.

'You bet. Just leave it to me.'

'And talking of you,' Ivor put in, 'what is your part in all this?'

Micky pulled out a chair and sat down. 'I'm the mastermind, ain't I? And I'll keep the duchess happy. Make sure everything is set up, that the money is in situ when she goes on holiday.'

'And your printer is trustworthy?'

'I'd stake me life on it,' Micky answered.

'You might have to, old chap, if anything went

wrong.' Miles looked hard now, his gaze un-wavering.

'Milo, I kid you not, this is a once in a lifetime opportunity. Nothing can go wrong.'

Miles nodded slowly. 'How do we gain entrance?'

'Simple. We climb in through a window. There ain't no alarms, only the old bloke who lives in the cottage and goes round once in a while, which is why we need the lookout. I'll suss it all out proper when I go up to see the duchess this weekend. When I get back we'll meet and if either of you want out, that's your prerogative. I'll take me idea somewhere else.'

Micky knew he'd said the right thing. Their eyes revealed their greed and all he wanted now was Ivor's money to put the plan in motion. And the sooner the better. After all, he couldn't exactly ask Ronnie to finance this little caper! McNee was an impatient sod and he wanted the hefty wedge that was owing to him. Micky wished yet again that he had listened to Ron. The Fortune was costing him dearly in protection. McNee was like a whopping great leech. Too big, too powerful to knock off his back. The frightener he'd had outside the club had made him realize the only way was to pay the black-hearted bastard what he wanted. Now that little goldmine in the country was looking even better than it had last week.

'Assuming success,' Ivor murmured, 'what is our cut?'

'I pay the printer his poke up front. So you get your investment back first, Ivor. Then we split the remainder.'

'How much each?' asked Miles warily.

'A couple of grand a-piece easy I'd say.'

'And the replacement funds – how good are they?'

Micky laughed aloud. 'As kosher as funny money can be.'

The three men looked at one another. Micky waited for the next question. None was forthcoming.

Micky reached down and took a bottle of whisky from the desk drawer. Savouring the moment, he poured them all a celebratory snifter. 'To Downey Manor,' he toasted, at last seeing an end to all his problems.

Bella was wearing a peach-coloured, full-skirted summer dress, with a slim white belt around her waist. As she checked her appearance in the bedroom mirror, Michael came in. 'Are we going yet?'

'Mummy's just putting on her lipstick.'

'How long will you be?'

Bella smiled into the glass as she smoothed the soft pastel colour on her lips. She looked down at her son.

'All finished now.'

'Uncle Ron said we can go to the park.'

'Pull your socks up and let me comb your hair, then.'

'It's like Christmas,' Michael said excitedly as she combed a parting in his thick, copper-coloured hair.

Bella laughed. 'Don't get too excited or you won't be able to eat your dinner.'

'Can we go now?' Michel screwed up his freckled nose.

'Yes. But don't run up the airey steps. Last time you ran up them you grazed your knee.'

But Michael wasn't listening. He couldn't wait to see his Auntie Joyce and his uncles, the first real family gathering in six months.

When they arrived upstairs the dinner was cooking. Sean was basting the meat and Ashley was preparing the trifle with a generous topping of cream.

'Go and sit down and have a drink,' Sean told them as everyone stood around breathing in the aromas. 'Ashley, get out the sherry and the Babycham.'

'Are we going to the park?' Michael asked Ronnie.

Ronnie grinned. 'Course we are.'

'Make sure you work up an appetite,' Sean called from the kitchen.

Bella knew they would come home sweating and ravenous, eager to eat after their game of football.

Ashley poured Babycham into two cocktail glasses. 'Go and have a chat, you girls.'

Taking their drinks into the front room, Bella and Joyce made themselves comfortable on the couch.

'I'll let you into a secret,' Joyce said softly. 'I've finally said yes to Ron, but don't let on I've told you as Ron is bursting to announce it today.'

'Oh, Joyce, that's wonderful news.'

'It's been a long time coming.' Joyce pushed back her dark wing of hair. 'I hope it's the right decision.'

'Of course it is. You and Ron are made for each other.'

'But Ronnie wants a family, a son in particular.'

'And you don't?'

Joyce laughed sadly. 'I never thought I would be a mother. And certainly not at my age.'

'You'll make a wonderful mum, Joyce. You and Ronnie are going to be very happy.'

Joyce smiled reflectively. 'When I caught your bouquet I never thought that marriage was on the cards for someone like me. I love Ron, but we are good friends first and foremost and neither of us want to change that.'

Bella nodded, recalling her wedding day and her beautiful bouquet of white carnations and pink roses that she had thrown into the air. Joyce had been shocked when they fell into her hands and even Bella had been surprised. Perhaps catching the bride's bouquet was the beginning of their romance? It was certainly the beginning of her own life with Micky. Could she now say the same as Joyce? Were she and Micky still friends as well as husband and wife?

Micky never talked about the club or the garage, or his hopes for the future or his amazing ideas anymore. He had once had so much lust for life and shared it with her. Now, they rarely sat down and talked. But was it because of her that things had changed? She hadn't been supportive of the Fortune and had complained about not seeing him enough. Even his New Year's resolution to keep her happy had fallen by the wayside. Was she expecting too much of her marriage?

'There's something else I'm worried about,'

Joyce added pensively, circling the rim of the glass with her little finger.

Bella frowned. 'What's that?'

'Ronnie wants to move back to Piper Street.'

Bella was surprised. 'I thought you were looking for a nice big house in the country?'

'So did I.'

'Why did he change his mind?'

Joyce smiled a distant smile. 'Sean and Ashley have bought the hairdressing shop and flat above off Ron. This place will be empty, apart from you and Micky that is.' She paused. 'If Ronnie suggested it, would you consider moving upstairs?'

Bella was caught off-guard by the question. 'I don't know, Joyce. I love the airey. It's where Michael's grown up and there's plenty of space. I have to admit though, that with Sean and Ashley gone, the house would seem very empty. There would only be Terry left upstairs and he couldn't stay on his own. He'd come down with us, I expect.'

'Oh, I see.' Joyce sounded disappointed.

'You were really looking forward to a fresh start, weren't you?' Bella said gently.

Joyce nodded slowly. 'Selfish of me, isn't it? I ain't no snob, but for once in my life I wanted to splash out, go a bit grand with my own place.'

'Have you talked about this to Ronnie?'

Joyce sipped her drink. 'I began to, but then I realized how much it meant to him to move back here, to his roots. Perhaps he's trying to recapture the past?'

Bella had given thought to this subject too. She had asked herself if the bond she had forged with

342

Teresa and her efforts to build bridges with Mary was an attempt to revisit her childhood. To put things back the way she would have liked them to be. But in her heart of hearts she knew that would never be possible. Was Ron trying to do the same?

'I don't know what you'll decide,' Bella said gently, 'but one thing I do know and that is that Ron loves you dearly. He won't make you unhappy and your life will become richer wherever you live.'

Joyce put down her drink and nodded. 'Yes, it doesn't matter where we live if we've got each other.' She looked round the room and began to smile. 'Though if we live here I can see Ronnie and I might have our differences when it comes to decoration. The furniture is as old as the hills. I've got my own taste, as Ronnie knows well.'

'I'm sure you'll make it look lovely,' Bella agreed as she heard the sound of Michael's laughter outside. 'And to think you and I will be neighbours. Oh, Joyce, I couldn't ask for more.'

'Do you mean that?'

'Of course I do.'

Joyce grasped her hand. 'Now don't forget to look surprised when Ronnie makes his announcement.'

Lenny was trying not to compare the squalid, cramped surroundings of Suzie's bedsit to the spotlessly clean accommodation of the café. He had never really appreciated Gina's housekeeping, mostly because he had been forced to maintain that standard. It was not in his nature to be fussy. At the warehouse he knew where everything had been, even though on the surface it looked a mess. When he'd been tinkering about with his formula, he'd been at his happiest, despite the occasional spat with Micky. As he lay on the back-breaking put-u-up, listening to the noise of the street below, the flashing neon lights lit up the dark room. The smell of beer and cigarettes rose up from the premises beneath, a strip club. Outside its doors there was always the local brass mouthing it off. Soho was alive twenty-four hours a day. It didn't sleep and nor had Lenny slept properly since he'd landed here two months ago.

Micky had promised to find him another gaff, but it had never materialized. He wanted to get out of this dump as soon as possible, but he had no money. He was used to nice clean sheets, a good cup of rosie and a substantial fry-up. Suzie's kitchen, which consisted of one cupboard, a draining board, sink and two electric rings, provided none of these. She called herself a singer and actress. Well, you could have fooled him. She brought more blokes home from the Fortune than she had hot dinners. There was always a permanent fag-fog in the room. Her bed was a tip and there was always someone ready to climb in or out of it. As the put-u-up he slept on was only hidden by a curtain, he was always on edge. As soon as he heard her come in he would crawl into his clothes and walk the streets. The only peace he got was when she went to work, from eight o'clock in the evening until two in the morning. He made sure he got some kip then. Though it was like sleeping on razors. He was ready to leap out of his make-shift bed the moment he heard her key in the lock. His nerves were in shreds. He never knew what mood she would be in. On a high or low, sober or sick. It was the drugs that Micky was giving her. Lenny hated them, what they did to people. He had seen a lot since he'd left Gina.

Lenny sat up, his ears alert for the sound of high heels on the rough wood of the stairs. As soon as he heard the swearing he knew it was Suzie. He jumped up and pulled on his trousers. By the time she opened the door, he was struggling into his vest. He grabbed his coat and shirt and pulled the curtain back.

'Who the hell are you?' an angry voice demanded.

Looking into the face of one of her punters, Lenny knew he'd had enough. This would be the last night he spent here.

'Oh, leave him alone,' Suzie shouted, pulling her customer away as he stepped towards Lenny. 'He ain't in my bed, is he? He's a paying guest.'

'You sure?' the mountain of flesh demanded.

Suzie put her hands on her hips. 'Well, what you waiting for?'

With as much dignity as he could muster, Lenny hurried out of the door.

He was going to find Micky. And he was taking the job he'd offered him. Principles in this life cost too much. He had left Gina to find his freedom. Now he had none at all. Micky promised that just one job would buy that coal yard he'd seen and show Gina the real man he was.

Lenny hurried out into the summer night, pushed his way past the women on the corner and headed for the Fortune.

Chapter Twenty-Three

The party was in full swing despite the damp and rainy August day. As Bella had promised the children, they were having a double celebration for their birthdays. Dolly's twins were dancing around the room, with paper hats on their heads, followed closely by Emma and Victoria Brown from next door. In hot pursuit was their seven-year-old cousin, Peter. All had to be restrained as the moment came to blow out the candles.

Bella clapped her hands. 'Are you ready?' She had made two iced sponges. One was decorated with six blue candles and the other, six pink.

'I'll blow soft,' said Teresa as she bent forward careful not to dirty the front of her new frilly white party dress. The table had been cleared of debris now that everyone had eaten, but the lemonade glasses were still fizzing.

'And I'll blow strong.' Michael puffed out his cheeks, flushed from having chased the girls.

'On the count of three, then.' Bella lit the last candle and all the children were suddenly silent. 'One, two, three!'

Every candle extinguished and the children clapped, filling the room with laughter. Bella began to slice the cakes whilst Dolly set the portions on plates and handed them out.

'I'll take your mum a slice,' Dolly said as she came back to the table. 'Do you think she's enjoying herself?'

Bella glanced across at Mary who was sitting in one of the fireside chairs, watching the children play. She wore a floral dress and smart sandals and no one had been more surprised than Bella when she had said she would attend the party. 'She's been chatting to Emma and Victoria's mum as though she has known her years,' Dolly added. 'I even heard her talking about vegetables!'

'Well, you can guess why,' Bella said meaningfully.

'You mean, the man who fumigated her house?' Dolly's eyebrows shot up. 'What's he like? Does Teresa like him?'

'Yes, it seems he's a good influence, as Teresa says she gets real carrots and greens on her plate, something unheard of before.'

'He's not married, is he?' Dolly asked with a frown.

'His wife died years ago, apparently. He told me all about himself one day when I was round there. He was born and bred on the island and worked for the council all his life. He seems to have taken a liking to Mum and she to him.'

'Has he got a car?'

'No. Only a bike and shanks's pony. He's coming to meet her this afternoon and stop for a cup of tea.'

'But I thought she couldn't walk far.'

'Her legs seem to be better now.' Bella smiled

ruefully. 'As you can see by the stockings and nice sandals.' Bella glanced again at Mary. In a soft voice she said to Dolly, 'And she's still keeping the prefab clean. I always have a look around when we call for Teresa to go to the park. You should see the back garden as well. Even your dad would be impressed. All sorts of vegetables growing there just like–'

'Doctor Carrot and Potato Pete!' both girls said at once and giggled together.

Bella's smile disappeared as she met Mary's gaze. 'You'd better take this over, Dolly.'

'Is one slice enough?'

Bella caught the tease in Dolly's eye. As she watched Mary accept the cake and smile up at Dolly she wondered if the improvement in attitude was down to the appearance of Gus. But whatever had brought about the change, Bella hoped it would continue. She wanted peace for the children's sake.

As the eating and drinking ended, Bella decided it was time for a game. She had wrapped some toffees in paper, making a huge ball tied up with string. She gave it to Terry who was sitting on a stool in the corner.

'Give this to one of the children, Terry,' she told him. 'We'll play pass the parcel and you can work the wireless.'

Terry clutched the big parcel and took it over. He loved being with the children but Bella had noticed he hadn't yet spoken to Mary. Not that she seemed to have noticed as she sat drinking and eating and enjoying the attention showered on her.

Bella reminded the children of the rules, leaving Terry in charge of the wireless. He liked music and knew that he was to turn the volume up and down at Bella's nod.

The music that burst forth was Guy Mitchell's popular hit, 'She Wears Red Feathers and a Hula Hula Skirt'. Dolly, Daisy and Mary began clapping along. Bella was astonished as suddenly her mother stood up and did a little twirl, waving her hands and singing loudly to the tune, obviously enjoying the party as much as the children.

It was almost dark and Micky looked both ways along the street before walking up to a terraced house in Hoxton. It wasn't a very salubrious area, but then Alfred Freshwater himself wasn't a very salubrious character. Bent from the toes upward, he was a man of many trades.

'What d'yer want?' A small woman opened the door cautiously. She looked like everyone's old mum, but she was unique in the fact that it was said she could also turn out a fiver or two. In the background he could hear a dog snarling.

'I wanna word with Alfred, Mrs F.'

'What sorta word?'

'A quick one,' he added with a wink. 'To do with what we was talking about last week if you get my meaning.'

The old girl squinted, peered over his shoulder, then let him in. Micky paused in the gloom, inhaling the smell of boiling cabbage and dogs. The Freshwaters kept a beast. It was growling up at him, all froth and fangs.

'Shut up, you bugger,' Mrs F shouted.

'You gonna put him away?'

'Nah. He'll do as he's told. Just don't make any quick moves.'

'Where's Alfred?'

'Same as always, under the boards.'

Micky waited for the old woman to take hold of the dog's collar, then backed down the corridor. At the end of it he pulled back the corner of a heavy rug. Lifting the trap door, he was blinded by a light from the bowels of the earth. 'It's me, Micky. All right to come down?'

'Yer.'

As always on his previous visits, Micky felt claustrophobic as he descended the wooden steps. The small room smelt of must and printer's ink. Alfred Freshwater was watching him closely from under his filthy tweed cap.

How did anyone breathe down here let alone work, Micky wondered uncomfortably. There was only one grille above letting in the air. It was even worse than Dad's old lock-up.

'How you doing, Alf?'

The master forger was smoking a fag. Micky watched him adjust his braces over his shirt and take a puff. He leaned against a large iron contraption that looked more like a trouser press than a counterfeiting machine.

'You won't get better than this,' Alfred said, handing him a one pound note. 'Not unless you know the Old Lady of Threadneedle Street personally.'

'I ain't had the pleasure,' Micky mumbled as he lifted the paper to the light. It looked just like an ordinary one pound note except it was too new.

350

'How many have you got?'

'How many do you want?'

'A grand at least. I need Lady Godivas too. Dirtied up a bit of course.'

'What you up to?' Alfred demanded curiously.

'I need it for an operation for me little crippled sister,' Micky answered.

'Pull the other one. Where's the job?'

Micky took the map from his pocket. 'This is the plan. It's foolproof.'

'That's like an actor saying Macbeth on the first night,' Alfred remarked as with ink-stained fingers he took the map and shambled over to a chair. For a long time he studied it, the circles and the crosses and the notes made beside them. He looked up at Micky, 'You know my terms, I told you last week. I want a monkey up front as insurance.'

'Two fifty.'

'I ain't gonna argue. It's five and two noughts or get your arse out of here.'

Reluctantly Micky handed over Ivor's stake. 'It's all there.'

Alfred counted them. 'When?'

'Like we discussed. The end of September when the duchess is away.'

'And you're sure this place is empty?'

'As the proverbial tomb,' Micky assured him. 'The nearest living soul is an old bloke who lives down the road and keeps an eye out every now and then. Trust me, all that lolly will be sitting there ripe for the picking. You only have to screw the safe, we make the switch and jump in the car.'

From upstairs there was a sound of barking and

growling. Micky jumped nervously.

'Who's that?'

'Could be the law.'

Micky froze. But his terror soon turned to relief as Alfred laughed raucously. 'It's only dinner time. The missus is feeding the lions.'

Micky could believe that as well. No wonder Alfred Freshwater had enjoyed a long and successful career; he didn't have any friends and consequently very few enemies.

Bella rose early before the rest of the household. The smell of autumn was in the air as she opened the window of the airey. It was a distinctive smell, one she loved, as the world hovered between seasons. September was a wonderful month to be married in, just before the heat of summer died. Friday September the sixteenth was a very special day, the day of Joyce's registry office wedding.

Like Bella and Micky they had chosen to have a civil ceremony. A service in church seemed inappropriate as they were already living together. Nevertheless, Bella had lots to do. First she must wrap up Joyce and Ronnie's gifts; a single gold pin with the letter J that Joyce could pin to her dress. Another with R, intended to be worn on the groom's tie. She also had a garter for Joyce in her favourite colour, purple, and a lace hanky of her own to lend her. All the traditions would then be observed; something old, something new, something borrowed, something blue. And last night Joyce had slept in the spare room, whilst Ron had stayed with Sean and Ashley.

But before she did anything, Bella opened the drawer in the sideboard. She took out her own wedding album and sat at the table. She knew she was being sentimental but this morning she couldn't resist a walk down memory lane.

All her own wedding photographs had been taken on Joyce's Box Brownie camera. May also had been a lovely month to be married in, as summer beckoned.

Her bouquet had hidden her bump and her white and buff wedding dress looked elegant with its little Peter Pan collar, which was, Bella decided, just as fashionable today. Micky was so handsome in his formal dark suit. He gazed down on her as she held tight to his arm looking up at him with love-filled eyes. Turning the pages slowly, she recalled each moment as Joyce had instructed, 'smile for the camera'.

Even Terry looked a grown man as he stood beside Ronnie who was dressed all in silver grey. Sean and Ashley's cheeky bow ties made her laugh as they posed against the big black cars with white ribbons and bows that had carried them back to the Blue Moon.

How special she had felt as she had shaken hands with all their guests at the reception. It was sad to think that the club would never open its doors to the Bryants again. She felt even sadder to see a snap of Lenny and Gina. What had happened to Lenny? Where was he now? How could he just disappear like that?

'You're up early!' It was Joyce, peering over her shoulder. She was wearing her dressing gown and turban. Bella knew that hidden beneath it were curlers, her thick dark hair to be styled by Sean later.

'I was going to bring the bride a cup of tea in bed.'

Joyce sat down beside her. She nodded to the album. 'That's what I call a lovely wedding.' They looked down at a photograph of Bella waving from the window of the car as it drove away. 'You looked so happy.'

Bella nodded as she closed the book. 'You'll be happy too, Joyce. Ronnie is a wonderful man and he'll take good care of you.'

'Yes, I know that.'

'No last minute butterflies?'

Joyce looked amused. 'Nothing that a strong cup of tea won't help. Of course, I can't guarantee what I'll be like when I walk into that registry office and sign on the dotted line. I still can't believe we're doing it. It feels like it's happening to someone else.'

'I can't wait to see you dressed.'

'Do you think cream is the right colour?'

'Perfect for you.'

'I never wear it normally.'

'You don't get married every day.'

Joyce laughed. 'No, thank God.'

Hanging in the bedroom was Joyce's gorgeous cream satin calf length dress. It had been made by the same seamstress who had sewn Bella's. On the dresser beside it was an exquisite sequinned hat and whisper of a veil. Her spray was made up of tiny white rosebuds hidden in fern with a big satin bow.

'We'll have a quiet cuppa before everyone gets

up,' she told Joyce who had picked up the album again and was browsing through it.

As Bella went to the kitchen, she felt very excited. Micky had taken the Friday off and she would have his company all day. To mark the occasion she had bought herself a slim two-piece in soft apple green. The colour complemented her coppery waves which she intended to pin up under the floppy brim of her hat. Micky had invested in a fashionable dark suit made of Italian cloth and young Michael was wearing a white shirt, navy blue short trousers and a little bow tie. He wasn't exactly a pageboy, but Joyce and Ronnie called him that.

When Bella brought the tea into the front room, Joyce was gazing into space. She had applied no make-up and looked pale and youthful. Bella knew from Ron that she had no family to represent her side. She wondered if Joyce was thinking about that now, but she was surprised when Joyce suddenly turned to her and said unexpectedly, 'I don't know if Ron's ever told you, but I had a child once.'

Bella sat down abruptly. 'No, Ron never said.'

'I was fifteen when he was born. He was two months early and only lived a couple of hours. I suppose he must have been too small to survive. My mum was a widow as me dad died when I was young. She sent me away to this home in the next town because it was seen as a big disgrace then. They just took him away and I never even knew what they did with him.' Joyce paused, her eyes far away. 'I never went back to where I lived. I heard my mum died of cancer a few years later.'

'Oh, Joyce, how sad.'

'Yes, it was really, because we never spoke again. I wished we could have put things right between us.'

'Did you come straight to London, then?'

Joyce nodded. 'Caught a train with the few bob I had and ended up in the East End. Bumped into this woman who offered me lodgings. I didn't know a pig's trotter from a cow's udder then. She was the one who turned me into a working girl.'

'Weren't you scared of an unwanted pregnancy?'

'She showed me ways to stop them,' Joyce said quietly. 'Sponges soaked in vinegar, pessaries and gels, that kind of thing. They don't always work, but a lot of times do. I never got pregnant anyway. Whether it was to do with my efforts or the fact it won't be easy to conceive again, I don't know.'

'You could always talk to the doctor,' Bella suggested tentatively.

'Yes, Ronnie suggested that. He says we can go up to Harley Street and see a specialist if nothing happens.'

'I don't think you'll need to,' Bella said with a little smile. 'I've heard that it's very romantic in Italy. Very romantic indeed.'

They both looked at one another and laughed. Very soon they were talking about the forthcoming honeymoon in Italy that Ronnie had booked. Bella was certain that with Ron to romance her in such magical surroundings, Joyce would relax and all her worries about having a baby would be forgotten.

'This is very nice,' Dolly remarked as they sat down on comfortable chairs in the reception room of the New Inn. 'Have you been here before?'

'Only once,' Bella replied as she watched the other guests file in. 'To help Joyce confirm all the details for today.'

'A reception like this would cost a lot of money I expect.' Dolly sighed softly as she gazed around the hotel's impressive interior. All was polished wooden floors, thick floral rugs and long Georgian style windows. The beautiful golden curtains on either side were gathered by heavy cords and tassels and guests were talking in a discreet manner as the waiters hovered with trays of champagne.

Micky and Percy, Terry, Sean and Ashley and all the other men were grouped at the bar. Even though there was champagne to drink, some preferred their pint glasses of ale. To one side of the room a long table was spread with delicious looking food. Michael and another little boy, one of the other guests' children, were playing outside in the garden where there were swings.

Apprehensively, Dolly fiddled with the buttons of her staid grey costume. The feathers in her hat caught the breeze from the open window. Bella noted it was the same saucer-shaped feathered hat that she'd worn to Bella's wedding, with a few more feathers stuck in here and there. Dolly's brown eyes looked tired and her colourful taste in clothes had apparently disappeared.

'Are they really going to Italy for their honey-

357

moon?' she asked wistfully.

'Yes, it was Ronnie's suggestion as Joyce has never been abroad before.'

Dolly sighed as she looked at Joyce and Ronnie shaking hands with their guests. 'Going abroad is all the rage these days. It was what me and Percy had planned this year. A camping trip, not a hotel of course. But we could've afforded to take the twins to France with a tent. But now with Percy losing his job at Burlingtons...'

'But he's got the new job in Albert Dock, hasn't he?'

'Yes,' Dolly said quietly. 'He's on the boats. They're two abreast down there, in all states. Some need mending, some painting, you can see the ships going on and on down the dock, and new sheds are going up to accommodate them. The United States Lines have even begun to put their own shed up as they've got so much work.'

'Really?'

'Yes, but it's unskilled work and less pay.'

'Are you managing all right?'

Dolly nodded silently, chewing on her lip. Just then Gina walked in the door and began to approach them. Suddenly Dolly got up. 'I'm just going to the cloakroom,' she blurted and hurried off.

'What's the matter with Dolly?' Gina asked with a smile as she sat beside Bella. 'Where are the twins?'

'They're with their grandparents for the day.'

'Only she don't look very happy.'

'Percy lost his job at Burlingtons,' Bella explained, wondering if she should go after Dolly.

'But he's got another one in Albert Dock.'

'Some of my customers work there too. It's very busy at the moment.'

'Yes, but Percy is a skilled fishmonger and he was looking at promotion at Burlingtons. Now he's at the bottom of the ladder again.'

Gina sighed and said softly, 'Well, he'd better make the best of it whilst it lasts.'

'What do you mean?'

'Burlingtons aren't the only ones in trouble so I hear. Many of my customers tell me the firms they work for are struggling. The machinery is old and in need of replacing. The factory sheds are like museums inside. Even the landing stages need renewing they're so rotten. Albert Dock is about the only place where new sheds are being built. Some blokes say that in ten years' time, if there's no investment, the docks will be on their knees.'

'But that's impossible, Gina!'

'Nothing is impossible in this life, love. I hear a lot in the café from all walks of life; the dockers and the union reps and the blokes passing through. We are going to need some serious redevelopment if we're to survive.' Just then Joyce came over with two glasses of champagne. 'Come on girls, drink up. Chin-chin.'

Gina smiled as she accepted her drink. 'What time are you lovebirds off?'

'First thing in the morning. We're driving to Dover to pick up the ferry.'

'I hope Ron knows his way,' Gina giggled. 'If that was Lenny we'd end up in Russia.'

They all laughed and although Bella knew Gina

missed Lenny she also knew her friend wasn't going to let it show. She looked stunning; she wore a striking black and white dress and matching hat with an upturned brim. She smelt of expensive perfume and her carefully applied make-up hid all the signs of her recent troubles. Bella didn't know whether to mention Lenny as she didn't want to spoil the day. But Gina didn't seem concerned as she continued to drink from the fluted glass. 'Congratulations, Joyce, you make a lovely bride,' she laughed gaily.

'Yes, really beautiful,' Bella agreed, sipping the champagne as the sparkles burst on the edge of her nose.

Laughing with her friends, Bella looked round for Dolly. It was unlike her not to join in the fun and the buffet would be starting soon.

Half an hour later, Bella found Dolly in the garden. She was sitting on a bench, watching the children play.

'Dolly, what are you doing out here?'

'I needed some fresh air.'

'I've been looking all over for you.'

'Oh, sorry.' She paused and said in a flat voice, 'Your Michael is getting a big boy. He's going to be tall like his dad.'

'I can't keep up with his clothes,' Bella answered as she sat down beside Dolly. She saw Michael and waved to him as he slid down a slide. 'Are you coming in? They're serving the food now.'

'I'm not hungry.'

Bella lifted the lock of hair that shielded Dolly's

face and tucked it behind her ear. 'What are you not telling me Dolly? You never go off your food. You look very pale and you were in the cloak-room ages.'

Dolly looked down at the table. The afternoon sun glanced across her face and she shivered. Bella noted that her lipstick had come off and she was clutching a hanky. 'Actually ... I ... do feel a bit sick.'

'But you haven't eaten anything!'

'I know.' Dolly stood up. She was now very white. 'I'll have to go back to the lav again.' And with that she hurried off.

'Mummy, is it time for dinner?' Michael had run over from the swings.

'Yes, I'll take you in.'

'Can I have anything I want?'

Bella smiled down at her hungry son. 'I don't see why not, except you might not know what some of the food is. Let's find Daddy to help us.'

A few minutes later Bella had left Michael with Micky and his Uncle Ronnie as they queued along the big buffet table. Quickly she went through the swing doors and out to the cloak-room.

Her suspicions were confirmed when she heard noises coming from the cubicle. 'Dolly, can I help?'

'I'll be out in a minute.'

Eventually Dolly appeared. She was wiping her mouth and looked ghastly.

'Here, throw some water over your face,' Bella suggested and Dolly leaned over the basin.

'How long have you been like this?'

'About a week.' Dolly sank down on a stool. Bella gave her a clean hanky from her bag. 'You don't have to tell me what's wrong. I know.'

Dolly looked up at her, nodding. 'I'm pregnant.'

'Have you seen the doctor?'

'I don't need to. I was sick like this with the twins.'

'But he'll need to work out the dates. And why are you so unhappy? Having a baby is a wonderful thing.'

Dolly grabbed Bella's hand. 'But I don't want it, Bella. I can't have it. Not now. Not with what's happened.'

'But Percy's got a job,' Bella protested gently as she went down on her knees and gazed into her friend's distraught face.

'Bella, it's the mortgage. We're struggling at the moment to pay it and are only just scraping by. If another baby comes along, we'll lose the house. And then where will we live?'

'Have you told Percy?'

'No.'

'Why not?'

'I don't want him to know yet.'

Bella gasped. 'Dolly – you're not thinking of doing anything silly, are you?'

Dolly burst into tears and put her hands over her face, mumbling words that Bella couldn't understand, until suddenly she jumped up and rushed back into the cubicle.

Bella sighed deeply. Why was it that people's lives became so complicated? Dolly was expecting a child she didn't want and Joyce was desperate to have one. Gina deserved to have Lenny beside her today, but he had vanished into thin air and she was forced into putting on a brave face.

As she heard Dolly retching, she made up her mind that before they left the cloakroom she would make Dolly promise to tell Percy about the baby.

Chapter Twenty-Four

The house and garden were quiet enough, but Micky paused, placing a cautious finger to his mouth. The three men accompanying him stopped abruptly.

'What's the matter?' hissed Alfred Freshwater, clutching a Gladstone bag to his chest. 'I thought you said the gaff was empty.'

'It is. But I'm just making sure.' Micky narrowed his eyes searchingly. But all he could see was darkness, the outline of trees and the curve of the wall. He would have to walk round it to approach the designated window. 'Wait here,' he ordered, raising his voice so that Terry and Lenny could hear him.

Micky stepped forward, his heart beating heavily in his chest. He was enjoying the rush of adrenaline more than he could ever have expected. What was there to fear after all? The duchess was long gone to her Scottish retreat, no staff remained in the house and as long as Lenny and Terry kept observation on the lane, breaking in would be a doddle. The sash window wasn't locked. He'd checked that only two days ago when he'd paid a visit, and unless the duchess had suddenly done a spot check, the entrance to riches lay before him. He pressed his back to the wall, pushed aside the ivy and trod slowly round. His heart did a little skip as a small figure darted out. The fox turned briefly to stare at him then slunk away.

Resuming his journey he followed the path and came to the point of entry. The manor was in total darkness, a woody silence enveloping the old stones and mortar.

A bird screeched, another flapped and a rustle came from the trees.

Instinct flattened him against the brick. His heart jumped into his throat. Was there someone in the shadows? He closed his eyes and opened them. The woolly hat he was wearing was making him hot. Sweat trickled down from his forehead. He should have worn a vest only, not all this clobber. What was over there in the darkness?

Gradually his eyes adjusted to the shape of a bush, its leaves waving in the September breeze. He licked his dry lips. Making his way along the border he came to the window. Sliding on his gloves, he pressed his fingers against the frame. For a moment he had another horrible shock. It was stuck. Then wiping the sweat from his lip, he composed himself. Taking a jemmy from his pocket he slid the tip into the space between frame and sash, careful not to damage the wood. With gentle pressure it released.

Ducking his head inside he listened. Not a dicky bird. He couldn't see a thing, but torches would take care of that.

He made his way back. 'All clear,' he whispered to the three men.

They crept to the window. 'In you go, Alf. You know where it is, under the ugliest mug you'll ever clock. Lenny, stay here and keep watch. Terry, follow me up the drive.'

Terry trudged slowly behind him. Micky wondered why the boy had to make so much noise as his big boots scuffed the gravel. He was still as daft as a brush, but at least he could be relied on to do as he was told. Micky stopped when they reached the gates. 'Now, you know what to do. Walk down the lane to the cottage. Watch that front door as if your life depended upon it. The old man ain't gonna stir after a week's slog at the manor. On Saturdays he's knackered, goes down the pub and comes home to put his feet up in front of the fire. I've been sussing him out on the quiet for over a month now and his routine never changes.' Micky took a deep breath. 'But *if* – and this is just an *if* – he ventures out for some reason and it looks like he's coming this way, leg it back to the car and tell Milo. He's parked in the bushes where we left him, right?' Micky gestured in the opposite direction. 'And he will give us a blast on the horn, like we practised at the garage.'

Terry nodded silently, his big square face hidden under the balaclava.

'You got that straight?' Micky asked again. 'You just got to watch the cottage, right?'

'Yer, Micky.'

'Good lad. Now off you go and after this is all over I'm gonna bung you a tenner all to yourself.'

Terry sniffed loudly. 'Terry needs a pee.'

Micky gave a little groan. 'I might have known it! Look, go in them bushes and be quiet about it.' He gave him a little push in the right direction and then when he could no longer hear Terry's footsteps, he made his way back down the drive.

Lenny was still standing by the window. 'Struth!' he gasped and visibly jumped as Micky appeared from the shadows. 'You scared the shit of me.'

'Calm down, Lenny. I told you, this is going to be a doddle.'

Lenny looked nervously around him. 'I don't like it here.'

'Why?'

'It's too – *easy*. I mean, no dogs or guards or anything.'

'She don't like dogs and she only trusts the old bloke down the road to look after the place and even in his case, it's drink yourself daft while the cat's away.'

'You shouldn't have brought Terry, Micky, that was a bad move. You sprung that one on me.'

'We needed someone to watch the cottage.'

'But not Terry.'

'Look, stop worrying. He knows what to do. Just keep thinking of the moment when you tell Gina you've bought yourself that little coal yard. She'll know what Lenny Rigler is made of then.'

'I ain't bought it yet.'

'You will have in twenty-four hours, once this job is done. Now, I'm going in to help Alfred with the switch and we'll be home and dry in no time at all. Just keep your eyes skinned, right?'

Micky sighed as he stepped back to the open window. Never again was he bringing Lenny on a job. He'd vowed he wouldn't before, but this was really the last time. What a pain in the backside!

Micky climbed in and pulled out his torch. The beam lit up the big table and chairs. He directed it slowly round to where Alfred stood with his ear to the safe.

'Turn that off.'

Micky did as he was told, making his way across the room in the darkness. 'Have you opened it yet?'

'Almost.'

Micky waited in silence as Alfred tried this combination and that. He began to grow a little worried as time passed. Shouldn't opening the box be a little more straightforward than this? The old girl had just twirled it round. What if it wouldn't open? What if she had put in a special code or something? Micky went cold at the thought.

Micky narrowed his eyes as he looked round the room. He could just make out the shapes of the chairs and shabby furnishings. It was like taking a gulp of air from a church vault. Like Lenny he didn't like this place. It was of a bygone era, like a mausoleum, worse at night than when he had seen it in daylight. He didn't believe in ghosts but if there were any on God's earth, this was the place to find them.

'Bingo,' said Alfred suddenly. 'It's open.'

'Thank Gawd for that.' Micky joined him at the

safe and flicked on the torch.

For a moment there was silence and then the little man croaked, 'Strike a light!'

'Bloody Norah!'

'You weren't exaggerating, were you?'

Micky stared in wonder at the overflowing interior of the safe. He could smell it from here, the scent of unlimited cash. Rolls of it, wads of it, packets of it, bursting to the safe's seams.

'What's going on?' Lenny demanded from the window. 'Have you got it?'

Alfred nodded. 'We've got it all right.'

'Right, let's get to work,' Micky said as they began to scoop the contents of the safe into one bag and replace it with forged notes from another.

'A good night's work,' Alfred observed as they climbed back out through the window.

'How much did we get?' demanded Lenny as they hurried up the drive to the car.

'I told you, I don't know,' Micky shrugged as he held on tightly to the bag.

'You said two grand each.'

'Yeah, well, we'll have to see.'

'You mean I've stuck my neck out for less?'

Micky stopped and with an exasperated shrug exploded, 'Do you want me to empty the bag here and count it under the moon?'

'You said two grand,' Lenny said as they began to walk again.

'Oh, put a sock in it,' Micky retorted. 'You give me earache. I got you a decent gaff at Suzie's and no, that wasn't good enough. Now you're moaning even before we done the job.'

'I just want my money.'

Micky was losing his temper now. Trust Lenny to start complaining even before they had counted what was left. He was about to make a suitable retort when there was an almighty bang.

'What the fuck was that?' Alfred gasped and they all froze.

'Gunshot,' whispered Lenny.

'Where from?' Micky looked both ways. He couldn't see anything. The moon had disappeared and the trees swayed darkly around them. Another shot rang out.

'It's the law,' Lenny breathed. 'They're on to us.'

'How could they be?' Micky declared. 'We've taken nothing. The funny money's in the safe. They don't know any difference.'

For a brief, desperate second, he thought the old boy might have been watching them all the time and was now coming up with the gun. But Terry would have seen him and Milo sounded the warning. No, it had to be something – someone else, but he didn't know who.

'Let's get out of here,' he said, as the cold perspiration trickled down his back. They began to run. Branches and twigs scratched his face. He tripped, pushing the sharp thorns to one side. He heard Lenny puffing behind him and the sounds of the night all around.

When they reached the gate Milo was waiting. Micky closed his eyes in relief. They'd made it.

But the back door of the car was open and a pair of legs hung loosely out. 'It's Terry,' Milo whispered hoarsely. 'He's been shot. There's a

369

hole in his back.'

Micky watched in disbelief as Alfred bent over Terry.

After a while he murmured, 'No pulse. This kid is dead.'

'But he can't be,' Micky objected. 'He's me wife's little brother.'

'He's her dead little brother,' Alfred corrected and poked a finger in Milo's direction. 'What happened, mate? You were the last person to see him alive.'

'It wasn't my fault,' Milo answered indignantly. 'I was sitting in the car and saw this figure stumbling up,' he continued bewilderedly. 'He just opened the back door and fell in.'

They were all silent until Micky blurted, 'I can't tell Bella he's copped it, can I? She thinks he's over at Sean's place for the weekend.'

'I should never have let you con Terry into this,' Lenny accused. 'It was a lamb to the slaughter.'

'Aw, shut up,' Micky yelled then. 'You are a flaming pain in the arse, you are.'

At this Lenny lunged forward. It took Milo and Alfred to pull him off. 'Listen, you idiots,' Alfred barked, 'fight amongst ourselves and we're finished.'

Micky caught his breath. Alfred was right. If they didn't work out a plan the job would well and truly backfire.

'Terry was shot in the back,' Micky pointed out, ignoring Lenny. 'All I can think is he went to take a piss and got himself lost. And who is poking about in woods at the dead of night? Why, poachers of course. They think he's game and take a couple of shots. Then they scarper.' He peered into the bushes. 'After all, no one ain't come after us, have they?'

'We're in a difficult position,' Milo said doubtfully. 'We can't exactly inform the authorities, can we?'

'No, but we could plant the body back in the trees and let someone else do it for us.'

'You wouldn't!' Lenny said horrified.

'You got any other suggestions?'

'The poor bastard,' Lenny gulped. 'He never hurt a soul. Can't we take him back with us?'

'And do what?' Micky demanded. 'Order up a coffin and a vicar? Oh yes, I can see that happening, I don't think.'

'What, then?' said Alfred impatiently.

'We take off his balaclava, dirty his face as if he's been hiding in the undergrowth and take him to the middle of the woods.'

'No,' Lenny shouted. 'I won't do it!'

'Who's asking you?' Micky snarled. 'Drive the car back in there till we're finished and wait for us.'

Micky felt anger flow through his body. He would like to land one on Lenny's fat nose, but he stopped himself. He had to keep his head. It looked as though they might still get out of this if they were lucky.

Micky kept the bag safely in his grasp. He would count this little lot out very judiciously. Alfred deserved his wedge. But Lenny didn't, nor did Milo, who should have kept Terry in sight. They didn't deserve any bees and honey. And they certainly weren't going to get it.

371

It was Monday evening and Michael was asleep in bed. Bella had just finished ironing the shirts, a labour of love. Young Michael was not like his father when it came to cleanliness, she thought ruefully. His shirts were always grubby round the collar. Perhaps little boys had a way of gathering dirt that was known only to them? The cuffs also got badly stained, but this was understandable as they used crayons and chalks at school.

As for Micky, well, he changed his shirt every day and there was hardly a speck on them. The one exception had been the vest that she'd washed this morning. It had been heavily soiled under the armpits and sweat had stiffened the back. He'd inspected a car at the garage, he'd told her, forgetting to put on his overalls. A rare occurrence for Micky who was always fastidious about his clothing.

Bella shook out the vest and folded it neatly. She was eager to watch the new television that Ronnie had purchased for them, much to her son's delight. Now a commercial channel competing with the BBC had started. It was putting on a programme called *Double Your Money* and Hughie Green was the compere. The paper said he was handsome and humorous and the contestants could win a lot of money.

She was about to put the dinner on as Micky said he would be home early, when there was a knock at the door. Expecting it to be Daisy from next door returning the cup of sugar she had borrowed early this morning, Bella hurried to open it.

The smile faded from her face as she saw a stranger standing there. He was tall and wearing a dark suit and he took off his hat when he saw her. 'Mrs Bryant?'

Bella nodded slowly. 'Yes, that's me.'

'My name is Reynolds, Detective Inspector Reynolds and I'm from Surrey police.' He showed her a small card. 'I knocked on the door upstairs but no one replied.'

Nodding to the airey he said in a gentle voice, 'I'd like to talk to you inside if I could.'

Bella saw the uniformed policeman behind him and her heart jumped. 'It's not my husband, is it?'

'No, it's not.'

The inspector entered whilst the constable stayed outside. When the inspector was seated, he said quietly, 'I'm afraid I have some distressing news for you.'

Bella felt the life drain out of her legs. If this wasn't about Micky, then who could it be?

The big man turned his hat round slowly in his hands. 'I'm very sorry to have to tell you that this morning, the body of a young man was found on a large private estate in Surrey. He had been shot and died from his injuries. Our enquiries led us to believe he is related to you. Your brother, Terence Doyle, in fact.'

'Terry?' Bella repeated. 'In Surrey? No ... no, that's impossible, you've made a mistake. He wouldn't even know where Surrey is.'

'We traced him through this,' the inspector held out a small photograph.

It was her and Micky, Lenny and Terry and

Sean standing on the registry office steps. Very slowly she turned it over and saw her hand-writing, faded, but still legible. 'For Terry. A day to remember. Our wedding, May the twentieth 1949.' Underneath this was Terry's own childlike scribble, the only words he could write, his name, Terry Doyle.

'We traced you through the records of the registry office,' the policeman continued. 'The only other things we found in his pocket were pieces of what appears to be nougat and a key. I took the liberty of trying it in the door above and needless to say, it fitted.'

Bella stared at the photo. This couldn't be happening. Terry had gone over to Sean and Ashley's. He was nowhere near Surrey. He never went off the island, at least not that she knew of.

'Mrs Bryant?'

She looked up. 'It can't be my brother.'

'We won't know that for sure until you identify him.'

'You want me to look at–' she stopped, unable to believe what he was asking of her.

'I'm afraid I'll have to ask you to come with me.'

'But it's not Terry.'

'Is there someone else who can be with you?'

Just then the door opened. Micky entered, coming over to take her in his arms. 'Oh Micky, they said Terry's dead.'

She listened as the policeman explained it all over again. She wanted Micky to snap his fingers and make the man go away, leave them alone so she could continue to make dinner and watch

374

Hughie Green and end their day like any normal day.

But when she heard Micky saying he would go next door to fetch Daisy and then they would go to the mortuary, she knew there would never be another normal day.

Not for a long time.

A cover was pulled back. She had heard it said that after death, people look peaceful, as though they were in a better place. But Terry just looked empty. He was a waxwork image, an empty shell, his eyes closed and the smile he always smiled, gone forever.

If it hadn't been for Micky holding her, she wouldn't have been able to stand. Her legs felt weightless. She couldn't cry as she stared down at the brother she had loved and protected so fiercely. The tears wouldn't fall. Why had he been taken from her? He had never done any wrong and wouldn't hurt a fly. Who had done this terrible thing to him?

The cover was replaced and Micky led her out. 'It's Terry,' he told the policeman.

After that, she let Micky take her outside. In the car he told her he was going to call Dr Cox. When he came, Bella swallowed the pills he gave her. She hoped they would make the awful place in which she found herself disappear. Even when Micky led her to the bedroom, undressed her and put her in bed, she was frightened to close her eyes. Would she see Terry in her dreams, that Terry who was not Terry – and try to wake him up and take him out of that terrible place?

A heavy sensation dragged her down. Her lids began to flutter as she looked up at Micky. She knew he was talking to her, holding her hand and telling her that he would stay with her. But it didn't seem to matter now. All she could think of was Terry lying in the cold place, with his skin the texture of china.

Micky was sitting with Bella and Michael in the front row of St Nicholas's Catholic Church. He was dressed in a black suit and tie for the funeral and like everyone else had shed tears as Father Johns had paid a glowing tribute to Terry. Although Micky was upset, the tears were for himself as his nerves had been stretched by the red tape at the inquest. What a palaver! But in the end the police had turned up nothing from the wood or from Terry's last known movements. He had been due to arrive at Sean's on the Saturday but never turned up. Sean and Ashley had simply assumed he might not have been well. The enquiries had come to a dead end and the verdict was death by misadventure.

Although he had managed a few tears, Micky was feeling on top of the world. His big worry had been the duchess. She was an unknown quantity in all this because she was a bit off her trolley. Alfred had assured him that he was worrying for nothing. Reminded him that his lordship had been one conniving old twister. The money in the safe didn't exist in the books of Her Majesty's taxmen. The duchess dipped into it for things like fixing the Jag. The funny money, crumpled and dirtied, tied up in string and squashed in bags, was only going to seep out in small quantities.

Micky passed his handkerchief to Bella, then smoothed a genuine wetness from his own eyes. To think what a close shave he'd had! But he was now ten grand richer – a miracle! He'd given Lenny and Milo half of what they'd expected, economized on Terry's cut, and given Alfred his full whack, which was only fair to a professional on the job.

Micky took hold of his wife's hand and squeezed it. He'd dealt with the undertakers, arranged the funeral and given Father Johns all the old bull on Terry. Bella wanted a good sendoff and if that meant he had to invent a few porkies, so be it. He had even stayed home for a few days. Until he couldn't stand the atmosphere any more!

Micky looked into his wife's grief-stricken face. She was taking her brother's death hard, but let's face it, Terry had been short of a full shilling. He would never have amounted to anything, would he?

Micky smiled at his son. Good-looking lad, but a bit wet behind the ears and leaning a bit too much towards his mother's looks. When all this was over, he'd try to toughen him up a bit.

There was best sherry and beer for the adults and lemonade and cream soda for the children. Spread out on the kitchen table were plates of dainty triangular-shaped ham and cucumber sandwiches, cheese biscuits, sausage rolls, pickles, gherkins, mince pies and two bowls of sherry trifle. Bella's heart hadn't really been in the preparation, but Gina had come over and helped. Joyce and Ronnie were only just back from their honeymoon and they had insisted they wanted to help her. But Bella had declined, saying it was just a small do for the mourners.

It was only a month ago they had all been celebrating at the New Inn. How could her life have changed so radically in such a short time? she wondered, as she placed the napkins on the side plates.

'I've given the children theirs first out in the yard,' Gina told her as she came in. 'Took it all out on a big tray. They can make as much mess as they like out there.'

'Thanks.' Bella went to the sink. She scrubbed the baking tray hard, a lock of hair falling over her face.

Gina came to stand beside her. 'I'm worried about you, Bella. You haven't stopped. Why don't you sit down and chat with everyone first.'

'No, I like to keep busy.'

'That's what I'm worried about. You'll exhaust yourself.' Gina touched her arm gently. 'Listen, no matter what has happened, Terry wouldn't want this, you working yourself to a frazzle.'

Bella didn't want to talk about Terry or her innermost feelings. She knew Gina was trying to help, but work was her only release, as then she didn't have time to think. 'Would you make the tea?' she asked, changing the subject and nodding to the kettle. 'Not everyone will want alcohol.'

Gina sighed heavily. 'Have it your own way, girl. But if you wash that pan any harder it will

378

dissolve down the drain.'

Bella kept scrubbing. She didn't want to think about what she would do next, say next, think next. She had found a way to cope by living in the moment. If she allowed her thoughts freedom they always returned to the dark wood where Terry had been found. He had died alone, shot by an unknown person and it was repugnant to her. Most of all, she blamed herself. It was her fault that he had gone off so much lately. Who had he seen? Where had he gone to? What crowd had he fallen in with? She had tried to persuade him to come downstairs and sleep in the spare room, but he had refused. What had been going on in his mind? Was he frightened of someone or something?

Bella realized she was staring at Mary who was being fussed over by Gus as they sat by the fire. Mary had cried throughout the funeral. Had been comforted by the priest and everyone else as the grieving mother. Now she was drinking from a glass, her cheeks red and her eyes bright as everyone paid her their condolences. Except of course Ronnie and Micky. She knew they were tolerating her presence and Mary was probably revelling in their discomfort.

'It was a lovely service,' Joyce said then and Bella came back to the moment as Joyce took one of the offered sandwiches.

'Yes, it was.'

'And a lovely tribute to Terry by the priest.'

Bella was aware that Joyce, like Gina, was trying to say the right things. She looked very beautiful with her golden Italian tan set off by her elegant black dress, but her face was full of concern.

'I'm sorry you came back to a funeral,' Bella said.

'I wish we could do something to help.'

'It's just nice that you're here. Now, can I get you a drink?'

'Ronnie's gone for one.' Joyce looked awkward. 'We are supposed to be moving in upstairs next week. But it doesn't seem very appropriate, not with ... well, what I mean is–'

'You don't have to worry on my account,' Bella said stiffly. 'I've cleared Terry's room out.'

'Oh, Bella, I was hoping to help you.' Joyce looked mortified.

'It was better to get it over.'

She had done it whilst Michael was at school and when Micky had gone back to the club. His fussing around had irritated her. She wasn't used to him being home and his presence seemed to accentuate the fact of Terry's death. Finally she had found a few moments to go upstairs. It was then she had let the tears fall. As she had placed Terry's clothes and personal effects in a box, she had wept. After that she had closed the door, ending a part of her life.

As more people arrived Bella went out to the yard. 'Would you like more to eat?' she asked the children. Emma and Victoria, Anne and Irene, Michael and Teresa were playing hopscotch. They didn't really understand the occasion. Even Teresa hadn't absorbed that her half-brother was dead. It was a relief to talk to them as they seemed to carry on as usual.

'Can we have some more mince pies?' Michael wanted to know.

'I'll bring some out.'

'Can we play Blind Man's Buff?'

She gave them her purple and black silk scarf that she had worn with her black dress. When they were occupied, she made her way back to the guests. Percy and Dolly were standing by the window. 'Thank you for coming,' she said.

'We are so sorry, Bella.' Dolly had tears in her eyes and a little bump under her black skirt.

'Thanks. Now you must have something to eat.'

She was glad when Ronnie came up and gave them something to drink. Dolly was her best friend, but Bella didn't want to talk to her now.

All she wanted to do was keep her hands and feet going. It was the best antidote to pain that she had found. Better even than the pills she was still swallowing, trying to numb the ache inside her.

Leaving Joyce to talk to Percy and Dolly, Ronnie slipped outside and went up the steps of the airey. The October night was as clear as a bell, the stars shone down from a deep blue sky. The weather had even turned a little warmer. He wondered if he should have brought Joyce with him. They hadn't had chance to look at the old house together and next week they were moving in.

He wasn't going to stay upstairs long. Just look around and make a few mental notes as to what was needed.

He took out his key and let himself in. Immediately he closed the door, he felt odd. He stood still, listening in the darkness to the deep silence. He had been so convinced it was the right thing to do. He was going to put in a telephone and make Joyce a modern kitchen to cook in. He had so many plans ... yet all of a sudden, the house felt more like a stranger than an old friend.

Switching on the light, he looked around him. The place was much the same as when Mum and Dad had lived here apart from a few coats of paint, new lino, different curtains. But essentially, still the same. Sean and Ashley had looked after it well. But it wouldn't be Joyce's choice.

Would she like living here? he wondered as he walked into the front room. Mum's big, polished table was no longer extended. Sean had dropped the sides and pushed it back against the wall.

He sighed, fighting the nostalgia. The family table. Family meetings ... the brothers who were going to make such a big name for themselves. The family firm...

And then, along came a spider...

The spider was time, Ronnie thought then. Time had caught up with them. They weren't kids any more, but men. Each as stubborn as the other. Too many chiefs and not enough Indians his old Dad would have said.

Ronnie went into the kitchen. He smiled, as for a brief moment he fancied he could still smell cooking. Mum's apple tart and egg custard with cinnamon sprinkled on the top. He wondered if Joyce would follow in her footsteps, with an apron tied round her waist, a willing slave to the stove. Somehow he couldn't see that. She'd more likely be nipping down the shop for something on

382

the quick. Or better still, going out to eat.

What was he doing, bringing Joyce back here? he wondered as the smile faded from his lips. You couldn't go backwards or you'd fall off the edge of the world was another of his dad's sayings. Yet here he was, starting married life with a quarter of a century of bachelor memories stacked under this roof. Financially, him and Joyce could afford to live anywhere. One minute they were set for the big gaff in the sticks, the next he was hightailing it back to Piper Street.

He turned quickly and went upstairs. It smelt of men up here. Polished leather and Brylcreem, newspapers and fags. Mum and Dad's room – he opened the door and memories flooded back. Surprisingly strong was the memory of Bella that night after the Indigo, when she'd had too much champagne. He smiled. Terry had kept guard, sleeping on the landing. Micky hadn't got a look in then.

The thought of Terry made him turn to the small room. This had been his own room once, the room Terry had seized for himself and had loved. The lad's own space. A possession he'd never had before. A few feet of absolute privacy.

Ronnie pushed open the door. He could smell Terry still. Mostly fags and what was it, he liked to chew? Those sweets – nougat, was it?

The room looked empty. Joyce had told him Bella had cleared Terry's things. His heart went out to her. What could he do to help ease her pain?

It was all such a puzzle. What had the kid been up to? Downey Wood – the end of the planet as

383

far as Terry was concerned! He must have been taken there. But by whom? And why?

'Ronnie?'

He turned. Joyce was smiling at him. He drew her into his arms.

'Well, have you decided?' she asked

'Decided on what?'

'Which room we're having.'

Ron lifted her chin. 'Are we doing the right thing? Coming back here? I mean, Terry was—'

'Terry's gone, Ronnie. There's just you and me.'

He felt the need to reassure her, or was it himself?

'Joyce, I love you, you know that, don't you?'

For her answer she stood on her toes and kissed him. 'Let's go back. We can work it all out next week.'

Hand in hand they went downstairs and Ronnie, if the truth be known, was relieved to shut the door behind him.

Chapter Twenty-Five

1960

A tall young man sporting sideburns, a quiff of Brylcreemed hair and a pair of crepe soles emerging below his drainpipe trousers, left his three friends to walk over to the jukebox. A blast of Little Richard filled the café and he returned to the oblong green Formica table overflowing with Pyrex coffee cups.

On the other side of the room sat the rival party of conventional dressers. These young men and women wore sharp navy blue blazers and polo necks, the girls flaunting back to front cardigans and pony-tails.

The warm steam fug of the café, even in June, was enhanced by the smell of Espresso coffee streaming from the shining chromium coffee machine. Behind it, Bella was stacking the shelves of glass cups and saucers. Above them rose a wall emblazoned by logos and black and white photographs of all the latest pin-ups. The Dallas Boys, Cliff Richard, Billy Fury and Elvis the Pelvis to name but a few. Every so often a customer would bring one in and up it would go, until the wall was covered and new space had to be found.

Gina's Coffee Bar was settling down after a mad Saturday morning. Bella knew that trade would bounce back in an hour, before the first showing of the main feature at the local cinema. Going to the window she smiled at another boy and girl deep in conversation as they sat on tall stools at the bar. They were obviously in love, whispering sweet nothings, whilst the other group were laughing and extrovert.

Bella lowered the blind as she always did after lunch, giving the interior a more intimate feel. After clearing the tables and chatting with the young people, she went to the kitchen. Here Gina was measuring the coffee beans. They sold gallons of Espresso and the expensive Italian machine that produced quantities of frothy milky coffee had paid for itself a dozen times over.

'If I hear "Good Golly Miss Molly" one more time, I'm gonna break that record over someone's head,' Gina warned as Bella set down the dirty glass cups.

'You'll have to beat me to it,' Bella laughed. 'That lad plays it all the time. Drives me nuts.'

'What did we do before juke boxes came along?'

'Search me.' Bella rinsed out the cups under the sparkling new taps and set them on the stainless steel racks. 'And it's not cheap to keep playing them. It's a wonder they've got the spare.'

'Oh, these youngsters aren't strapped for cash.' Gina lifted the large glass flask onto the chromium container. 'They make anything up to twelve quid a week, you know. One of them Teddy Boys was telling me last week he works in a factory making motorcycles. All that clobber they manufacture is custom made.'

Bella nodded. 'Michael is already fussy about what he wears. He likes nice clothes to impress the girls at the youth club. Some of them at Docklands look very grown up and wear make-up. The youngsters grow up so quick these days.'

'His father should know about that,' Gina nodded.

Bella didn't comment. Michael was a happy-go-lucky boy but on the rare occasions he saw his father, he was always quiet and withdrawn. He was as confused as she was over Micky's irrational behaviour and mood swings.

As far as the romantic side of their marriage was concerned, it was non-existent. No hugs or cuddles or fond words. The last time they had made love was a disaster. She'd tried to please him, but he'd pushed her aside irritably when he gained no satisfaction. She no longer worried where he was when he didn't come home. She knew. He almost lived at his new club, the Flamingo.

Gina glanced her way. 'So what is Michael doing this morning?' They never stayed on the subject of Micky long.

'He's gone to Saturday morning cinema with Teresa. And then they're going down the Docklands. Him and his mates have got a skiffle group started. They only muck about with an old tea chest and washboard, but he loves it.'

'A bit different to going up the market like the old days.'

Bella nodded. 'That would bore him now.'

'One day he'll be coming in here.'

Bella laughed. 'Then I'll have to pay for the coffee I serve him!'

As she said this, Gina put down the cloth and frowned at her. 'No, you needn't, not if you was the owner.'

Bella stared at her in surprise. 'What did you say?'

Gina grinned. 'How do you fancy being a joint owner of a coffee bar?'

'This place?'

Gina nodded. 'The bloke that owns the freehold is selling. Would you come in with me?'

Bella smiled incredulously. 'You're joking of course.'

'I'm deadly serious. I want a real partner who understands the business.'

'But how much would it cost?' Bella asked doubtfully.

'He wants three grand. That means one-and-a-half apiece.'

'That's a lot of money.'

'I don't know how you're fixed? Would Micky help?'

'I don't know.'

'It's a good investment.'

Bella frowned. 'What would you do if I said no. Could you still afford it?'

Gina shrugged. 'I'd raise the money somehow.' She paused. 'It's not just the money, Bella. It was you that helped me to turn the café into a modern business. I was at an all-time low after Lenny did a bunk and then the tea urn went on the blink as well! It was you that said why didn't I install one of those new-fangled coffee machines you'd seen up the Brompton Road, remember?'

Bella smiled. 'Yes and you asked me to come and operate it.'

'To help you get over Terry, really,' Gina said gently. 'I knew working here would get you out of yourself. Apart from that, I was glad to have you back again. We work together well and understand each other. Will you give my proposition some thought?'

Bella felt a curl of excitement in her stomach. 'All right, I will.'

'Good girl!' Gina exclaimed, raising her voice above the noise of the hissing coffee machine. 'Don't forget, Espresso is big and coffee bars are the in-thing. We've got good heads on us, Bella, let's make them work for us.'

As more young people filed in the door Bella tried to imagine that the shop was hers. It was a big responsibility. Not the same as keeping the accounts and being a part-time waitress. But she was independent now. Ronnie had taught her to drive and she had a little car. Why shouldn't she branch out?

Bella could see a big opportunity ahead. But what would Micky think of it?

Micky was on a trip. He had been for the past twelve hours. He had arrived at the Flamingo with look-a-like Leyla as he dubbed her, in the early hours and taken her to the back rooms. As it was his club, all bought and paid for thanks to the duchess, he could do exactly as he pleased, a heady sensation and a novelty that hadn't yet worn off. Let the others run the club, that's what he paid them for. His manager and doormen, the little chics behind the bar and the high-class tarts who paid him fifty per cent of their tote.

He was happy as Larry here in the back room where the beautiful colours flowed in and out of each other and there was the sensation of being in a different time and space. The LSD tablets had never given him a bad trip as they had some people he'd dealt to. As he relaxed beside the beautiful young black woman who could have been Leyla but for the fact Leyla had overdosed and departed this mortal coil three years ago, he was in psychedelic heaven. He had found Nirvana. He had also found a satisfying flow of income from the drugs. All these bourgeois arty types trying to score from dodgy cockney villains

389

to impress their friends ... well, he was their man.

He grinned foolishly. And the pot smokers, too! Roll on the beatniks and the musicians and the long-haired radicals. The dopes had actually convinced themselves they were going to change the world. As God hadn't managed to do it in the long aeons of ownership, what hope had they? The revenue he was generating from these monkeys was going to stack up the vaults again. The duchess's money was long gone, and that bastard McNee was at his old tricks again. He'd been hoping that the Krays, with whom he had a nodding acquaintance, would put paid to McNee and plant him ten feet under a flyover. But unfortunately Reggie had gone down this year and Ronnie was having a ball on his own. Still, all that would change if Reggie was out with good behaviour in half his time. Then let's see McNee get his just desserts!

Feeling satisfied, Micky felt the urge to run his hand over Leyla-Mark-Two's flat stomach. She was totally out of it still, her eyes seeing into some other world. He would have a joint or two with her in a minute and pulling her to him, he roused her softly. She awoke with a way-out smile on her face.

Baby, if this was what tripping was all about, he wanted more of it.

Percy had painted the yellow front door of 24 Chapel House Street, emerald green. The horse-shoe knocker had been replaced with a glinting lion's head and the square of grass at the front was neatly tended as was the border of flowers.

The Shines had moved in four years ago when Mr Taylor died and although the house was small, it was Dolly's pride and joy.

She had replaced the lace curtains with frilly nets, the old lino with carpet and all the beds were doubles. One for her and Percy, another for the twins and one for five-year-old April and three-year-old June. Widowed Mrs Taylor, burdened with arthritis, slept on the bed settee downstairs.

Bella dropped the heavy knocker and there were yells of delight from inside. The door swung open and Dolly and two little girls flung themselves forward. The next in line for attention was young Michael, who barely flinched as they clung to his legs. The ten-year-old twins looked shyly out from behind Dolly's plump shoulders.

'Come in, come in,' Dolly beckoned, all flying frizzy hair and plump bosom. She pulled Bella inside and kissed Michael on his cheek, much to his embarrassment. 'Tea's all ready in the kitchen,' she gushed, urging them down the hall. 'Anne and Irene have made fairy cakes and April and June helped stir the custard. Now Michael, go and tell the girls what you'd like to drink and we'll all sit down soon to eat. April, June, go and wash your hands and faces, please.'

Giggling the two little girls ran off. The twins escorted Michael out to the kitchen and Bella followed Dolly to the front room. She was surprised to see that Mrs Taylor's chair was empty.

'Mum's gone to Raymond's for a month,' Dolly said by way of explanation. 'It won't be much of a holiday I'm afraid as she has to put up with all his brood. Me and him have ten between the two of us!'

Bella sighed. 'And there's me with just one.'

'Don't speak too soon,' Dolly warned as she made herself comfortable on the settee. 'You're only twenty-eight, there's plenty of time yet.'

'I've always wanted a big family,' Bella replied wistfully as she sat next to Dolly. 'But it just hasn't happened and now I'm beginning to think I'm better off as I am.'

She didn't enlighten Dolly on the way things were at home with her and Micky although she knew that Dolly had guessed. Even though she wanted another child, she knew it would be unwise to have one. Their most recent quarrel had been over the coffee bar. When she'd told him about Gina's suggestion he'd flown off the handle. Gina was trying to get money out of them to keep the café going, he'd insisted. When, ill-advisedly, she had tried to explain the potential, he'd told her she was a gullible fool and Gina wasn't getting a penny.

'Dolly, I'd like to talk to you about something. I want to ask your advice.'

Dolly's eyes widened. 'Wait a minute, I'll send the kids into the garden to play.'

Bella opened her bag and took out the sums she had been doing. When Dolly returned, she passed her the notes.

'What's this?'

'Dolly, I'm thinking about going into business.'

'Who with?'

'Gina. She has a chance to buy the coffee bar. This is a summary of the takings.'

Dolly examined the paper. 'I'm afraid I'm hopeless when it comes to figures, but you seem to be doing all right.'

Bella nodded. 'The kids spend as much on coffee as the dockers and labourers used to on fry-ups. They like different food too, easier to prepare as the bakery delivers most of it. Pastries, fancy breads and quick snacks. Not only have we changed the menu, but our reputation for good coffee has got around. Sometimes there's standing room only. Last Saturday morning we had a queue outside the door–' she broke off, grinning. 'I'm only seeing the good side, as you can tell. That's why I wanted your advice.'

'What can I tell you?' Dolly chuckled. 'I don't know anything about coffee bars. But I can see you're very enthusiastic.'

'I am.'

'You like working there, don't you?'

'I always did. Even when it was a café. But now it's even better. The young people are entertaining and the coffee brings all sorts together and breaks down barriers. It all started with the coffee machine and then the juke box. Teenagers need somewhere to go, drink coffee and listen to their music. In a way, it's an extension of the old youth clubs.'

'A bit of a change to the Docklands youth club, though?'

'As the kids get older they want something else.'

'I don't know if I'd let my girls go in a coffee bar.'

'They're young yet. But you probably won't be

able to stop them when they get older.'

Dolly sighed. 'Percy already has the shotgun under the bed when it comes to boys.' She giggled. 'If the girls come in your coffee bar, you can report to me on what's happening.'

They laughed and Bella tilted her head curiously. 'So do I get the thumbs up?'

'You don't need me to give an approval,' Dolly grinned. 'But yes, I think it's a wonderful idea.'

Bella felt excited. At least she had Dolly's support. All she had to do now, was work out the money with Gina. Would the coffee bar be a wise investment? If she didn't give it a try she would never know!

If Bella had any worries about the success of Espresso, she soon lost them. Over the summer, trade increased to the point where they had to employ help. Tina, the young girl who had helped in the café days, returned to work.

Bella had come to a decision and she had invested all her savings into the coffee bar, every penny that she'd saved over the years. The family was happy for her, but not Micky, who had warned her she would regret it. Even Mary and Gus who were now living together in the prefab, called in to see what the coffee bar was like. Bella served them knickerbocker glories from the new ice cream machine and Espresso afterwards. Gus played the juke box and Bella was amused to see Mary talking to the teenagers.

In September Bella became an official partner. There was a small celebration one Saturday morning. Bella had prepared twice as many sandwiches as usual and the baker had delivered large trays of coconut Madeleines and rum babas.

Ronnie and Joyce entered just after half past nine. Joyce wore a French pleat as her dark hair had grown longer. Her face was perfectly made-up with Max Factor Pancake and her eyes enhanced with artistically applied mascara. As usual, all heads turned when she walked in. Even the youngest boys stared at her whilst the girls giggled as Ronnie smiled at them. Dressed in a blue blazer and clean-cut white shirt, he looked very handsome.

'Congratulations you two,' Joyce said as she hugged Gina and Bella. 'Do you know they're lining up outside?'

'We could do with more seats,' Gina chuckled. 'There are plenty of bums to sit on them.'

'Then knock down that wall and move into the kitchen,' Ronnie suggested and everyone stared at him. 'It would make the place more modern.'

'Are you offering?' Bella asked.

Ronnie grinned. 'I've knocked down enough walls for strangers and you're family. So if you want it done, it's done.'

'Yes, please,' Bella and Gina cried together. 'We want to look like Moka in Frith Street and the Mocamba in the Brompton Road.' Bella had gone up to the City and tried to bring ideas back. The food was easy, but not the decoration.

The following day, Sunday, Ron sent his men. A month later, it was all done, with no interruption to the business. The customers were as excited as Bella and Gina.

They opened to their busiest week ever. Soon

they were attracting the City custom: musicians, beatniks and people who seemed to spend their lives drinking coffee and writing their life stories.

The teenagers loved it, crowding in to meet the new element. Bella hoped that Micky would take more interest now they had got the business off the ground. But there was no sign of that.

'You'll come to us for Christmas dinner, won't you?' Joyce asked her as the holiday approached. As usual, Michael and Ronnie had gone to the park with the football and Joyce and Bella were dressing the tree in the front room.

'I'd like that.' Bella didn't mention Micky. She didn't know if he would accompany them or not. She was very worried about him. On the rare occasions he was home he drank heavily and smoked a strong tobacco, leaving a smell on his clothes that followed him around the house. As a result, she was forced to leave the windows open even if it was very cold.

'You know,' Joyce mused as she hung a dainty silver bell on the Christmas tree, 'this house really seems like home now. I didn't think I could ever be satisfied playing at the little wife. I always thought I'd get back to doing something, other than helping Ron with the business. But the past five years have been so happy that–' she stopped, a little flush coming to her cheeks. 'I've discovered I'm happy being Mrs Ronnie Bryant.'

Bella knew she loved Ronnie dearly. They were content living in Piper Street when they had had the choice of living anywhere they liked. If only she and Micky still felt the same, Bella thought longingly. She wanted to make a fuss of him like she used to. Like Joyce did with Ron. She wanted to cook him dinners and watch him sit in front of the television with Michael and drink mugs full of hot cocoa. Bella was so proud of their son. He was now at the grammar school. Micky didn't seem to realize how bright he was.

Then there was the coffee bar. She longed to boast a little and win Micky's approval. She wasn't jealous of the Suzies of his world as she knew they came and went. She had long ago become resigned to Micky's amours. But if they tried hard, if she could make him see what joy a family could bring, could love be revived?

Bella gazed around Joyce's enviously. Everywhere there was evidence of her fresh and modern taste. All Mrs Bryant's old furniture, except the big polished table, pushed into the alcove with a bright red tablecloth over it, had gone. Lively colours had replaced the gloomy old ones that had made the house seem so old-fashioned. A sofa and a tub-shaped chair had replaced the couch. Coloured squares on the curtains and squiggles on the pottery made the room look stylish. One of the walls had a splish-splash design that looked almost like coloured rain. Bella sighed softly. Perhaps, despite Micky's insistence that he hated the modern fashions, she should try to gain his attention by redecorating the airey?

'Ron's mum wouldn't approve of the changes,' Joyce admitted, breaking in to her train of thought. 'Ron told me his dad was never allowed to bring in new things. She liked the house as it was. She was really house-proud.' Joyce bent down to clasp another little bell. 'I never knew

397

her but I would have liked–' Suddenly she put her hand to head.

'Joyce, are you all right?'

'Yes, I just came over a bit dizzy.'

'Sit down.' Bella helped her to the sofa. 'Are you doing too much?'

Joyce blinked and carefully rearranged her dark hair.

'Actually, I'm praying this is good news.'

Bella looked at her and then a smile slowly formed.

'You don't mean–?'

Joyce nodded. 'I've missed a period. I know it's early days, but what if it's true? Oh, Bella, I long to have a baby. More now than ever.'

'Joyce, that's wonderful.'

'I'm not going to tell Ron until Christmas Eve. It will be my Christmas present. I'll see the doctor first, to confirm it of course.' She looked at Bella, her face full of hope. 'Oh, I'm so sorry, this is selfish of me. I know you and Micky would like another child.'

'I'm quite happy as I am,' Bella said lightly, taking Joyce's hand and squeezing it.

'You mean a working woman?'

'Yes. Babies aren't the top of my Christmas list. Only your baby. I'll be an auntie! Now I can go out and buy lots of baby clothes.'

'But only white or yellow!'

Suddenly they were laughing and hugging and Bella knew that this Christmas, with or without Micky, was going to be a very special one.

Lenny stood in the shadows. He had watched the

café for months now, careful never to let himself be seen. It had become part of his life, ever since his release. The evenings had drawn in and the darkness gave him good protection. Each night he watched all the youngsters laughing and talking as they left the café and said their goodbyes on the street. Sometimes he heard the music drift out and this made him sad. It made him think of the days when he and Gina used to lie in bed on a Sunday morning and turn on the wireless. Gina had a lovely voice when she sang, throaty and full. He'd never forget the way she felt beside him or the way they had made love. The strange thing was he'd been blinded by lust and hadn't known he'd loved her until he'd been incarcerated. Then he'd had time to work it all out. To come to the realization she was a good woman. Loyal and giving. The bossiness was just her way of getting things done. He'd resented that. Resented her success as he had never had any of his own. Other thoughts had tormented him in prison. Had she found a new man? Was there a new love interest in her life? Had she replaced him?

What a fool he had been! The regrets were legion. Why had he let Micky convince him he was wasting his time in the café? He'd been happy there really. Micky had put ideas into his mind. Massaged his ego in order to get what he wanted. 'You're letting her rule you,' or 'she'll drive you into the ground, you're worth more than the brush she sticks in your hand to push each day.' Micky had finally convinced him that stealing from an old girl who was half barmy was the way to go. The irony was that yet again he had escaped detection. Just like the warehouse. Instead he had frittered away the money and been caught trying to nick a lorry. A lorry of all things! What was in his mind? It was full of old tyres and he'd had this notion he'd get money for them. Two years he'd gone down for. For a load of old rubber!

Lenny turned up his collar, threadbare and rough. He watched Gina move amongst the tables, washing them down, lavishing care on that bloody great machine behind the counter. He smiled then. That was his Gina.

He watched every night. Watched until the lights went out. Then he was tempted, oh so tempted to go down the side and into the yard. What would she say to him? What would he say to her?

He remembered every inch of the yard, which wasn't surprising as he'd cleaned it so often. He knew every brick, every stone, every dustbin. He knew what it was like to walk in the back door and see Gina there, her black hair swept up behind her head, her eyes flashing, ready with a quick answer and more often than not, ready to lay into him. But how he missed her. He missed everything about her. He was forty-six now, a down and out with a receding hairline, empty pockets and a gut full of ulcers.

He was an ex-con living in a hostel, reviewing his life which amounted to sod all without Gina. Still, he couldn't turn back the clock. He'd better get moving if he didn't want his collar touched. The coppers would think he was casing the joint.

Shrugging his shoulders under the old coat, Lenny moved carefully away. The shops were full of bright Christmas lights, some kids on the corner were singing carols. He didn't want to be round here any more. He had to move on with his life. But he was lost.

And Lenny couldn't find his way back.

Chapter Twenty-Six

The big, polished table was extended and set for Christmas dinner. Joyce and Bella were in the kitchen preparing the food and Michael and Ronnie were watching television. The smell of roast turkey was pervading the house as Sean and Ashley arrived.

'Happy Christmas one and all!' They bore armfuls of presents and smelt highly of lacquer as the wind blew them through the front door.

'Happy Christmas!' Bella kissed them under the mistletoe and there were rude comments and much laughter. The Christmas tree was surrounded by carefully wrapped parcels that Michael had examined earlier to see if he could guess what was in them.

'It's nice to be cooked for,' Sean told them when he had taken off his coat and hung it up. 'But if you girls want a hand in the kitchen let us know.'

'Thanks, but we're five minutes away from dishing up,' Joyce said over her shoulder. Ever since Joyce had moved in she had insisted she cook dinner for the family and Sean and Ashley had been happy to accept. They knew it was important to her to carry on the tradition.

'How efficient.' Sean made a little wave with his hand. 'Next year you'll have to come over to our place for cocktails,' Ashley purred and everyone laughed as he put on an exaggerated voice. 'I mean it. We'll have it all decorated by then with a fantastic new cocktail cabinet in the lounge.'

'He's only showing off,' Sean admonished teasingly.

'We'll come if you do our hair,' Bella grinned. 'You can give us our drinks whilst we sit under the dryers.'

'That's blackmail!' Sean screeched as everyone laughed again and the Christmas spirit began to take effect.

Sean and Ashley were very fashion conscious and had employed an interior designer to decorate the salon. Everyone seemed to be smartening up their homes, Bella pondered as she stirred the gravy. Perhaps she should really do something about the airey? No one had mentioned Micky and Bella knew they wouldn't. They didn't want to embarrass her.

When they were alone she turned to Joyce. 'Do you think downstairs could do with smartening up?' she asked as she poured the rich brown Bisto into the gravy boat.

'We could go up to town to the January sales and look for ideas,' Joyce suggested as she lowered the roasting dish to the oven.

Bella liked that idea. 'I'll arrange a day off from work.'

Joyce frowned thoughtfully. 'It's a shame Gina couldn't come today. I don't like to think of her on her own.'

'Neither do I, but you know what she's like.' Bella had tried to persuade Gina to join them, but each Christmas was the same. They always asked her and she always found an excuse. Bella knew that Christmas was still a difficult time for her.

'I wish she'd find herself a man,' Joyce murmured, expressing Bella's own feelings. 'Surely you must have some eligible customers?'

Bella sighed. 'Gina laughs and jokes with them all, but keeps them at a distance. She's not interested in men in that way. Not after Lenny.'

'She must have loved him a lot.'

'I think she did.'

Joyce sighed and drew her hand across her forehead. 'I'll just sit down for a minute. It's very hot in here.'

'You should be in the other room with your feet up.'

'And spoil Ron's surprise?' Joyce laughed softly as she sank down on a chair and folded her hands over her stomach. 'I feel so fortunate, Bella. I have all a woman could want. A family around me, a husband like Ron and a baby on the way. Who would have thought that Joyce King, Madam and brothel owner would be given the chance to change her life like this?'

Bella looked into Joyce's flushed and radiant face.

'No one deserves happiness more than you, Joyce, and Ronnie is going to make a wonderful father.'

Joyce giggled. 'I can't wait to see his face.'

'Neither can I,' Bella wagged her finger. 'And next year it will definitely be me who's going to cook the Christmas dinner. Baby Bryant will be wanting attention and you won't know a moment's peace.'

Both women looked at each other and Joyce managed to whisper as tears of mirth and happiness filled her eyes, 'And Ronnie, poor lamb, will have been up all night, looking after him!'

The dinner had been eaten and the dishes cleared away, with the dining table once again back in the corner. They had opened all their presents and were enjoying a slice of Christmas cake in front of the fire.

Michael's head was buried in a book called *Dennis the Menace*. Bella felt a wave of nostalgia. The comic annual, amongst all his other presents, seemed the last from childhood. All his other presents were very grown-up. A leather football from Ron and Joyce and a fashionable blue polo-neck sweater from Sean and Ashley. She herself had bought him the most grown-up present of all. A Dansette record player.

The salesman who had sold it to her had explained this model was cutting edge. Unlike all previous models, it played 12 inch, 10 inch and 7 inch records at different speeds. Throughout the afternoon they had been listening to Frank Sinatra and Doris Day, some of Ron's old collection that was almost worn smooth by the clumsy needle of the cumbersome radiogram. The record player could sit on a shelf or table and was light to operate. Michael couldn't wait for the shops to open. He wanted to buy recordings of Lonnie Donegan and Tommy Steele, his musical idols. Luckily Bella knew what they sounded like, as she'd listened to them many times on the jukebox.

'I've got some of Crosby's here,' Ronnie suggested as he began to blow the dust off a pile of large, heavy records. But it was Joyce who took the record from his hand and made him sit down. 'Before you play that,' she murmured as she sat beside him, 'there's something I'd like to say about your present. As you may have noticed, you haven't got one.'

Everyone laughed and Ronnie made a face. 'What! No socks this Christmas!' Everyone chuckled again, but Joyce's voice shook slightly when she answered. Bella knew this was the moment Joyce had been waiting for all Christmas.

'No, you haven't got socks.'

'A tie, then?' Ron looked puzzled as he met his wife's dark eyes.

'No, it's not a tie either.' Joyce reached out for his hands. 'I can't give it to you yet, as, in a way, it's on order. And I'm afraid you'll have to wait about seven months till it arrives.'

The room was silent until Sean jumped up. 'Joyce, you don't mean? You don't! You *do?*' Suddenly he and Ashley were rushing forward and hugging her. It was only Ron who sat with a straight face, unable to comprehend.

'Ronnie,' Joyce whispered softly. 'I'm expecting.'

His jaw fell open. 'A baby?'

'Of course a baby.'

'A baby,' Ronnie repeated. 'You mean I'm

going to be a father?'

Joyce nodded. 'That's the general idea.'

He reached out for her. 'I just can't believe it. Are you sure?'

'I've seen the doctor. He doesn't seem to think there's much doubt.'

'We're going to be uncles,' Sean said emotionally, looking at Ashley.

'What will I be?' Michael asked.

'You'll be the baby's cousin, young man,' Ashley grinned. 'And as such, will be given the privilege of changing the first nappy.'

There was another burst of laughter and Ashley ruffled Michael's hair teasingly as Sean hurried off to the kitchen in search of the glasses and the unopened bottle of cream sherry.

It was the last Friday in December and all through the week Bella had been at a loose end. She missed the busy hours at the café. The time between Christmas and New Year had never seemed so long. Even though she had brought the accounts up to date, given the airey a spring-clean and was now entertaining her mother.

Mary had called with Teresa whilst Gus dug over the garden before the frosts. 'I suppose you'll be celebrating the New Year,' Mary hinted heavily as she parked herself by the fire. Teresa and Michael disappeared into the bedroom to play the Dansette.

'I've no special plans,' Bella shrugged as she poured the tea she had made into the best china. 'Just a quiet night in.'

'Good,' Mary said bluntly, 'as Gus and me are

going up to the Rose and I thought I'd leave Teresa here.' As she was eating the slice of sponge cake that Bella had cut her, she added sourly, 'Not that after Christmas there's any money to buy a drink with.'

'I didn't think Gus liked the pub.'

'Sure, where else should we go, if not to the boozer? It's New Year's Eve, ain't it? And I'd like to buy the poor bugger a drink seeing as all he's done for me.'

Bella opened her bag and took out three pounds.

'You'd better have this. But be sure to buy food first.'

Mary took it quickly, raising her eyebrows. 'I can't work miracles on a few quid. There's the larder to fill and I ain't been back to work yet.'

Bella took out another two pounds and Mary grabbed it. As she was closing her bag there were footsteps outside.

'So he's home, is he?' Mary scowled as Micky burst in the door.

Micky glowered at the sight of his mother-in-law.

'What's she doing here?' he demanded angrily.

'It's Christmas, Micky, or haven't you noticed?' Bella stared at her dishevelled husband.

He ignored her and strode into the kitchen. Bella followed. 'Where have you been all week?'

He took a bottle of beer from the cupboard and opened it. 'Where I go or what I do is my business. I've told you that before.'

'But the last time we saw you was Boxing Day.'

He drank greedily from the bottle. 'What was

the point of coming home?'

'To see your son, of course.'

Micky laughed at her words. 'Michael wouldn't care if he never saw me again. You've turned him against me and you know it.'

Bella was shocked. 'That's not true, Micky.'

'You married the wrong brother, Bells, why don't you admit it?' He pushed his face up to hers. 'Michael thinks more of his uncle than he does of me. And who was it who done all that? I am looking at her now, standing right in front of me. What else has gone on behind my back?'

'Micky, stop it. You don't know what you're saying.' Fear crept up into her throat as he grabbed hold of her.

'You're hurting me.'

His wild eyes stared into her face. 'How much money have you got in your bag?'

'Wh ... what do you want it for?' she stammered uncertainly.

'I need it, that's all. I'm short of ready cash and I know you must have some from the coffee bar.'

'But it's not mine to—'

'Where is it?' he demanded, shaking her. 'You'd better cough up, Bells, because if you don't, I'll chuck that old bat and her kid out and then I'll turn this place upside down till I find it.'

Bella felt her blood run cold as she returned his gaze. This wasn't Micky. It was as if someone else had stepped into his body. What had happened to him? And why did he want money?

'All right, I'll get you some,' she said quietly. 'But please don't cause any trouble as the children will hear.'

'Then you'd better hurry, hadn't you?' He reached down into the cupboard and snatched up another bottle.

Bella didn't look at Mary as she went through. She didn't want her to witness how frightened she was. She prayed the children would stay in the bedroom playing their records.

There was fifty pounds in the cash box. She took it from her dressing table drawer. The amount was sufficient to pay all the January bills at the coffee bar. She began to take out some of it when a hand gripped her.

'So this is where you hide it.' Micky grabbed the box and pushed her down on the bed. 'Quite the little hoarder, aren't we?' He took out all the notes and thrust them inside his coat. 'Is that the lot?'

'Micky, you can't take it all.'

'Why not? Look at how much I've given you over the years! It's about time you started paying your way. I'm fed up with watching my hard-earned money frittered away on that old soak you call a mother.' He pulled out the drawers of the dressing table searching for more. 'Anyway, Gina can afford it. She's loaded.'

When all her belongings lay on the floor, he glared at her. Then without a word, he turned and strode out.

Bella slowly replaced her things. She was shaking when Michael came in. 'We've played all Uncle Ron's records,' he told her. 'I wish we had some of our own.'

'You can buy some soon.'

'Are you all right, Mum?'

She nodded and sat on the bed. 'Come here.' She took his hand and drew him close. She wanted to be reassured. Micky had said some dreadful things. Did he really believe she had turned Michael against him?

'I've put on Doris Day,' Teresa cried excitedly as she ran in the room. 'We can dance to this one as it's fast.'

'Go on and have some fun,' she told Michael.

He smiled at her. The smile that was so like his father's.

When they had gone, Bella put her head in her hands in despair. What was wrong with Micky? He looked so strange. Why had he been so rough with her? Now she had to face her mother and pretend nothing was wrong.

'You've got trouble there, girl,' Mary predicted when she returned to the front room.

'I don't know what you mean,' Bella said shortly.

'Of course you do. Sure I can see right through the eejit, always did. I tried to warn you, but you'd have none of it.'

'Don't speak about Micky like that, Mum.'

But Mary wasn't listening. 'Your old man had a face like a bag full of spanners when he walked out. I ask you, is that any way to treat his mother-in-law when he sees her?'

Bella picked up Mary's coat. She didn't want to listen to any more. And now she had overheard those angry words, Mary was happy to leave.

Bella woke early the next morning. She had slid the bolt on the airey door last night but even then she slept lightly, waking at the slightest noise.

It was New Year's Eve and the radio was full of nostalgia. As she prepared breakfast for the children, she listened to the broadcaster describing the events of the past year. Alfred Hitchcock's film *Psycho* had caused a sensation with a gruesome shower scene. The Olympics had taken place in Rome during the height of a blisteringly hot Mediterranean summer. And charismatic John F Kennedy at only forty-three years of age was now the new President of the USA. But none of this really interested her. There was only one thing on her mind – Micky, and what had happened last night.

She hadn't decided what to do. The coffee bar had been closed all week and wasn't opening until Monday. Perhaps she should go tomorrow and explain to Gina. She knew she would be very angry with Micky and the money was a big loss. There were bills to pay at the beginning of the year. They would have to draw money from the bank, leaving them short in the account.

Bella placed the plates and the bread, butter and marmalade on the table. She was still considering what to do when there was a screech of wheels outside. She hurried to the window and looked up. Was Micky returning? Her heart started to beat fast. But no one appeared and carefully she opened the door.

She could hear voices and went to investigate. She was surprised to see Dr Cox's car parked behind Ron's. As she hurried up the steps she was met by a white-faced Ron.

'It's Joyce,' he told her as he pulled on his coat.

'An ambulance is on its way.' He looked very haggard as he added, 'She started to bleed in the night, not very much at first but then–' He raised his hands in confusion. 'It was all so sudden.'

Bella's heart sank. 'Is the baby all right?'

'I don't know. She got this bad pain and we thought it was just a stomach-ache. But then it got worse and the bleeding started.'

Bella tried to think calmly. 'Shall I come with you? I can ask Daisy to have the children.'

'No. It's all right. I'm going in the ambulance with her.'

Just then Dr Cox came down the stairs. He nodded to Bella, but his face was very grave. All too soon the ambulance came and as Joyce was lifted in, Bella could see she was very ill.

'I'll keep you in touch,' Ron told her hurriedly as he climbed in and the doors were closed in her face.

Bella stood and watched the ambulance roar off followed by the doctor's car. Suddenly Micky and the money didn't seem important. Joyce had looked so still and pale. Tears began to fill Bella's eyes. She could do nothing now but wait.

It was after the children were in bed that night that Ronnie knocked. 'They're operating,' he told her, his voice weary as he sank heavily down on the chair. 'She's lost a lot of blood.'

'What happened, Ron?'

'They said the baby was growing in a tube and they have to–' he stopped, burying his face in his hands. 'To take it away.'

'Oh, Ron. I'm so sorry.' She couldn't help him,

he was completely devastated.

'They told me to come home and get some sleep. They won't know anything for a while. But I can't ... can't go upstairs...'

'Would you like to stay here, then? Rest on the couch, perhaps.'

He nodded, but he just sat, gazing into the embers of the fire. It was New Year's Eve and the Christmas decorations were still up and strung around the room. The firelight glanced on them and across his face, making Bella remember the last time they had sat here alone together years ago. So much had happened since then.

'I'll make you a hot drink.'

He didn't reply and she left him staring into space, his features set like a mask. He looked much older, his shoulders drooping as though life had beaten him.

When she had made a cup of cocoa she brought it back to the fire. He'd fallen asleep with his head on the back of the chair. Bella put the cocoa in the grate to keep it warm. There was nothing she could think of to help. She thought of what Joyce had told her in confidence, of her doubts and fears about the life she had led. It was almost as if Joyce had known...

She closed her eyes and tried to pray. 'Hail Mary, full of grace,' but she hadn't prayed since she was a child. Memories flowed back of Bow Street. Of Mary and of *him*.

He was gone now and couldn't hurt her. But where was Terry? Where had her little brother gone? After all this time she still missed him.

If only Micky was here to talk to. The old Micky

who could make anything right.

When she woke, daylight slipped softly through the curtains. The mantel clock was striking six. Ron groaned softly in the chair. 'You sat up all night with me?'

'I slept on the couch.'

He stood up, confusion and fear in his face. 'I must go to the hospital.' He thrust his hand through his untidy hair. 'I shouldn't have slept so long.'

'You were exhausted. Do you want to wash and shave before you go? And eat a little breakfast?'

'No. There's no time. I want to be with her when she comes round.' He stopped when he got to the door.

'I suppose Micky's not home?'

'Not yet.'

'Thanks, Bella...'

'What for?'

He patted her arm.

The frosty morning air floated down the steps of the airey. Ronnie took them two at a time.

What would happen now? Bella wondered as she listened to Ronnie drive away. Had Joyce's operation been successful? When the children were up she would go upstairs and phone Sean. Surely he would be able to find Micky?

It was New Year's Day.

Micky was higher than a kite. He was also waiting for McNee's collector. The Flamingo was empty, last night's revellers gone, leaving the air stale with smoke and drink. The chairs were turned up on the tables and the floor was still littered with cigarette packets, balloons and a few party hats. The women had celebrated rowdily, causing an affray in the street below. Old Bill had been called as usual. But Micky had been tripping, smoking and drinking, and trying his best to sleep with a new girl at the club. She was far out now, away with the fairies.

He wanted to satisfy McNee for a while. Would have done so by now if the LSD had arrived on time. The quality was sharp and would blow his punters' minds. It would fetch the best price on the streets without even trying. Till then he was enjoying a ride on his rainbow. Would enjoy it even more when the woman beside him opened her eyes.

Suddenly there was a voice outside. If it was McNee's boys, he would bung them the hundred quid he'd cobbled together. Then they'd leave him alone and he could space out some more.

'Who's that?' he called as he pushed himself up on his elbow and narrowed his eyes at the door.

'It's me, Mr Bryant,' said the old man who swept the floors. 'You've got visitors.'

'Well, show them in.' Micky took a drag on the pipe and filled his lungs.

To his surprise Sean walked in. His little brother of all people. Now where was the little fairy he knocked around with? Micky rested back, his vacant eyes watched the tall form glide towards him. It *was* Sean – or was it? He laughed stupidly, assuming Sean was part of the experience.

The next thing Micky knew he was being lifted under the armpits. Now that was novel. The girl was still on the couch and he was flying above her. Sean's voice was somewhere in his head, but now he couldn't see him. He wasn't so sure he liked that.

It was too close to home.

Although Micky was not aware of it, he was riding in the back of Sean's car. Ashley was sitting beside him and in silence they pulled into a hot dog stand. They poured coffee down his throat and he gagged, bringing it up in the gutter. Each time they poured more, until finally they stopped.

The colours were fading now, as was his sense of wellbeing. Micky made a mental note never to buy from the African again. He'd stick to Leyla-Mark-Two who always provided the best.

He never had a bad trip with her stuff.

And looking at the back of Sean's head as they sped through the streets, Micky decided this was one hell of a trip.

Definitely too close to home.

Sean and Ashley were waiting impatiently. If Micky didn't sober up, they'd have to go on their own. Bella had just rung the hospital from upstairs. Joyce was very ill.

'You'd better go without him,' Bella said as she came into the room, her arms full of Micky's dirty clothes. 'He'd be no use at the hospital. What was he drinking?'

Sean and Ashley shrugged. They weren't going to tell her that Micky was probably full of every illegal substance he could lay his hands on.

'We'll go on our own then.'

'I'll come as soon as I can.'

Sean kissed her gently on the cheek. 'Don't worry. Look after yourself and him indoors now.'

'Bella doesn't know about Micky, does she?' Sean asked Ashley on their way to hospital.

'No, and we're not going to tell her.'

'What about Ron?'

Ashley sighed. 'He's your brother. I wouldn't know what to tell him.'

'Whilst Joyce is ill, I'm staying stum. But it was a shock finding him like that. I would never have believed it if I hadn't seen it with my own eyes. Would you?' Ashley shuddered. 'What a dive that Flamingo is!'

'And the girl. How can he do that to Bella?'

'I don't know. And thank God she thinks it's just the booze.'

'Let's hope it stays that way.' But Sean knew Micky was out of control. Just like he had been at the still. Well, they'd all had another chance after that. Micky might have nine lives, but by Sean's reckoning he was down to the last one.

Chapter Twenty-Seven

It was Sunday and Gina was working hard in the café, cleaning the surfaces and shining the mirrors. She had put on the kettle for a cup of tea and soon she would sit down and relax. She was humming to the strains of 'Only the Lonely' by Roy Orbison. It had been a big hit last year and she knew the words off by heart. The sentiments couldn't be more appropriate for her, as though she wouldn't admit it, she had been lonely without Lenny. Even though it was him that had done the dirty on her she missed his presence, still did after all this time.

In her heart she knew she was half to blame. Their lives had become a case of All Work and No Play. They hadn't spent enough time fooling around, as Lenny had pointed out more times than she could remember.

Roy Orbison's voice trembled on a high, clear note, sending a shiver along her spine. Was she too old to find romance again? She could see a grey hair, more white than grey, snaking over her head. Pulling the tweezers from her pocket she aimed them at the root. Each time she did this she knew two would grow in their place. Sean had warned her when she last went to the salon.

'Let me colour it for you,' he'd advised as he pinned up her shining black chignon. 'Henna will do the trick and you'll still have a full head of hair when you're ninety.'

Gina turned sideways in the mirror. Perhaps Sean was right. She could do with something to give her a lift. No double chins yet but she wouldn't see thirty-eight again. It was serious upholstering from here on in. And your hair was your crowning glory although keeping up with the fashions was important. Black and white was nice for the coffee bar, slacks or a straight skirt and a smart little top like a crisp white shirt. Shoes were high on her list too. Preferably high heels as she still had good legs. Each night she cleansed her skin and moisturized away the wrinkles. Yes, she still took good care of herself and intended to keep doing so.

Her customers appreciated it, often complimenting her on her appearance. The bohemian types regaled her with homespun poetry. The artists amongst them asked her to model. But she never took them seriously. It was all good fun, a lot of verbal and hot air, but they made her feel young.

Tomorrow the café would be open. It was a new year and the kids would pile in, talking about the music and their dreams.

Well, she wasn't too old to have dreams too, even if she didn't have a man. Gina and Bella's Coffee Bar was going to be famous one day. As famous as the Moka in Frith Street. Everyone knew the Moka. It had been opened by her namesake, the voluptuous foreign actress, Gina Lollobrigida. The Moka and the 2is in Old Compton Street were decorated in the same style as she had chosen for this place. All linoleum floors and Formica tables. They didn't have a battered old piano like the 2is but sometimes the kids brought their guitars in.

Deep in thought, she almost missed the figure hovering outside. An older man with a beard, dressed in a baggy coat. For a moment she smiled. He looked disreputable enough to be one of those talent scouts you saw in the newspaper

Then Gina froze. Unable to move she stared into the eyes that were only remnants of the person she had once known.

The kettle began to boil. She reached out to

419

turn it off but when she looked back there was no one there.

She rubbed her eyes and blinked. Then she dropped her cloth and ran to the door. Unlocking it hurriedly, she went outside. The street was deserted.

Her brain was telling her she was mistaken. But her heart was telling her it was Lenny.

Ronnie was staring at the doctor. This just wasn't possible. Hospitals these days were so well equipped. Miracles happened daily. People were saved by new drugs, new techniques and wonderful inventions. He had read it often enough in the newspapers, even knew of a few rapid cures himself. Joyce had been alive a short while ago, as fit as himself.

'I'm sorry, Mr Bryant. There really was nothing more we could do.'

'But why–' Ronnie demanded, anger and desperation in his voice as he stared at the older man sitting on the other side of the desk. 'Why did it have to happen to her?'

The doctor paused, his voice patient but firm as he replied. 'As I have been trying to explain, there were complications caused by the pregnancy. We tried to stop the internal bleeding but I'm afraid it was too late.'

Ronnie finally heard what was being said to him but he didn't understand. All he could do was keep shaking his head, his mouth open as the dry hospital air poured in.

'These things happen very quickly sometimes.'

'But I thought – *we* thought – it was just a bad

420

stomach.' Ronnie suddenly felt himself crumble. In his mind he could hear himself trying to persuade Joyce to let him get the doctor. And each time she had said no. If only he'd done as he thought best.

Ronnie dragged up his eyes. 'Where is she?'

He followed the doctor down the corridor and entered a small side ward. Joyce was lying there, his Joyce. Her eyes were closed and her black hair combed around her head. She looked very small.

'Would you like me to stay with you?'

Ronnie shook his head and after the doctor left, he sat in the chair. 'Oh, Joyce, what have I done?'

He took her hand and whispered he loved her. Their life had been sweeter than he imagined possible. They had been friends as well as man and wife. If he hadn't wanted a son and heir so much, she might still be alive.

He pressed his lips on her forehead and whispered, 'Wherever you are, Joyce, I love you.'

Emotion filled him as he looked at her face. Even in death she was beautiful. He didn't want to be without her.

Why had this happened?

He was not a man to give in easily to emotion. But now the tears seemed to come all at once.

Micky was on a high, sweating a little with the rush of the fix, but on a high.

It was a cold, cloudless Saturday in January and the earth in the churchyard was hard with frost. The mourners at Joyce's funeral were gathered round the open grave wrapped up in their expensive black coats.

Micky narrowed his eyes thoughtfully at his grief-stricken brother, centre stage. It was the opportune time to put his plan into action. Today he was going to redeem himself with the family.

He was going to eat humble pie if it choked him. If the clubs had worked out, he wouldn't have to grovel like this, but a run of bad luck had dogged his footsteps since the job at Downey Manor. It was that Terry who had started the ball rolling by going and getting himself shot. And then Milo, the ungrateful bugger had to be silenced. Not that Micky had done the deed, but he'd had to pay full whack for a result.

And now he was being shafted by McNee! Most of his ilk were wearing concrete boots under the Thames. But McNee had survived, a law unto himself. Micky pulled back his head self-righteously. Some things in life just didn't seem fair.

As Micky stood beside his wife, he was planning his strategy. He'd have to make it right with Bella first. Much to his surprise, she was on to a winner with the café. All those young kids had money to burn. The problem was he wasn't seeing any of it. He'd almost burnt his boats that day when he found Mary Doyle sitting in *his* chair in *his* house scoffing *his* food. A man's home was his castle or supposed to be. But there sat the money-grabbing old crone, her hand hot on Bella's rubbles. Cash that he was fully entitled to.

As the coffin disappeared, he heard a few sobs. Personally, he didn't understand what all the fuss was about. Funerals gave him the creeps. They were expensive and time consuming. Take Terry for instance, buried just a few plots away. No one ever came up here now except Bella. He was forgotten, remembered only as a half-wit, a lame duck. If he had done what he was told and not wandered off that night at Downey, he would be alive today.

People brought trouble on themselves. Like old Joyce. She was nice enough, but it was her choice to latch on to Ronnie and have a kid. If she'd gone back on the game, she'd still be alive now.

Micky glanced furtively at his brother. Ronnie should think himself lucky. He was a free man now and not short of a few bob. He didn't have to kowtow to McNee or squeeze a living out of two poxy clubs. Sympathy where sympathy was due. And Ronnie didn't deserve any.

He felt Bella stir as Ronnie cast down a handful of earth.

'She was a good 'un was Joyce,' Micky whispered to his wife. 'Like Terry. Salt of the earth. It just ain't fair, is it?'

His wife glanced at him, a flash of surprise on her face.

'It's Ronnie I feel sorry for now.' He managed this lie with dexterity since he had been practicing it for the last five minutes. 'I'll take a bit of time off work to see he's all right.'

Bella's smile was faint, but she reached for his hand. He squeezed her fingers, smiling supportively.

It was so easy with women. The right touch and you were home and dry.

Bella looked up when she heard Micky come in. He was still wearing his black suit from the

423

funeral and he rubbed his hands together as he sat by the fire.

'How's Ronnie?' she asked anxiously. 'Did you ask him to come down to eat with us?'

'Course I did. But he wouldn't have none of it. Said I'd go up before we went to bed though and say good night.'

'It must be awful without Joyce.'

'Yeah, don't seem right she's gone. First Terry then her.'

'At least Father Johns gave Terry a good sendoff,' Bella sighed. 'But there was only a few words for Joyce that didn't express what we all felt.'

'Ronnie wanted it over and done with,' Micky pointed out. 'Neither of them was religious. It wasn't like they went to church or anything.'

In spite of the austere funeral arrangements, Bella had been amazed at all the floral tributes for Joyce. A beautiful wreath of red roses from Ron and dozens of sprays from many others. She had sent a large posy of white roses, just like her wedding bouquet, the one that Joyce had caught. She had also taken a big bunch of chrysanthemums for Terry as she hadn't been to the cemetery for over a month.

'It doesn't seem possible that Mr and Mrs Bryant and Auntie Gwen and Terry and Joyce are all buried there now,' she murmured sadly. 'I wish we knew what happened to Terry.'

'It wouldn't make no difference if we did,' Micky replied quickly. 'Take Ronnie for instance. He knows what happened to Joyce but it ain't helped. If you knew who shot Terry, it wouldn't bring him back.'

'But someone would be punished for the crime.'

'Yeah, but I don't see that happening,' Micky answered hastily.

Bella nodded. It was over five years now since he'd gone. The police had closed the case a long time ago. But sometimes it still seemed fresh in her memory. She understood what Ronnie was going through. He had to find an outlet for his grief now, like she had done at the café. Everything around him would remind him of Joyce. They had so many plans for the baby. Joyce had told her the small bedroom that had once been Ron's and then Terry's was going to be the nursery. It had made Bella happy to think a new life would fill it. That Terry might be watching over the baby in the room he had loved so much. But now that would never happen.

'I think I'll make supper.' She wasn't hungry but she didn't want to dwell on these thoughts. Life was for the living and now they all had to get on with it.

But Micky caught her hand. 'Sit down. I've got something to tell you.'

'What is it?'

'I'm sorry for taking that money off you. I must have given you a fright. I'll repay you every penny when I'm flush.'

She sat down then. 'Why did you do it, Micky?'

He looked so remorseful that Bella believed him when he shrugged and shook his head. 'I can't really explain, Bells. I've no excuse only that I'd had a bad day and a few drinks.'

'You've been drinking a lot lately.'

'I know. But only because I've been worried.'

'What about? Are you in trouble?'

'No, course not. But business ain't all that brisk.' He looked down. 'The honest truth is, I'm not seeing a return on the clubs. The custom is harder to come by, what with all these new dives opening up. Everyone's out for a quick few bob these days. There ain't no classy joints left. People want sleaze and I ain't prepared to provide it. I have standards, you know.'

'Micky, why don't you sell the clubs and buy another garage? You always did well there and you could get another salesman like Milo.'

He nodded slowly. 'I might do that. But I want to get shot of the Fortune and the Flamingo first. But that's my problem not yours.'

Bella looked into his eyes. 'I didn't tell Gina about the money because I'm going to try to replace it. I don't like keeping things back as she trusts me you see.' She softened her voice as she continued. 'But I haven't forgotten that you've been generous in the past and helped Mum and Teresa.'

'She's family, ain't she?'

'Please let's try and get on like we used to.'

'I've said I'm sorry and I mean it. I love you, Bells. I might not have shown it lately, but I intend to change. I'm getting out of the clubs and that's a promise.'

He took her into his arms and slid the pins from her hair. Burying his face in its thickness, he whispered tender words. She couldn't recall how long ago it was they had last made love, but she felt wanted and loved again.

She linked her arms around his neck as his kisses took her to the place in her heart where they had once been happy together.

When the clubs sold and Micky had found some real work, they would be able to lead normal lives again.

Chapter Twenty-Eight

Summer had started late, but it hadn't made any difference to business. Bella was clearing tables only for them to be taken immediately. It didn't matter if it was boiling hot, lashing with rain or snowing, the kids kept pouring in. Today it was a simmering Saturday in July with big white clouds scudding across a clear sky.

'It would be nice to have something a bit more exciting on the menu,' Gina said thoughtfully as Bella put down the tray of dirty cups and plates. 'I was thinking of spaghetti bolognese, as we have an Italian flavour with the Espresso. I could knock a few dishes up with a bit of practice.'

'Yes, but all they ask for is ice cream.' Bella turned her attention to the machine which was making a mouth-watering aroma throughout the café. 'But in the winter spaghetti bolognese would probably go down a treat.'

Gina sighed as she placed two coffee cups and a banana sundae on a chromium tray. 'It's like the jukebox. Espresso, ice cream and music all go together.'

Bella laughed. 'If we didn't have the box there, we'd be empty. There's been a man launched into space this year and Stirling Moss has won the Grand Prix but all the kids want to know about is music.'

'Like this new dance, the Twist.'

Gina nodded. 'I like it.' She began to fill a leaf-shaped glass dish with pink, green and chocolate ice cream, sprinkling a few nuts on top. 'That Chubby Checker's got a really good voice.'

'I thought you were a Roy Orbison fan?'

'Yes, but the Twist is good for the figure.' Gina did a little demonstration and Bella laughed.

'You'll have them dancing round the tables in a minute.'

'We're not licensed for it unfortunately,' Gina giggled as she pushed the tray towards Bella.

'It would be a good idea, though. If only we had a bit more space.'

Gina deftly stripped the skin off another banana, sliced it down the middle and covered it with ice cream. 'Don't tempt me. I'm always thinking what we can get up to next. Which is why I thought I'd tart up the menu.'

Bella smiled as she poured the coffees. 'I'm thinking of taking Michael and Teresa and some of their friends to the zoo for their birthday. D'you fancy coming?'

'Count me in, yes.' Gina frowned. 'Ain't you having a party, though?'

'It's not the same this year without Joyce. And anyway, the kids are getting older and want a change.'

Gina nodded thoughtfully. 'How is Ronnie

these days?'

'He's thrown himself into his work.'

'He's not at the house much, then?'

'Not a lot. He still takes Michael up the park on Saturdays and stops for tea after. But he's not his old self and don't ever talk about Joyce.'

'What about your Micky, then?' Gina said, raising her eyebrows. 'Is he coming to the zoo?'

Bella spluttered. 'You must be joking!'

Gina burst out laughing too. 'No, I can't imagine him in his mohair suit feeding nuts to the monkeys.'

Bella joined in the joke, but she knew that whatever celebrations they had in mind for the two birthdays, they would happen without Micky. It hadn't taken long after Joyce's death for him to fall back into his old ways as he spent more time than ever at the clubs and yet was still short of money. She had managed to replace what he had taken in January but it was only her wage that now supported them. He took it for granted she paid the bills and kept the home running.

Bella took the coffees to the table as Gina prepared more dishes. When all the orders were done and fresh coffee made, she began to clean the empty tables.

Suddenly there was a crash. All heads turned to look at Gina. She was standing over the shattered glass dishes, her face white.

'What happened?' Bella asked as she ran over.

'There was a man looking in the window.' Gina's hand went up to her throat. 'I could have sworn it was Lenny.'

'Lenny? But it couldn't be, could it?'

Gina shook her head. 'No, it must have been a double. This bloke was wearing a uniform.'

The children were playing with a ball after spending all their pocket money in the souvenir shop. The twins and their little sisters, June and April, had spent their pocket money on food for the animals, ice creams and sweets. Teresa and Michael had been more thrifty and bought books that had lovely colour illustrations of the zoo's animals.

Dolly, Bella and Gina had found a spot on the big green where they could sit down under the trees. The park was full of adults relaxing as the kids sucked ice blues to alleviate the heat of the August day. Bella had brought a Thermos of tea, two bottles of Tizer and a picnic, guessing that six children and three adults would end up very hungry and thirsty at the close of the day.

Bella opened her bags and set out the food. In the distance they could hear the monkeys and the high-pitched screeches of the tropical birds. A keeper was walking slowly up and down making sure everyone behaved themselves and left no litter.

Dolly clasped her bump as she collapsed on the grass. Her maternity dress was like a tent as she patted it down around her. 'I'm not due till November but I'm as big as a house. Even the twins didn't compare to this.'

'Mummy's got an elephant in her tummy,' six-year-old April laughed as she came back to retrieve the ball.

'No, it's a Chi-Chi,' giggled four-year-old June who had been fascinated by the sight of the big panda, the scene-stealing star attraction of London Zoo.

'I hope it's a baby,' Dolly informed her daughters, 'or your father is going to send it back if it's covered in black and white fur. Now go and play with the others, the food isn't ready yet.'

'If this is another girl, you and Percy are on your way to a netball team,' Gina teased as the little girls sped off.

'Yes, and no rude remarks about goals, please!' Dolly warned her two friends.

Bella knew that Dolly and Percy were struggling to make ends meet, but that hadn't stopped their family from enlarging.

'You ain't going on this Pill, then?' Gina asked as she helped herself to one of the sandwiches.

Dolly nodded, her face serious. 'I'm giving it some thought, actually.'

Bella poured the tea from the flask into three plastic cups. 'But don't you have to take one every day?' she said before she had time to think. 'That can't be good for your system.'

'Some of us don't have a choice,' Dolly replied sharply.

'We're all inclined to be sceptical about something new,' Gina broke in, 'but I read that a lot of women say it's changed their lives.'

Bella handed Dolly a sausage roll which disappeared almost immediately.

'It's different for you, Bella,' Dolly said off-handedly, unwilling to let the subject drop. 'You've only got Michael and can spend as much

431

time as you like on your career.'

Gina quickly passed Dolly another sandwich. 'Oh well, at least you two have done your bit towards procreation. Left up to people like me there wouldn't be a next generation.'

There was a scream behind them and they all looked round. June had fallen over and was holding her knee. Dolly rolled her eyes and got to her feet, lumbering awkwardly over to her daughter.

'Don't be upset,' Gina whispered as Bella looked crestfallen. 'Dolly's very sensitive at the moment.'

'I didn't mean to preach.'

'You weren't. You were just expressing an opinion. Dolly has forgotten that life don't always work out the way you want it. What's getting on her nerves is the house. There's too many people crammed under one roof.'

'I wish I could help.'

'A win on the pools might do it,' Gina smirked as she pushed a piece of bread pudding into Bella's hand. 'But then, a few more bob would solve all our problems, wouldn't it?'

It certainly would for Micky, Bella thought but didn't say as she opened another bag of sandwiches. 'Has that man outside the café ever appeared again?'

'No...' Gina said hesitantly, her expression thoughtful. 'But the funny thing is–' She stopped, rolling her eyes. 'Oh, I'm daft, I am.'

'What?'

'It's just that sometimes it looks to me as though someone's been tidying the yard a bit, but I can't be sure...'

Bella frowned. 'Who would do that?'

Gina laughed, flapping her hand. 'No one, of course. I told you, I'm going barmy.'

Bella was still thinking about this when Dolly walked towards them. All the children followed her like the Pied Piper and she sank down on the grass with a big sigh.

'We're hungry!' they all complained.

'You don't need to tell us that,' Dolly answered, rolling her eyes.

'Feeding time at the zoo!' Bella exclaimed as she unscrewed the top of the Tizer bottle. A plume of liquid sprayed out, missing the children and covering Dolly. Her mouth fell open silently as she shook the Tizer from her hair. It even dripped from her eyebrows.

Everyone stared at her.

Then Dolly began to laugh. All the children joined in, Bella and Gina too, until tears filled their eyes.

Wiping Dolly's sticky face and arms with a cloth, Bella dabbed at the wet bump too.

'It's definitely a boy,' Bella giggled as the baby kicked under her touch. 'When I had Michael it felt the same.'

Dolly smiled into Bella's gaze, their small spat forgotten. 'I'll call him Tizer if it is.'

Once more, everyone broke into laughter. Bella leaned forward and hugged Dolly. Her careless remark about the Pill forgiven.

Neville Raymond Percival Shine was born on the morning of Friday the seventeenth of November 1961. Percy came round with the news the

433

following day, Saturday. 'He's ten pounds and nine ounces,' Percy said proudly as Bella made him sit down. She had just come in from the café and Ronnie was out with Michael.

'Where's Micky? Is he in? I wanted to wet the baby's head.'

'I don't know when he'll be back.' Bella poured the tea and placed a cup on the table by Percy's chair. She sat down beside Percy. 'What colour hair has he got?'

'Light brown, like mine.' He grinned, rubbing his shiny head. 'Well, what's left of it.'

'Is Dolly all right?'

'She had him at home, ten minutes after the midwife arrived. She says Dolly gives birth as easy as shelling peas,' Percy replied, gulping his hot tea. 'Her mum's with the girls. They can't wait to walk the baby in the pram. So I thought I'd just have a quick one with Micky. But if he's not here–'

At that moment Ronnie and Michael walked in.

Percy stood up, a big grin on his face.

'Don't tell me, it's a boy!' guessed Ron and walking to Percy gave him a manly hug.

'A whopper and all, Ron,' Percy burst out. 'Arms and legs like blooming balloons.'

'Congratulations, mate.'

'What's his name, Uncle Percy?' Michael put down his football.

'Neville – after Dolly's dad – Raymond – after her brother – Percival after yours truly. Bit of a mouthful, ain't it?'

'A bit long,' Michael agreed thoughtfully. 'But

Nev's all right.' And they all laughed.

'Dolly asked me to ask you all over tomorrow. Just for tea like, and to see the baby.'

'Are you sure?' Bella asked. 'Don't you want a little time to yourselves?'

Percy guffawed. 'I've forgotten what that is.'

Bella looked at Ronnie. 'Can you come, Ron?'

He hesitated for a moment, until Michael said eagerly, 'We can have a kick-about on the green near their house if you do.'

Ronnie brushed his hand through his nephew's dark hair. 'Well, why not?'

'You fancy coming down the pub now for a quick one?' Percy asked eagerly. 'I ain't had chance to celebrate yet.'

'All right,' Ronnie agreed as Percy kissed Bella on the cheek.

'Thanks for the cuppa. See you tomorrow, then.'

Bella went to the door and watched the men go up the airey steps. Would visiting Dolly tomorrow be uncomfortable for Ron? It was almost Christmas. In January it would be a year since Joyce died.

What was Ron going to do at Christmas? Should she offer to cook dinner upstairs? Or would Ron want to be by himself? Sean and Ashley were going to Switzerland on holiday. She knew they had tried to get Ron to go with them, but he had refused all their offers.

'Uncle Ron asked me what I'm going to do when I leave school,' Michael said as he wiped his dirty cheeks with the back of his cuff.

'What did you tell him?'

435

'I said I wanted to be a builder like him.'

Bella looked at her son in surprise. 'Is that true?'

'The first house I'm going to build is for Granny, Teresa and Uncle Gus. Then a huge one for Auntie Dolly. And if you want a house, I'd build one for you, too.' He patted his tummy. 'Is tea ready yet?'

'Yes, but go and wash your dirty face first.'

She was about to go to the kitchen when the door opened again. This time it was Micky. He looked as though he hadn't shaved in days.

'Micky, what's the matter?'

'I'm in trouble,' he muttered as he closed the door hurriedly.

'What kind of trouble?'

'It's that bastard McNee.'

Bella felt the blood drain from her face. That name sent a chill down her spine. 'What does he want?'

'I need money to pay him off. How much did you bring from the café?'

'None – none at all.'

'You're lying!' He took hold of her and began to shake her. 'Open your purse.'

With shaking fingers she did so. 'Here, you can have it all if you need it that bad.'

He swept it out of her hands. 'A couple of quid will go nowhere. You must have more than that.'

'Mum?' Michael was standing there.

'It's all right, Michael. Go and eat your tea. I want to talk to your dad.'

He walked slowly into the kitchen. When he had gone she looked at Micky. She was angry

436

now. 'Can't you see you're frightening us?'

He didn't seem to hear as he pushed past her. As she stood wondering what to do next, she could hear him in the bedroom. Just like last time he was pulling out drawers and banging around. A minute later he reappeared.

His eyes had that wild look. For a moment she thought he was going to grab her, but instead he stormed out of the house.

Michael was sitting at the table. 'Has Dad gone?'

'Yes. He was in a hurry.'

Michael pushed away his plate. 'I'm not really hungry.'

She sat down and hugged him. What else could she do?

The following day, Ronnie drove them to Dolly's. 'Are you all right?' he asked as they pulled up at the Shines'. 'You're both very quiet.'

Bella nodded but she'd had a sinking feeling ever since Micky had left. She had tried to act as normal, but Michael was old enough to know there was something wrong.

'I hope you don't mind visiting Dolly,' she said quietly.

Ronnie shook his head and smiled. 'Percy was a bit merry when I dropped him home last night. He went skipping up the path like a two-year-old.'

Percy didn't look like one when he opened the door. He was surrounded by little girls, all struggling to get past him. He raised his eyes to the ceiling as his family began to jump up and

437

down with excitement when they saw who it was.

'Come in, come in,' Dolly cried from the front room. Everyone went along. There was hardly any room to move, let alone sit. Mrs Taylor had given up her chair for Dolly who was nursing the baby. The four girls began talking and shouting at once and the baby, wrapped in a big white shawl, started to scream.

Mrs Taylor clapped her hands. 'All of you go out to the back garden and play.'

'It's cold out there.'

'Then put on your coats.'

The children ran off and Percy, Ronnie and Bella sat down on the couch. There were white fluffy nappies and baby clothes everywhere.

'He's just had his feed so you can hold him if you want,' Dolly said, about to get up.

But Bella stopped her. 'You should be resting. Here...' She slid her hands under the white bundle. Neville's little black eyes opened as she rocked him.

'He's a big baby, Dolly.'

Dolly laughed. 'No wonder I was always eating for two.'

'Look he's smiling!'

'It's probably only wind.'

'Oh, I'm sure it's a smile.' Bella tipped him up in the crook of her arm for everyone to see.

'He wanted a feed every few hours in the night,' Dolly pointed out, frowning at Percy.

'That's my boy for you.' Percy puffed out his chest.

'And someone – not to mention names – slept through it all!'

'I was out like a light thanks to Ron,' Percy chuckled and Ronnie grinned as Mrs Taylor called out 'Tea's ready,' from the kitchen.

There was chaos for the next half hour as food was dispensed and eaten on laps or wherever there was a space. Mrs Taylor took the baby and at last he went off to sleep.

After tea, the men took the children to the park. Dolly showed Bella the new clothes she had knitted for Neville in blue wool. Most of the girls' clothes were pink, which explained the rose-coloured bootees on Neville's tiny feet. Bella had brought a lemon and white matinée coat and gloves to match.

'They're lovely,' Dolly said eagerly. 'He'll need those this winter.'

'We'll go up to the market for some wool after Christmas,' Bella promised.

'What are you doing on the twenty-fifth?'

Bella shrugged. 'I'm not sure. Sean and Ashley said they're going away for Christmas and Ron just told me he's having dinner with a friend.'

Dolly looked surprised. 'Who's that?'

'He didn't say.'

'Didn't you ask?'

'No, because I know the real reason is he doesn't want to be in the house without Joyce.'

'So what will you do?'

'Just cook for us, I expect.' Bella hoped she wouldn't ask any more but she did.

'How's Micky?' Dolly enquired just as Mrs Taylor brought in the screaming Neville.

Bella was glad that the baby's loud yells made it impossible for her to reply.

It was Friday the twenty-second of December and Sean and Ashley called at the café on their way to the airport. They brought Christmas presents with them that were to be put under the tree. Sean was excited about their holiday in Switzerland and showed Bella the travel brochures. Skiing was the in-thing as many of their customers had told them. Sean was keen to take lessons whilst Ashley was content to ride on the ski-lift.

'Don't break any legs,' Gina warned them. 'I want that nice hair-do you promised me, Sean. I'm fed up with all these grey hairs.'

Ashley grinned. 'It'll be me who has the grey hair, watching him try to ski down them slopes.'

'I'll be all right, as long as I don't meet an avalanche,' laughed Sean.

There were more rude comments and finally they left for the long-awaited holiday.

'Why don't you take tomorrow off?' Gina suggested at five o'clock as they cleared the tables. 'Take Michael out to do some Christmas shopping. He must get a bit fed up in the holidays.'

'I take him to Mum's, not that him and Teresa ever stay in. They're off down to Docklands all the time.'

'Well, the offer's there. You could even have a day to yourself. You've been looking a bit tired lately.'

'But tomorrow's the last day for the kids to get out.'

'I'll have Tina here, remember. You ain't indispensable, girl.'

Bella laughed. 'I know that.'

'Look, do as I say for once. I've got nothing but the café to think about. You've got the family.'

Bella hadn't said anything about Micky. So she gave in gracefully. 'Well, I have got a bit of shopping left to do.'

That night, whilst Michael was at the youth club, Bella thought about Micky. Should she try to look for him? But she was reluctant to drive up to the clubs. She had never set foot in the Flamingo and remembered what the Fortune was like.

Unable to settle, she picked up the newspaper. She read it through and was about to close it when she noticed a small article. 'Fire at Downey Manor'.

Downey Wood was where Terry had been found! She read the few lines as her heart beat rapidly. There had been one casualty, an elderly woman who had died in hospital. Amongst other treasures that had been rescued from the house were a number of oil paintings.

Bella closed the paper, wondering who the woman was and how that place seemed to be ill fated.

Christmas Day passed quietly. Bella listened out for more news on Downey Manor but there wasn't any. She cooked dinner and after unwrapping their presents, she and Michael listened to the Queen. As she told of the many countries she had visited in 1961, Bella's thoughts strayed. Where was Micky? Was he coming home? And if he didn't, what was she going to do?

That night Bella let the tears fall. She had to keep a brave face for Michael. It was only when she was alone she could give way to her sorrow. Her marriage was a failure. She had to try to think what to do for the best. If only Micky would change his ways. Sell the clubs as he'd promised. They would manage on her wage from the café until he found something else. If he was free from the worry of his debts, she was sure they could be happy again.

Early on Boxing Day morning there was a knock at the door. 'Who's there?' Bella asked before unlocking it.

'Detective Inspector Reynolds.'

Her heart missed a beat. It was the policeman who had investigated Terry's death.

'I'm sorry to intrude during the holiday, Mrs Bryant. Is your husband at home?'

'No. Why do you want him?'

'Just an enquiry. May I come in?'

Michael came out, still wearing his pyjamas. The policeman smiled at him. 'Hello, young man.'

'Sit down.' Bella nodded to the chair.

Removing his hat, he sank into the chair. 'As you may know, there was a fire at Downey Manor, the estate where your brother died.'

Bella nodded as her heart beat very fast. 'I saw it in the paper.'

'We are looking into the circumstances of Lady Downey's death.'

'What's that got to do with my husband?'

'We have some evidence that suggests he knew Lady Downey.'

Bella sat down quickly. 'What kind of evidence?'

'A receipt from a garage in London signed by your husband. It was recovered from a wall safe at the premises, untouched by the fire. Through subsequent enquiries we believe the garage was owned by Mr Bryant.'

'He did have a garage,' Bella agreed. 'But he sold it.'

'The new owner has confirmed the date of change of ownership. This receipt states that a Jaguar car, a very expensive model, was sold to Lady Downey by Mr Bryant just prior to your brother's death.'

Bella could only stare at him. Micky had never told her anything about this.

'I take it you can't help me with any information?'

Bella shook her head.

'It's surprising, isn't it,' the inspector said slowly, 'that Mr Bryant never brought this to light when we were investigating your brother's death?'

'Micky would have said something,' Bella protested, feeling bewildered. 'Are you sure it wasn't Milo who signed the receipt? The salesman who worked for Micky.'

'That would be a gentleman by the name of Miles Heath-Gash?'

'Yes, that's right.'

'No, Mrs Bryant. The signature is your husband's. Unfortunately...' the policeman paused again, 'Mr Heath-Gash, we discovered, was involved in a road accident shortly after leaving your husband's employ and died of his injuries.'

'Miles is dead?' Bella was shocked.

'We need to speak to your husband to clear up this matter. Do you know where he is?'

Bella gave a slight nod. 'You might find him at one of his two clubs. Either the Fortune or the Flamingo in Soho.'

He nodded slowly. 'I'm sorry to have troubled you. I hope I won't have to bother you again.'

Bella followed him to the door. 'Inspector, is Terry's case still open?'

'Obviously this is a new development, Mrs Bryant. We're following up every lead we have.'

'It might just be a coincidence that Micky sold the car at the same time.'

'Yes, but your husband omitted to disclose the connection. Why would he do that? And there is something else, another line of enquiry...' a frown spread slowly over the big man's face. 'Along with the receipt a great deal of money was discovered. And most of it was counterfeit. Obviously we would like to find out why it was in there and where it came from.'

'But Micky wouldn't know anything about that!' she blurted.

'I hope you're right, Mrs Bryant.' He stared at her for a while as though trying to read her thoughts, then slipped on his hat as he went out. 'If you think of anything that could be useful to us, please ring me on this number.' He handed her a card.

Bella watched him walk up the airey steps.

Michael came to stand beside her. 'Why didn't Dad tell them about that car?' he asked as they went back inside.

'I don't know, Michael.'

444

'What does counter-feet, mean?'

'It means false,' she replied shakily as she tried to make sense of what the policeman had told her.

Chapter Twenty-Nine

Alfred Freshwater stood in his empty cellar for the last time. Other than the old wooden table on which the printing machine had stood, a few piles of dust and the mould that was beginning to creep up the brick walls and mask the smell of ink, it was like any other cellar. But he was leaving part of his life down here, under the boards. He felt as though he had unassembled himself at the same time as he'd taken the plates apart and hammered the rest of the contraption flat. Now his life's work was just a pile of metal in a Hoxton scrap yard. It was one of the hardest things he had ever had to do, other than burying Gyp.

Well, no use looking back. He still had Nellie. If he was honest – which he wasn't – the thing that saddened him most was the fact that no one appreciated the real skill of his work. He had turned out masterpieces on an antiquated printer and fooled the most professional eyes of the country.

He was hardly likely to boast about that though, was he?

How much of his work was still locked up in vaults and undiscovered? Odds on, the odd pound or two was still in circulation. Not that he'd worked since the Manor. He wasn't *that* committed to his trade. No point in running a risk when he had enough kosher lucre to see them through the rest of their lives. That Micky, mad bastard though he was, had set him up with a tasty pension. His one regret was Terry. He was only a kid and hadn't stood a chance with the bugger who shot him.

Alfred trod slowly up the stairs. He flicked off the single bulb hanging from the ceiling and lifted the trap door. His wife came down the hall to meet him.

'Are you ready?' His voice was gentle, because he knew the answer.

'I put his blanket over him.'

He followed her through the kitchen to the basket in which the animal had slept for the past sixteen years.

Funny that, the Manor going up in flames and Gyp pegging out shortly after. Like a message from heaven to get on his bike, but it still wasn't easy.

Alfred lifted the animal, not altogether a light-weight, and made his way into the garden. Together they lowered the last of their life in Hoxton and sixteen years of memories, into the hole. When it was all done, he threw the spade aside.

'What time's the taxi?'

'What's wrong with the bus?'

'Nothing, I suppose.' They could afford to buy a bus if they wanted, but Nellie had her eye on the ackers. A thrifty woman, was his Nell, which, he freely admitted, had worked in their favour.

But today they were travelling to Dover. Catching a cross-channel ferry to Calais.

'Here we come sunny Spain.'

She nodded. 'No more flaming wet weather.'

'Better be off then.' A villain he knew had sold them a villa, would you believe? No, he answered himself, he wouldn't, not till he got there and saw it for himself. 'What about our bags?'

'We've only got one.'

He smiled. They were travelling light. The way travellers should really travel. 'I'll buy you a nice Spanish dress when we get there.'

'No ta. I ain't into frills and fancies.' Nellie grinned up at him, her brown wrinkled face and small, shrewd eyes making him remember the girl she once was when he married her.

They went into the house and he put on his coat. 'Well, it's cheerio England, then, ain't it?'

When they got to the gate, a bus whooshed by.

'We've missed that bloody one,' his wife complained. 'Now we'll have to wait half an hour for another.'

'Told you we should've got the taxi.'

She threw him a frown. 'You always was a spendthrift. At least when we get to Spain you won't know your pesetas from your pound.'

But Alfred smiled to himself. He wasn't quite ready to lay down and roll over yet. He had already been to the library and taken a gander at the Spanish currency. They had pictures of some very interesting banknotes.

Lenny watched the red bus drive past.

It was the first day of 1962. Like the man sitting

up there in the driving seat, he too was part of the London transport services. True, he hadn't been a driver for long, four months to the day in fact. He'd only signed up for the job in order to pass the café on a regular basis. But in those four months he had started to believe in himself again. He was driving his passengers up and down the City roads, enjoying all the rabbit and pork, at the wheel, in charge, a bloke, doing a bloke's job.

He had all the lingo off pat. The times of departure and arrival and he knew his route blindfolded. He had even put in for overtime. Not that he'd have got the job if he'd revealed the truth, that he was an ex-con. But he'd taken the risk and found himself issued with a uniform, a cap and his number. The best blooming bit of luck in all his life.

Now his shift was over and he was standing in the perishing cold on the first day of the new year, drawn like a moth to a flame. The café was closed and the kids had gone. This was the time he liked best, when the lights flooded out into the dark street and Gina was on her own. Sometimes she played the jukebox, doing that little wiggle with her hips. He'd got sick to the teeth of 'Only the Lonely'. But he liked to watch her. She was a lovely mover.

As Lenny turned up the collar of his coat, he saw a car pull up. It screeched to a halt and the driver leapt out. Lenny's eyes narrowed. He knew that silhouette. His heart raced as the figure banged on the door.

Gina let him in. Lenny saw her expression

change. He could tell she was getting angry. Then she was backing away, struggling to distance herself.

Lenny jumped into the road. A car passed by inches away from him. He jumped back again. When he looked up, they were behind the counter. Gina was trying to drag the man away from the till. He pushed her off. She tried again and this time he hit her.

Lenny ran again. Headlights blinded him, a rush of wind tore at his coat. An engine roared in his ears and a horn blasted. Gina was on the floor when he burst in.

The next thing he knew he had his hands round Micky's throat, had pinned him down on the floor. Lenny heard Gina screaming but his hands were locked there. Micky's face turned red, then blue, his Adam's apple squashed under his thumbs.

Then suddenly a gun appeared. Lenny let go as he gazed down the barrel.

'Where did you spring from?' cried Micky, his hand shaking as he levelled the gun. 'I thought you was in clink or six foot under by now.'

Lenny climbed to his feet, a snarl on his face. 'Like that poor bastard Milo?'

'I never laid a finger on him.'

'No, you made sure of that.'

'He was just a loser anyway.'

Lenny had always had his suspicions. Now he looked into Micky's bad eyes and saw the truth. 'I suppose you would've come after me too, if I wasn't sent down.'

Micky raised the gun. 'It ain't too late, is it?'

'Use that thing and it's the end of the line,'

Lenny said as calmly as he could fake it. 'I wrote everything down. It's all on paper, tucked up nicely for Old Bill if anything should happen to me. Every last detail. The Strattons, the Manor and the money. *And* what we did to Terry.'

Lenny watched his words take effect. Micky's face paled. His eyes sprang about in his head, crazier than ever. Lenny could feel his legs trembling as the gun wavered up and down.

'Take what you want and get out,' he added gruffly as Micky's finger pressed on the trigger. 'Me and Gina ain't going to grass on you. You got a chance. Now take it.'

Lenny braced himself. Micky was madder than the proverbial hatter. The shooter was waving everywhere.

Suddenly the shop door opened. Two young kids stood there. Lenny closed his eyes. When he opened them Micky was running. The young people stood with their mouths open as he rushed past.

'Far out, man,' the young man grinned as the car roared off.

'Not far enough if you ask me,' Lenny muttered, taking the boy's arm and guiding him into the street. 'Forget what you've seen, it was just a misunderstanding.'

'You want us to hang around?'

Gina's voice was a whisper as she came up. 'No, thanks, love, I'm closing now.'

After they'd gone, Lenny locked the door.

'So it *was* you I saw out there?' Gina breathed.

'Yeah, it was me.'

Gina sank down on a chair. 'Christ, Lenny, he

nearly put a bullet in you tonight.'

'If it was loaded.'

'You took a big chance.'

'Not as big a one as facing you.'

Lenny didn't know what would happen next. Either way, he was still standing. In Lenny's book, it was a definite result.

Tomorrow, Tuesday, was the anniversary of Joyce's death. A year gone by already. Ronnie was taking her roses, white ones, like she liked. He'd bought them today and put them in the bowl in the sink to keep fresh. Meanwhile he kept himself busy. Not that he was home much, but he remembered to clean the grate now and then, push a cloth round occasionally and wash up the dishes. As soon as tomorrow was over he was going to…

His thoughts came to a halt as the telephone rang. He went into the hall and answered it. Two minutes later he was dragging on his coat and rushing down to the airey. He banged on the door.

'Ronnie!' Bella stared at him.

'Thank God for that.' He felt relief flow through him.

'Is something wrong?'

'Have you seen Micky?'

'No.'

He looked back up the steps then went for it. 'I'm afraid he's in trouble.'

'Is it to do with the fire?'

'What fire?' he asked, confused.

'That Inspector Reynolds called round on Boxing Day. There was a fire at Downey Manor.

They found a receipt for a car signed by Micky a few weeks before Terry died.'

'Are they sure it was Micky's signature?'

'Yes, they went to the garage and checked up the dates. The Inspector also told me that Milo was killed in an accident a little while after it was sold.'

Ronnie shook his head, pushing his hand through his hair. 'I don't know what this is all about but we've got to get over to the café.'

Bella frowned. 'To the café ... why?'

'Micky was there earlier and tried to rob Gina.'

Bella stared at him. 'Oh no! Is she all right?'

'According to Lenny, yes.' Ronnie put up his hand when he saw her surprise. 'I'll tell you the rest in the car. Can we leave Michael with Daisy?'

'I suppose so, but I don't understand what's going on.'

'That makes two of us.' But Ronnie had a feeling that soon they were going to find out.

The café was in darkness.

They went down the lane to the yard and the gate creaked open. Gina unlatched the back door.

'It's only us,' Ronnie said quietly.

Bella hurried forward. 'Oh, Gina, what happened?'

'I'll live, girl, don't worry. Come on in.'

Lenny was sitting at the small wooden table in the kitchen surrounded by crates and boxes. He wore a big coat and had grown a beard. He looked much older now as his black hair had turned grey. He stood up when he saw them, an

452

anxious look on his face. 'Hello, gel.'

'Lenny! Where have you been all this time?'

He spread his arms. 'It's a bit of a long story.'

Gina laughed without humour. 'You can say that again.'

Bella didn't ask any more questions. All she wanted to know was that her friend was unharmed.

'Are you really all right, Gina?'

'Yes, apart from a lump on me jaw. That maniac came bursting in, said he wanted everything I had in the till. Of course I told him to sling his hook. The next thing I knew I was on the floor.'

Bella looked down. 'Oh, Gina, I'm sorry. It's all my fault he came here. If I'd not told him I never kept money at home—'

Gina reached out and took her arm. 'Slow down, love. Let's take the weight off our feet whilst we talk. My legs are still like jellies.'

They all sat down at the table. 'For a long time Micky's been short of money,' Bella began. 'He told me he's in debt to McNee.' She looked at Ronnie. 'I'm sorry to spring this on you, Ron, but it's true. Micky came to the café because I don't keep any money at home now. Not after he took some before.' She turned to Gina. 'It belonged to the café but I put it all back. I wish I had said, but I thought keeping quiet was the best thing to do at the time.'

Gina sighed. 'Well, it's been a night of surprises, so one more don't make any difference. The biggest one being *him*.' She flashed a dark glance at Lenny. 'When your old man was about to stuff his pockets with our hard-earned takings, this one appeared and grabbed him by the throat.'

Everyone looked at Lenny. 'I was standing over the road.'

'Doing what?' Ronnie asked.

Lenny looked awkwardly at his dirty hands. 'I come here to watch the café sometimes. Only after everyone's gone like, when it's closing time. I don't do nothing, just watch, see how she's getting on.'

'So it *was* you Gina saw before?' Bella murmured.

'Yeah, but I didn't have the guts to come in.' Lenny glanced nervously at Gina. 'She'd send me off with a flea in me ear.'

'Too right I would after the way you buggered off,' Gina said angrily.

'Go on,' Ronnie nodded, 'what happened next?'

'Like Gina says, Micky turned up and hit her. I lost me rag, run over and would most likely have throttled him if he hadn't stuck this gun in me face.'

Bella gasped. 'A gun?'

Lenny nodded. 'And I thought he was going to use it.'

'We never found out if it was loaded, thank God,' Gina sighed. 'Lenny told him that if he pulled the trigger the shit would hit the fan as he'd written everything down on paper for Old Bill to find.'

'What do you mean *everything?*' Bella said looking from one to the other.

Gina lifted her eyes. 'Go on, Lenny, you'd

better tell them what you told me.'

Bella listened to Lenny speak in a low, halting voice. She heard how Micky had organized a robbery and got Terry, Milo, Lenny and another man to help him. When Lenny told her about the safe at Downey Manor and the counterfeit notes she knew it was true. Detective Inspector Reynolds had already told her about the forged money. But when Lenny came to the part about Terry being shot, tears filled her eyes.

'How could you let that happen, Lenny?'

'I swear I didn't know he was coming on the job. Micky sprung it on us.'

Bella sniffed back her tears. 'You should have stopped him somehow.'

Lenny wiped his own eyes. 'I know. I'm sorry, girl, I really am.'

'What good is sorry now?' Gina said. 'It's too late for remorse.'

For a moment everyone was silent.

'What made you do the job in the first place?' Ronnie asked as Lenny tried to compose himself. 'I would have thought after the warehouse you'd learned your lesson.'

'I dunno,' Lenny said miserably. 'It's this devil I've got sitting on me shoulder. Micky took me to this coal yard that was for sale. Said he'd seen all this money in this old girl's safe and after we'd done the Manor, there'd be enough for us all to have what we wanted. He said the old lady would be none the wiser and I could buy the yard and prove to Gina I was successful.'

'Is that why you left me?' Gina demanded. 'Because you thought you wasn't successful?'

Lenny shook his head wearily. 'I don't know why I left. I was all mixed up with what Micky kept telling me.'

'So you're putting the blame on him?'

'No, course not.' Lenny's head sunk lower.

'What a fool you are!' Gina exclaimed, red spots of anger on her cheeks.

'What mystifies me,' Ronnie said wearily, 'is how you all got away with it.'

Lenny swallowed noisily. 'Micky said we'd never be rumbled if we put back funny money. He knew a bloke that printed it. An Alfred some-one.'

'Where is he now?'

'Ain't got a clue, Ron.'

Bella dried her tears. Now she was angry. How could Micky do such a thing? He'd kept quiet all through the investigation. 'Do you know who it was that shot Terry?'

'It was like the police thought. A poacher or someone. There was a couple of shots before as if they was after animals.'

'What did Micky mean about Milo?' Gina asked.

Lenny drew his hand over his face. 'Milo was the driver. Micky only bunged him a few quid from the job and they had a blooming great row. The next I heard he'd been killed.'

'Inspector Reynolds told me it was a road accident,' Bella said.

'Did Micky put the finger on Milo?' Ronnie sounded shocked.

Lenny looked straight at him. 'You'll have to make up your own mind on that one, Ron.'

Ronnie clasped his hands together. Looking pale and angry, his grey eyes full of sadness, he shook his head. 'You are a fool, Lenny, but it's Micky who has to answer for all this.'

'What are we going to do?' Gina asked anxiously.

Ronnie sighed heavily. 'He'll be at one of the clubs. I'll try the Fortune first.'

'I'm going with you.' Bella stood up.

'No, I'm going alone.' Ronnie's refusal was final. 'I want you to stay with Daisy until I get back. Lenny, lock up after we go and don't open the door to anyone.'

Gina drew Bella to her. 'Do as he says and take care of yourself,' she whispered against her ear.

Bella sat quietly in the car as Ronnie drove back to Piper Street. She was afraid. Would he find Micky and what would happen then?

Chapter Thirty

Bella watched Ronnie drive away. Inside Daisy's house she could hear Michael and the girls' laughter drifting from the top window. She knocked on the door.

Daisy smiled as she opened it wide. 'Come in. The children are playing upstairs.'

Bella stood in the hallway. It was a house just like their own with two floors above ground and one below. A pleasant smell of cooking was coming from the kitchen and Daisy's husband,

Leonard, strolled out, his tall, thin body clad in a pair of dungarees. He was a dustman and often brought home things for the home, hence every corner was filled with an ornament of some kind.

'Hello, Len,' Bella smiled.

'Wotcher, girl.'

Daisy frowned when she saw Bella's strained face. 'Come into the front room... What's happened?' she asked when they were alone. 'Is Gina all right? What was it all about?'

'I'll tell you later. But could I ask one more favour?'

'Course you can.'

Bella hesitated. She knew that Ronnie would be annoyed if she followed him, but she couldn't help herself. She had to find out the truth.

'Would you have Michael a bit longer? I wouldn't ask, but I must do something important.'

'That's not a favour, it's a pleasure. But it's you I'm worried about. You look dreadful. Would you like a bit of supper first?'

Bella shook her head. 'No, thanks all the same.'

They went to the front door. Daisy patted her shoulder. 'Don't worry about Michael. He can always sleep on the put-u-up.'

It was beginning to rain as Bella took the car key from her purse. There was a heavy, tense feeling in her stomach as she climbed in and began the drive to Soho.

Bella was driving along Tottenham Court Road, recalling the night she had spent here with Micky. She had wanted him too much to care about their squalid surroundings. He was everything to her

458

and her love knew no bounds. What had happened to them over the years? Micky had watched her grieve over Terry and admitted to nothing. How could he have led Terry into danger and left his body in a wood?

Bella parked the car near Wardour Street, tears pricking at her eyes. All the memories came flowing back of the night Micky brought her to the Fortune. She had thought they were going to see *The Barefoot Contessa* and had worn her new blue dress for the occasion.

The club had been a big disappointment. Was it still as seedy as it had been all those years ago? Everywhere she looked now, the buildings were old and dirty. The gutters were overflowing and the neon lights of the gambling clubs and strip joints reflected in the water. Women and men stood on corners and smoked cigarettes in the rain touting for custom. They stared at her as she passed by and some made remarks. How could Micky ever want to be in a place like this?

The Fortune looked even dirtier and smaller than she remembered. As old and disreputable as all the other clubs in the street. Posters of semi-clad women were peeling off the walls and water plopped noisily from the broken pipes. A man in a shabby suit stood outside.

'Is Micky here?' She gripped her bag tightly as though it might be snatched away from her.

'Micky who?'

She glanced inside. 'Micky Bryant. He owns this place.'

'He don't any more, love.'

'You must be mistaken.'

The man looked her up and down, a leer on his face. He wore a red bow tie and his brown hair was greasy, hanging on his collar. 'You should come inside, love, and I'll put you in touch with the gov'nor.'

Bella was suddenly aware they were quite alone. 'Who is that?'

'Billy McNee,' he answered. 'Now just you come in out of the rain and we'll get acquainted.'

She took a step back, then turned and walked along the street her legs feeling weak with fear. Her footsteps became faster until she broke into a run. When she came to a corner she hid inside a doorway trying to catch her breath.

Billy McNee had taken over Micky's club! Where was Micky? What had happened? People passed by, hunched in the driving rain. Her breath caught in her throat. What should she do next? She didn't know the exact address of the Flamingo, only that it was close by.

When she had calmed a little, she stepped out. Frightened she was being followed, she looked behind her. The cars roared by, spraying water from the puddles over her as they went.

It was when she turned down the next street that she saw it. The 'F' was missing from the sign 'Flamingo', but the rest of it still hung lopsidedly over the door. For a moment she hesitated, then crossed the road. It was very quiet now. No one was about.

The door was bolted and barred, with graffiti sprayed over it. Steps led down to a cellar but it was clearly deserted.

There was no sign of Micky.

An alley ran beside the building. Relief washed through her when she saw Ronnie's car. As she walked past it she could smell the overflowing dustbins and drenched rubbish piled against the filthy walls. A cat hissed at her and sped away.

She came to a door and found it open. Feeling her way along the dark passage, she listened for sounds. There were none, only the scuffle of things around her feet.

At last she came to a large, dimly lit room. There was a bar at the far end, but all the chairs were broken, fallen on their sides, without legs or backs. Someone had smashed all the mirrors. This must have once been the Flamingo Club!

What had happened here? Where was Micky? She was so frightened she could only hear the beat of her heart.

Then there were voices. Following the sounds she walked through another passage at the end of which there was a crack of light.

Pushing open the door, Bella entered.

Ronnie's face was gaunt in the pale light as he bent over Micky who was sprawled on a couch. His jacket was open and a bright red stain was spreading across his shirt.

Bella ran to them.

'Come and join the party,' Micky croaked as blood trickled through Ronnie's fingers. Micky nodded weakly to the array of bottles on the table beside him. 'What do you fancy, Bells?' He raised his eyebrows slowly. 'Oh, pardon me, I forgot. You ain't much of a drinker, are you?' He laughed, a sound that soon became a cough.

'Oh, Micky, what have you done?'

'It was McNee,' Ronnie told her, exposing the wound in Micky's chest. She gasped, dropping her bag. Ronnie looked at her. 'I need something to put over this.'

Bella managed to stand up. She felt sick and faint. But she went to the small room adjoining the office. It was a kitchen of sorts and she opened a drawer and found a cloth.

Ronnie pressed it against Micky's chest. 'I have to get a doctor, Micky.'

But Micky held Ronnie's arm. 'That bastard will pay for what he's done to me. I swear it, Ron. He drained me dry. Then when there was nothing more to take he trashed me club.'

'You should have got out of it, Micky. The writing was on the wall years ago.'

Micky nodded slowly, a thread of blood on his lips. 'You know how he does it? Just changes the names and with a bit of hooky paperwork he's the new owner.' He coughed. 'At least you got a fair whack for the Blue Moon in the days when McNee was half a businessman. But the racket is out of control now.' He tugged Ronnie's cuff. 'I should have got out like you say but I did my head in with that bloody stuff. The booze and pills made crazy.' He looked at Bella. 'I'm sorry, gel, for what happened to Terry.'

'Did you take him to Downey Manor?' She had to hear it from his lips.

'I wish I never had. That job only brought me trouble. Most of it went to line McNee's pocket anyway. I just saw the money sitting in the old lady's safe doing nothing... Terry must've gone off for a piss or poke around in the bushes...' His

462

voice drifted away as his face drained of colour. His head rolled to one side as his eyes stared sadly up at her. 'I – I–'

Ronnie lifted his brother's head. 'Don't talk any more, Micky. I'm going for help.'

'It's over for me, now...'

Bella took his hand. 'Don't say that, Micky.'

'Remember the rats, Bells?' he whispered, gripping her fingers tightly. 'Them fat great buggers ... the ones down the docks ... by the bridge? One day they're gonna dig up the bastard there. I've seen to it. Given the nod to some friends of mine...' He began to choke and Bella took him in her arms. She held him, laying her head next to his. For all he had done, he was still Micky, the man she had fallen in love with all those years ago.

'Tell, Michael ... tell him his dad said to remember Robin Hood, eh? The good old days–' His lips trembled as he looked up at her. 'You was a good girl, Bells, the best...' His hand dropped from hers.

Bella looked at her dead husband and felt the grief flow through her. She would never see him again in this life, or talk to him. They had become strangers, but still at the end, they were man and wife.

Ronnie placed Micky's arms by his side and closed the lids of his eyes.

'There's nothing more we can do now. But when I find that bastard McNee–'

She gripped his arm. 'No, Ronnie, don't say that. Micky said he had taken care of it.'

'It shouldn't have ended this way.'

463

'Micky only had himself to blame. We all loved him, but it wasn't enough.'

He gripped her arm and helped her up from the couch. 'We have to call the police now, but first we must decide what to tell them.'

'I don't want to talk about Terry or implicate Lenny. None of that will bring back Terry, will it?' The tears were wet on her cheeks as she opened her bag and took out a card. 'Here is Inspector Reynolds' number. Though I never expected to use it.'

Chapter Thirty-One

25th December 1965

The airey was filled with bright, sparkling decorations. With Michael's help Bella had strung the paper chains across the ceiling, secured in each corner with balloons. The tree glistened in the corner, silver, red and blue tinsel entwined in its branches. The fairy lights twinkled and the star on top was dotted with silver glitter, reflecting the rainbow hues of the room. Mistletoe and holly hung from the lights and doorways. All the presents were under the tree as yet unopened.

The turkey was in the oven and Bella was putting the last touches to the trifle when Michael walked into the kitchen. For a moment Bella was taken aback. It was Micky standing there, the son as tall and handsome as his father had been at sixteen. A mirror image even though his hair was a dark auburn and he wore it in the fashion of his favourite group, The Beatles, there was no doubting he was a Bryant.

'I'm off to church then, Mum.' He was going to the eleven o'clock Christmas Day service with his girlfriend and her parents. 'Me and Francesca will be back this afternoon for tea.'

'It won't be ready till six.'

'Good. I'll have time to let Mrs Sullivan's dinner go down first.' He laughed Micky's laugh, bending to kiss her.

'Wish the Sullivans a Happy Christmas from me.'

'They've invited us for New Year's Eve.'

Bella nodded slowly. 'That will be nice.'

'Can Uncle Ron come too?'

'Is the invite for him as well?'

'Mrs Sullivan said if any of the family want to come…'

Bella hadn't realized the young romance was getting so serious. 'All right. You can ask him yourself later today.'

They went outside and up the airey steps. She shuddered as a cold breeze whistled past them. Michael climbed on his bike. She put her hand on his arm. 'I wish you would let me take you in the car. The weatherman said snow's on its way.'

'I like a bit of fresh air. And Mr Sullivan will put me bike in his boot when he brings us home.'

Bella gave in, watching him cycle off. Her brown eyes under her short, neat bob went proudly over her son. He was growing up fast and was fiercely independent. But out of all the girls on the island,

Michael had chosen Francesca Sullivan for his first steady girlfriend. The Sullivans were an Irish family and devout Catholics. For the last six months, Michael and Francesca had been seeing each other every free minute they had. The Sullivans lived in Blackwall and Ciaran and Molly Sullivan were hard-working people with a big family. Francesca had four brothers and two sisters. Ciaran Sullivan ruled his family with a rod of iron. It was a sin to eat meat on a Friday, or to miss Mass on Sunday, or to omit a weekly confession. Of course, Mary had been delighted that her grandson had found the faith again. An irony, Bella thought, seeing the catastrophic lapsing of the Doyle household!

If the Sullivans knew anything of her chequered past, they had never said, Bella mused thoughtfully. Not that she knew them well, only in passing. The New Year's get-together would be interesting...

A car pulled up, the first of several that would arrive today. Gina and Lenny climbed out, both wearing smart heavy coats and hats. 'Take care on that contraption, young Michael,' Gina shouted. 'And say one for us.'

Michael waved before he turned the corner. 'I thought it was Micky,' Gina said breathlessly as she greeted Bella. 'He's the spitting image.'

'Yes, in some ways.' Bella kissed Lenny on the cheek. 'Happy Christmas, Len.'

'You too, gel. Is Ron in?'

'I should think so. His car's there.'

'Do you mind if I go and have a beer with him first?'

Bella pretended to look disappointed. 'I was hoping you was going to help me stuff the turkey.'

Gina rolled her dark eyes and pushed him up the steps. 'Go on, you lemon, I'll give Bella a hand with dinner.'

Half an hour later, when all was prepared, Bella and Gina were seated beside the glowing fire. There were carols on the radio and Mrs Bryant's big, polished table that had now been moved down to the airey was extended to it fullest and laid with shining cutlery, linen napkins and tall stemmed glasses. Although Sean and Ashley were taking their annual skiing holiday, Mary, Gus and Teresa were coming for dinner and this year the Shines were joining them too. It would be a full house and Bella and Gina were enjoying the calm before the storm.

Gina raised her ruby red glass of cream sherry. 'Chin-chin, girl.'

Bella did the same. They sipped and smiled at one another, old friends and working partners, comfortable in each other's company as the mellow feeling of Christmas enveloped them.

'Did you see about McNee in the paper?' Gina ventured, as though she was reluctant to say the name.

Bella nodded. 'The report said it was a gang-land killing. That McNee's body had been under the demolished bridge for at least two years.'

'No wonder the police couldn't find him after Micky.'

Bella nodded as she gazed into the fire. Time had helped to heal the wounds since Micky had died that rainy night in Soho when Ronnie had used the card she had in her bag to call Inspector Reynolds. After they had taken Micky away, she and Ronnie had given their statements, but much to their bitter disappointment there was no other evidence to support Micky's claims. During the next few weeks McNee disappeared. Now it seemed as though Micky's bone-chilling prophecy had come true.

'You know, Lenny ain't forgotten what you and Ronnie done for him – kept stum about the Manor.'

Bella smiled at her friend. 'Lenny is a good man at heart, Gina.'

'Yes, but the good took a long while coming.'

'It did in the end.'

'He still feels bad about Terry.'

'It wasn't his fault, it was Micky's. And although Lenny could have said no, it was for a good motive. He wanted to impress you.'

'He didn't need to. I loved him as he was.'

'He served his time for the lorry, Gina. That was punishment enough.'

Gina sighed. 'I still worry the coppers will come knocking at the door.'

'Why would they? Milo, Micky and Terry are dead. That man Alfred Freshwater has disappeared. And Lenny certainly won't tell anyone.'

Gina grinned then. 'It's funny what the future holds. I'd never have believed he would become a bus driver. Or that you and me would have got ourselves as good a reputation as the 2is. Or that...' she held up her left hand and displayed the gold band on her finger, '...I would become

Mrs Rigler in January 1965!'

Bella grinned. 'To be honest, I never thought I'd be seeing Michael cycle off to Christmas Day Mass instead of spending it at home, playing his records on the Dansette and pretending to be one of The Beatles.'

'He's got it bad for her, then?'

'The Sullivans have invited me over for New Year. Michael wants Ronnie to come too.'

Gina sat forward, narrowing her eyes. 'No need to ask why.'

'He's very fond of Ron.'

'The question is, are you?'

Bella felt her cheeks warm. 'We're just good friends, always have been.'

'It's more than that. You can't hide it from me.'

'Hide what?' Bella asked innocently.

'You and Ronnie. Honestly, girl, there's walls dividing you, not a mountain range. You live with your memories of Joyce and Micky and are frightened to live in the present.'

'I don't know what you mean.'

Gina held out her glass for a refill. 'Course you do. You're a beautiful young woman–'

'Not so young. I'm thirty-three, Gina.'

'That *is* young, ducks. Young enough to start again. Me and Lenny did it and we were geriatric compared to you and Ron. You have to let Micky go. Ron is a father to Michael, in all ways but one.'

'Gina, I don't want to get married again. I'm happy with the business and looking after Michael.'

'He'll be working full-time soon,' said Gina,

unwilling to let the subject drop. 'You can bet if this Mr and Mrs Sullivan have anything to do with it, they'll want him signing on the dotted line for their daughter before he even kisses her.'

Bella's mouth fell open. 'He's too young for marriage!'

'Yeah, but he don't know about life, how this is just puppy love. He needs someone like Ron to give him a bit of a whisper.'

Bella smiled at her friend as she replenished her glass. 'You mean you think I'm too protective?'

'It's only natural with what's happened. But personally I think your lad should sow his oats a bit.'

'Well, I can't stop him from seeing Francesca. And frankly, I'd rather him be with a nice girl and have a steady job and–'

'Listen to yourself, girl! You know what all the kids are like that come in the café. They come to you with all their troubles and you are the first to tell them they are young and have their lives before them. Don't forget how much your Michael loves his music. He's got a lovely singing voice too and Daisy has done a good job teaching him the old joanna. You never know, he could be one of these pop stars one day.'

'That's what he's always wanted.' Bella didn't say that she was also worried that Michael was taking Francesca too seriously. For six months now she had missed the noise of his record player always at full volume. They never sat together in the evenings any more watching *The Avengers* or *Ready Steady Go,* his favourite programme.

Suddenly the front door latch went. Two fifteen-year-olds burst in, Anne and Irene in their Carnaby Street clothes, short skirts and piles of marmalade-coloured hair. They were followed by ten-year-old April, eight-year-old June, also of similar colouring, and at last four-year-old Neville. The room erupted into bedlam as Dolly and Percy appeared, bearing gifts. Lenny and Ronnie soon joined them and half an hour later Mary and Gus arrived with Teresa. Bella always marvelled at her half-sister's beauty. Her hair was a rich brown like Michael's and at sixteen, she was tall and slim. Anne, Irene and Teresa often came to the coffee bar on Saturday mornings. Dolly approved of this only because Bella kept an eye on them.

Mary was now walking with the aid of a stick. They lived in a council house in Poplar on a new housing estate. Like Michael, Teresa had left school last September. Whereas Michael was only doing a part-time job of delivering meat and looking for something permanent, Teresa had begun work as a typist. Bella knew that with her stunning looks it wouldn't be long before she had a boyfriend.

The family was growing up fast. What would happen in the next few years?

When dinner was over and everyone was opening their presents, Bella went to the kitchen. Many hands had made light work of the clearing up and there was only the hot drinks to be made. As she was putting on the kettle, Ron joined her. He looked very handsome, his grey eyes older and wiser, but the little lines that creased out from his eyes gave him a charm that only came with years. She could see very little of Micky in him. In fact it was Sean who resembled Micky more these days.

'Let me help,' Ronnie said as he watched her fill the kettle.

'Set the tray if you like, as many cups and saucers as it will hold.'

Ronnie carefully did as she asked, but his expression was distracted.

'Bella, there's something I'd like to ask you about Michael.'

She turned, lifting her eyes. 'Have you been talking to Gina?'

'No, not about Michael.'

She smiled. 'She thinks he's too sheltered.'

Ronnie frowned. 'I wouldn't say that. But do you know what he wants to do? Has he found anything that interests him yet?'

Bella leaned against the cupboard and folded her arms thoughtfully. She was wearing a new figure-hugging sweater and a skirt that was the shorter length with high heels that boasted of the new, pointed toes. She liked to be fashionable and kept up with the trends at the café. She and Gina were always talking about clothes and make-up, the latest cosmetics as well as the latest blend of coffees. She saw Ronnie studying her and she blushed.

'No, other than being besotted with Francesca.'

He grinned. 'I had noticed.'

'Have you got any ideas, Ron?'

He nodded, leaning his hip against the draining board, his white shirt exposed and his conservative tie making him look very masculine. She knew that under that shirt was a reminder of the past. A large scar which had never really faded. One day last summer, she had seen him working in the back garden dismantling the old shed. It had been quite a shock to see it on his otherwise healthy and strong body. 'I'd like him to come in with me but I don't want to put him under pressure. He could learn the business from the bottom up. It's hard work, but the rewards are there as you know.'

Bella tilted her head. 'The building trade...?'

'It's not a white-collar job, but I think he'd take to it. He's been out a few times with me on the sites. He hasn't said anything to you, has he?'

'No, only about his music and even that's taken a back seat this year.'

Ronnie nodded. 'If he joined the firm he could do his music at the weekends. I wouldn't ask him to give it up.'

Bella nodded slowly, a twinkle in her eye. 'Now I've got a question for you. The Sullivans have asked us over for New Year.'

Ronnie gritted his teeth and groaned. 'You're joking.'

'No. Michael's going to ask you about it.'

'It ain't my cup of tea, Bella.'

She raised her eyebrows teasingly. 'Or mine. But I'll do it for Michael.'

He was smiling as he looked down at his shoes, then back to her. 'It might not be such a bad idea after all.'

'What do you mean?'

'It's the New Year – new beginnings and all that. I was hoping for you and me too.'

She felt the colour rush into her face. A chorus

473

of laughter went up from the next room at the comedian on the television. The kettle began to boil. Ronnie reached across, his arm brushing against her as he turned it off.

'I think a lot of you, Bella. A great deal in fact. We're good friends and have a lot in common–'

'That don't sound very romantic, Ron.'

He stared at her, a slow smile on his lips. 'No, it doesn't, does it?'

'Try again.'

'All right, what about this?' He took her arms gently. 'Bella, I'm in love with you. In fact I'm crazy about you. And I am about to burst if I don't say it.'

'That's a little better.' She kept a straight face.

'I'm so in love with you that I want to hold you to me and kiss you.'

She laid her hands on his broad shoulders. 'What if someone comes in?'

'It don't matter to me, if it doesn't to you.'

'We won't find out till we try,' she whispered as she lifted her mouth.

Bella looked into his eyes, into all her past, into their lives that had touched and burned and cooled and was now glimmering like the stars on a Christmas night. She knew her love was different too. It wouldn't be like the one she had for Micky, all the passion and excitement of youth. No, this was sweeter, a love that had been growing slowly as the years had passed by. It hadn't really taken Gina to make her see that.

She had known it in her heart for some while now. As he kissed her, the wings of a butterfly seemed to touch her heart. As though it was dancing there, in the place that had ached so bitterly and yet had still survived.

It was love that had brought them to this moment. A special kind of love that didn't deny Micky or Joyce but set life and memories in just the right places. She believed that if she wanted to take it, there really was a new beginning.

A little giggle came from behind them. Neville was standing there, his face awash with chocolate.

'Uncle Ronnie's kissing Auntie Bella,' he yelled.

Bella and Ronnie smiled as they heard Dolly's calm response. 'That's what people do at Christmas, ducks. Now come here and let me wipe your chops.'

Piper Street had come back to life again. There would be many more Christmases like this one. The house would be full of fun and laughter. She would see to that. And she knew she would have Ronnie by her side no matter what.

They had weathered the worst of times. And now the years ahead were going to be the very best.

The publishers hope that this book has given you enjoyable reading. Large Print Books are especially designed to be as easy to see and hold as possible. If you wish a complete list of our books please ask at your local library or write directly to:

Magna Large Print Books
Magna House, Long Preston,
Skipton, North Yorkshire.
BD23 4ND

This Large Print Book for the partially sighted, who cannot read normal print, is published under the auspices of

THE ULVERSCROFT FOUNDATION

THE ULVERSCROFT FOUNDATION

... we hope that you have enjoyed this Large Print Book. Please think for a moment about those people who have worse eyesight problems than you ... and are unable to even read or enjoy Large Print, without great difficulty.

You can help them by sending a donation, large or small to:

**The Ulverscroft Foundation,
1, The Green, Bradgate Road,
Anstey, Leicestershire, LE7 7FU,
England.**
or request a copy of our brochure for more details.

The Foundation will use all your help to assist those people who are handicapped by various sight problems and need special attention.

Thank you very much for your help.